The Inscrutable Mr. Yang

A NOVEL

LINDO FORBES

NAPART INC.

The Inscrutable Mr. Yang

Copyright © 2025 by Lindo Forbes

All rights reserved.

No part of this publication may be reproduced, distributed, or transmitted in any form or by any means, including photocopying, recording, or other electronic or mechanical methods, without the prior written permission of the publisher except in the case of brief quotation embodied in critical articles and reviews.

Without limiting the author's and publisher's exclusive rights, any unauthorized use of this publication to train generative artificial intelligence (AI) technologies is expressly prohibited.

The story, all names, characters, and incidents portrayed in this production are fictitious. No identification with actual persons (living or deceased), places, buildings, and products is intended or should be inferred.

EBOOK ISBN: 978-1-7381463-2-1

PAPERBACK ISBN: 978-1-7381463-3-8

Book Cover by Zandra Murray, Zandragon Designs.

First edition 2025

Also by

The Insufferable Mr. Fletcher
The Indomitable Mr. Temple

To those who've been taught to seethe in silence, give voice to your rage

Chapter One

"**O**h my god, your hair!"

It was the first day back from the August Civic Holiday, and Claudia Sano had been through this song and dance no less than a dozen times today. She would probably have to go through it a dozen more. She pasted on a smile for the intern and gave her hair a playful little flip. "It was time for a change."

She stood in the generously appointed break room of Morenal, Smith & Sano, putting her assorted drinking vessels in the dishwasher. Every day she swore she would be better about accumulating cups and mugs and glasses, and every day she ended up with a shelf's worth scattered around her workspace. Today she'd managed two mugs, three glasses, and a teacup.

"Oh, of course! Your birthday was last week—you're a Leo! It's a Venus retrograde in Leo summer. It makes perfect sense!"

A couple of years ago, her birthday was met with lots of welcomes to her 'Dirty Thirties'. Then last year people congratulated her on entering her 'Jesus Year'. She'd thought thirty-four would arrive without fanfare, yet here this young woman was, fanfaring.

Claudia kept her smile bright despite the stream of astrology she didn't subscribe to. "Exactly!"

Agreeing was easier than admitting she'd been losing hold of the reins and needed to do something to regain a semblance of control. Cutting eight inches of her hair off, leaving it to its natural gentle curl, was the least drastic option available at the time. Not that she would explain it to the eager-eyed intern.

"We're going to the spot for drinks after work. You should totally come!"

"Ugh, I wish I could!" Claudia matched the young woman's vocal fry, pouting her disappointment for all that she'd rather walk naked down Yonge Street than be out in Toronto's nightlife. Gesturing vaguely in the direction of her office, she sulked, "I'm up to my tits in deadlines, but have a drink for me, okay?"

The intern bounced out of the kitchen, waving exuberantly. The beaming smile she received was worth the sin of lying to the young woman. Returning her smile, Claudia pulled her phone out of her pocket to make a note to call the local bar they frequented at the corner to cover their tab when she heard a scoff behind her.

It was the new Doberman-faced custodian. Howard and Valerie, the owners of the cleaning company, had needed to step back for health reasons and there had been a few new faces as a result. She'd noticed him immediately. Tall, medium-built, with a rangy frame and a caramel complexion, his raspy voice always sounded like it was rusty from disuse. His hair was long enough to be braided in an ornate style along his head and he wore a gold rope chain and a thick gold bangle on his left wrist. As far as she was concerned, it only added to his overall sinfulness.

"Hi, Ian!"

She got the same gravelly grunt she'd come to associate with the taciturn janitor. Claudia worked really hard at not letting her mask drop at work. She couldn't afford to be seen as anything other than the bright, bubbly Portfolio Manager in her uncle's firm. Among the ways she managed was not engaging other similarly grumpy people. The last thing she needed was to let his surliness reach out and touch hers, luring hers to the surface, no matter how much she wished she could.

"I'm here for another hour or so." She and the other five members of her team often kept the cleaning and maintenance staff apprised of their movements since their irregular, inconsistent hours were an occupational hazard of watching global markets.

"Working on your deadlines?" Ian asked, air quotes heavy in his voice.

"I'm sorry?" She'd shared some small exchanges with the man in the three months since he'd started. Nothing in-depth or insightful. Barely enough to be considered pleasantries, really. But they were generally inoffensive. This... tone? This was new.

"You lied to that girl. 'Deadlines'," the derisive air quotes again, "are not the reason you aren't meeting them for a drink."

"Oh, really? And how would you know that?"

He gave a noncommittal shrug. When it became clear his lifted shoulders were his answer, Claudia crossed her arms around her chest and held his gaze. Being five foot three wasn't the obstacle people made it out to be. High heels and an attitude, both of which Claudia possessed in spades, effectively leveled the playing field.

"Well?" She asked him, one brow raised expectantly. She had inherited her abuela's steely-eyed gaze, which she employed to great effect now.

Ian used his whole body to sigh, as though she'd started this. As though she'd forced him to initiate this conversation. "Your laugh."

"What about my laugh?"

"It was fake."

"My…" Claudia's mouth hung open with her disbelief. She blinked through her shock and demanded, "You think you know when my laugh is fake?"

He gave another full-bodied shrug, eyes half-lidded, and explained, as though it was the most obvious thing in the world, "You laugh with the tall, flirty woman that comes here sometimes. And the Director of Software Development. You laugh with her, too."

Her cousins and closest friends, Junior and Alma.

Well, shit.

"Should I be concerned about how much attention you pay to my comings and goings?" There might have been a teasing lilt to her voice, but she wasn't sure she was joking. She'd put too much time into perfecting her workplace persona to have it unraveled so easily by a relative stranger.

"Not at all," he said simply. "I shouldn't have said anything in the first place. My apologies."

"Oh, no. It's too late for that. What else have you noticed about me?" *Tell me where the mask is slipping; show me where I need to shore up my defenses.* The desperate thought came unbidden.

If a Black man could look green around the gills, this one did. He didn't squirm or fidget, but it was plainly obvious he'd rather be swallowed by a sinkhole than remain in this conversation with her. If she wasn't working on quelling the new, low-level panic bubbling in her gut, she might have empathized.

Whatever spirit had possessed him to open up had vanished. He did not seem pleased to be left holding the proverbial conversational bag. His only reply was a curt, "Nah, nothing else."

The way he studiously avoided eye contact and focused on organizing the items in his cart said he wasn't telling the whole truth but would speak no further on the matter. Claudia made a mental note to tighten the lock on her facade and took a deep breath. Exhaling quietly, she tried to shake her worry off. Now was not the time to unravel. She had an hour or two left before she could go home, unwind, and work her way through the impending spiral. Instead, she let her trademark smile spread over her face.

"Okay," she said, her bright, cheery tone masking her rising panic, "Let me know when you think of something!" And with that, she headed back to her office, where she could freak out in peace.

Chapter Two

"What were you thinking, bro?" He muttered to himself as he watched Claudia walk away, damning himself for engaging the tiny dynamo.

Ian hadn't planned on saying anything. He'd been doing so well. But she'd shown up today with her new haircut, a bob that left her full curls tousled above her shoulders, so different from her severe updos, he'd lost all restraint.

She looked so soft, so touchable, so damned beautiful, he forgot himself and spoke his thoughts aloud. *Dammit.*

He supposed it was bound to happen sooner or later. He was drawn to her, but for the life of him, he couldn't shake it. Yes, she was beautiful—bronze-skinned and stacked, with a pouty mouth that might be the result of a small overbite, and large dark eyes that hid a galaxy of secrets—but she was also very clearly at the top of her game. She had a sweet setup in a corner office, which meant, if nothing else, she was a force to be reckoned with. That meant she was absolutely off limits.

Yet still he wondered. Still, he hovered, trying to figure out which version of the curvy beauty was the real one. Was she the woman who met the world with a wide smile, an infectious laugh, and a tailored suit? Would she come home to share all the wild and wonderful things she saw in a day, all the ways she was moved and inspired? Or was she the woman who silently schemed and plotted to bend the world to her will? Did she need to regroup to tend to her proverbial bruised and battered wounds before heading back into battle? Both? Neither? No matter how he tried, he couldn't shake the fascination.

And he really did try.

Every day, before each shift, Ian looked himself in the mirror for a stern talking-to. The words he used might have changed over the last three months, but the gist was the same: do not engage. He was here, cleaning up after these seemingly regular but obviously wealthy people because his dad had a stroke and his parents couldn't afford to lose this contract. They'd worked so hard to get it—jumped through endless hoops with security background checks—and in the process had shed all but their most loyal original client list. If they weren't able to keep up at Morenal, Smith & Sano, they could lose everything. In this economy, people were tightening their budgets against expenses deemed extravagant. Trying to find new clients wouldn't be impossible, but the time it would take to regain the lost income could prove detrimental.

So here he was reminding himself to keep his head down and do his job. It was a temporary detour from his own life plan to help his parents. He would not ruin this for them with his penchant for chit-chat. Ian was a hard worker; no one could dispute that. What also couldn't be disputed? Ian's exuberance for all things. A landscape architect by trade, his supervisor and mentor routinely chided, 'Work and talk, Ian. Work and talk'. The very last thing he wanted was for someone to complain about his flapping gums, so he didn't speak to almost anyone at all.

It didn't mean he wasn't paying attention, wasn't taking it all in. From what he could tell, this place was a rarity. He thought he'd lucked out by being hired right out of school by his professor and given the opportunity to design instead of being sucked dry at some soulless firm as a nameless, faceless CAD drone. And while he understood, intrinsically, there had to be other great places to work—employees happy with their jobs, employers who were good to work for—he hadn't ever imagined a place like this.

A finance firm with over a hundred employees that felt like... he didn't know the word. It wasn't anything so trite as 'family'. No, it was more like the staff here were all hired because they were the best at what they did, and, as such, they were treated competently. Basic, thoughtful amenities were supplied without comment or fanfare because it seemed the management understood productivity increased when people were treated with humanity and respect.

It took all of his will to not stop to ask about the planters in the hallway, the brand of coffee in the break room, the carpet in reception, and the art that hung throughout the space—Ian could talk for hours about any subject at all. He'd done it before, and he'd do it again. Just not here.

Which is why he was kicking himself. Claudia was obviously some type of uppity up who had members of the C-suite's ear. One word from her and things could end terribly for him. While she didn't seem the vindictive type, he knew there was more to her than her bright smiles and bubbly laugh. There were little sparks, tamped down before anyone else seemed to notice—though how they didn't remained an eternal mystery—that he found captivating.

No, this chapter would close, and he'd return to his regularly scheduled programming. His exposure to the woman who was entirely out of bounds, who'd occupied too much of his time and attention, would end, and he'd be free of this... obsession.

His phone buzzed in his pocket, and he looked around to make sure he was alone before he pulled it out.

"Jonathan?"

"Hey, man!" Jonathan Bendea, his professor turned boss and mentor, was one of the few people in his life who called instead of texted. "Do you have a sec?"

He didn't really, but there was no point in wallowing in it. Instead, he answered with a breezy, "Yeah, what's up?"

"I'm calling to try to convince you to attend the groundbreaking at the site next week." Ian made a frustrated sound in his throat, but Jonathan pressed on, "I know you're taking a leave of absence so you could focus on helping your parents. A clean break makes sense. We support you fully."

"But?" The word came out on an exasperated exhale.

"But *I* want you to experience this. It's your first design coming to life. I don't want you to miss this chance. This is a big deal, Ian. You need to witness it—embrace it—it's a feeling like no other."

"I'll think about it. I promise."

"That's all I ask." Jonathan's easy charm, the same charisma that held the rapt attention of class after class of undergrads, made him very difficult to refuse.

True to his word, Jonathan didn't linger. Still, for all its brevity, the call was a well-timed gut punch. Painful, yes. But necessary.

Ian needed to remember what was at stake if he didn't see this through. He had willingly walked away from his career, from his life, to help his parents. He chose this. He was no longer the Ian who could afford to be distracted by beautiful women and their bubbly masks, where only he would pay the price for any fallout. This was his parents' company, their legacy, and if he failed, his entire family would suffer.

No, he wouldn't let it happen. Which meant his fascination with her ended now.

Chapter Three

Claudia checked the notification when her cell lit up.

Picking it up, she sighed wearily, "Yes, Nanda?"

"Is everything okay?"

Her sister Fernanda joined a conservation excursion in Costa Rica after university. She married the founder, pushed out four boys, and never looked back. So her solution to 'sistering' was to institute weekly 'catch-up' calls. It used to be just the two of them, but had since evolved to a separate call for her kids to regale their tía with their adventures. Fernanda thought she was so clever. These twice-weekly video chats were Fernanda's way of checking in on Claudia without being obvious about it since, apparently, their constant texting wasn't a reliable enough barometer of Claudia's state of being. Except, if they missed a scheduled call, Fernanda slipped into a mild hysteria, convinced something catastrophic had happened.

"Tranquila, Osita." She really wasn't in the mood for her sister's histrionics.

"You know I hate being called that." Fernanda grumbled.

"But you were like a little grizzly bear. Muy cute."

Her sister scoffed, while rolling her eyes, "All babies are hairy, Claudia. It's called lanugo, and it's perfectly normal."

"You'd know," Claudia laughed. At her sister's outraged expression, she rushed to add, "because of all the babies you've had, not because you were a Sasquatch!"

"Moving on," Fernanda's haughty sniff told Claudia everything she needed to know. Namely, her sister was gearing up for a lecture. "I've been reading up on lymphatic drainage. It's supposed to be really good for relieving swelling and ridding the body of toxins. Have you heard about it? Reducing inflammation can boost brain function. I think you should look into it."

The fact they were on a video call didn't stop Claudia from making a face. Her sister was always trying to find a way to 'help'. Whether it was newfangled diets, increasingly niche exercises, or trendy new age practices, Fernanda had convinced herself the right combination of things existed to fix Claudia's brain.

While it was true she suffered from depression and anxiety, and that her brain's chemistry needed constant monitoring so she could function, the reality was much simpler.

Claudia Sano, like Bruce Banner before her, was always angry. Her rage was what propelled her through the world.

She had a close-knit, nominally dysfunctional family; a solid education given to her by both books and life; and a challenging yet rewarding job she fought to get and keep. She knew she was, objectively, doing well. What she didn't know was how people looked at the world around them—the imbalance, corruption, and pure, soulless greed—and not want to scream until they were hoarse? What response could be more appropriate to the sight of dead babies and exploited civilians than unfettered rage?

She knew there were other people like her, people who moved through the world ranting and railing against the unfairness of it all. She also understood that the average person was doing their best to stay afloat, to survive. But it was the hypocrisy that drove her insane. The quote attributed to an Irish philosopher, for example, made her grind her molars to dust. How could they be considered good men if they were doing nothing while evil triumphed? The very fact they were getting credit for goodness in the face of their indifference was galling.

It was an insult to her injury that, as a Black woman, her own fury was used as a cudgel. Her every action was seen through a filter, casting the most innocuous emotions as angry. She wasn't considered sad, disappointed, or heartbroken. She was never weary or exhausted, only angry. Simply minding her own business could be perceived as 'an attitude'. Drawing boundaries for herself? 'Hostility'. Correcting someone for their avoidable mistake? 'Arrogance'. So, her justified anger? Well. She wasn't allowed to be angry. She wasn't allowed to snarl and spit. The world was constantly telling women to sit pretty, play nice, and she hated it.

It was a double-edged sword, of course. She understood sweet and bubbly was more attractive than snarling and nihilistic, but unfortunately, being a beautiful ray of sunshine too often translated to trivial and insignificant, and she didn't have the strength to fight this fight on both fronts. It was all she could do to get through the day without being consumed by her impotent rage.

"No."

"No, you haven't heard of it?"

"No, Fernanda, I'm not interested. I don't need it, and I want you to stop presenting these crackpot theories as solutions."

They had a version of this conversation at least twice a year. Fernanda would lay off for a while, but, bless her, her younger sister couldn't help herself. Honestly, Claudia wasn't even mad. Not really. She understood Fernanda was coming from a place of love, no matter how suffocating it felt in the moment.

Besides, it's not like Claudia didn't understand what was wrong with her. She'd found ways to cope, to compensate. She'd found ways to fight. Ways to rebel.

Her job was her proudest act of subversion. She used all she knew of both history and the ways money functioned to give the working class a small bit of security that would otherwise be denied them. Regular people were meant to be fed to the machine, not achieve meaningful, long-term benefits from their labor. They were supposed to work themselves to the bone to power the system that kept the elite at the top and everyone else fighting for crumbs. She did everything she could to ensure her clients, who were generally overlooked and underestimated, had a future to live off of when the time came. Relying on the government was as much a mistake as believing big business saw them as anything more than grist.

She didn't begrudge the rest of her team for chasing flashy accounts. She just knew the only reason she was able to accomplish the few hours of restless sleep each night was because she was doing her small part to restore a semblance of balance.

But the price she paid was steep. Looking into the abyss day in and day out so she could forecast trends and predict pitfalls meant she was constantly fighting her demons, constantly trying to keep her head above water so she didn't succumb to the anxiety that clawed at her during every waking moment.

No, Claudia had to keep hold of her anger lest it carry her away. Which meant she controlled every facet of her life to the best of her ability. She didn't pursue anything more than casual hookups, she didn't socialize outside of work, and she didn't, under any circumstance, let strangers in. Once a person saw behind the mask, it was impossible to go on as they had before. People generally had no idea what to do with a furious woman because the world didn't make space for them, and she was tired of trying to explain it. Instead, she let her big eyes, big boobs, and big laugh act as a diversion so she could seethe in peace.

But with her sister blathering on about inflammation... her peace was fleeting.

Cutting Fernanda off mid-sentence, Claudia asked, "Did you know Australia is wider than the moon?" Her sister snapped her mouth shut in confusion. Good. "It's not important. I just want to talk about literally anything other than your *tonta* cures for my brain."

Why people—her family, especially—thought she could smile or exercise or fresh-air her way out of a mental health issue was an eternal mystery. It was probably why she went out of her way to keep it a secret, right on the heels of social stigmas and prejudices.

"Fine. What do you want to talk about?"

"Junior and Davis—"

"No! I don't want to hear it!" Fernanda shuddered, pressing the ball of her palm into her eye socket. "She accidentally video called me last week while they were... busy. Why she was reaching for her phone while *that* was happening, I have no idea, but I will be forever scarred by the experience."

Claudia couldn't help but snort her laughter. How upset could she be at her cousin when she was a product of her environment? Everyone knew you didn't go looking for Junior's parents if you didn't want to see things best left unseen. It was standard practice to call out for Jaime and Yesenia and wait for them to come to you. Even as a child, Claudia understood her aunt and uncle were not like other grownups. Their... passion... for each other was just one of the many ways they were different.

"Get your mind out of the gutter, perv. I was going to say they're starting the reno now that the permits have been approved. Diego sent a team to the house."

"Sure, like you haven't had her sex life inflicted on you."

"Sometimes the stories are entertaining. Dare I say informative? Por ejemplo, did you know the left testicle usually hangs lower than the right for right-handed people and vice versa for los zurdos?"

"Really?"

"Claro. Interesting, right?"

"Pero, *how* she knows this is the problem!"

Claudia shrugged. "I've learned to not think too much about it. Makes passing Davis plates at Sunday dinners easier."

Fernanda groaned her laughter, and they moved on to other topics.

When she wasn't fretting, Claudia enjoyed these chats with her sister. She was proud of the life Fernanda had built for herself and the beautiful family she and her husband had together. If only she could get Nanda to see her life didn't need to be fixed, that she had found her own contentment without all the trappings of convention.

Sure, someone could want the bubbly, sunshine-y version she projected, but the mask only worked for so long. What would happen when it slipped, when she needed to close herself off from the weight of the everyday? How long before the reality of her sunk in and the truth came to light? She refused to be made a burden or a project. Refused to live someone else's life simply to go along to get along.

So, no. Husbands and babies and picket fences were all well and good; they just weren't for Claudia. Neither were the group assignments of partnership and community. She didn't like when too many elements were out of her control, and letting majority rule meant sometimes the most attainable option was also the safer, more palatable one.

Claudia didn't want safe and palatable. She wanted change, which came from doing the work. It's why she went through the steps to fight the only way she knew how.

The sooner everyone accepted it, the better.

Chapter Four

I an knew it was a mistake to be here.

No, not a mistake. More... it was rubbing his nose in the life he'd walked away from to help his family, and the wound hadn't healed enough to withstand this salt being tossed at it. He hadn't had enough time to build up the callus.

Jonathan, his boss and mentor, insisted he be here for this. *'This is a big deal, Ian,'* he'd said, *'you need to witness it—embrace it—it's a feeling like no other.'*

So here he was, standing at the demolition site, blocks away from his day job, surrounded by high-tech machines and the skilled workers who operated them, looking out at what was to be his project. A design he'd toiled on for the better part of a calendar year. And now they were finally ready to take the first steps to actualizing his vision.

"Hey, man! It's been a minute!"

Ian turned to see Diego Sano grinning his wide, welcoming smile. "Oh, shit! If it isn't the young king."

Diego's construction company, Sano Princes Contracting, had earned him the moniker. He wasn't as tall as Ian and had a slightly stocky frame, though he carried himself as though he were seven feet tall and ripped. His light brown skin might have hinted at a possibly mixed heritage, but he'd heard Diego identify as Black without any qualifier too many times to dwell on it.

"It's good to see you." Diego clasped Ian's hand, bringing their shoulders together. "Word on the street is you had some family trouble. You good? You look good."

Was he good? Ian scoffed to himself in what his sister would call church clothes, looking down at his polished, leather oxfords, pressed slacks, and dress shirt. He supposed 'family trouble' was easier than saying, "My otherwise hale and hearty father had a stroke three months ago and might never regain his full range of motion and currently requires almost round-the-clock care that my mother insists on providing, thereby putting herself under immense strain as she tries to manage both his health and the business that keeps a roof over their head. So I indefinitely stepped away from my dream job as a landscape architect to help them."

Less of a downer, too.

Ian cleared his head and repeated the words that had become a mantra—*it could have been worse; Dad is alive, he's stronger every day, it could have been worse*—before putting an agreeable smile on his face. What was done was done. It wasn't as though he wasn't going to help his family through this. There was no point in wallowing. "Yeah. Stepping up for the family. You know how it is."

"My abuela always says, 'When we reach together, we can achieve anything'."

"Exactly." He'd said the line with such rote familiarity, Ian briefly wondered what kinds of things charming, handsome Diego would ever have to sacrifice. "Do you have the build contract for this?"

"I wish. Nah, we're doing some of the install later. It's a big enough job for us, though, so I'm looking forward to getting up in it."

That made sense. If Ian's plans remained unchanged, and by all accounts they had, there was lots of work to go around.

The two men stood, shoulder to shoulder, surveying the space that would become a parkette in memorial to a prominent member of the Indigenous community in Toronto. Ian had stood here, in this very spot, for months, looking out at the vacant lot, planning and thinking and imagining the best way to make the client's request a reality. Now, the ground was broken. Phase one was about to begin.

Ian loved being an architect. He loved everything about it. The way a space could come alive or be given the sense of movement with a well-placed stairwell or atrium. He loved thinking about the design of every little detail, the way they'd complement and elevate each other as part of the greater whole.

He'd specialized in landscapes because he found beauty in incorporating live elements while making a space that was meant to evolve with its environment over time. Choosing the flora that only grew under certain conditions, soil compositions that could not be adjusted, views that needed to be preserved, enhanced, or mitigated all spoke to something fundamental within him. The power to create—working at the nexus of style and function—while recognizing the responsibility to future generations by maintaining a focus on sustainability kept him energized and motivated.

This project was meant to be his calling card. His first major design was coming to life. The space he would use as a springboard to hang his own shingle. He was so close to having it all in the palm of his hand; he still felt the phantom weight of it like an itch he couldn't quite reach.

Jonathan was right. It might have been a bitter pill, but standing here, the August sun bright in the sky, Ian felt triumphant.

He pulled out his phone, knowing full well no single picture could do the feeling justice. He just hoped when he looked back on the image, he'd be able to remember how transcendent it felt to be standing there witnessing this moment of his history.

"It's so unreal," he said more to himself than to Diego. Holding his phone out, he tried to capture as many angles and panoramic shots as possible.

"Don't laugh, but I legit have goosebumps. There's something in the air, man."

Ian nodded his agreement.

Attempting a better angle with which to get the most complete shot of the site, he started to inch closer to the edge of the dig site. He looked down and wondered about the darkness of the soil, convinced their initial tests came back as Luvisol. Crouching on his haunches, he rubbed some between his fingers and made a note to ask about it.

I might as well take a pic or two while I'm down here, he thought to himself, taking photos for both research and posterity. Satisfied, he started to rise when he heard Jonathan's voice.

"Good, you're here!"

Turning to greet his friend and mentor, Ian lost his footing. Windmilling his arms for balance, he righted himself, taking a relieved breath at the near miss. Smiling widely at Jonathan, he called out, "That was close!"

As if on cue, the earth beneath his left foot shifted, sending him sliding unceremoniously down the small, muddy incline as assorted cries and startled shouts accompanied him on his journey.

His embarrassment wanted him to stay where he was to avoid eye contact with his once and future colleagues, but the potentially ruinous cocktail of Toronto's filth now soaking through his clothes had him up and on his feet with a quickness. Ian's entire left side was caked in sludge. He felt the cold, clamminess seeping through to his skin. It took all of his concentration to not gag in front of the dozens of onlookers.

"Holy shit, man! Are you alright?" Diego, sporting sensible work boots, extended his arm to Ian. "Does anything hurt?"

He gripped Diego's forearm and got himself back on solid ground. "Just my pride."

"Pride nothing." Jonathan, tall and lean and darkly handsome, was at his side in two long steps. Taking Ian's shoulders in each large hand, his former professor gave him a thorough once-over. When he was satisfied with his own assessment, Jonathan pulled Ian to his side, the dry one, Ian noted, for an embrace. "Your instincts were good, Yang. I would have done the same thing."

"Likely with way less spectacle." Ian felt the mud drying as his skin cooled further.

Jonathan lifted his right foot for Ian to see. Though they were dressed similarly, he had on a pair of Terra boots instead of dress shoes. "Another rite of passage, Yang. Footwear must be chosen for function over style when on site!"

"Those look pretty stylish to me," Diego teased.

"Claro," Jonathan gave a mischievous grin and shrugged in concession to his vanity, "pero fuerte también!"

Diego and Jonathan lapsed into rapid-fire Spanish, of which Ian could only pick out the occasional word. *Sucio. Trabajo. Pronto. Cambio.* They were very obviously discussing his current situation and felt no compunction about doing so. He was used to it. Even though he knew Jonathan was born in Canada, English was his third language, and he often slipped both Spanish and Romanian into daily conversation. He might start his day with a hearty "Neața!" but wish you an "hasta mañana" when he left. It could be "bon provecho" as you went for lunch just as easily as he might offer a "poftă bună". There was no telling.

"My dad's office is close to here. I'm pretty sure he's out all day." Diego pulled his phone out of his pocket, typing out a quick text.

"That's okay, man. I work in the neighborhood. I have a change of clothes; I just need to figure out a way to clean this mud off without being late." He gestured to his side and tried valiantly, again, not to hurl as his mouth filled with saliva. "How much do you think one of the fitness places down here would charge to use their shower?"

Finding a gym in this part of the city wouldn't be difficult. It was teeming with every kind of facility imaginable. Finding one that would let a muddy man shower for a reasonable price would be the real challenge.

"Nah. My dad's office has a full bathroom. Private. I can slip you in and out before you head to work. MS&S is four blocks that way. You don't even need to move your car if you don't want to."

Diego's dad had an office with a private bathroom at MS&S? There were only five offices with that luxury in the building and only two men named Sano. Which meant Diego was from an altogether different class of people. Ian had never made the connection. Why would he? He was a Yang, and while he didn't know any other Yangs he wasn't directly related to, he knew it was a common enough surname. Why would he think any differently of Sano? Until this very moment, it had never even occurred to Ian to connect the Sano on the side of Diego's truck with the Sano etched in marble over the doors of his current workplace.

If he wasn't already sick with embarrassment and covered in mud to underscore it, a new hot, bitter mortification flowed through his system. Right now he and Diego were peers. Colleagues. They'd seen each other at various work sites over the years and had maintained a friendly acquaintance. Once they walked into the offices of Morenal, Smith & Sano, that would all change. Sure, they both had keys to the kingdom, but Ian's dangled off a janitor's ring while Diego's were plated in something rare and expensive.

Young King, indeed.

Ian did not like this new train of thought. Was he honestly standing here embarrassed of the work his parents did? The work that put him and his three siblings through school? The work that kept them fed, clothed, and housed? The work they took immense pride in for its ability to provide for their family?

He'd fall into a mud puddle a hundred more times before admitting this momentary weakness.

"That's actually my new spot. My parents have been the custodians for years. I took over for my dad while he's recovering from his stroke."

"Word?" Diego's surprise seemed more about the smallness of their worlds than any perceived change in Ian's station. "Then let's go."

"Perfecto!" Jonathan clapped. "Problem solved."

Ian took a deep breath and let it out slowly. Holding his one side still, he tried, no matter how futilely, to minimize the amount of mud that came in direct contact with his skin. He turned to look in the direction of the MS&S building.

"I'm already parked there. My plan was to walk back when we were done here, but…" He gestured to the general state of himself, trusting no other words were required.

Fortunately, the two men got the message.

"We could…" Diego trailed off, trying to come up with a solution to ferrying a muddy Ian to his job without destroying the interiors of his pickup truck.

Jonathan raised his hand, finger pointed to the sky, "Ah! I have a tarp in my trunk."

"Should I ask why?" Diego smirked

"No, you should not." With a cheeky wink, Jonathan took off to grab the layer of protection for Diego's seats.

"I gotta say, Yang," Diego gave him his trademark grin, "you sure know how to make shit interesting!"

Ian shook his head in mild chagrin before returning his friend's smile. "So, what you're saying is you miss me?"

The two men collapsed on each other, snickering at the absurdity of it all.

Catching his breath, Ian groaned, "All this and I still have a full shift of work!"

"Fuck!" Diego doubled over in uproarious laughter. "At least it can't get worse!"

No, it couldn't. Thank God for that.

Chapter Five

Claudia looked at the unanswered text she'd sent her brother for the third time. Why did he need to confirm their dad would be out all day? Wasn't Diego supposed to be on some job site? He'd gone on and on about it when he stopped by her place last weekend. Was he passing through? He almost never came to the office, always cracking about how he wasn't meant to be tied down to the monotony of office work.

Her curiosity, always a rabid and demanding thing, had her up and out of her seat before she could think better of it. Though her father's office was on a separate floor with the more customer-forward boardrooms and meeting spaces, Diego would still need to check in with security before being allowed in. If he was here but not answering her texts, she was going to throttle him. She did not take kindly to being ignored.

Smiling gamely at her father's assistant's assistant, Claudia pointed at the door. "Is he in there?"

Jorge, seemingly startled by both Claudia's sudden appearance and interest in the goings on of her father's office, squeaked out an "Uh...he, um—"

"It's okay." Claudia waved her phone at the young man by way of explanation. "He's expecting me."

She let herself into the office, closing the door firmly behind her. She wasn't sure what kind of soundproofing her father's office had, but this conversation was for her brother's ears only. Crossing the space to where the bathroom door stood ajar, steam from the shower creating a foggy barrier, Claudia started in on her brother.

"Diego, please tell me you didn't come here for a whore's bath in between your conquests."

"Yo! Don't you knock?" Diego shifted himself in front of Claudia as she pushed her way into the bathroom. "Excuse you. I know you know a whore's bath is a pits and bits situation. I blame your exposure to Alma for this pearl-clutching."

Diego's voice barely registered as a wet, practically naked Ian standing by the sink captured Claudia's full attention. He had a towel wrapped around his waist and another hanging off his shoulders. His skin was still damp, and small droplets of water made trails down his shoulders, following the path of beautifully carved muscle.

The riot of voices in her head rose to a cacophonous din as all-encompassing *want* flooded her system. Through the chaos and upheaval in her mind, the newly elected Minister of Horniness materialized, muscling Anxiety out of the way of her brain's controls.

Was it only a week ago he'd told her her laugh was fake? Now she stood eye level to his collarbone and was overtaken by an intense urge to clamp his nipple between her teeth and lash at it with her tongue until he whimpered.

There was no scenario where Claudia was prepared to see an almost naked Ian, so him standing there, all taut brown skin, glistening pleasingly under the warm lighting, in her father's office. It was simply inconceivable. Yet it was happening. Her eyes roved all over every exposed part of him until she made her way to his face, where he watched as she ogled him.

Brazening it through, she turned abruptly to her brother, who had also noticed her reaction, if his arched brow and shit-eating grin were any indication, and said, "You didn't answer my text."

"Because I was busy."

Claudia reared a bit. Was Diego... did he and Ian... here? At *work*?

Sensing the direction of her thoughts, her brother scoffed, "Calmate, Chismosa. No need to start tapping out a telegram. It's not that kind of party."

"Not yet." Ian's raspy voice drew her eyes back to him.

"Ay!" Diego bumped his fist to Ian's, cosigning his contribution to this absurdity. "If I were into dudes, you'd be my perfect man."

Ian nodded magnanimously with a shrugged, "Your loss". The motion loosened his towel, and Claudia was equally thrilled and disappointed to note the waistband of his boxers. Shifting to secure his covering, he turned to the pile of clothes on the toilet seat and pulled a shirt over his head before pulling the towel that was on his shoulders up through the neck like a makeshift hoodie.

"Diego!" Claudia couldn't do anything about the waspish bite to her words. She was decidedly out of sorts and needed to put this lid back on its forbidden box. "What are you doing in here with the janitor?!"

Ian's flinch was small. The barely noticeable inhale, along with an accompanying squint, made her insides curdle with shame.

"Fuck off, Claudia." Diego's sincerity made things infinitely worse. He turned to speak to Ian over his shoulder. "I'm sorry, man. She's usually cool."

Claudia closed her eyes and tried to regroup. She'd stared down bigger problems than a beautiful, half-naked man unlocking an errant swell of horniness in her core. It wasn't the end of the world. She simply needed to regain control of things. Taking in a deep, cleansing breath, she tried again in her most pleasant, customer-friendly voice.

"I didn't mean it in a disparaging way, Ian. I'm trying to reconcile finding you undressed in my dad's private washroom with my brother." There. Calm. Collected. She sounded like a woman completely at ease.

Ian held her gaze. She felt his attention sear her skin but held her ground. Instead of answering her or acknowledging her words in any way, Ian turned to Diego. "You're siblings?"

"Yes." They answered simultaneously, though Diego's came out more resigned than Claudia's assured reply.

She understood why Ian was asking. Claudia didn't look like a single member of her immediate family and only bore a passing resemblance to three members of her extended family if you squinted in the right light. When they were children, born with only 38 months between the three of them, they used the same grade of crayon to distinguish themselves. Claudia was brown, Fernanda was mahogany, and Diego was tan. The differences didn't end with their complexions. Diego and Fernanda both had wild, gorgeous, curly hair, whereas Claudia didn't. Diego managed to be tall at 5'10" in comparison to his two barely 5'3" sisters. Fernanda was lithe in a way she and Diego were not. If they hadn't grown up together and spent every day of their childhoods together, a case could be made for the three being genetically unrelated to each other for their lack of shared physical characteristics.

The furrow in Ian's brow told Claudia he wasn't convinced. "You have different dads?"

Diego looked confused for a moment before understanding dawned. "I'm Manuel Santiago Sano Pérez. This teensy tyrant," he dodged the punch Claudia threw at his side before continuing, "is

Claudia Regina Sano Pérez. She likes to believe using our maiden name somehow prevents people from knowing she's the boss's daughter."

"He didn't need our full government names, Diego." Claudia scolded with a narrow-eyed glare. Did Ian even understand the Latine practice of putting your mother's maiden name last? Diego was recklessly sharing their entire lineage willy-nilly.

"Por qué no? Manuel Santiago es muy sexy. Everyone should hear how good it sounds!"

All the calm serenity Claudia had wrangled was evaporating like the steam from Ian's shower.

Damn it! She did not want to think about Ian's shower. Or, she did. She wanted to spend a lot of time thinking about it, possibly with a toy buzzing away inside her. This simply wasn't the time or place.

Instead, she focused on her brother's excellent attempt at evasion. Why wouldn't he answer her very reasonable question? Well, two could play that game.

"Shouldn't you be at work, Diego?"

"I make my own schedule, Chismosa. I only answer to myself."

"Claro que sí," Claudia nodded in agreement while she pulled out her phone and pressed the speed dial. Maintaining eye contact with her brother, she brought the phone to her ear and said brightly, "Ma? Guess who stopped by for a visit?" Their mother's voice bounced around the small space. "I know. He must have a day off or something. It's been a long time since I've seen him, too. Yeah, he's right here!"

"Traitor!" He hissed. Claudia held out the phone to her brother, who scowled down into her face before snatching it out of her hands and stomping out of the washroom.

"Big talk from Mr. I Make My Own Schedule!" She said to his retreating form. He flipped her off in response as he backpedaled with their mother about his availability.

With her brother out of the way, she asked Ian directly, "I don't suppose you'll tell me why my brother let you in here to shower."

"I got dirty. Diego offered to help me clean up."

Inside Claudia were two wolves. One wanted every detail about what kind of dirty Ian had been, and the other didn't want her intrusive sex thoughts to hover anywhere near thoughts of her brother. Luckily the second wolf won the standoff.

"Fine. Don't tell me. It's not like it matters what type of mess the two of you make since you're conveniently already here to clean it up."

Shit, damn mother fuck! What was wrong with her? The words had barely left her mouth, and she already wanted to take them back. It wasn't what she meant, and Ian's nodded acceptance scalded.

If she'd been dangling bloodied from a crane over shark-infested waters, she would have sworn she didn't care about things like this, yet here she was, making derisive comments twice in the last 10 minutes. All she could do was turn on her heels and leave before she made things worse. As it was, her displays of snobbery had appalled everyone present. The last thing she needed was to further cement the idea that she was some type of elitist.

She went to the window where her brother was wheedling his way out of whatever their mother was asking for. Taking some pity on him, and hoping to return her karmic scales to neutral, she mouthed, 'Put it on speaker'.

"Ma? Ma! I have to go back to work." Claudia interrupted while taking the phone from Diego.

"Qué?"

"Diego left his phone in the truck, but I have to go back to my office," her quirked brow and his wry smile announced her the unspoken winner of this particular game of sibling tonterías. She walked out of her father's office with her mother still trying to get her children to commit to a joint visit. "He'll call you back. Después. Claro. Sí. I will. Ciao."

She made it to the elevator before their call finally ended. Even with her mother's voice still ringing in her ear, the game of chicken with her brother, and every reminder possible that she was at her place of employment, the only thing on her mind was the tiny sliver of waistband under Ian's towel and what it hid.

Fuck.

Chapter Six

Claudia wasn't sure how spending her Saturday at a field in Brampton constituted 'appreciation', yet here she was, sitting in what she supposed were the fancy seats watching a cricket tournament. To be fair, she'd only recently arrived and had no idea how much game was left.

She purposefully arrived late to most social functions. Over the years, she'd struck the perfect balance between *I have so much to do, but I simply* had *to make an appearance'* and *'my anxiety doesn't want me to be here at all, so be thankful for this scant offering'*. In most cases, her display of enthusiastic enjoyment was enough to smooth any feathers ruffled by her tardiness.

Yet today, as late as she'd arrived, she'd been watching cricket for a half hour and still didn't really understand what was happening. She did, however, appreciate the plethora of athletic men in fancy uniforms on the field as she'd shimmied her way through the spectators to her seat. Her own outfit might have veered a little more Wimbledon than was strictly necessary, but she looked cute in her sleeveless white linen sundress, wide brown leather belt, and wide-brimmed sun hat, which was all that mattered.

She'd barely settled in when her antennae picked up the familiar timbre of a hushed exchange. The two women directly in front of her sat in mirrored postures—both brown in a way that could mark them as Black, South Asian, or a combination of the two—happily catching up on the ins and outs of various players' lives.

"Do they suspect foul play?" The woman in a canary yellow jumpsuit asked.

Her co-conspirator in a sporty visor shook her head. "No. It sounds like they were blindsided by budget cuts and didn't have the ability to pivot. They apparently sent out an email to crowdfund, but I haven't seen any follow-up."

"I was there last weekend. It was packed, yet I didn't see a single thing about it. No volunteers with donation buckets. Not even a sign at either entrance."

"There isn't anything on their social media either. I'll be surprised if they're solvent by their fiscal year end." Sport Visor said, taking a sip of her soda.

Claudia listened as the women spoke. This was the real benefit to these outings. Some called it idle gossip, but she didn't. As far as Claudia was concerned, there was nothing idle about it.

Calling the exchange of information gossip, no matter how simple or catty or frivolous it may seem, was reductionist and dangerous. This type of unloading was how many women survived. Knowing which exec to avoid being alone with, which store would help you when funds were low, which doctor actually ran tests when you complained of an ailment instead of focusing on your last menstrual cycle and 'ideal' weight, or how to get a discount on a much-needed service were all vital exchanges.

It was no surprise to Claudia that women have been discouraged from this behavior for generations while men congregated in their clubs doing the same thing. An informed woman was a powerful woman, and the system only worked when that power was curtailed with baseless claims of grace and propriety.

A group of washerwomen working over a communal basin organically leads to a conversation about how much each is getting paid. A widow confiding in the women from the neighborhood about her new financial reality perhaps spurs an audit of their own finances. The weekly bridge game turning to the downfall of the local high school hero could be the thing that prompts a woman to look for signs of substance abuse under her own roof. A hushed conversation about a scary diagnosis might inspire a trip to the doctor.

The sharing of information was essential. No one would be able to shame Claudia out of the search for more.

Like most things, gossip itself was inert—it had no intrinsic value. What she did with it, how she applied it, was what mattered. Claudia wholeheartedly believed it played a part in her success in both securing new clients and reading the market. As far as she was concerned, all the training and education in the world could only take you so far if you hadn't honed your gut instinct, and Claudia's gut needed details. Lots of them.

When Claudia tuned back in, her attention torn between the array of well-built men in their smart uniforms and her love of chisme, the women had moved on to more personal matters.

"...they thought they were pregnant," Jumpsuit whispered.

Claudia cringed.

"And?"

"No."

Phew! Claudia thought, relieved for this unknown woman.

Sport Visor tsked sympathetically, "Too bad. They've been trying for a while now, right?"

Oh. Of course. Abject terror wasn't the only response to the possibility of procreation. She knew that. *Obviously.*

Her rumination came to an abrupt halt when the crowd burst into a mix of cheers and groans. Claudia looked to the field, unsure what was happening. An outfielder was strutting back to his position, and one of the batsmen was leaving the field. The incoming batter brought the people to their feet as he sauntered over to the... wicket? She was pretty sure that's what the three sticks in the ground were called.

Everything about the way he moved was riveting. Lithe and graceful, he held his bat in an easy grip, twirling it casually as the muscles in his forearm flexed. His steps were long and confident, something Claudia found rather impressive considering the bulk of the shin pads he wore. She couldn't see his face through the helmet, but his hair, dark and curly, poked out at the bottom.

When he got into place, he did a limbering bounce on his toes, shaking his limbs loose before getting into position. When gameplay began again, the two women in front of her practically drooled their appreciation for this specific player. Claudia watched him as they divulged detail after detail about the man. Everything from his family and their assorted connections, the opportunity to play for another more lucrative league abroad he'd allegedly walked away from, the many women who'd tried and failed to ensnare him, and his recent career change to help manage some unspoken hardship.

"It's such a shame," Sport Visor said.

"Terrible." Jumpsuit agreed.

"You have to admire a man who's committed to family."

"He'll make some woman very happy."

"Very."

All the while, Claudia couldn't take her eyes off him. He'd hit every ball that came his way, running between the wickets, his body agile and powerful. He radiated a focused intensity she felt all the way in the stands. His body's contortions, twisted torso, knees and elbows at all angles, didn't seem to impede his speed in any way. At one point, Claudia thought he'd hit the ball out of bounds, but the stadium went wild, cheering and stomping and whistling. It seemed like his turn was over, and in response, he dropped his shoulders, letting his head tip back for a brief moment before allowing a little celebratory shoulder shimmy.

Something about the move struck her as familiar. Sure, it was common enough, but her brain latched on to it like a snippet of a melody she couldn't quite recall.

Claudia gasped as the realization landed.

"Excuse me," she asked Sport Visor, "What's happening? Is the game over?"

Both women turned to her, smiling. "Yes, can you believe it? He batted a century!"

"He...what? Who did?" Claudia had hoped asking about the game first would make her interest less transparent. No such luck. Jumpsuit gave Claudia a knowing look and then looked to Sport Visor to answer. Before the woman opened her mouth, Claudia knew what she was going to say.

"Ian Yang."

Claudia smiled her thanks. When the women turned back around, she closed her eyes, absorbing the blow. As a rule, she didn't lust over men. She could admire an attractive one, could acknowledge when one sparked any semblance of arousal in her. But carrying torches wasn't something she did. But she'd noticed Ian from the very first moment, and each interaction only fanned the flames of her interest.

If she'd only had to battle the image of him wet and glaring in her father's office last week, she might have stood a chance. But now she had to add incontrovertible proof of what his body was capable of? The stamina, the strength... the *flexibility!*

Still reeling from Sport Visor's confirmation of the thing she knew in her gut, the batter pulled off his helmet to run his fingers through his hair as he tipped his face to the sun. There he was, flushed and sweaty, soaking in the raucous roar of the crowd. When his teammates made it to him, he was swallowed in a tangle of back slaps, head rubs, and a particularly vigorous embrace that ended with a comically exaggerated kiss on the face.

He received it all with good humor and easy grace, gripping forearms, bumping fists, with that long, easy gait on display.

His co-batter threw an arm around his neck and shook him playfully, the both of them leaning into each other, laughing.

Then, as though he could feel her, Ian looked up in the stands and directly into her eyes, the connection slamming into Claudia with a jolt. It was impossible. He couldn't see her from all the way down there, could he? But he could, because there she was, looking right at him, too.

If she thought he was handsome before, and the good lord knew she did, his smile made him lethal. It wasn't that it changed his face; it had the same dimensions and contours as before. It was that his smile fooled you into believing he was attainable, that you could simply reach out and access his beauty for your very own. Without his forbidding glare acting as a warning, a person was likely to stumble right into ruin without caution. His smile made the transition from '*I did not give you permission to come*' to '*Let's grab a couple drinks. If all goes well, you can end the night on my face*' jarring.

His wide smile faded, no doubt from the shock of seeing her there, out of place, colliding his worlds. Not knowing what else to do at that moment, she wriggled her fingers at him in a small wave.

He lifted his chin in reply, one side of his mouth tipping up in a wry grin, before returning his attention to his teammates.

The whole interaction passed in mere seconds, but Claudia slumped in her seat from withstanding the pressure of it.

Unfortunately, their moment had witnesses, and she felt Sport Visor and Jumpsuit's attention. Taking a deep breath, she prepared to stave off their impending questions but was saved by her client, Gita.

"What did you think of your first cricket game?" Gita picked her way carefully through the seats, extending her hands for Claudia to take. "Of all the games for you to see, what a play!"

Gita's family started a collective for women who needed a fresh start by offering a living wage to train and work in one of her day spas. They'd started a scholarship of sorts for the women who wanted to go back to school to pursue business ventures of their own. It started as a soft place to land for survivors of domestic violence and grew into something bigger.

One of Claudia's existing clients introduced them. Gita showed up to the meeting with fourteen years of financial statements and a shareholder report. Claudia was so impressed by the woman's competence, her clear intention to capitalize on the opportunity, Claudia committed to helping grow their portfolio—after having her own auditors look between the proverbial couch cushions, of course.

Ownership in this cricket team, it turned out, was a passion project of Gita's to honor her late husband.

"I'm still not entirely sure I was following, but it was definitely fun!"

If she didn't already know Sport Visor and Jumpsuit had been eyeing her, Claudia's familiarity with the woman who was part owner of the team only made her more of a curiosity.

"The season is almost over, but you'll have to come to more games next year."

"I would love that!" Claudia beamed, knowing she would likely make it to the exact same number of games as she had this season.

As Gita led her out of the stands, Claudia turned to give the two women a bright, friendly, 'Have a great day', but the words got stuck in her throat.

Ian Yang was staring at her from the dugout—or was that the pavilion?—pads removed, his long, rangy body in contrast with the flurry of activity around him. His usual, Dobermann-faced sternness was on full display.

All the reasons she stayed away from him at work came rushing to the surface. A Saturday in Brampton didn't make this less of a professional outing. She needed her game face on to make sure Gita had her full attention. Her resolve restored, Claudia lifted a shoulder in a show of unruffled indifference and followed her client into the stadium.

If there was fallout to be had, it was future Claudia's problem.

Chapter Seven

Claudia watched as her cousin flirted shamelessly. Even with the obnoxiously large green stone on Junior's finger, Claudia was sure their server was doing a quick risk-reward calculation.

"I'll have the Niçoise and a glass of the house white, thank you." Claudia said pointedly, bringing the woman's attention away from her flirtatious cousin and back to the more urgent matter of Claudia's grumbling stomach.

"Of course."

When she was out of earshot, Junior gave a contented sigh.

"You have a boyfriend. That you live with." Claudia knew her cousin wasn't contemplating adultery. For all her vixen ways, Junior had always been staunchly monogamous. She just wasn't in the mood for Junior's brand of hedonism today. "Keep it in your pants until you get home."

It had been almost two weeks since she'd watched Ian play in the cricket tournament. Even the distraction of the Labor Day long weekend hadn't helped clear her thoughts of the man. Junior's ever-present libido was only adding fuel to the fire she'd been unsuccessfully trying to put out.

"Do you think Fletcher would let her watch? I think I'd like it if she watched."

Case in point.

"I don't want to know more about your sex life than I do, por dios."

"Yesterday, we—"

"Cállate, Hammer, por favor!" Claudia begged. She hoped using the childhood nickname Junior hated would distract her from further oversharing. The last time she let Junior wax poetic, she got a detailed earful about his thumb and an elastic band that would haunt her until her last breath.

Junior was their paternal grandmother Regina's first granddaughter and older than Claudia by four months. They grew up together, as close as sisters, even though they had almost nothing in common.

Junior was a tall, only child with a dazzling smile and an overt sexuality she was never taught to be ashamed of. She was also a literal heiress to her maternal grandfather's shipping empire. Claudia, on the other hand, was the oldest of three, short, busty, and plagued by anxiety. They had similar complexions, but their only shared feature was their eyes, if anyone bothered to notice. It was second nature to add, "Our dads are brothers, but we look like our mothers" immediately after stating that they were cousins.

But that wasn't entirely true, either. While Junior looked almost exactly like her mother, Claudia's father, Manuel, had married a woman with a similarly complicated bloodline—the biracial Regina Sano also had an Indigenous paternal grandmother—so Claudia and her two siblings, Fernanda and Diego, didn't look like each other and didn't look like anyone else in the family, either.

Another difference between them? Junior kept everything close to the chest; her life was shrouded in secrets. Claudia was an open book. The problem was most people didn't know how to read it.

People understood the kind of anxiety that led to self-harm. They could, conceptually, empathize with the feeling of hopelessness that brought about those types of ideations. It was much harder for them to follow the path Claudia's mind took. Her problem wasn't that she wanted to hurt herself; Claudia struggled with knowing who was a threat, with identifying who was a source of harm.

There were millions of people milling around the city every day, and, at any given time, she could be sharing space with a bigot. She could be making chit chat while she waited in line with a class traitor who voted against their own interests in the name of a wealth they'd never achieve. How was she to know if that woman was prioritizing her proximity to whiteness at the expense of her reproductive rights? Have those queer people excluded their trans brethren for the lie of gender essentialism despite their own marginalization? Did that visibly ethnic man fall into the trap of the 'model minority' and prop up the tools of the oppressor?

The possibility of it haunted her. That they could potentially feel validated by her pleasantries was too much. It made her suspicious and kept her on edge so that going out to do everyday things was much more difficult. Her brain was constantly warning her of the perils of her fellow man, and she couldn't do much to counter the narrative because it was absolutely true. People sucked. Not being able to tell which people sucked in which specific way until it was too late, until they'd revealed themselves to be a problem, spun Claudia out.

The more times society moved regressively right, the more times the Overton window shifted to normalize some new atrocity where society didn't say *No* or *Stop* or *Enough*, sent her anxiety into overtime wondering who among them was culpable.

She wanted them—those who lied and cheated and stole at the expense of others who were smaller and weaker—to suffer. Make them face their victims. Make them live the life they created for others. Make them ashamed and let them wear that shame for all to see.

And if that didn't work? She wanted to burn their lives to the fucking ground.

Junior's phone lit up on the table, drawing both women's attention. Junior picked it up and started swiping through pictures. "Ooh, what have we found now?"

Claudia shamelessly leaned over to get a better look. Every single member of her family called her La Chismosa. If they didn't want her to know something, it was on them to keep it from her. "Why do you have a picture of Ian?"

Junior looked at her with narrowed eyes. "Ian?"

"Him. On your phone. How do you know him?"

"How do *you* know him?" Junior challenged.

"He's one of the custodians at MS&S."

Everything about her cousin's body language changed. She went from languid laziness to full alertness between one breath and the other. "How well do we know him?"

"Why?" Claudia's reputation for being a gossip meant she was often pumped for information. It didn't bother her, per se, but occasionally the power was in what you held back. She also liked to be able to tailor the details to the situation, so knowing why someone wanted the details mattered just as much.

Junior scooched her chair closer, explaining as she scrolled through the images. "This guy," she pointed to a handsome, heavyset Black man, "is Quincy Temple. He's interested in one bakery and bookshop proprietress."

"Leigh has a secret admirer?"

"It's not even remotely a secret. He's giving a full-court press."

"Aw, that's nice." Claudia had always liked Leigh Bridger. She was kind and funny and was the living embodiment of the word forbearance. In all their years of friendship, Claudia had never known Leigh to date or even have a casual fling. "She deserves it."

"That's what we're trying to find out. Up until a week ago, we didn't have a last name to do any real background work. But if you know one of his friends…"

"Uh, 'know' is doing a lot of work there, prima. I sparkle at him, and he sort of grunts in return." Claudia thought of all her interactions with Ian Yang. She could probably count the sum total of words they'd exchanged. Even when he was wet and shirtless and… well, even then he'd stared stone-faced while she babbled incoherently. "Ask Diego about him. They seem to be friends."

"Diego, your tonto brother?" Junior asked as though Claudia had lost her capacity for reason. "When I texted him to ask if we needed a buttress, he sent me a picture of his nalgas. Never in the history of humanity has there been a less serious person."

Claudia couldn't, wouldn't, argue the charge of her brother being a fool. It was objectively true. The odds of him reporting anything useful to her cousin's purposes were slim to nil. But, still, "And if he doesn't want to talk?"

Junior sank back in her chair, a wide, dazzling smile spreading on her face. "Dale, Chismosa. *Make* him talk."

Something slick and molten swept through Claudia at the idea of *making* Ian do anything. She had to school her reaction lest the lust sweep her away. The memory of the way the water glistened on his skin, small beads trailing down his torso, now joined the memory of his body in motion, batting in the cricket game, and making her mouth water. His clenched jaw and corded muscles on full display challenged her to pick a focus. She felt her face heat in a furious blush, cursing her brother again for his part in Ian's shirtlessness in their father's office, an encounter she had yet to shake off, which was the catalyst for the whole thing.

She cleared her throat. "You'll owe me. Big."

"Don't I always?"

Claudia didn't feel like engaging with her cousin's smug reply, but as Junior set her napkin in her lap while their server placed her lunch in front of her, Claudia focused on the challenge before her. Getting Ian to talk was a thing she wanted. And, for better or worse, 'getting what she wanted' was Claudia Sano's core motivator.

The problem was she wasn't sure what would happen in her attempts to get the intel. She already struggled with proximity to the man and the way he vacillated between truly seeing her and looking right through her. She had no doubt he knew more about her than whether her laugh was fake. It made approaching him a potentially risky prospect. Her whole shtick was a house of cards held together with smoke and mirrors. Getting close to Ian, if she even could after the whole debacle with her brother, might upset the whole structure.

But if it didn't... "I'll take one swing at it. If he shoots me down, then it's over."

"Your best effort is all I ask," Junior said before taking a bite of her lunch.

Chapter Eight

"Good morning, Ian!"

He was standing on the executive floor, on the other side of the frosted glass wall behind the reception desk. He watched as Claudia made her way from the break room, beaming her smile at him. It didn't mean anything, he knew. She smiled at everyone that way—wide and open and completely fake. No matter how much he wished it were real, that her joy was directed at him particularly, it simply wasn't the case, so, instead, he waited for her to breeze on by after he grunted his reply.

But she didn't swish by him. No, she teased a light, playful, "I had no idea we had a cricket star in our midst! Do you play any other boarding school sports? Polo? Lacrosse? Jai alai?"

Ah. He'd wondered if she was ever going to bring it up. He certainly had no intention of doing it. Seeing her there two weeks ago, gorgeous in the sunlight, had been too much, too impossible. He still hadn't really wrapped his head around it, so he swept it under the rug where it could build community with all the other inconvenient thoughts he didn't have time for.

"No." He'd hoped keeping his answers brief would discourage further conversation. He reminded himself for the hundredth time not to engage, not to loosen the reins on his inner Labradoodle. To not give her the history of the sport and his relation to it, to share with her this thing he loved. Again, despite the herculean feat of remaining impassive in the face of her unrelenting cheer, she doubled down.

"Guess what?"

His younger siblings would have been falling over themselves to answer 'chicken butt'. He fought to keep a straight face.

When he didn't answer, she continued gamely. "Looks like we have some friends in common!"

Even at his very best, Ian was not equipped to resist this level of perkiness. His was a temperament best suited to giddy enthusiasm. With as much as he liked to chitchat, he needed two more mugs of tea in his bloodstream before he was strong enough to stay the course. This was exactly what happened when he veered from his normal routine. Now, because of a snooze button, he was under-caffeinated and ill-prepared to engage the discipline required to maintain his work face.

"Doubt it." His normally raspy voice was even scratchier from disuse.

"So, you're not friends with Quincy Temple?" She asked playfully.

God, what he would give for her attention to be genuine. Everything about this woman fascinated him.

"I am." He narrowed his eyes at her. Even factoring in the surreal experience of seeing her in the stands at his cricket game, knowing that she'd watched him play, this full-scale charm offensive at eight in the morning, her beaming at him and asking about Quincy, was too bizarre. "Are *you*?"

"That's what I wanted to talk about."

"With me?" His suspicion had him on high alert, and he didn't bother trying to hide it.

"Yes, of course you, Silly!"

What was happening right now? Ian looked around, trying to figure out if he was being pranked. Maybe there was a gaggle of execs standing behind a pillar snickering to themselves? Or perhaps there was a bet of some kind that she'd lost?

"You want to talk to me about Quincy Temple." He said it again, slowly, hoping she would hear the inherent ridiculousness of the statement and abandon whatever this was. "Why?"

"It's always fun to find out you have friends in common, right? I just wondered who else we might know."

Something was rotten in the state of Denmark. Anyone who knew him and Quincy knew that theirs was a tertiary connection at best. Some might even generously consider them friend-in-laws. Ian was paternal cousins with Quincy's childhood best friend, William, and, in a fluke so random it seemed statistically impossible, maternal cousins with his university housemate, Domenic. For all the times he and Quincy spent together, it was always with either of his cousins present as intermediaries.

No, something was up. He wasn't going to fall victim to her sweet, bubbly act. Claudia Pérez—no, Sano. He mustn't forget—was a pufferfish. Cute but deadly.

"Nah, I'm good."

Claudia blinked rapidly, a little unbalanced, before regaining her composure. "You don't want to talk to me?"

"About our personal lives on company time?"

Her blank, uncomprehending stare was worth his caffeine headache. He hadn't known there was joy to be had in fighting his nature. Every day he'd worked to keep his exuberance in check was a bit of a struggle. But this, bedeviling the usually unflappable Claudia with his taciturn persona, was a goddamn delight.

"Are you serious?"

Ian forced himself to count to five before answering. "From what I understand, wage theft is a big problem for corporations. I don't condone stealing of any kind."

Claudia's mouth fell open, and he had to bite his cheek to keep from laughing. He started to move with a curt, "If you'll excuse me."

He'd only made it ten steps before she put her tiny, curvy body in the way of his cart.

"You're being serious." Her eyes darted all over his face as she reckoned with the unspoken question.

"I am."

He wasn't sure if it was hubris, if she truly couldn't fathom a man not being willing to lollygag for her attention, but it was an interesting development all the same. The woman was shrewd and calculating, and Ian was willing to bet some of her reaction was a simple case of her missing the mark, of needing to recalibrate her next attempt.

"What was that word your brother called you?" He was by no means fluent in Spanish. Spending time with Jonathan meant he had a couple dozen words that were mostly slang and mildly derogatory. It wasn't a word he'd heard before, not that he could recall everything that had ever sailed out of his friend's mouth.

She gave her head an adorable little shake as she tried to follow his wild change of topic. "It's a family nickname."

"Does it mean something like... short stack? Small fry?"

Her affronted gasp was a battering ram to his composure. To keep a straight face, he bit his tongue so hard he tasted blood. He hoped she didn't think she was fooling anyone. Without those fancy shoes she always wore, Ian was positive she didn't stand taller than his chest.

"It means gossip. Literally 'gossipy woman'."

Realization dawned, bathing everything in the cold light of understanding. "Oh, I see."

"No, you don't."

"I think I do." He insisted; a fissure of disappointment curdled his stomach. "You figured you could interrupt my work, pump me for information, and I'd have no say in the matter because you're the boss's daughter?"

"What? No!" Her hand came up to her mouth, as if she were scandalized by the very reasonable words he'd spoken. "Look, I get that I didn't make a good impression the other day sticking my foot in it like I did, but I'm not like that."

Her horrified expression didn't seem fake, so he was inclined to believe she wasn't intentionally throwing her weight around. But still... "Prove it."

"How can I prove something like that?"

"Easy. If you want to talk to me, you can meet me somewhere public and sit down to a civilized conversation."

"Fine. What time are you finished tonight?"

"Not tonight. I have a headache." It was caused by a lack of caffeine and rather easily alleviated, but she didn't need to know that. Besides, the frustrated sound she made in her throat was worth all the withdrawal pains.

"Okay. When would be a good time?" The words came out with forced calm, and he wondered what an unleashed Claudia looked like. He decided to push a little more, just to see what would happen.

"Slide into my DMs. We can work something out."

"I don't know your handle."

"How hard can it be to find a janitor on the 'gram?"

Claudia gave an exasperated huff, "How many times do I have to apologize for that?"

"Once would be great." He hadn't realized just how much it would hurt to be dismissed for doing an honest day's work. The work his parents had prided themselves on. Her stricken look wasn't enough to make up for her disdainful comments.

She closed her eyes, letting her chin drop to her chest. He watched as she heaved a silent breath, in and out, probably doing some centering-type exercise. He kept his focus on her face—for once, her heaving breasts weren't enough to hold his attention. When she met his gaze, he saw a new resolve in her eyes.

Claudia made her way around the cart and stood directly in front of him, the top of her head not even reaching his chin. She tipped her face up to his and locked eyes. He was so captivated by the depth of her black coffee gaze, he almost missed her words when she started to speak.

"I am not embarrassed that you're a janitor. I don't think you should be embarrassed to be a janitor. I don't think being a janitor is in any way something to be ashamed of. Furthermore, I don't honestly believe that what you do here can be summed up as something so pedestrian as janitor. I'm sorry for my insensitive words, and I am appalled that I gave you the impression that I held such elitist views. I don't."

Ian nodded his acceptance. He wanted an apology, and, dammit, she had delivered. She genuinely seemed horrified by the whole thing, and, as much as it had stung, it was no less than he'd thought about himself, muddied and embarrassed, when Diego suggested coming here to get cleaned up. If he were being really honest, it was a big part of why her thoughtlessness had landed the way it did—Ian hadn't reconciled the ugly part of him that thought he was better than this, and Claudia's careless words highlighted a bias he didn't even know existed.

He hadn't spent any real time thinking about what it meant for his parents to have a cleaning company. He grew up surrounded by other working-class families who did all manner of jobs, from clerical to service to manual labor. His friends were raised by people who ran the gamut between orderlies, cashiers, secretaries, bank tellers, bus drivers, and homemakers. Whenever it came up in his youth, his parents' job was met with a simple 'For real?' or a 'Like Molly Maid?'. Even the rare jackass who had something derisive to say never made him feel embarrassed, only defensive.

It shamed him to realize somewhere along the line, he'd acquired airs, as his mother would call them. He'd spent many an afternoon over the course of plenty summers scrubbing toilets or dusting shelves to earn a bit of extra pocket money, and he prided himself on knowing five different ways to remove stains from fabric. The sense of completion from walking away from a newly cleaned space was rivaled only by washing, folding, and *putting away* a load of laundry in the same day.

He'd wrestled with this, the endless loop of the argument running in the background of his thoughts, and he was no closer to an acceptable explanation. Instead, he decided to answer the question she'd asked weeks ago. "We were at a construction site not far from here for a project I designed when I slipped and fell into a ditch. I was covered in mud. Diego offered to help me out by sneaking me into his dad's private washroom."

He watched as the words landed, as she slotted the pieces around in her mind.

"You and my brother work together." She said it more to herself than anything else. "Why didn't you just say that?"

"I've known your brother for years now. I picked a side."

She laughed a quiet, genuine laugh. The sound was like a soothing balm on his frayed nerves. She smoothed the fabric of her skirt over her hips, an action he might have considered a nervous tic on someone else, and said, "I look forward to you changing allegiances once you get to know me."

Ian wanted that to be true so badly. "I guess we'll see."

"I guess we will!" Claudia gave him a cheery salute before heading to the elevators.

Chapter Nine

It had taken Claudia all of three hours to get Ian's number from Diego, two days to work up the nerve to text him, and eight days for him to finally suggest a meeting. The possibility of it, of them being together socially outside of work, loomed over every one of the eleven intervening days.

At some point, Claudia had to admit to herself that she was no longer in this for her cousin. Yes, Junior set her on this path, but the truth was she wanted to know more about the inscrutable Ian Yang. The man she knew—the man she thought she knew—was taciturn and severe. He didn't fill silences with mindless blather, and he certainly didn't start conversations. Yet she'd had glimpses of a different man at the cricket match. One who was playful and effusive. One who seemed to like a bit of silliness in his day.

Her family always teased her for her insatiable need to know. They called her a gossip and made big shows of keeping things from her to keep their precious secrets safe. Please. Like any of those bobos knew a thing about secrets.

The simple truth was society didn't like women to have information because it was currency. Power. The very last thing a woman was supposed to be was powerful. But Claudia wielded the knowledge she accrued like a scalpel. Knowing a thing was the first step. The real power was in the application. Holding back, pressing forward, searching for patterns—all of the ways the world bent to the will of the knowledgeable were at the root of Claudia's endless quest for details.

Now, with the pieces of Ian Yang not quite lining up, she wondered what more there was to know because, like it or not, the knowing was its own form of protection.

She pulled into the mega grocery store parking lot at Kennedy and the 401. Why Ian wanted to meet her here was another piece of the puzzle.

He was sitting in what looked like a cafeteria, wearing basketball shorts and a Sade hoodie—the late September weather still teetering between summer and fall—chatting with an older Chinese man.

His raspy voice carried through the space. "Like this?"

The man did a lot of miming and gesturing to the available bottles on the table. Following along, Ian gamely added the sauces as instructed and shoveled in a large mouthful.

"Mmm. Good!" Ian gave a small bow.

The man grinned widely, nodding his approval, before shuffling off to, presumably, continue about his day.

The smile on Ian's face dimmed a little when he caught sight of her. She wondered if it was her presence specifically or something else that raised his hackles.

"Odd choice for a meet-up, Yang." Claudia lowered herself into the seat across from him, making sure to smooth the skirt of her dress. She crossed her feet at the ankles, placing her purse on the table in front of her. "Care to explain?"

Ian leaned back to better assess her. Weekend Ian, it appeared, had a looser posture and a penchant for smirking. "Not particularly."

Claudia was proud of herself for not rolling her eyes. She needed information and she hadn't yet figured out how to play this. Perhaps the direct route was best. "Well, I'm here. Start spilling."

"I have conditions." He said, around another mouthful of what appeared to be a beef noodle soup.

Claudia's raised brow was her only response.

He swallowed, wiping at his mouth with the balled-up napkin in his fist. "I'm serious. I won't divulge things that are private or harmful. I'm only telling you things that are theoretically public knowledge."

"Fair. What else?" She was riveted by the sight of him eating. The way his mouth slurped his noodles, closed around the spoon, the bobbing of his Adam's apple. All of it had her transfixed.

"For every question I answer, you have to spend time with me."

That snapped her out of it!

Claudia reared in her seat. "I beg your pardon?"

"I think you heard me just fine."

She leaned back in her chair, taking him in. Leveraging information for personal gain was a game she knew well. What she didn't know was whether Ian Yang would turn out to be a keen negotiator or if he was swimming in deep waters.

Claudia did a quick calculation. What this information was worth to her directly versus how she could use it to help a woman she genuinely liked and respected. Would she be willing to spend the currency of her time if the intel Ian had proved useful?

"I know you're not suggesting I barter sexual favors for a harmless bit of backstory," she enjoyed how his eyes bugged out at the suggestion, "so define spending time with you."

"I'm definitely not suggesting anything of the sort! I'm not asking you to go on dates with me; I'm trying to get you to know the janitor."

"Why?"

"Because," he put his elbow on the table and leaned in, "I'm a damn good janitor."

She couldn't help the laugh that bubbled out of her. Her body's reaction to the smile he gave her was another thing she couldn't help.

Claudia cleared her throat and tried to reclaim the distance between them. She spent as much time as she could by herself to compensate for the amount of effort she spent being 'on' in public. Even the version of herself she showed her family was draining. He couldn't know how much work she put into appearing easy and effortless, how much putting on her outside self cost her. That she was willing to pay that price to spend time with him, wager or not, was something she was actively refusing to think about.

"Counteroffer."

Ian magnanimously waved his hand for her to proceed.

"'Spend time' is too nebulous. If I agree, for every question you answer with useful information, I will spend one hour with you doing a pre-approved activity."

"Who decides if the information is useful?"

"I do. But I will be honorable."

"What if the thing I want to do takes more than an hour? What if I wanted to go on a hike, for example?"

Claudia laughed right in his face. She couldn't stop it. "First of all, I would not agree to go on a hike for any length of time. But, yes. If something takes more than an hour, we can address it on a case-by-case basis."

"Alright."

They stared at each other across the small bistro table, a mini face-off, while they took each other's measure. His jaw claimed her full attention as it clenched and flexed, pulling the tendon in his neck taut, daring her to run her tongue along it.

"Will you tell me why you want to know?"

"Does it matter?" Claudia asked, leaning back in her seat in a paltry attempt to clear her head. The muscles in his jaw worked, and she used all her discipline to keep her thoughts from straying to the dark, sweaty corners of her imagination the Minister of Horniness was gesturing towards.

This kind of haggling was new. Normally, Claudia retrieved information in more subtle ways. She had a face people trusted. They felt comfortable casually unburdening themselves to her unprompted. Sometimes she'd ask a seemingly casual, innocent question and be filled in with more facts than she'd bargained for. Other times, she opened the door by dropping a smaller, inconsequential tidbit, thereby allowing the juicier facts to come forth. Her favorite, of course, was applying Cunningham's Law. Men loved correcting women, loved it even more when they were beautiful and appeared young. One false statement uttered with an innocent batting of her lashes was all she needed for him to spill his guts, allowing her to make her escape with the person being none the wiser.

Thinking about how spectacularly her bubbly gossip approach failed, she decided she appreciated the straightforward interrogation style. The key was to always look at all the available pieces before making a decision. It wouldn't do for everyone to know what she was about, but it was certainly effective in this situation.

The sounds of the spoon clattering in the bowl snapped her out of her reverie. Now finished his soup, Ian asked, "Will you tell me what you're going to do with the information?"

"What do you want to hear to make this easier on your conscience?"

Ian's crooked grin made her belly flutter. "Say you agree to the terms to spend some time with me."

She ran through the details again, checking for any loopholes or unforeseen traps. Feeling fairly confident she'd covered her bases, she reached her hand across the table. "I agree."

Ian gave her hand a wary look before taking it in his. It was warm and soft in a way she found surprising. He had calluses, yes, but not where she expected them for someone who labored all day. When he let go, she almost whined at the loss.

"Okay, Claudia Sano. What do you want to know?"

She fairly quivered at the inherent invitation to the question. She wanted to know all sorts of things, and her brain's Minister of Horniness did not disappoint. Starting with, but not limited to, whether he had any interest in being pegged and his opinions on orgasm denial. She wanted to know if he preferred to be in control or if he minded ceding the reins to his partner. She wanted to know the weight of him on her body and wondered what exactly the physique she'd glimpsed in her father's office was capable of handling.

Instead, she asked, "What is your relation to Quincy Temple?"

"Diving right in, eh, Gossipika?"

Claudia giggled—giggled!—at his butchering of chismosa. He'd rhymed its English translation with Costa Rica and given it an accent of some sort. It was the most adorable mistake she'd heard since her nephew said backback whale when he'd meant humpback whale. She had no intention of ever correcting him.

"No time like the present, as they say."

"Indeed."

Ian launched into the particulars, explaining his relation to Quincy, what he knew about him through personal experiences, and details gleaned from his cousins. He liked the man, based on the way he spoke of him, and Claudia made a mental note of that, too. He scrolled through the pictures Junior had sent her and supplemented more of his own. At the core of it, Quincy seemed loyal to five men in particular since childhood and another three people from university. The rest were a cluster of satellites attracted to their orbit. To hear Ian tell it, most of them were good enough people, if a little shallow and clout chase-y.

"How old are you?"

Ian's face scrunched. "What does that have to do with anything?"

"It's something I want to know."

"You're playing a dangerous game. By my estimate you owe me at least 20 hours."

Claudia scoffed playfully. "Twelve at best. The details provided from your tangents, while informative, were not a result of my direct questioning and therefore cannot be factored into the final total."

"I thought you were a money person. What's this lawyer-talk about?"

"I'm merely reminding you of the terms you set." She raised her shoulder in a show of casual indifference. It wasn't her fault he was so chatty. They'd agreed to a straightforward one-to-one exchange, and he'd blithely divulged valuable intel. It was equal parts endearing and appalling.

"Pufferfish," he muttered to himself.

Claudia canted her head to the left. "I'm sorry?"

"Nothing. Never mind." He waved his hand in front of his face as though he were clearing a swarm of midges. "In light of your very astute observation, I don't think I should answer any more of your questions." He began to gather his trash, indicating the end of their visit. Then one side of his mouth kicked up. "Unless you care to join me, I really need to get started on this list."

He was obviously taunting her, but she stopped to consider. Did she care to join him? She was with a man who'd extorted her time for his information in the most wholesome way possible: over a plate of deli counter noodles at a random Asian grocery store in Scarborough. Her curiosity demanded she find out what else would happen during this unconventional visit.

She picked up her purse and prepared to stand. "What's the produce like here?"

Ian's open-mouthed double take was worth it.

Stepping away from the table, she goaded him further, "I assume you have an actual list of some sort?"

"It's my mother's." He seemed so stunned by the turn of events, the words dribbled out of his mouth.

"Well. Might as well get to it." Claudia said, heading toward the corral of shopping carts.

She hid her pleased smile at the trance-like way Ian followed her.

Deciding to tackle the store systematically, from end to end, they each grabbed a cart and started shopping. Claudia moved them briskly through the aisles, judiciously adding things to her cart while keeping an eye out for things from Ian's list.

"You save a dollar if you buy two." Ian gestured to the fettuccine she held.

"I only need one."

"But the value—"

Claudia held her hand up. "I'm going to stop you right there. It doesn't save me money to buy more than I need. Further to that, ask yourself why the store has offered this 'deal'." She emphasized the word with finger quotes. "There's obviously a benefit to them somehow. Don't let yourself be taken in by hyper-consumerism."

He seemed to consider her words before asking, "What about coupons?"

"Same." She shrugged. "They're usually just a loss leader."

Before he could challenge her assertion, a South Asian woman entered the aisle with a baby in the car seat on the handle, a small child in the cart itself, and a girl of about nine trailing her in her soccer uniform, unsuccessfully making her case.

Claudia had no idea what language they were speaking, but she understood the international posture of indignant child and beleaguered mother. There was obviously something the young girl was upset about, but her mother had given it as much attention as she'd planned to and was now trying to get her daughter to pick another topic.

Ian looked on sympathetically, smiling at the kids in turn.

"Do you have a brand of crushed tomatoes you prefer?" She held out two containers with similar labels. If he was this easily distracted, it was no wonder he needed help getting simple chores done. People at the grocery store did not require her attention. The collective goal was to get what you needed without getting in the way and, if the gods were on your side, find a checkout lane that was moving briskly. "Or are they basically the same?"

Claudia was looking at the various sauces, unconcerned with the familial drama playing out behind them, when she heard the sound of the mild commotion. Turning to make sure she wasn't going to get caught in the crossfire of a tantrum, she guessed the child in the cart had stood up and quickly lost his balance, landing heavily on a loaf of bread, toppling the once neatly stacked items around him. The woman went to settle the upset toddler, ignoring her fuming daughter.

The girl crossed her arms and scowled at the packages of pasta. Claudia had definitely been there. Countless times she stood alone in her rage while her mother tended to her siblings, imploring her to cheer up or to simply get over it.

Ian managed to get the child's attention and gave her a look filled with such pitying commiseration, he might as well have said, 'Smile, it will be okay!'.

The girl obviously felt the same way because she gave Ian an eye roll for the ages. Its execution and degree of difficulty demanded accolades and ovations. When she turned her furious face to Claudia, almost daring her to also suck, Claudia did the only thing she could think of: she leaned forward to bring herself in the girl's direct sight line, curled her lip, and snarled.

Claudia was aware of Ian's gasp but didn't acknowledge it. She wanted to give this girl the permission she never had, a roadmap to navigate her feelings in a way her own family hadn't managed, in a way society would never allow. This child was angry. About what, Claudia had no idea, but it didn't matter. Her thick hair was falling out of her lopsided ponytail, she had dirt and grass stains on her uniform, and her tiny body vibrated with outrage.

What Claudia had needed when she was in this child's shoes was for someone to explain to her that she had a right to be upset, that her rage was valid because they'd recognized the same injustice she had. Or, at the very least, believed her reaction to it was justified.

She thought back to the vindication she'd felt when she read Mrs. Whatsit whispering, *'Stay angry, little Meg. You will need all your anger now'*, and lived her life trying to pay that feeling forward. Rising to her full height, Claudia gave the girl a quick, decisive nod. She returned Claudia's gesture and, fists balled at her side, stomped off after her family.

"Now," Claudia held up the two cans to Ian again, "which one do you want?"

Chapter Ten

"**D**id… did you just snarl at a child?" His disbelief made his voice shrill. He completely ignored the two cans of crushed tomatoes she proffered, waiting for someone to tell him he'd imagined the whole exchange.

Nothing about this day was going according to plan. He'd asked Claudia to meet him here because he truly was booked solid. Between checking in on his father, which meant trying to police his mother, and getting his own affairs under control, this weekend didn't leave much in the way of leisure.

He'd almost put it off until he had more time, more freedom of movement, but he had no idea when that day would come. His curiosity had gotten the best of him, as it always did. When Claudia agreed to come to Scarborough to meet him, he figured he could carve a bit of time for himself amidst all the chores and errands he had.

Ian wasn't sure what compelled him to ask Claudia to do groceries together, but he was having a great time. He loved watching her navigate the ingredients that were normally deemed 'ethnic' or 'weird' with a simple "2.99 a pound for chayote?!" when balancing a squash in one hand. Arguing with her about the names of things turned out to be a highlight of his day. As a child, he'd always struggled with the names of things in 'English' when his family used the Caribbean words. How many times had he asked for balanjay when he should have said eggplant or bhaji when he wanted spinach. For all that he grew up speaking English, the nuances of the language as it evolved from the Caribbean melting pot meant there were still words considered foreign. Having Claudia add the extra layer of Spanish for words he already had to 'translate' was fascinating. Her calling cassava yucca, for example, made him want to go through the produce section and label each item one by one to see if any overlap between their two worlds existed.

Another thing he hadn't expected? Claudia baring her teeth at a child in the middle of the canned goods aisle.

"She was upset." Claudia answered simply. "Now she knows it's okay."

"What's okay?"

"Being angry. Girls are conditioned out of anger almost immediately. It's a real problem. I try my best to validate young girls' anger whenever possible."

Ian thought about the way the child's eyes widened in shock before melting into starry-eyed awe. "Does it always work?"

"No," Claudia admitted with a shrug, "but when it doesn't, it keeps the embers of rage glowing a bit longer by giving them something else to be angry about, which also suits my purpose."

Ian wouldn't say that he spent any considerable time seething as a child, but he did remember needing his mother's attention and not being able to have it because his younger siblings needed her more. He also remembered being made to feel childish or inconsiderate for not instantly subduing his own needs and wants for the greater good.

"But," he knew what he wanted to ask but wasn't sure how to vocalize it. "But how do you know they're getting it? How can you be sure your message is being received?"

Claudia looked thoughtful for a moment. She was so beautiful he sometimes lost sight of the fact that she was also wildly intelligent and, apparently, a keen observer of the human condition.

"In an ideal world, I'd be able to explain it to them in a quick, digestible sentence or two." She scoffed, mostly to herself, and said with a curled lip, "Who are we kidding? In an ideal world, they wouldn't need to be taught to embrace their anger."

Ian nodded his understanding. In an ideal world, many things would be different.

"But, barring that unknown utopia, I think just seeing that it's okay to be angry, to be recognized without being made to feel like it was wrong and impolite," she fairly spat the word, "is enough counterprogramming to the false sugar and spice messaging."

Ian opened his mouth to answer but closed it again, too taken with the woman and how her mind worked to know where to begin. Deciding to follow her down her own path, he asked, "Is it weird that you have a..." He winced a little, trying to find a better way to phrase it. "An unflattering family nickname when you have such subversive opinions?"

She made a face that straddled amused and disinterested. He wished he knew exactly what she had been thinking to generate it.

"First," she said without looking at him, scanning the shelves for the evaporated milk his mother wanted, "I'm Latina. Most family nicknames are some highlight of your insecurities. Flaca if you're skinny, Tetona if you're busty, and Gordita if you're chubby are fairly common in Latin American households. Being called a Chismosa is relatively tame, all things considered."

She bent at the knee to look at a brand of coconut milk. Not finding what she wanted, she rose and looked him in the eye. "Second, I don't take it as an insult to be called a Gossip."

He didn't know what to do with the challenge in her eyes. Since both hauling her body to his and kissing her senseless, and falling to his knees to submit to her bidding were equally inappropriate, he ignored it. "Why not?"

"Why should it be?"

He thought about it, seriously pondered the issue of being considered a gossip. Before he could come up with something, she hit him with a barrage of questions that almost had him raising his hands to fend off.

"Who does it benefit to keep information hidden from the masses? Why should I be made to feel immature for seeking out the details and fact-checking sources? When has it ever been in the interests of the people to blindly trust what we're told to accept as gospel? Hmm? Don't you find it weird that 'gossip' is a charge levied against women for the simple act of talking amongst themselves? Why is that?"

Satisfied she'd made her point, she turned on her ridiculous heels and kept going down the aisle.

"So, you think you're performing an act of rebellion?" Catching up to her, he noticed her looking at the pre-made soups.

"I think painting gossip as a moral failing when it is in fact a millennia-old practice of sharing information and preserving histories is an obvious attempt at keeping a certain segment of the population in the dark. I won't be shamed for insisting the lights be kept on."

On the surface he understood what she was talking about. It was definitely something that had always been cast in a 'feminine' light. It wasn't as if men didn't do it. He could admit it was true—as soon as the subject matter turned to something...impor tant, the jovial guys talk on golf courses and in smoking rooms the world over was re-framed as 'gossiping like a bunch of women'. Still, "For millennia?"

"What's the difference between me asking you some questions and repeating what I think is relevant to interested parties and a griot of old?"

He wasn't prepared to have this conversation in the middle of the cereal aisle but since it was happening, he took a deep breath and charged forth.

"Griots were keeping stories and histories alive. They weren't spreading rumors."

"Says who?"

"Literally everybody!" He spread his arms wide as if to encompass the totality of human history.

She rested her hand on her cocked hip and tilted her head. Leveling him with dark, steely-eyed intensity, her voice was both hard and soft, a determined encouragement like the kind used for leading a fourth grader through the rules of BEDMAS. "What's the difference between a griot announcing the birth of a child and a random person at the market commenting on the family's new addition? Why does it matter that the story comes from an official source if the details are the same?"

He didn't have an answer for her. It had never occurred to him to consider it but, laid out like this, what argument could be made against her point?

"Gossip saves lives. It always has."

God, but she was amazing. "Who *are* you?"

"I beg your pardon?"

"You look like Claudia Pérez, Portfolio Manager at Morenal, Smith & Sano but you haven't ooohed or giggled once, and, let's not forget, you literally snarled at a child four aisles over."

He saw the words land and regretted them instantly. Though he'd said them playfully, her eyes widened with awareness. The fiery, whip-smart, insightful woman he'd spent the past hour with disappeared behind a wall of unrelenting pep, and he knew nothing he said or did would get her back.

"It's been a long week; I'm just tired. A good night's sleep will fix me right up!" She smiled at him, big and bright and fake. He'd never been more disappointed to have a beautiful woman's attention.

Claudia traipsed through the rest of the grocery store, cheerfully pointing out interesting, new-to-her items, *ohmygosh*-ing whenever she found something to put in her own basket. He thought he'd gotten her back when she reached for a bag of dried sorrel with a stunned "No. Way! They have jamaica here?" When he tried to engage her on the name of the ingredient—the hibiscus flower called jamaica in Spanish and sorrel throughout the Caribbean—he gave him a saccharine "Cool!" and kept moving.

She shimmied to the music, using her fettuccine as a microphone to sing along to a particularly wrenching ballad.

When they'd finally made it to the cash register, they'd, by silent, mutual agreement, chosen one of the two open lines instead of self-checkout. She checked out the magazine covers while he cursed himself, again, for chasing her away. Looking aimlessly around, he spotted the young girl from before. Her mother was no less harried for the fact her three children seemed calm and settled.

The girl dismissed him with a sniff, apparently still unimpressed with his efforts at commiseration. Her attention was focused on Claudia, taking in her clothes, her heels, and her general *presence* as though she were committing every detail she could to memory. Claudia must have felt the child's eyes on her because she turned to meet her slightly awed gaze. She nodded once, with proud determination. Claudia returned the gesture, a colonel's approval of her soldier's ready alertness, before returning her attention to the tabloid headlines.

"I was wrong."

Claudia looked up, waiting for him to elaborate.

"You can put her away now. I was wrong and I'm sorry." He gestured at the girl who was now engrossed in a smartphone. "That's who you are. I shouldn't have teased you about it."

Her response was a raised brow that miraculously managed to convey a snorted *'whatever'*.

Instead of engaging him, Claudia turned to the cashier and buried the woman under a veritable tidal wave of bubbly enthusiasm. She asked if she was having a good day before gushing about her hair and nails, asked if she had much longer in her shift, and if things were better or worse with the new self-checkout stations. Between the two of them, they chattered nonstop. He didn't see an end to the bombardment of glitter and sparkles and unrelenting cheer until finally Claudia produced a foldable bag from the ornament dangling on her purse.

"That's so cute!" The cashier smiled, handing Claudia her receipt. "Now you'll never forget it in your car!"

For her kindness, she got a beaming, "I know, right?" from Claudia.

When the cashier turned to start scanning Ian's goods, Claudia gave him a haughty, narrow-eyed 'take that' look before setting about to bag her few groceries. He shook his head, laughing to himself.

Claudia Regina Sano Pérez had handed him his ass in 4-inch heels and a sundress, and he'd deserved it. More than that, he was looking forward to her doing it again.

Chapter Eleven

Claudia followed her cousin Alma into a baby boutique, the promise of Peruvian ceviche the only thing keeping her compliant. Alma had done extensive research on double strollers and was ready to kick some literal and figurative tires before making a purchase.

It had only taken eight minutes for Claudia to huff, "Why am I here again?"

"Because you hate babies." Alma rolled her eyes as if the answer were obvious.

"I don't hate babies." Claudia scoffed. Not wanting to pass on a legacy of mental illness did not a hater of babies make. One could argue she was protecting all future babies that may have been born from her chemically imbalanced loins. She was a full-on saint, actually.

Her entire family worried about her to varying degrees. Her sister's constant video chats, her parents' unsubtle entreaties for her to move back home, and her abuela's endless chain of rosaries prayed for her wellbeing. Even Diego, the youngest of her siblings, who didn't think it weird that his sister was basically a shut-in, was prepared to slay her dragons should she require it.

Alma thought she covertly monitored Claudia's welfare because she worked in the same office and had easy, casual access to her, but Claudia had recognized the attempts for what they were. The truth was, only Junior let Claudia be however she wanted. People liked to say it was because they were so similar. They weren't. Yes, Junior had struggled with loneliness as a child, but it wasn't anxiety-fueled. Yet somehow, when Claudia was having an episode, it was Junior who knew how to get through to her when almost nothing else did.

Even as a child, she'd needed her anxieties assuaged; she needed to be told exactly what to expect every step of the way before she could begin contemplating the activity. If four-year-old Claudia was told she was going to the bank, then the dry cleaner, and then the grocery store, woe befall anyone who thought to save the bank for last or, worse, skip it altogether. Did they really think she wasn't aware of how much harder it made things for her? That if she were able to attain even a modicum of flexibility, she would have done so by now? She didn't choose to be intractable. She didn't want to be hobbled by anxiety. She simply didn't know another way. The best she could do was to manage it, to find a way to live within her limitations.

Someone was always checking on her, always making sure she hadn't gone off the deep end unnoticed. She figured if she had to endure their scrutiny, if she had to leave the comfort and security of her home, the very least she deserved was a delicious meal for her trouble.

"Fine. You don't hate them, but you're not particularly enamored of them either." Claudia nodded her acceptance of that truth. "I don't feel like fighting off the many opinions of the parents. If I have to hear about how it was done 'back home' one more time, I swear I will commit actual crime."

Claudia snickered, knowing exactly what poor Alma was talking about. Their family was Panamanian, and Alma's partner Eddie's family was from Peru. There were a lot of 'old world' practices already being foisted on the couple's young son, Lalo. Another baby wasn't going to make them calm down.

Alma continued to explain Claudia's presence as she browsed through the stroller options. "Junior doesn't appreciate scale or moderation of any sort, Silvana is too young to be helpful, and I don't want to deal with any stinky boys today, which means our brothers are out. You, Chismosa, are the perfect blend of informed and indifferent for this outing."

Claudia gave a small laugh at Alma's spot-on assessment of their Toronto-based cousins. "Fine. I accept."

"Good." Alma gave the handle a shake. "What do you think of this one?"

Claudia didn't know the first thing about stroller needs, but she knew about being a single woman, so with that in mind she asked, "How easy is it to put together when you're by yourself?"

Alma considered the mechanisms for folding the stroller, keeping the reality of two babies in mind, and scratched it from her list. They kept shopping, Alma touching and shaking strollers, Claudia looking at the larcenous price tags.

"Junior said she threw you at some guy at work." Alma's non sequiturs were legendary.

"Junior said? But you call me the gossipy one."

"You are the gossipy one. She was talking about something else entirely. Which is why I'm asking you. What guy?"

"Ian Yang, the new janitor." Claudia didn't cringe so much as shudder at her word choice. She reminded herself to come up with a better word. Custodian, maybe? Cleaner? She never called

Harold or Valerie janitors. She didn't know how she'd ended up in the habit with Ian.

"Oh, *him*!"

Claudia took a deep breath. "What does that mean?"

"Please. Are we pretending he isn't hot as sin?"

Claudia's eyes widened. She was used to debauched commentary from Junior; it was practically the woman's stock in trade. But Alma was the serious one. She didn't usually participate in that type of bawdy locker room talk. Even acknowledging Ian in that relatively harmless way was off-brand for Alma.

Raising a haughty brow, Claudia sniffed, "If Junior told you why I was 'thrown at him', then what he looks like isn't relevant, is it?"

Alma gaped at her, mouth open and eyes wide. "Claudia?" Alma reached to put her hand on her forehead as if testing for a fever. "Are you alright?"

She swatted Alma's hand away before it could contact her admittedly flushed skin. "Stop! I'm fine. I'm just..." She heaved a weary sigh, which earned her another shit-eating grin. Allowing herself to deflate a little, she admitted to the ceiling, "I don't know!"

"Go ahead, tell me what's happened."

And, because she didn't know what else to do, because she was still a little unbalanced from yesterday's grocery trip, she unburdened herself to her cousin. Starting with how he told her about her fake laugh, the incident in her father's office, the cricket game, and the wager. She told Alma about doing groceries together and how close to her regular self she'd allowed herself to be before he'd asked her who she was. She explained how startling it was to have him ask and how upset she'd been to have to answer.

"When are you meeting next?"

"I don't know. He hasn't set a date yet."

"But you're going to go?"

"I mean..." Claudia shrugged helplessly. What could she say? She didn't want to go. She really wanted to go. Every answer was the wrong one for the right reason.

Alma stopped fussing with the stroller to look at Claudia. "Could he be trouble?"

She knew what Alma was asking. Could this Ian, this man who had disturbed her equilibrium, become a bigger threat to her carefully ordered world? Could he be trouble *for her*? She didn't think so. Not more than he'd already done by occupying her fantasies and infiltrating her dreams.

Instead of giving voice to it, she shook her head.

"And you're okay with this... exchange?"

"I am. It's just..." Claudia made a vague gesture to indicate herself, "He already sees through it."

"They aren't that different, prima. I know you think they are, but you're wrong."

Alma had been trying for years to convince Claudia that her 'outside' self, the one suited in the armor of tailored clothes and high heels, wasn't vastly different from her 'inside' self. But Claudia wasn't sure Alma understood that her 'inner' self still wasn't her final form. There was a version of herself who was more like a bridge troll, disgusted with humanity and plotting ways to make the villains pay for their sins. The version of herself ruled by intrusive thoughts and questionable impulses.

The version of herself that wondered if maybe–just maybe–she'd sleep better at night with a little blood on her hands.

The few times she managed to speak these thoughts out loud, she was always reminded there were other ways to go about things. Claudia used to rail at the very idea—why should she use those methods when they didn't work?—until she realized those methods were touted specifically *because* they don't work. Which only made her angrier.

She wanted it all to stop. She wanted all aggressors to pay. They wouldn't if they weren't forced to receive the pain they'd caused. If they didn't suffer for their sins, then they were essentially getting away with it. This was the loop that literally kept her up at night. As far as she could tell, humanity's capacity for mob-think meant it would be all or nothing. They as a society couldn't withstand the all, and Claudia's brain chafed at the nothing. She wanted to lie down and close her eyes until it was over. She wanted to wage a battle in the streets. She couldn't do both. She wouldn't do either.

"I appreciate the—"

"Don't make polite noises at me, Claudia." Alma interrupted irritably. "I'm going to keep saying it until you get it through your thick skull. You've convinced yourself you're too much because tía Elena is a worrywart. But having sharp edges or an acerbic tongue isn't some fatal flaw. There are truly unlikeable people walking around hand-in-hand with their boo. You don't have to pretend to be someone else if you want to get close to this man."

"Bueno. Pero..." Claudia sighed helplessly. "Even if being with him like that was an option, which it is not," she steamrolled over whatever Alma had opened her mouth to say, "I go for uncomplicated men for a reason, prima. I work so hard at regulating my mood, at finding the balance for my sharp edges, as you call them. A man like Ian would pull me in the wrong direction."

"How?"

How? Claudia laughed to herself. It was a bitter, twisted sound that caught in her throat. She'd tried being with someone as angry, but it only sent her spiraling. They fed her nihilistic tendencies without offering a productive outlet for her anger, and Claudia needed to be mindful of her behaviors falling into compulsions. She'd tried men who were aware but not actively consumed, but they would tut and tell her it was 'the way things were'. She'd even made the critical mistake of being with a man who was angry at the unfairness of the world only because it was changing before he got his turn at the top of the ladder.

The proverbial backbreaking straw was when she'd been told she was too beautiful to worry about such heavy topics. It had sent her into the arms of kind but simple men who drank fair trade coffee, avoided fast fashion, but had no true understanding of the level of destruction the G6 nations were wreaking in the name of 'national security'.

"You've seen him. Has an angrier-looking man ever walked among us?"

Alma snorted her derision, "As you have pointed out a bajillion times, problematically angry men look like they play squash at a country club and are called Chad or Steve or Brett."

"In fact," Claudia interrupted, "I said those kinds of men are especially *dangerous*."

"Well, men that look like Ian belong on magazine covers. His type of angry bends you over some furniture to provide an *attitude adjustment* when you've bratted too close to the sun, if you know what I mean." Alma said, while giving a suggestive hip thrust.

Claudia's scandalized gasp bounced off the walls of the small boutique. "Alma, estás ahí?"

"Yes, I'm in here, drowning in pregnancy hormones."

"Jesuscristo. Add it to the list of why I don't want to get pregnant!"

"I know. Poor Eddie is exhausted. There are two entire trimesters still to go!"

"*Eddie* is exhausted? You're making a people! The least he can do is be ready with a wet tongue and a hard dick for you to avail yourself of at any time of the day or night!" Claudia decreed, annoyed at the mere suggestion a man was being inconvenienced by his pregnant partner.

"Oh, that part he handles like a champ!" Alma literally winked and nudged Claudia. "It's the mood swings, sore body, and general sense of worry for my overall health that's got him losing sleep."

"What's wrong with your health?" Claudia asked, concerned for her cousin while also moderately relieved to hear Eddie remained one of the good ones.

"Nothing out of the ordinary. Eddie watched a documentary on the Black maternal health crisis. He's now convinced I'm in mortal danger. He can't be reasoned with." Her annoyed huff was full of love for her college sweetheart.

"Isn't your imminent death more reason for him to be here? He should have a say in the stroller he'll be stuck using as a widower with two young kids, no?"

Alma guffawed, holding her belly. "Too dark, Chimosa!"

"Okay, pero en serio, you're good?"

"Do you think I'm a fool, Claudia? Why can't you date Ian if he's interested?"

Fuck. Claudia wasn't actively trying to change the subject; she was just happy that it had organically veered away from her and on to Alma. She should have known her steadfast and resolute cousin wouldn't be so easily swayed.

Claudia took a deep breath and told the truth, even if it was just this once. "He makes me feel out of control."

Alma pinched the back of her arm. She hissed over Claudia's yelp of pain, "I asked you if he would be trouble."

"I thought you meant something different!" Scowling, she yanked her arm away as she rubbed the abused flesh.

"Como qué? What other kind of trouble could I mean, Claudia?"

"I don't know, Alma! He's not going to be trouble because I'm not going to let it, okay? We're going to spend these hours together, and his intense stare and his dangerous good looks won't be a factor anymore."

Alma made a dismissive sound, muttering something under her breath that Claudia was too exhausted to deal with. Let her grumble. It didn't matter because this arrangement was temporary. Once it was done, so too would her interest in him be done. There was no other way.

She knew from experience that getting close to men whose outsides telegraphed the disdain and antipathy coursing through her insides was dangerous. So, no, there was nothing to see where this man was concerned, no matter how she wanted him to adjust her attitude. It was too dangerous. *He* was too dangerous.

Letting Ian Yang get close, *closer*, was a mistake she had no intention of making.

Chapter Twelve

"He can't be serious," Claudia muttered to herself when she pulled up to the address Ian had texted. She had agreed to another 'chore' because, despite everything, she had enjoyed last weekend's grocery shopping. Well, it was more she enjoyed that she didn't have to work as hard to be around him. He seemed to understand that she wasn't the sunny cheerleader she pretended to be at the office and didn't ask too many questions about it. After she'd gone out of her way to make her point, she felt fairly confident he wouldn't make any more pithy comments either.

She could admit she'd perhaps gone a little overboard, but he had only himself to blame. He'd said he knew when her laugh was fake, correctly pointed out the difference, then had the nerve to ask where the ditz had gone? She'd had no other recourse. It was that or admit how much it had hurt, and she wasn't prepared to go down that road.

Now, she was cursing herself for not asking more follow-up questions as she took in the massive laundromat she was meant to spend the next hour of her Saturday.

Pulling her purse from the passenger seat and settling the strap across her torso, she swung her car door shut and went in to find Ian. The cavernous space hummed with the motors of the industrial-sized machines. The air smelled of a weird mix of stale and chemical, with a lingering hint of 'mountain fresh' tacked on for shame's sake.

She found Ian at the end of the row of chairs lined against the one wall, spread indolently while scrolling on his phone.

"You want me to watch you do laundry?"

He looked up, startled, then took her in from head to toe. She would have sworn in a court of law that she felt his gaze, cool and feather-light on her skin. His eyes roved over her form, cataloging everything from her heeled sandals to where the hem of her skirt hit her thighs to the flounce of her blouse's sleeve. It was a point of pride that she didn't fidget while enduring the sheer force of his attention.

"Do you need help unloading your car?" He stood to perform the same limbering bounce on his toes as he'd done on the cricket pitch.

"No." Claudia stretched the word out, failing to follow his words.

"You didn't bring any stuff." It was three parts observation, one part accusation, with a question thrown in for garnish.

"Stuff? Like what, a sudoku book?"

They traded confused looks, their befuddlement bouncing between them like dice on a Craps table.

"No, like your clothes and sheets and so on." He moved his hand in a vague rolling motion, as if jump-starting her memory. When she continued to stare at him blankly, he added slowly. "So, you can wash them?"

Claudia's hand flew to her chest. "Here? Now?"

"Yes, of course, here, now. I sent you the map link. What did you think we were going to do at a laundromat?"

What *did* she think they were going to do today? She might have given it some consideration, been more prepared, if she'd bothered to look at more than the major intersection on the map before agreeing to meet him. The way he'd returned to his taciturn gruffness after they'd spent the day shopping together gave her whiplash. He wasn't rude to her. Or, she guessed, not more than he'd been before. But... well, she thought they'd share some idle chit-chat when they happened upon each other in the common areas of the office. She'd thought they'd leveled up their acquaintance.

Instead, he'd given her the same old grunt and nod and went on about his business.

"I..."

Ian's mouth curved in a wicked grin. "You had no idea you were coming to a coin wash, did you?" He looked her up and down pointedly, huffing out a chortling sound. "Not judging by your outfit, you didn't."

She looked down at herself, then at him. He was wearing lilac-colored track pants and a long-sleeved white t-shirt with a pink teddy bear on it.

"Even if I knew you invited me to the laundry, I still wouldn't have shown up in my pajamas."

It was his turn to look down at himself. "These aren't my pajamas."

Though she knew his voice was naturally raspy and he didn't mean anything salacious, her brain's now-established Ministry of Horniness got straight to work conjuring images of Ian in bed, tangled in his sheets. Naked.

Clearing her throat, and hopefully her filthy mind, Claudia made a show of looking around. "Where are your things?"

"Already started. They take a bit longer to dry." He added that last, as though Claudia had any idea how long a load of coin washing took to complete.

Feeling a little out of sorts, Claudia shifted her weight from one foot to the other. She had no idea what to do with herself. She wished she really had brought a sudoku book.

"So…" She trailed off, looking pointedly at the busy patrons moving between the rows of machines. "What now?"

"Now we wait. And chat."

"Chat?"

"Yeah, chat. Visit. Catch up."

She narrowed her eyes as she searched his face for sarcasm. Finding none, she crossed her arms over her chest and grumbled "Oh, now you want to talk to me" under her breath.

Obviously tired of looming over her, Ian spread himself back in the chair. Everything about Ian was loose and languid, so different from his closed-off posture at work. He sat up straight and muttered to himself, "I'm sitting down and we're still almost eye-to-eye," then went back to his sprawled posture.

Claudia flipped him off as she lowered herself into a seat, leaving a space between them. She crossed her feet gingerly at the ankle.

"Let's start with your outfit. What did you think you were gonna be doing dressed like that?"

She'd wanted to take advantage of these lingering days of summer by wearing a tiered skirt and long-sleeved boho blouse. "What's wrong with my outfit?" At his arched brow, she huffed. "I'm outside. These are my outside clothes. I might not have worn such a flouncy blouse, but otherwise," she waved her hand over her person, "this is it."

Ian nodded, digesting the information.

"I'm perfectly happy to skip the backstory on your rainbow bear t-shirt in favor of getting some clarification on why you're here."

Ian gave her an affronted glare. "This," he pulled the hem of his shirt, "is Cheer Bear. From the original lineup of Care Bears. Her belly badge is a symbol of hope and happiness!"

"Her belly badge..." Claudia trailed off, stifling her laughter. She continued. "Let's table that and focus on my more pressing concerns."

"I thought it would be a good idea to take advantage of the long weekend, y'know? I thought it would be quieter since it's not recognized provincially."

Ah, yes. The National Day for Truth and Reconciliation. How typically Canadian to make a performance of restitution to the Indigenous peoples but fail to stick the landing by not making it mandatory to observe the holiday nationwide.

"I'm getting ready for winter. Culling the summer clothes and pulling the heavy stuff out of their hidey-holes. I can't wash my comforters properly at home, so I came here." Claudia nodded slowly, taking in his explanation. He continued, "I thought you might also have comforters and such to wash, so I offered the opportunity to do it together."

"Because I would have checked the destination and prepared accordingly. Right." Okay, so it was actually rather thoughtful. "I don't have comforters, so it's not a missed opportunity. Thank you, though."

"What do you mean you don't have comforters? What do you sleep with during the winter?"

Sleep with? Was that another adorable misspeak or something more Freudian? Because she'd spent entirely too much time curating a list of ways she could *sleep with* Ian, and not a single one of them involved slumber.

"Um, I have weighted blankets. I use a heating pad when it's really cold."

He made a small, 'huh' sound. "Is it because you run hot?"

She wouldn't get into what it took to get her brain to settle long enough for her to get to sleep. Instead of launching into the laborious sequence, she sniffed a prim, "Not particularly."

"I do. Or so I've been told." He rubbed the back of his neck after rolling his head from shoulder to shoulder. "But I like to be snuggly."

His was not a voice meant to be discussing teddy bears and snuggly blankets. The disparity kept her feeling unbalanced and on edge.

"You never did answer me. Do you play any other sports besides cricket?" She figured bringing it back to something neutral and un-bedroom-related would help.

He rolled with her subject change. "I mean, who doesn't enjoy a pickup game of ball at the park, y'know? But no, only cricket at that level."

"Do you regret not going further with it?"

"No, I like where I'm at right now."

She nodded thoughtfully and opened her mouth to say something else when the penny dropped. "Wait. Why would you think I had something to regret?"

Whoops. She wasn't meant to have those details, wasn't supposed to know he'd walked away from a chance at a more lucrative career. It would be too weird if she laid out all she'd learned about him, most of it by sheer happenstance, but she didn't want to lie to him about it, either. She chose a truth that was closest to reasonable.

"Oh, you were playing for a national team in a fairly competitive league, so I figured…"

He seemed to accept the explanation. "Yeah, I guess. But what if I wasn't good enough to go further?"

An elaborate eye roll was her only response.

"I suppose you formed this opinion based on your extensive knowledge of the sport?"

Claudia snorted her laughter, "I know exactly nothing about the sport. It doesn't take an expert to recognize how good you are. It was obvious that you are a star player."

He tipped his head to one side, assessing her through a half-lidded gaze. His mouth curved into a slow, pleased smile. "Thanks."

Claudia's eyes bounced around, desperate to land her attention on anything other than Ian's handsome face.

He continued talking, with no concern for her inner turmoil, "It's a byproduct of British colonialism, I guess. Guyanese people love them some cricket. I've been playing since I was a boy; I had no choice but to be good at it. But at thirty-one, my body can only take so much more abuse."

When he winked at her, the duly elected Minister of Horniness was at the ready, providing images of him kneeling in nothing but his shin pads and his filthy smile. Worried she would do something inappropriate like stick her hand in her underpants while leaning over to lick his mouth, she barreled forth, "Is that how you know Miss Val, because your family is also Guyanese?"

He leveled her with a disbelieving look. "Are you being funny?"

Claudia took a moment to replay the conversation in her mind. No one had ever accused her of being funny. It had been argued that she might not even have a sense of humor, so she'd obviously done something wrong, but she had no clue what. Had her horniness blinded her to a faux pas of some sort?

"...No?"

"They're my parents, Claudia. Howard and Valerie Yang? They are my parents."

She frowned, trying to recall everything she knew about the children of the lovely couple who took care of the office. Slowly, she listed the details. "Their eldest works for an offshore drilling company and is away traveling the world with his job most of the time. Their youngest two are still at school, studying to be a lawyer and a physicist. Their middle son is a gardener."

Ian ran his hands down his face, groaning his frustration. "I'm a landscape architect. My mother has always conflated it with landscaper and, over time, distilled it down to 'gardener'."

Claudia's eyes were wide with delight. She covered her mouth to keep from cackling at such a fabulous crossing of wires. Ian gave her an aggrieved huff in response.

"If it makes you feel any better, she is very proud of your achievements. You won an award after graduation?" The way her shoulders shook negated her valiant efforts to stifle her laughter. It sputtered out of her regardless, the tendrils of mirth stealing her breath.

"I have to load the dryer," he grumbled under his breath and stormed away.

Claudia watched him as he shook the items out, detangling them from the effects of the spin cycle as her laughter died. Almost immediately, the pieces slammed into place. She was gripped with a pang of sympathy so sharp her stomach dropped. If she weren't already sitting, she might have stumbled from the force of it.

"It'll take thirty-ish minutes," Ian announced as he threw his body back in the chair.

She was overcome by the reality of everything she now understood; she stammered a helpless, "Ian, I... I'm sorry."

His frown made it clear he had no idea what she was apologizing for or why she sounded so heartbroken. "She does it all the time; I shouldn't be surprised."

"No. I mean... I didn't put it together, and I should've. Your dad had a stroke. You're helping your parents while he recovers." Sighing, Ian closed his eyes and tipped his head against the wall behind him. "That's why you asked me to meet you here and the grocery store," she was talking to herself now as more of the pieces slotted together, "because you're—"

"Impossibly busy," he finished for her, eyes still closed and voice heavy with exhaustion.

"Are you okay? With everything, I mean."

"Mostly." He turned to face her, his head still leaning on the wall. "I keep reminding myself that it could have been worse, that he's getting better every day. Less chance of succumbing to a pity party that way."

"I guess now we're even," she smiled.

"How so?"

"You didn't know Manuel was my dad, and I didn't know Howard was yours."

He made a sound that could pass for laughter. "You don't use the same last name as yours!"

"Sí, pero I'm not sure I knew Howard's so... samesies."

Ian leaned forward with his forearms on his thighs, hands clasped in the space between his knees. "I can't decide if it's a good thing or a bad thing."

"What do you mean?" She tilted her body towards him so she could hear over the din of the machines.

He gave her a once-over out of the corner of his eye, then returned to his hands.

Claudia nudged his shoe with the toe of her sandal and insisted, "What? Tell me."

He heaved a heavy, soul-weary sigh. He did that a lot, she noticed. It seemed to her that Ian was in the habit of saying things, then getting evasive when pressed to elaborate further. She waited for him to organize his thoughts. When he was ready, he turned to her, still unable to sit while keeping his body within the confines of the chair's borders. Really, did the man need to take up so much space?

Ian gestured to her with his forefinger. "That."

"What?" Claudia's face scrunched in confusion.

"That look. Before you knew, you looked at me like I was just a guy. A menial laborer who you had to lower yourself to speak to because you wanted information, but 'just a guy' all the same." She bristled as indignation straightened her spine, but he kept going before she could retort, "Now you're looking at me all 'poor Ian'. I don't know how I feel about it."

"Would you rather discuss the many people who've informed you that you 'run hot'?"

"I didn't say it was many people."

"Full disclosure," Claudia raised her hands in a placating gesture, "I learned a lot about you from the two very appreciative women sitting in front of me at the cricket game. They seemed to believe you could have a different body being warmed in your bed each night if only you'd say the word."

Ian scratched his stomach. The hem of his t-shirt had ridden up as he contorted in his seat. Claudia was mesmerized by the trail of dark hair that disappeared beneath his waistband. The urge to nuzzle it with her cheek was shocking in its intensity.

"That's a huge exaggeration," he said, still idly fondling his stomach.

Did the man have no regard for her nerves?

Clearing her throat, Claudia asked, "Really? A huge exaggeration?"

He caught his head in his hands, his elbows on his knees, and made a frustrated sound in his throat. "Yes! God, I can't believe people still bring it up. It was so long ago, right? I was scouted, in my youth, to go pro."

"Yes, they mentioned that, too." Claudia nodded sagely.

Ian huffed his annoyance, continuing as if she hadn't spoken, "It was a contract thing. A way to lock me in until I was old enough. I was only meant to train before being picked up, but the pickup was all but guaranteed. There was no consideration given to my actual education, no concern for my academic success. The school I attended was an afterthought. All that mattered was I showed up to practices and sat on the bench during game time. While that was happening, women tried to latch on to me, thinking I was their express pass to the WAG life."

"Ah. But you weren't interested in being a meal ticket."

"I was not." He agreed vehemently.

"Which has earned you a reputation as a man whose standards are so impossibly high, women's hopes have been dashed against the rocks of your indifference."

"Jesus Christ, Claudia! Why would you say it like that?"

She laughed, the sound loud and disruptive, bursting out of her. Ian shook his head in a grand display of aggrievement, which only made her laugh harder.

Shoulders still shaking, she wiped a tear from under her eye and gave Ian a gentle shoulder check. "Do you like 'cruel Ian' better than 'poor Ian'?"

Ian kissed his teeth. The mmcht sounded like the crack of a whip as he stomped over to the dryer, mumbling to himself about pufferfish. Claudia couldn't help but trail in the wake of his affronted dignity, marching along so the click-clack of her heels could be heard over the rumble of the machines.

"It can be both if you like!" She clasped her hands under her chin, batted her eyes, and put on a high-pitched, simpering voice, "Oh, poor Ian has to fight them off with a stick. Poor Ian can't have a moment's peace with all the women throwing themselves at him. Won't someone think of Poor Ian who's positively drowning in strange—"

"Here." He interrupted, passing her two corners of a comforter. "Make yourself useful; hold this side. But maybe lift your arms higher so it doesn't drag on the ground."

"You... ugghhh!" The exasperated sound she made was the only warning he had before she launched the comforter at his face.

Laughing, he made quick work of folding the blanket and putting it in his hamper. "Okay, okay. No more playing around." He looked at his watch. "I need to get this done so I can finish up the rest of my running around before my shift at the food bank."

That information was like a record scratch in her brain. Shift at the food bank? It would appear those two women from the cricket game didn't know everything about his comings and goings.

"You volunteer at a food bank?"

He did that thing again where he introduced a topic then seemed inconvenienced by follow-up questions. She'd have to get to the bottom of that. Right now, she was particularly interested in this story.

"I just," he sighed heavily, "sometimes it feels like donating to charity isn't enough. I mean, I know it helps, and I'm committed to my monthly contributions, but I also need to *do* something."

If she wasn't absolutely sure he didn't have access to her private life outside of these scheduled visits, she would have accused him of pandering to her. How many times had she thought the same thing? The act of giving was good, of course, but it also absolved the giver of any further demands to contend with the problem. It was good and right and just to give to an organization like

Covenant House, say, but to her mind it rang a bit hollow if you never reckoned with *why* the youth were on the street to begin with.

"Why the food bank?" The more time she spent with this man, the more fascinated she became.

"Dunno," he shrugged. "Feed Scarborough was started by a guy who wanted to do something to help. That's it. A dude saw a problem and thought to try to help fix it. Seemed like a good enough reason."

The answer was good, but the way he averted his eyes as he methodically folded sheets said there was more. "So it was that guy specifically that caught your attention?"

More shrugging. More darting eyes.

She settled her weight into her heels, crossing her arms over her chest. Her posture was unmistakable, screaming 'I can wait all day' to anyone who saw her.

Ian threw his hands up and blurted an exasperated, "People shouldn't go hungry!" He turned and pulled another blanket out of the massive dryer, fitting the corners together. "Food is a basic human necessity. You should be able to climb a tree and feed yourself from its fruit if all else fails. All the bullshit about shoplifting and petty crime on the news but never a single word about how hunger can drive you to acts of desperation, no word about why people are in such dire straits. That's why."

"Oh." Claudia didn't know what else to say. She agreed with him wholeheartedly and was surprised and impressed by the fiery way he spoke on the subject. She also liked the angry edge to his voice as he spat out the words more than was reasonable, though she suspected the Minister of Horniness had a little something to do with that. "What time is your shift?"

"Not until four, but I have stuff to do for my folks first."

"With all you've got on your plate, have you considered suspending your shifts?" She wasn't entirely sure why she asked. It wasn't any of her business, and it was probably impolite, besides. She just wondered if he'd be less... harried if there was one less ball for him to juggle all the time.

He looked down at her, and a muscle in his jaw twitched. "I willingly walked away from my life to help my family – my job, my social life. All of it. I don't regret it. The only things I kept were cricket and the food bank. Cricket's done for the season, so all I've got left for myself is one four-hour shift a week. So, no. I haven't considered it." There was no self-pity, no woe is me lurking behind the words. Only a defiant determination.

"Okay," she nodded, her voice full of compassionate understanding. She, of all people, understood the need to get her hands dirty. The need to feel like your actions were making a net positive difference in the world. "Then let's get you out of here so you're not late."

Together, they folded up his sheets, towels, and the duvet for which he said he couldn't find a proper-fitting cover so went without one. She reorganized his hamper, settling the items in a neat, compact stack. He gathered his few things before hefting the load and following her out into the afternoon sun.

They got to her car first. She stood on the concrete parking block and turned to face him. Her breath hitched at his nearness. They were eye to eye, and Claudia couldn't help but steal a few glances at the curve of his sinful mouth.

"I, um, had fun at the laundromat," She said, twisting her fingers together bashfully, "Who'd've thought I'd ever say that?"

"Thanks for all your help, Gossipika. It definitely made the time more enjoyable."

Was it her imagination, or was he also stealing furtive glances at her mouth? Out of habit, she caught her bottom lip in her teeth. Yep, he was watching. But only because she was so close, right? Only since they were momentarily the same height and not because he wondered what they'd look like stretched around his dick. Right?

She stepped down off the block of concrete, and Ian didn't react. Didn't lean forward or shift to stay close. So it was only her imagination. Too bad. It was for the best, though. Nothing good could come from them crossing any lines.

"See you around, 'poor Ian'." She teased as she settled into her car.

"See you around, Gossipika."

She pulled out of the parking space. When she checked her rearview mirror, Ian was still standing in the same spot watching her. He stood there, unmoving, until she pulled into the flow of traffic, and Claudia wondered—not for the first time—if she might be playing with fire.

Chapter Thirteen

He looked at his phone again, tearing his attention away from the endless crowd of people going about their business in the late October sun. God, he loved people-watching. A million stories floated around in the lives of perfect strangers. Hundreds of fascinating tales of lives lived with joy and triumph and hardship and loss, all milling around untold. Unknown.

"I swear, if your plan is to take me to Little Canada, I will impale you with my heel."

Ian didn't even try to stop the smile from spreading across his face, slow and easy like maple syrup. It had been almost a month since they'd had one of these 'contracted outings'. Their schedules had been particularly incompatible, with Claudia at a wedding in Miami over the Thanksgiving long weekend and him with... all his regular commitments.

"I specifically told you to wear comfortable shoes, so there shouldn't be any risk of impalement. But, seeing as you're here," he brought his hand to just under his chin, "instead of your probable natural spot here," he lowered his hand to below his armpit, "you've clearly disregarded my note."

She scoffed at his approximation of her actual height. "I'm outside. These are—"

"Yes, yes," he interrupted, "your outside clothes."

She flipped her sunglasses onto her head so he could receive the full scope of her scowl. He wanted to taste her curled lip, nibble at it until it gave way to breathless kisses. Instead, he looked her up and down, appreciating that while she wasn't in anything that could qualify as casual, she was dressed down by her standards, in monochromatic navy: cigarette pants, a cashmere crew neck, and a mid-length trench coat. Except for those damn heels, this was as simple as he'd seen her.

"Okay, so...if we aren't experiencing the breadth of Canada through the art of miniature, what are we doing?"

Directly across the street from where they stood were major attractions—a huge multiplex cinema to the north and a humongous shopping mall to the west. They were around the corner from a century-old playhouse that famously ran the Phantom of the Opera for the entirety of the 90s, and they were a block away from recently renovated concert venue Massey Hall. They were literally surrounded on all sides by every caliber of restaurant the city of Toronto had to offer. Had she run out of ideas after Little Canada?

"Did..." He cleared his throat and started again, trying to keep his tone neutral, "Do you want to see the miniatures?"

"Huh? No." Claudia dragged her attention away from the busker playing buckets and said more firmly, "No. As you so helpfully pointed out, you went out of your way to mention my footwear. If we were going to a movie or play, or restaurant, my shoes wouldn't have been an issue." She used the pointer finger of one hand to count off the fingers on her other hand as she itemized her points. "You didn't come all the way down here to go to the Eaton Centre when there are only maybe a half dozen stores here that you couldn't find in the three malls that are just as close to you with better, freer parking. Little Canada is supposed to be the size of two ice rinks. That, coupled with your habit of commenting on my height—"

"Claudia, please, I'm begging you," Ian's breath caught at the way her gaze clashed with his. It was sharp and fiery and gone in an instant, but he saw it. He felt it, and he was going to take his time to unpack it all. Later. When the potential for a full mast erection wasn't such a threat. Fighting to regain his train of thought, he put his hand flat under his chin and swept his arm in a wide arc, easily clearing the top of her head. "Be serious."

She crossed her arms over her chest in a showy huff and grumbled, "Whatever."

The urge to pull her into his embrace and hold her close was so strong, he felt the muscles in his arms twitch. He took a half step to the side, enough to be out of arm's reach of the woman who occupied so much of his thoughts, and asked, "You ready to unlearn what Valerie told you?"

She looked around Yonge-Dundas Square uncomprehendingly. "You're going to need to elaborate."

"This. This is an example of landscape architecture." Ian spread his arms out to encompass the four thousand square meter space. "This is what I do."

She looked around again, taking in the rows of lighted fountains set directly into the pavement and low, circular stone planters on the western side of the square. She took a couple of steps to his left to look at the drinking fountain behind him.

The revitalization of the space happened more than twenty years ago. He wondered what she saw when she looked at it. "This is the easiest example of what landscape architecture is. I wanted to show you some of my favorites."

That managed to recapture her attention. Good. He always preferred it when she was looking at him. When her dark, steely gaze dared him to underestimate her.

"You have favorite slabs of concrete?"

Was that all she saw here? Granted, the Yonge-Dundas Square was built as an open public space and event venue didn't really register as landscape architecture the way other sites did, but it still most definitely qualified.

"I have a favorite plenty of things. Today, we're going to see how slabs of concrete," he stressed her words, "can be incorporated into the community. Are you going to be okay walking in those?"

She looked down at her shoes. "Yeah. I've lost almost all nerve endings in my feet after puberty failed to provide me the final prayed-for inches."

He gave her heels a wary glance. It was the perfect day for walking: sunny, dry, and cool. Still, he quickly revised his plans, removing HTO Park and Sherbourne Common from his route, worried she'd be hobbled within the hour otherwise. He'd save the Village of Yorkville Park for another time. "Okay, this way."

They cut diagonally across the square toward Victoria Street, making their way one block north. The first stop was the Devonian Square on the Toronto Metropolitan University campus. "Welcome to Lake Devo!"

"Let me guess. This is your alma mater?"

"Nah, the school of architectural science here is amazing, but the landscape program had shuttered by the time I was ready to enroll. I still stayed local and went to UofT." Maybe he could have gone away to school, but his parents had already worked so hard to give him this shot at an education without the crippling debt; going more than a subway ride away seemed like gilding the proverbial lily. He had summer job savings on top of the academic and athletic scholarships. With his parents' help, he was able to enter the workforce with nothing but his diploma and letters of reference instead of the debilitating amount of red many of his peers had in their bank balances. "I put that Metropass to work!"

Her small huff of laughter ricocheted through him. Every time he earned her real, genuine laugh, he felt like a superhero. "Now look around. What do you see?"

He looked over her head—remembering, again, with a small amount of glee, she was unable to obstruct his vision even in heels—and tried to see what she saw.

It was with a small parkette dominated by an oval-shaped reflecting pool that turned into an ice rink in the winter. Massive boulders imported from the Canadian Shield, some of them forty cubic meters or more, dotted the northern and southern edges of the space.

"Honestly? Another slab of concrete with a splash pad instead of fountains."

He would have felt demoralized if not for her palpable frustration at not being able to get it.

"Yes, there is definitely that." He cocked his head, gesturing for her to follow him so she could look at it from a different angle. "Think about all the afternoons spent at a piazza, stopping for a quick break, or a little snack."

"What makes you think I—"

He cut her off with a heavy sigh and said in a bored monotone, "Claudia, have you ever been to a plaza in Spain, a piazza in Italy, or a place in France?"

She gave him one of her now-familiar indignant sniffs and tilted her nose in the air in answer.

He wanted nothing more than to grab her face and kiss her haughty mouth. This woman was a test of every restraint he had and many he didn't. "As I was saying, think of one of those, and now look again."

Claudia looked around, turning slowly with his new directive.

"When people talk about missing university, it's usually just a twisted sense of nostalgia. What they really miss is *community*. They miss the only aspect of European life we've ever managed to successfully recreate: living in a walkable 'city' with plenty of designated third spaces."

She nodded. Whether she was agreeing with him or signaling her comprehension, he wasn't sure, so he continued, "This park is small; it's not even a hundred square meters. But do you see how the academic buildings line up on that one corner?"

She tilted her head, following his hand as he pointed to the area in question. Leaning over her, he pointed to the opposite corner "And how the honey locusts over there are planted?"

Their leaves were the golden yellow of autumn.

"You mean the way the trees are on both streets in a kind of L pattern?"

"Exactly." He smiled down into her beaming face. "They complete the frame."

They watched as the pedestrian-only section of Gould and Victoria streets bustled, people crossing through the tables and chairs, while others relaxed in the noonday sun.

Taking a deep breath, filling his chest with the city's unique brand of vibrant, chaotic energy, Ian continued, "Architecture has always been where the science of designing buildings meets the philosophy of art. It's what I love about it. A building will always be a building no matter how stunning or avant-garde the design, but it can evolve, change with the times. Sure, it might start as a factory but end up retrofitted into a school, or a bank into a restaurant. The reason I chose to specialize in landscapes is for this," he gestured at the reflecting pool. "Using live elements to add color, depth, and texture to concrete and steel? The combinations are endless. The only limits are my imagination. And soil type. And zoning bylaws. And sun exposure. But mostly my imagination." He let the cheeky grin spread on his face, knowing she would recognize his ultimate point: there was so much opportunity for creation to be had if you were willing to do the work.

Claudia looked around, and he waited with restless anticipation for her thoughts. It was becoming increasingly clear to him that Claudia Sano was a woman who liked to know things. There was no detail too small, no aspect too obscure, to be considered insignificant in her eyes.

Giving her a bit more time to work through her thoughts, he wandered to one of the backless concrete benches. "Something like this evolves with the space; it grows and changes with its environment, allowing its surroundings to dictate its purpose."

"How so?" The gentle furrow in between her brows told him she was still processing.

"Take these boulders, for example." He ran his hand over one of the two-billion-year-old rocks. "They're a design element to be sure, but they have also been used as gallery walls during May's CONTACT photography month, where large, colorful, abstract images are glued to the rocks."

Claudia nodded. "Evolution."

"Evolution." Ian agreed.

"This was always meant to be a reflection pond slash skating rink," she started slowly, and Ian nodded his encouragement, "but, over time, it became more. Its uses grew to fit the needs of its environment."

"Right. And?"

She looked at him, all the pieces now in place and her pride of comprehension glowing in her eyes. "And it can keep changing to meet the community's needs as long as it exists because that's the ultimate point."

"For me, yes, that's the ultimate point." He was so helpless against the force of her smile, pleased and delighted, he didn't bother fighting it. He allowed himself to fall back onto the bench, his limbs sprawled akimbo.

"Har har. I might have been a bit slow on the uptake, but I'm getting it now."

He allowed her to think his antics were about her ability to grasp these new-to-her concepts instead of the inescapable truth that she made him weak in every conceivable way. His composure, his will, his knees, and his heart all suffered from her ceaseless assault.

Sitting up, he gave her a playful, lopsided smile. "You think you can handle more?"

Her spine straightened, she arched her brow. "I can do this all day."

God help him.

"Alright, Gossipika. Let's go."

Chapter Fourteen

Somewhere between the Devonian Square and Nathan Phillips Square, it occurred to Claudia that Ian suffered from a classic case of mistaken identity. His resting bitch face and gravelly voice gave the impression of a grumpiness that simply didn't exist. This man was a non-stop, chattering ball of energy.

She was so amused she forgot to be upset by the betrayal. Almost.

Maybe betrayal was too strong a word, but there was definitely an adjustment period required to deal with as they walked all through the downtown core. She was cynical and mistrustful, and had thought she was opening herself up to a like-minded soul. Discovering Ian was a look-on-the-bright-side optimist was worrying. She'd spun herself out thinking about what two negatives getting together would bring; she didn't even consider the alternative. This thing between them, whatever it could be called, might be over before it really began.

At the grocery store and laundromat, they were preoccupied by the task at hand, only making general chit chat while skirting around deeper, more somber topics. This was the first time they'd done an activity that was just for the hell of it. This change of pace, this deviation from the status quo, meant she was getting the real man as he discussed his real passions.

He waxed poetic about Trinity Square, which they'd cut through to get to Old City Hall. When he told her about how the church and square were threatened by demolition to make way for the Eaton Centre in the '70s but the parishioners of the church successfully preserved the church by forcing the mall's design to be changed, she crossed herself. Though her extremely Catholic abuela's mistrust of Anglicans was legendary, it seemed sacrilegious for even "those Godless heathens" to have their place of worship torn down to make way for a shopping mall.

Protests from Toronto's citizens also led to the preservation of Old City Hall around the same time, he'd said, and explained how Nathan Phillips Square was a forecourt to City Hall, a distinction Claudia hadn't ever considered. As far as she knew, it was all one outside space—you walked *through* Nathan Phillips Square *en route to* City Hall.

To drive home how mistaken she was on the matter, Ian pointed out all the ways the original design elements had evolved—sections people chose to use as seating, parts that were once solely structural now used in all manner of decoration, the advent of the Toronto sign now ubiquitous on social media—before stepping into a grimy hole in the wall for an order of pan-fried dumplings.

He'd gesticulated wildly as they walked, laughing and smiling as he pointed out other architectural details of the city. Buildings and houses from the late nineteenth century, Toronto's misguided tendency to dispatch the older buildings for boring, soulless glass towers, and the heartbreaking lack of vision and foresight when it came to maintenance and restoration.

She was fascinated by the way he applied history to his references, so different from how she viewed them. When he explained architectural styles existed in a cyclical nature, she laughed, saying, "Imperial tyranny is also cyclical". When he referenced the Neoclassical era of France, she brought up how the fall of Robespierre led to the rise of Napoleon. When she wrinkled her nose at a squat cement block of a building, commenting on it looking like communist lodgings, he defended the beauty of the Brutalism style that existed long before the communist embrace of it. She, in turn, pointed out the chaos of Yeltsin's reign ultimately made way for Putin. Their brains seemed to have the same information yet applied it to entirely different ends.

He was smart and engaging and so very passionate about this subject, she couldn't help but be swept up in his wake.

"Are those columns Corinthian?"

"They are!" His joy at her rudimentary grasp of architectural elements made her want to enroll in some type of continuing education course at one of the local colleges. For a fleeting moment, Claudia thought he was going to grab her face and place a loud, smacking kiss on her mouth. Hoped he would. Wanted him to. When he didn't, when he held up his hand for a high-five, Claudia hammed it up, adding an over-the-top fist pump for good measure instead of acknowledging the small spike of disappointment that sizzled through her bloodstream.

"I'll make an architect out of you yet, Gossipika!"

For all the reasons Claudia loved the rich, warm brown of her complexion—the way it glowed in the sun, how fabulously it handled jewel tones, the agelessness it bestowed—the way it hid the heated blush that erupted anytime Ian called her Gossipika was definitely gaining in rank.

Down Bay Street, along Adelaide, they weaved their way through their fellow pedestrians until they arrived at an Italian restaurant that had locations all over the city.

"Are you still hungry?" It was a genuine question. A person as energetic as Ian probably burned a lot more calories than the average human.

"This," he said with an indulgent smile, "was formerly the York County Courthouse, built in 1852. Right through those doors is now the restaurant's Enoteca, a great spot to stop in for cocktails."

Catching on, Claudia nodded, "The space has evolved."

"Yes. The 19th-century exterior elements remain, but inside is pure 21st-century modern. That's the beauty of architecture. It's why I love it."

Ian Yang in love must be a sight to behold, she thought. The way he tapped into an endless reserve of enthusiasm for the things that moved him, she wondered if any woman would be able to resist his attentions when he was ready to apply a full-court press.

"Come on." He grabbed her hand, and the surprise of it in no way diminished the thrill of feeling large hands curl around hers.

He led her around to a small courtyard and she was embarrassed to admit that, though she'd been to the restaurant before—it was walking distance from her home—she'd never wandered back here. Impressed with how much there was to see in the small space, Ian walked her from feature to feature, explaining what he knew and what he most enjoyed as they went.

There was a garden area enclosed by trellises where the plantings were designed to be historical and educational, and at the core of the plaza was a black granite stage, used for impromptu performances or casual seating. He pointed out how the water feature distracted from the traffic noise to create a little oasis in the heart of the city and the openness of the square also allowed for spontaneous gatherings. All the while, Claudia remained keenly aware of their still joined hands.

When she asked about the sculpture of large granite books on the stage and incorporated into benches, he explained it was a nod to the space's origins. "This used to be the site of public hangings and other punishments. The last public execution happened in 1865."

Claudia shivered thinking about it.

Ian noticed and walked them over to sit on the granite stage. "How are those feet doing?"

Hoping to mask the loss she felt when he let go of her hand, she kicked her feet up with a cheerful, "A-okay, thanks!"

"I have no idea how you manage in those all day."

She canted her head, unsure what to say. She wore heels as part of her preparation for being outside, as part of the armor she donned to face the world. Even her winter boots had a wedge heel. Claudia prided herself on rarely being caught 'flat-footed' in her work, and it extended to her wardrobe, too. She liked the way she looked and moved in them. She liked the way they sounded as they click-clacked on the ground. She liked that they made her feel powerful in a world that was constantly trying to make her powerless.

Ian leaned back on his hands. Claudia wasn't sure if the way his new position blocked the late autumn sun from her eyes was intentional, but she appreciated it all the same.

A pair of small children ran through the courtyard, coats abandoned somewhere along the way, gleefully squealing and chasing each other. They both had longish hair, and their bodies and voices still had the beautiful androgyny of youth, but Claudia guessed it was a boy and a girl. As they raced out of view, she heard the familiar cacophonous plonk, plonk, plonk of piano keys being bashed indiscriminately.

"There's a piano outside?" She craned her neck to see where it could be.

Ian also looked toward where the sound originated. "On the restaurant's terrace, maybe?"

Claudia frowned. "That can't be good for the piano. They are notorious for not liking moisture, heat, humidity, lengthy exposure to direct sunlight, or being moved around. And honestly? Same."

Ian looked at her with an amused grin. At least she thought it was amused. It could also be patronizing, she supposed, but that didn't seem as likely.

"Why do you know so much about pianos, Gossipika? You been holding out on me?"

"Hardly. I took piano lessons for eight years because my mother thought it would help with my—" She cut herself off. There was no need to get into all of that right now. Her mother's never-ending attempts to cure Claudia of her *moods* weren't pertinent information at this juncture. "Piano lessons are good for kids, y'know?" She cleared her throat and said in an officious voice, "It helps with enhanced cognitive skills, boosts self-esteem and confidence, and can also help develop motor skills, discipline, and social skills." Claudia winked at him and finished in her normal voice. "That's what the article my mother read claimed, anyway."

She basked in the sound of his gentle laughter.

"Do you have a favorite composer? Mozart? Chopin? Tchaikovsky?"

"Are you just listing random composers?"

He gave a sheepish grin. "Maybe?"

"Beethoven." Claudia smiled her answer.

"Because he was Black?" Ian leaned over, playfully nudging her with his shoulder.

"That's legit one of my favorite urban legends! There is no genealogical evidence he was Black. It's all racist conjecture based on his swarthy complexion and coarse hair. My other favorite is

Chevalier, who is actually Black. No, I like Beethoven because he's the coolest." Claudia gave an affronted gasp at Ian's barked laughter. "I'm serious!"

"The coolest? Really, Claudia?"

She tipped her nose in the air in response.

"Okay, okay," Ian raised his hands in front of himself. "Hit me with it. Why is Beethoven the coolest?"

"If you have to ask..." she sniffed.

He made prayer hands and batted his lashes at her. "Please, tell me, Claudia. Pretty please?"

That did it. "Well! First of all, you have to understand the times. Mozart is this prodigy who came out of nowhere, blowing everyone's mind and taking the world by storm. Hadyn and Scalieri are already at Viennese court, but then here comes this brash upstart who befriends the former and antagonizes the latter."

Ian rubbed his hands together with anticipation. "Royal drama is always so messy."

That little bit of genuine interest was all Claudia needed to launch into her favorite details about Ludwig van Beethoven.

She started with Beethoven's father being obsessed with making him the next Mozart. How Beethoven was given lessons by an eccentric who woke the child up in the middle of the night to practice. She explained how, because he grew up with his father's nightmarish treatment in the name of his bottomless ambition, he never received a proper education, was allegedly dyslexic and terrible at math, and had to support himself from a young age because his father drank the family's money away.

"Shady." Ian tsked

"Totally." Claudia agreed. "Now, from all this strife there is actual talent. Except the man has grown up to be distrustful and ornery. Rumor has it he was an impossible slob with appalling hygiene and an inability to 'understand human behavior.' So he's mean, he's filthy, he gets into fights with friends and foes alike, but it almost doesn't matter because he's busy pioneering composing for piano!" She finished triumphantly.

"What do you mean?" Ian asked, hands clutched in his lap and almost breathless from the suspense. It seemed Claudia's enthusiasm for the subject was contagious.

"At the time, his peers and predecessors composed symphonies for harpsichord. Beethoven was the first to write for the piano specifically."

"All that, and he kept going after he went deaf? I stand corrected, Gossipika. Your man is pretty cool."

Claudia nodded smugly.

"So? Were you all," he made a dramatic pantomime of playing a piano, "dun dun dun dunnnnn?"

Claudia laughed gleefully at his rendition of Beethoven's 5th Symphony. "See? You do know his work!"

"I mean," Ian grabbed the back of his neck, averting his eyes, "Bugs Bunny really broadened my horizons, y'know?"

"A real man of culture!" She teased, acknowledging that many people's exposure to classical music and opera was a direct result of a rascally, carrot-chomping rabbit.

"Okay, tell me about your favorite piece." Ian prompted.

"Opus 129." The answer came easily and without hesitation.

"Yeah? How come?"

She opened and closed her mouth. "Oh, well... I—"

Claudia had no intention of getting into the many ways her life choices were influenced by her mother's hand-wringing about her mental health. How some of his moodier, more somber pieces would have been fun to perform but would have sent her poor mother for the smelling salts with worry about her daughter playing such 'dark music'. How she, even at a young age, practiced the art of subversion.

"Better yet, play it for me!" Ian's smile was wide and winning.

"What? No!" Claudia gave a horrified shake of her head, shifting her body away from his. "I haven't played in ages. It will be terrible."

"I don't believe that for a second."

She scoffed. "You should."

Ian hopped onto his feet and extended his hand. "Come on. For me. Please?"

In the end, it wasn't a choice at all. The simple fact of the matter was Claudia Sano wanted Ian Yang to hold her hand again more than she didn't want to play the piano.

She made a big show of getting on her feet, huffing a put-upon "Fine!" and a "This is on you!"

Ian, for his part, took her hand in one of his and mimed zipping his lips with his other. After a bit of confusion, they finally found the piano. It hadn't been outside but in the restaurant's lobby by the large glass doors that opened onto the terrace. This section of the restaurant wasn't very busy, but it wasn't the empty Claudia would have preferred for this impromptu recital.

"Uh," she started, but Ian cut her off.

"Don't even worry about it."

"Easy for you to say," she grumped.

"I'll stand right here to block you from view. As tiny as you are, they'll think it's being piped in from the speakers!" He teased as he led her to the bench, holding his hand out for her coat. She settled herself in front of the keys as he added quietly, for her ears only, "They don't matter. Just play for a little bit for me, okay?"

Claudia nodded and took a deep breath. Giving her fingers a quick stretch, she played the simple run of scales and arpeggios that had started every piano lesson of her youth. The instrument was in tune and the keys were responsive, even though her own fingers felt thick and clumsy. She gave her shoulders and back a quick stretch before muttering, "Here goes nothing."

She dove right into Beethoven's Op. 129. It hadn't been that long since she'd played—she and her siblings were often called upon to 'play something' whenever the family gathered in the vicinity of a piano—but it had been ages since she'd played for strangers. Fernanda was the most technically proficient of them, Diego had the most showmanship, but Claudia's strength had always been in the way she poured her emotions into the music.

This piece was a favorite of hers. It was quick and jaunty, which her mother approved of, but was called 'Rage Over a Lost Penny', which Claudia appreciated. Rage wasn't always grim and stormy and pounding. Sometimes rage was bouncy and repetitive and deceptively complicated, and she wished more people understood that.

The last chord was still echoing when raucous applause broke out, jolting her out of the trance playing had put her in. Startled, she looked around to see people had been drawn from the different corners of the restaurant to watch her play. She pressed her hands to her cheeks when she found Ian smiling down at her in wonder. He mouthed, 'That was amazing,' as he clapped even louder.

Standing, Ian guided her around the bench and raised her hand to the crowd like a winning prize fighter. The applause intensified, and Claudia dipped into a quick, slightly embarrassed curtsy before taking her coat and purse from the man who was happily leading this display.

The crowd seemed to disperse almost as suddenly as they'd appeared. Claudia was still reeling from the experience. She hadn't intended to play the whole thing, hadn't intended to make a scene of any kind, hadn't wanted to be noticed. She hadn't intended for the laws of physics to completely abandon her, or she'd have remembered that sound travels. All she was thinking about was sharing this love of hers with Ian, the way he'd shared his with her all afternoon.

"You wanna grab a drink?" Ian's voice, closer than expected, startled her all over again.

She couldn't stay. She was starting to unravel, her messy thoughts jumbling and morphing in a way she knew would keep her up at night. Already she was replaying her 'performance', picking it apart, wondering what Ian heard and saw, what the other patrons of the restaurant thought. Were her transitions smooth? Did the pedal stick? This was the cost of her carelessness, of loosening the reins without thought to the consequences.

"I need to get going."

"Yeah, okay." Her reluctance was reflected in the subtle catch in his voice.

She popped up on her toes to press a quick peck on his cheek. Ian must have thought she was only going to hug him because he put his hand at the small of her back, turning his head ever so slightly. The kiss landed at the corner of his mouth. Claudia wanted nothing more than to settle into the feeling, to linger in it. The way his large hand flexed against the small of her back made her want to lean into his embrace. But she couldn't. Stepping away, she fidgeted with the ties on her coat.

"Thanks for playing Beethoven for me. I loved it." Claudia couldn't deal with his quiet intensity; she couldn't think about Ian loving anything of hers.

"Uh, thanks. For the lesson. About landscape architecture. I learned a lot." She babbled.

Ian nodded mutely.

Claudia mumbled a nonsensical "I'll see you around" and turned on her heel before she could say or do anything else to further embarrass herself.

Her mind tumbled and spun and twisted every step of the almost kilometer walk home. By the time she was safely indoors, settled on her couch with a hot mug of tea, divested of her outside clothes, the truth of her situation was undeniable.

Ian Yang had officially become a problem for Claudia Sano.

Chapter Fifteen

Claudia wasn't having a good day.

Most of her days were managed with regimented control and the sheer force of her will. Managing her anxiety meant keeping things as routine and curveball-free as possible. Usually, she was able to get out of the house without complete system failure.

Today was not that day.

She had no idea what triggered it. Maybe turning the clocks back last weekend was a factor? She'd slept, she'd meditated, she'd been diligent about her eating habits and staying hydrated. All the things she knew she needed to monitor to keep herself level had been in order, and yet, the idea of getting dressed and going outside filled her with such dread, her head pounded so furiously she almost vomited.

And, as always, the episode came on at the absolute worst time. The Paradise was screening *Everything Everywhere All at Once*, and she'd told Ian she'd go with him. He'd gone on about the film when they were waiting for his mother's car to get serviced. The adorable way his eyes bugged out when she said she hadn't seen it, that she didn't generally go to the movies all that often, made her laugh so hard she'd worried a little splash of pee slipped out.

That was six days ago, with nine of their negotiated hours under their belts. It had taken just over two months of sporadic visits for Claudia to forget a time when she wasn't doing some type of random errand with Ian Yang.

Now? The thought of getting dressed to sit in a room full of people made her feel nauseated.

She'd been fighting this feeling all day. Time was running out to tell Ian she couldn't make it. She wanted to. God, how she wanted to. The memory of his ebullient rambling about the beauty of the film while they were at the mechanic would pale in comparison to his post-viewing rantings, wouldn't it? He'd be animated and have exact moments to refer her to when making his grand declarations.

Would he have leftover popcorn? She imagined him gesturing wildly, leaving a little trail behind him like some fairytale protagonist. Or maybe he'd wave Twizzlers at her for emphasis, adamant she only needed to hear him explain it one more time for her to see the error of her ways.

But what would she say? These random outings of theirs, borne of an old school payola scheme, were now something she looked forward to if only for the sheer randomness of them. Ian obviously had a lot on his plate and thought to tackle as many birds as possible with one stone. A huge part of her understood the inclination. Respected it, even.

Aside from their city tour three weeks ago, their time had been spent multitasking. Always toward another purpose, achieving another end. Surely, he would understand about being overwhelmed. He certainly experienced the day getting away from him unexpectedly, right?

And worse, he'd accept it. He'd understand and be gracious and ask nothing more of her. Maybe he'd go to the screening anyway. Maybe he'd take someone else.

It was the potential someone else that clawed at her.

For all the time they spent together, there was absolutely nothing about it to indicate the possibility of a "someone else". They both could very well be working through an entire roster of someone elses, and there'd be nothing anyone could say about it. No trust had been broken. No confidences betrayed.

The fact she'd spent an inordinate amount of time imagining holding him down and using his face like a seat was no one's problem but her own.

Telling him her broken brain was the culprit wasn't an option. As distasteful as it was, she'd much prefer him think her a flake than a head case.

Could she... could she tell him some of the truth? Most of the truth?

She decided to pull the bandage off and sent a simple text. **Hey! I know it's kinda last minute, but I can't make it to the screening. Sorry.**

There. Straightforward and to the point.

Her phone buzzed in her hand.

"Everything okay?"

Was this the first time they'd spoken on the phone? It must be. Claudia would have remembered the sensation of having his raspy voice directly in her ear otherwise. She would have prepared herself for it rioting through her by putting the phone on speaker or something. Though she didn't know if having the sound bounce around her loft would have been better or worse.

"Yeah, I'm fine. I can't get my shit together, that's all."

"Been there."

There was a lot of rustling and movement on his end of the call.

"What are you doing?"

"Snaking the drain in my parents' bathroom."

A surprised sound sputtered out of her. "That's... not what I expected you to say."

"Yeah, well, it's not what I expected to be doing." His laugh, a low, broken chortle, brought an answering smile to her face, and she marveled at the way he managed to disarm her.

There was a loud clanking followed by the familiar mmcht of Ian kissing his teeth. Claudia filled the silence with a rushed, "I'm really sorry about the movie. I know you were looking forward to it. I was too."

She heard him sigh and was somehow certain it wasn't directed at her but at his plumbing exploits. She couldn't say how she knew, only that it didn't make her feel any better about needing to cancel.

"It's all good, Gossipika. It's not like I haven't seen it a bunch of times already. Hell, I might turn it on now to keep me company while I finish here." Whatever he was doing settled because his voice sounded closer. "There'll be other chances to broaden your cinematic horizons."

Of course he was being kind. Of course he was generous and understanding without demanding she explain or elaborate. It was exactly what she expected, which is why it chafed. Why did this have to happen tonight, of all nights? At least she could take some small, immature comfort in knowing there'd be no *someone else* taking her place at the cinema. She'd take all the silver linings she could get, no matter how selfish or petty.

It must have been the petty selfishness speaking because Claudia heard herself say, "You might as well come here and watch it if you're just gonna stream it on your phone."

Huh?!

"Huh?" Ian asked, clearly surprised at her offer.

Yeah, buddy, that makes two of us, she thought as she cursed herself and her new penchant for impulsivity. "I mean, if you still want to watch it with me. No pressure." She tried to backpedal, "Or we can do a watch party depending on the streaming platform."

"Nah. If it's cool, I'll pass by."

Claudia didn't remember the rest of the conversation. Didn't remember how they'd settled on the time or what had possessed her to offer in the first place. She certainly hadn't *planned* to invite Ian, and the idea of him in her space wasn't something she was prepared to navigate. But he'd agreed to come over, and it was absolutely too late to back out now. Especially not after she'd already begged off going to the actual cinema.

The gnawing restlessness settled a bit when it became clear she was no longer contemplating leaving the house. It vanished completely when she started her evening ritual of making herself a cup of herbal tea. Whatever had agitated her subconscious seemed satisfied and retreated into the cave of her mind, where it festered until otherwise needed.

A gentle knock echoed through the unit. She gave one last look around, smoothed her jersey knit jumpsuit, fussing with the cuff of her sleeves in a nervous gesture before making her way to the door. Forgoing the screen in her foyer for the peephole, Claudia rose onto her tiptoes to confirm it was Ian at her door and opened it with a breathy, "Hi!"

Why did she sound like she'd just run up six flights of stairs? How lame. Just because a man was standing at her door in a burgundy ribbed knit sweater with a wide collar, a matching t-shirt underneath, and perfectly worn-in jeans that hung deliciously from his hips did not mean she had to lose her head.

"Hi." His voice was hesitant. If Claudia didn't know better, she'd say it was shy.

A gust of cold November wind snapped her into action. She stepped aside to ushered him inside. "Come in, please."

"Thanks. This is for you."

She peeked inside the bag he handed her. He'd bought an assortment of movie-style snacks. Popcorn, candies, chocolates, and—she'd guessed it—a large pack of Twizzlers.

"Thank you! You didn't have to."

"My mother would bust my ass if she ever found out I showed up to someone's house for the first time with my 'two long arms swinging'." He said the last in a perfect imitation of Valerie's accent.

"The next time I see your mom, I'll be sure to tell her your arms were very full."

"You joke now but when I call you to be a character witness, you won't think it's so funny."

She laughed at his faux affront, the sound dying on her lips as an awkward silence threatened to take hold.

They collided awkwardly into each other when Ian leaned in for a hug and Claudia proffered her cheek. Laughing off her nerves, she reached up on her toes and hugged him. If she lingered a little with his arms wrapped firmly around her, well, there wasn't anything to be done about it. It was all she could manage to not sigh contentedly as she rubbed herself along his body like a tabby cat.

The moment might have gone on a beat too long, just long enough for Claudia's embarrassment to raise its head and take stock of its surroundings. Luckily, Ian chose that exact moment to tease, "Didn't I say you wouldn't come up to my chest without those heels on?"

Grateful for the reprieve, she swatted his arm with her nose tipped in the air, and they laughed off the residual nerves.

Making a show of looking around, Ian said, "Nice fireplace."

She knew what he saw. The entire space was an endless array of moody neutrals with a large gas fireplace facing the staircase. Her loft made an excellent first impression. It was, after all, what sold her when she was house hunting. Its stunning 16-foot ceiling and expansive windows flooded the space with natural light, creating an airy and inviting ambiance. The open-concept kitchen, dining, and living area suited her needs perfectly and worked well for the type of entertaining she did.

"Yeah, let me give you a quick tour." And it was quick. She led him further into the living room. "There's a washroom there; that's the laundry room," she indicated the two doors, "that's the guest room."

"It's two bedrooms?"

She nodded, "Two bed, two bath. Though, depending on who you ask, it's a one-bedroom plus den."

Up until last month, her youngest cousin, Silvana, lived with her. She'd since decided to share an apartment with Davis's sister Danielle now that he and Junior lived together.

It was weird to exist in the intersection of missing her young, vibrant cousin and being happy for the blessed quiet of solitude. Silvana's living with her had been a mutually beneficial situation for all. Silvana's super overprotective parents wouldn't let her live in residence if she was staying in Toronto, but she didn't want to move away for school. And, the part no one had to tell her because Claudia just knew it intrinsically, Silvana acted like an 'inside man' looking out for Claudia.

Sure, it wasn't a position Silvana knowingly took. Claudia was positive she didn't even realize it was expected of her. The reality was much simpler: it made everyone feel better to know Claudia wasn't spending all her evenings and weekends alone.

Except now she was, and it was glorious.

"And upstairs?" Ian was inspecting the banister.

"My bedroom and en suite." It overlooked the entire main floor, earning her space its loft designation. "And my walk-in closet," she added nonsensically. What did he care about whether she had a closet, much less if it was a walk-in or not. Gah! She was already being awkward, and he'd only just arrived.

"It's nice. Suits you."

It was nice, and it did suit her, but she knew enough about Ian by now to know he was probably choking on the words he was holding in. "Diego already lectured me on the missed opportunities for more usable space, if that's what you're thinking."

He gave her a sly, sidelong glance. "I wasn't."

She raised her eyebrows expectantly.

"But you could easily fit some additional storage under the stairs, just so you know."

His impish grin was so adorably silly, she couldn't contain her laughter. Ian joined in, both of them cackling uncontrollably. It was so perfectly Ian, so exactly them, the last of her nerves dissolved. She knew how to hang out with Ian, how to laugh and have a good time; the location being her living room changed nothing. She could do this.

Wiping the tears from her eyes as she got her breathing under control, she tilted her head toward the kitchen, "C'mon, Goofball." Ian made his way over and leaned on the breakfast bar as she pulled bowls and trays out. Together they started plating their snacks and making drink choices.

Settling themselves on the couch, Claudia picked up the remote. Looking at Ian, she asked, "Ready?"

"Ready," he nodded.

Here goes nothing, she thought, as she pressed play from where she'd cued the movie.

Almost immediately, Claudia was captivated by the story of a woman trying to file her taxes getting roped into a universe-saving scheme. There were so many crazy subplots and transitions she couldn't help but give the movie her full attention. It was fun and funny. Until it wasn't. Then Claudia was gripped by a profound sadness that stole her breath. A daughter so unhappy, so lost, she searched the multiverse to find a version of herself her mother could love and, believing none existed, decided the only solution left was infinite darkness.

She'd been there. Maybe not in the interdimensional way station hidden in the hole of a bagel, but definitely wondering if she could be different, if she were somehow other, maybe her mother wouldn't worry so much. Wouldn't be constantly wringing her hands, fretting at the state of Claudia's life.

If having an existential revelation in the middle of this movie with a considerable subplot about a teppanyaki chef controlled by a raccoon wasn't bitter poetry, she didn't know what was.

Claudia snuck a glance at Ian to see he was equally enthralled, staring at her screen with undisguised awe and wonder. He didn't ponder if there was a different life out there for him, didn't seem gripped by the inescapable fear humanity might very well suck in all versions of the universe.

She felt her rising anxiety and knew she couldn't stop it, couldn't halt its progression. She also knew it wasn't fair to ruin this night for him, to have him think he'd been the cause of her upset. So she did what she always did when she felt too much but couldn't safely express herself: she stilled, and imagined she was all alone in an endless field of soothing yellow. She hugged her knees close to her chest, tipped her face up to the perfect, cloudless sky, and waited for the dandelions to turn to white puffs where her tears could blow away like seeds in the breeze.

Chapter Sixteen

"What's wrong?" His voice was closer to a whisper. She was so still. Still in a way that was eerie and concerning. She didn't answer, only flinched in acknowledgment of his voice as she stared straight ahead. A shiver of alarm stole up his spine. He cleared his throat and spoke louder, "Claudia? What's wrong?"

She looked at him, face blank, and somehow he knew. He knew, and he was sick about it.

"Claudia, are you crying?"

Wincing, she wiped her face and showed him her dry fingertips. "I'm not crying."

"Claudia," her name came out on a sigh that was worry as much as it was frustration. "Come here, please."

"I'm okay, I swear."

"I'm not, though, so will you please come here?"

He waited patiently—as patiently as a man whose heart was racing in his chest could be, anyway—for her to decide to indulge him. He lost his tenuous patience with her slow slide across the couch, and when she was within reach, he leaned over and scooped her into his lap, cradling her as she curled into his chest.

"Talk to me, Claudia. What's wrong?"

"The movie." Her voice was small and watery, setting Ian's teeth on edge.

"You didn't like it?"

"I didn't think it would be so sad."

"You think it's sad?"

She nodded, sniffling.

This had been his favorite movie of last year, and he'd seen it dozens of times since then. Between the acting, set design, action sequences, and storytelling, there was always a new element to appreciate. In all his viewings, he'd never classified the movie as sad. In fact, the emotional elements—the exploration of roads not traveled, the mundane becoming the profound—made the film's central theme more poignant. To Ian, it was the very best of cinema: creativity and imagination working together to tell a story of hope.

Yet that's not at all how Claudia was experiencing the movie.

But he'd learned this about her already, hadn't he? When he waxed poetic about France's contributions to architecture, she countered with the rise of Napoleon's tyranny and continued with the cruel practice of France demanding a tax from its former colonies, appropriating about 85% of said former colonies' annual income to the tune of close to 500 billion dollars.

Claudia viewed the world through a lens free of artifice or bright sides. She embraced the cold, harsh reality of the situation, stared it in the eye, and refused to flinch. Refused to accept change wasn't possible, that we weren't allowed to demand more. Demand better.

She still hadn't moved her face from the cocoon of his chest, and he chastised the small part of himself that relished the feel of her curled against him even in this time of her distress. He placed his hands lightly on the small of her back, holding her in place.

"Can we talk about it?"

"About what?" She kept her face in his chest, her body curled comfortably against his.

"Claudia," though it was delivered in a voice barely above a whisper, it was clearly an admonishment. "Why were you... I don't even know what to call it. Dry crying?"

He was rewarded with a barely there chuckle that shook her small frame. Her hands fisted into his shirt, as she inhaled loudly.

"I—" She exhaled a long, measured breath as though mentally preparing herself for what came next. "I don't always feel *allowed* to express myself in public. When that happens, I imagine a field of flowers and I sit there and feel whatever it is until it's safe to come out."

The words were spoken into his shirt, but he still heard them. He still felt them land like a left hook to his jaw.

"Why aren't you allowed to express your emotions?"

Claudia exhaled noisily, letting all her reluctance out. "My mom was engaged to someone else before she met my dad."

He knew better than to question the seemingly random change of topic. One of the things he'd come to understand about Claudia was that she didn't rush to fill silences with small talk. She was about to share something with him, and he held her closer as he settled in for the story.

"She's always been a bit high-strung. She was one of nine in a family that didn't have much. They worked hard and loved their kids, but my grandparents weren't visionaries. Women only had so many options in their eyes, y'know?"

He did know. It never ceased to amaze him how vast the differences still were in the Caribbean. Sure, girls continued their schooling with much more freedom and frequency than in his grandparents' time, but for many people a woman's worth was still tied to finding a man and raising his kids.

Claudia continued, "She took the way out available to her: she fell in love with a man who promised the moon and stars." Ian stiffened, preparing himself for this story to get worse before it got better. "It was the way things worked in her small town—you met a boy, he worked to provide for you and the kids while you kept a clean home, and hopefully he kept his hands to himself when life got too hard."

"What changed?"

"Gossip." Ian heard rather than saw her smile. "The neighborhood ladies were talking about her fiancé, about how it was too bad she was so desperate to be in a relationship that she'd put up with a no-good, spendthrift, philandering man like him. The women spoke too many details for her to deny, too many truths to ignore. My mom, who was on her way home to him, learned things she'd had no clue about. Facts that put a bit of steel in her spine. She decided to leave that very afternoon while he was at the bar with the few dollars she had to her name, and her pride."

"Gossip saves lives." He repeated her words from the grocery store that long-ago day.

She nodded silently. He let her order her thoughts, sensing that she needed to figure out how to say what came next.

"Even though those ladies ultimately saved her, my mom became obsessed with what people were saying about her. It occupies her every thought. If she looks a certain way, if her kids misbehave, if her husband is too friendly with another woman, if her sister-in-law gifts too extravagantly—she is constantly worried about what people are saying. A woman like that with a daughter like me.... A daughter who didn't smile easily, who was never entirely right? It's a bad combination."

He didn't know what to say, and the knot of emotion now clogging his throat would betray him even if he did speak. So, he ran his hand aimlessly up and down the length of her spine.

Her voice had the wry detachment of one who'd accepted their fate "It was one thing when I was a baby. Babies are mercurial by design. But by time I'd reached adolescence, it was more than my poor mother could bear. What would people think about her daughter who scowled and raged all the time? What would people say if her daughter couldn't smile and play nice? So, I learned how. It's easier to storm in secret than to bring upheaval to my mother's pristine, orderly world."

Ian hated the resignation in her voice. The abject certainty this persona she'd created was her only viable solution.

"You're allowed to cry, Claudia. You know that, right? It doesn't make you bad or weak or troublesome."

"But maybe it does. Ever since I was little, I would get in these moods. I'm sure there's a more medically acceptable term for it," her laugh was a cold, mocking sound, "but my mother didn't know what else to call it when her daughter would become lethargic and listless. My abuela would hold me close and rock me while she peppered me with kisses and prayer until it passed. Sometimes it was a couple hours, sometimes it was an entire day." She shrugged her acceptance of her circumstances. "On a few occasions, my cousin would barge her way into our abuela's arms and read to me from one of her million storybooks while our abuela held us both. It's always been this way. I don't remember a time when it wasn't."

Ian's hands stilled as he absorbed the full scope of Claudia's words.

"I just..." She let out a hopeless, weary sigh. "I would also raze the multiverse if I thought I could find a version of myself my mother didn't stress about."

And then he understood. Claudia, like Joy in the film, was exhausted by trying to fit into a mold to appease a mother who could not be appeased.

Ian knew this was a momentary flare of emotion brought on by the movie. He knew deep in his marrow, without any specific supporting evidence, Claudia didn't walk around feeling down about herself this way. Yet, even though he knew it was temporary, he didn't want her to wallow in it now.

"One of the things people get wrong about my work is just how much input from nature, from ecological resilience, goes into the design. The thing is, every element of biodiversity should be considered. How much can an ecosystem withstand from both nature and humanity before it can no longer recover from the damage? How long will it take to regain its balance?"

Claudia sat up in his lap, wiping her eyes with the cuffs of her sleeves, completely engaged in his words. This woman. Even in her distress, her thirst for knowledge took precedence.

He settled his hands on the small of her back and continued, "We look at which flora can be introduced to varying soil and light conditions as well as how it would react to the local fauna. And you know what?" She shook her head, letting her hands fall into her lap. "With some obvious exceptions, a lot of things can put up with a lot of things. It might take a while, and you might not recognize it, but nature endures."

The smallest curve tilted her lips.

Unable to help himself, unwilling to try, Ian tucked Claudia's hair behind her ears and lightly held her face in his hands. "What others might see as broken is often a period of transformation and adaptation."

Claudia looked to the ceiling as her eyes filled with tears. Tears of his own formed in sympathy. Ian would have given anything to spare her this, anything to lighten this load. When she'd found a measure of calm, her eyes searched his. He wasn't sure what she was looking for or what she saw, but he was content to simply hold her attention. It was what he'd wanted from almost the very beginning, for her to look at him and see him and deem him worthy of her notice. Even with her eyes glassy and lashes clumped with her tears, he couldn't look away.

"Resilience is just another kind of strength," he insisted, trying desperately to give her some of her fire back.

A small puff of air, barely a gasp, was the only warning he had before she leaned in to kiss him. His breath caught, and his twisted sense of self-preservation kicked in, causing him to pull away. He'd spent all their time together doing everything in his power to keep his desires to himself, to not cross any boundaries; his brain didn't recognize the gesture as consent.

At her wide-eyed horror, he stole a quick, chaste kiss to stop her from getting the wrong idea. He definitely wanted to kiss her. God, he couldn't remember a time when he hadn't wanted her lips on his. But it had to be real. He couldn't stand it if it was anything less than certain on both their parts.

"Stop the clock." Ian was hanging on by the very thinnest of threads, and he didn't want to cross the line while she was crying. He couldn't stand it. "Claudia. Stop the clock. Please."

He waited for the understanding to dawn. Prayed for it. If he had to explain to her what he meant, he wasn't sure he could accomplish it with any type of clarity. He'd wanted to hold her, kiss her, from the moment he first laid eyes on her. But these visits, their bartered outings, weren't about his unfulfilled desire. He truly wanted to show her the other version of his life.

It was an act borne of desperation, yes, but he would never conflate the two. If she was going to allow him to kiss her, he needed it to be outside of their arrangement.

He looked up, her glassy eyes searching his, and he breathed a sigh of relief at her small nod and barely whispered, "Stop the clock."

Unwilling to waste another moment, Ian rose up while pulling her to him, their mouths met in the middle in a consuming kiss. He'd wondered, obsessed, over the taste of her and was frustrated that their first kiss was seasoned with the salt of her tears. Still, he refused to part from her, refused to break for even something as essential as breath, not so long as Claudia was in his arms, giving him this gift of her kiss.

"Ian, I—"

"Shhh..." He kissed a trail down her throat and back up to her mouth. "It's okay."

Her head jerked in what he supposed was a nod and then they were kissing again. This time with more fervor. Searching hands joined grinding hips as they learned this new aspect of their friendship. The soft, full curves of her body in his palms was better than his every imagining. She was lush and warm and writhing in his lap, making needy little noises in his mouth. He didn't think he'd ever been harder.

A fleeting thought skittered across his mind about paying his parents back for a portion of his tuition. His imagination, honed in the hallowed halls of higher learning, failed him so spectacularly in the face of the reality of holding the bounty of Claudia in his arms. But then she sucked on his tongue, and the thought dissolved like sugar in a mug of hot tea.

His arms had chosen to divide and conquer, and he couldn't be happier with their decision. One hand cradled her head, while the other palmed her ass, pulling her as close as their bodies could manage while still fully clothed. He poured all his longing into his kiss and let her moans and whimpers guide him.

He'd never been more sure about anything than he was about the fact that being in Claudia's condo, dry humping on her couch, about to come in his pants like an adolescent, was exactly where he was supposed to be right now. Swallowing her sighs, drinking from her lips, and breathing from her lungs had become his life's work.

"Ian, I... I'm... it's—" Claudia's words came out in a tangle of shocked disbelief, seemingly as surprised as he was to find himself at the precipice of climax.

"I know." He pulled her bottom lip into his mouth, sucking gently before letting it go. "Me too."

She wrapped her arms around his neck, pressing her chest fully against his, and there was no more time for talking because she was dragging her hot little body up the steel rod of his erection as he spilled in his jeans.

He groaned as the last of the tremors worked their way through his system, enjoying the small intimacy they'd shared with each other. It had been a long time since something so simple had been so arousing.

"Oh, my God!" Claudia let her head fall back as her own climax took hold.

Then he heard it. It was a hitched sob that ended on a sigh, long and low, and sounded like relief. Claudia Sano had found a moment of peace in his arms, and, in that moment, his heart broke and was put back together. Reshaped. Given new contours and borders. Rebuilt.

He'd decided right then and there; he would be this woman's shelter, a port in the storm of her raging mind, for as long as she'd let him.

Gathering her in his arms, Ian pressed a gentle kiss to Claudia's forehead as they both slumped together on her couch, panting.

Ian kept his mouth on her skin, lips pressed lightly at her temple, soft and delicate under his lips. Her warm skin radiated the mild hint of lavender he'd come to associate with her.

"I've wet your shirt with my tears; how embarrassing."

"That's not the only thing you've made wet." He moved his hips against hers in a playful taunt.

"Stop!" She buried her face in her hands after smacking his shoulder in a scold that lacked all heat.

"Don't be embarrassed." His lips moved against the side of her face as he spoke, "It was incredibly hot. I can't remember the last time I indulged in a little *frottage*. It's underrated."

Claudia exhaled noisily, burying her face in his chest once more.

"Hey," Ian turned so he was facing her. "What's the matter?"

"Nothing," her frown suggested otherwise. "Thinking about tomorrow. About how you'll go back to ignoring me, even after this."

"I don't ignore you." If only she knew just how much bandwidth she occupied, how much of his days were spent thinking about her, she might never let him get close to her again.

"You certainly don't talk to me."

"Claudia, all I want to do is talk to you. That's the problem." He kissed her again, taking advantage of this liminal space where they were allowed to kiss each other without having to address the fact they were kissing each other. "If you haven't noticed, I don't speak to anyone."

"Why not?" This time she leaned forward and kissed him. The thrill of it was in no way lessened by how many times he'd tasted her.

How could he explain it without making her feel like a chore? His life stopped being his own the moment he answered his phone, his mother's voice saying the words he knew he'd hear for the rest of his life, incomplete yet indelible *Dad's in the hospital... A stroke... It was sudden... The doctors say...* Jonathan had driven him to the hospital and sat with him and his mother while they waited for updates.

When the worst was over, and truly, it was an ever-evolving scale of worse, he'd already made his choice to step in with the business. Every day since, he'd been doing the work of three people: the physical custodial work; the administration of ordering supplies, paying bills, and managing their small staff; and support worker, watching over his mom while she took care of his dad. All of which was made infinitely harder because his mother refused to fully relinquish control of the day-to-day management, insisting on wading into affairs he'd already handled.

Ian didn't want to say any of it. He didn't want pity, nor did he want praise. There was no other choice. His younger siblings were too young, still in their junior year at university. His older brother lived far away with his own complicated life.

But Claudia was in his lap, her big, gorgeous eyes trained on him, waiting for an answer.

"It's been a lot. Stepping in for my folks?" He allowed the feel of her fleshy thighs in his grip to center him. He took a deep breath and admitted a truth he'd been suppressing. "It's been a lot."

She cupped his jaw, her thumb gently tracing his cheek, and he leaned into her touch. He closed his eyes, letting his head flop back on the couch, unable to withstand the feel of her and still achieve the higher functioning required for speech.

"In the beginning, I had so many things to remember. It's been years since my folks dragged us to work, y'know? It's not a skill you forget, of course, but the process of it? The rhythm of it? It's different than when you're cleaning your own house. There were so many pieces I needed to consider, all the little things the rest of the team just knew that I didn't. I was too focused on getting up to speed to talk."

Claudia had moved from his jaw to running her hands along his chest, and he let the soothing motions seep into his skin. "And now?"

That was the question, wasn't it? He knew she meant them specifically, why he didn't stop to chat *with her*. But the answer was bigger than her in a way he still hadn't been able to reconcile.

"And now... now I don't want to jeopardize what my parents built. I don't want anyone to find fault with me or my work or the staff under my leadership. Talking—*visiting*—while at work is off limits."

Her eyes widened briefly before her chin wrinkled. She opened and closed her mouth, pressing her lips in a tight line.

"What?" She obviously had something to say. He had no idea why she suddenly felt compelled to censor herself.

"I..." She gave her head a small shake and started again, "I don't know how to ask this without seeming rude."

He couldn't help but laugh, a belly-rumbling sound that chased the morose weight that had begun to settle. Claudia Sano had snarled at a child in a grocery store as an act of solidarity. The bar for what she considered rude was leagues different than his.

"Don't laugh! I'm trying to be respectful."

Calming himself, Ian wiped his eyes with the heels of his palms while taking a deep, cleansing breath. "I've been forewarned. Go ahead. Speak your mind, Gossipika."

He couldn't be sure, but the way Claudia's eyes fluttered—a quick lowering of her lashes before steeling herself and bringing them up again—made him wonder how she really felt about him using her family nickname.

"It's just, well... have you met your mother?" She gave a helpless shrug, as if imparting information he didn't have about the woman who'd brought him into this world. "That woman likes to chat."

His smile was wide and fond. "You don't have to tell me."

She arched her brow as if to say, *'So then?'*

"It's her company. She can do whatever she wants with it. While she's entrusting it to me, and I use the word trust loosely because she is all over me when she supposedly took a step back to focus on my dad, I don't want to do a single thing that might cost them what they've built."

There was no truth bigger than that. His responsibility to his family was more important than any water cooler chit chat. He needed to get them through this crisis, help guide them to the other side, no matter what he had to sacrifice. If there was a version of this where he could have Claudia too, he'd take it and be grateful. But his life wasn't his own at the moment.

All he could do was wait until it was.

Chapter Seventeen

Ian heard her laugh ring out and smiled to himself. It was the laugh he'd come to recognize as her real one. The way it petered out in a small sigh before the final giggle settled was so unlike her fake boisterous one; it amazed him how anyone was fooled by it.

He'd had the pleasure of hearing it a dozen times since they came together on her couch two weeks ago, and it felt like a reward every time.

Making his way through the building's main entrance, he heard other voices with Claudia's. She was huddled together with the tall, flirty one and the IT one he knew was named Alma. He'd seen them around, the tall one less frequently—he was fairly certain she didn't work there—and liked the way Claudia was when she was with them.

"But it's the day after Mother's Day!" The tall one grumped. "Why would a company run by Panamanians schedule the gala for December 9th? What's next, a staff retreat on November 3rd?"

"Are you seriously only realizing this now?" Alma asked with a raised brow. "It's been decided for ages. The invitations went out almost two months ago!"

"Don't bug me with logic, Alma!" The tall one snapped. "I've been busy with cohabitating. My holiday brunch is on the 2nd, and now I have to have an entire weekend of family bonding the very next week?"

"Con cuidado, prima. You might hurt my feelings."

"Por favor, Claudia, I thought you'd be on my side with this. Mother's Day on a Friday means a drive-by to see Abuela at the very least but more likely a meal. Saturday would be more involved with my mom and probably yours, too. Then the gala at night and Mass on Sunday? There is no way I can 'I have to work' my way out of church for Mother's Day." The last she'd whined to the ceiling. "That's the entire weekend in outside clothes!"

"Poor Hammer," Alma pouted, "has to put her dukes and earls away for a weekend to leave her house."

Claudia scoffed. "Please. I bet there's one open on her phone right now. She's never too far from a 'yes, milady'." She put her hand out to the tall one, "Dámelo. I'll show her."

Ian could clearly see the bit of challenge in the tall one's eyes and decided to make himself known, if only to prevent an all-out fracas.

He gave a dramatic clearing of his throat. "Do I need to call security?"

Claudia whirled at the sound of his voice. "Ian!"

The pleased smile on her face coaxed an answering one on his own. He bit it back before he forgot himself and did something goofy like pull her into his arms and kiss her in the lobby of their workplace.

"Just a family meeting of sorts. Nothing to worry about." Claudia cut her eye at the tall one, who rolled her eyes in response.

He stared at the three women, wondering how they were related. The tall one had the same complexion as Claudia, and maybe they favored each other around the eyes a bit. Claudia and

Alma only seemed the same height until you looked at their shoes. Alma's soles were so thin she might as well be barefoot, while Claudia teetered on her trademark heels. Claudia definitely didn't seem like she was from the same family.

He didn't have extensive knowledge about women's clothing, but even in this, their differences were obvious. It was late November, and the tall one was wrapped in a large scarf and a well-made floor-length wool coat, a vision of comfortable luxury. Alma was a study in practicality. She wore a blazer over her large tunic, and though her pants might not be leggings, they were from the same family. And then there was his Claudia. He'd started thinking of her as his the night she clenched her tiny fists in his shirt and bawled her broken, exhausted heart out. She stood magnificent in one of her many tailored knee-length column dresses.

"Jaime Sano." Ian took her hand with some hesitation.

"Jaime Sano? Like..."

"Yup. He's my dad. I'm a source of great confusion."

"She always says that. Call her Junior like everyone else does." Claudia explained with barely contained exasperation. "This is my cousin who beat me to the title of first-born granddaughter by four months."

"It's true. I'm a pretty big deal." Junior nodded agreeably. So this was the cousin he'd heard so much about. She said it with such exaggerated cockiness, he couldn't help but smile. This woman was obviously used to attention and used that attention to control the narrative around her.

"She's also an agent of chaos." Alma added wryly.

A dazzling smile lit Junior's whole face. "That's also true!"

"And this," Claudia gestured to the woman he recognized as the Director of Software Development, "is my cousin Alma, who you already know. Younger than us in age but far older in spirit."

"The bar is on the floor." Alma's put-upon sigh underscored her dry delivery. "You can't imagine the trouble their mouths have gotten them into over the years."

He had no trouble believing it. Claudia's repeated claims of gossip's value and legitimacy, and her unflinching interpretation of world events were high on the list of provoking behaviors he'd witnessed.

"If you'd put your mouth to work, you wouldn't be in this situation. Again."

"Ay, Claudia! What if the baby can hear you? Está bien, muñeca." Junior splayed her hand protectively over Alma's belly, as if to shield it from Claudia's words. "Don't you listen to her, Alma. Make as many babies as you want. I'll be here for you."

"That's not the endorsement you think it is, Hammer. Lalo is obsessed with that stupid bandana buddy elephant you bought. He drags it everywhere. I can't wait for something else to capture his tiny attention so I can throw it out!" Alma complained, giggling at her cousin's outraged face. "Besides, my mouth is exactly what got me in this situation." She tipped her head up at Claudia in a frat boy nod. "Again."

Junior's uproarious laughter filled the space. "Funny how that works, eh?"

"This maturity you speak of," Ian trailed off, making a show of looking between the three women.

Alma shrugged. "Like I said, it doesn't take much to be more mature than these two."

It didn't escape his notice that for all their teasing and carrying on, Junior and Alma had positioned themselves in such a way that he would literally have to go through them to get to Claudia. He wondered if their posture—Alma in front, her right side lined up with Claudia's left side; Junior mirroring Alma, protective without obstructing—was a conscious decision or something borne of years of instinct. He liked knowing they were ready to fight for her. Fight *with* her if it came to it.

Yet they were here, laughing and teasing, making it easy to see why these cousins were also her closest friends.

Junior turned to him, her smile bright and inviting. "I wanted to thank you for your service. Your notes were impeccable, which I certainly appreciated."

"It's your friend that's gettin' wit' Q? He's a good guy." Ian took a wild guess. Junior herself was sporting a giant green rock on her ring finger; he felt it was a safe bet the information wasn't for her personally. He didn't want to spend too much time thinking about how few details he asked Claudia for before singing like a canary.

Junior demurred, hand on her chest, "It's none of my business."

Ian didn't know the woman at all, but just in this short interaction he was certain there was nothing she wouldn't insert herself into if she felt it necessary. "Respectfully, if you weren't making it your business, you wouldn't have had Claudia ask me any questions."

Alma didn't even pretend to hide her laughter.

Junior turned to Claudia, beaming, "Smart. I like him."

Claudia lowered her head, a hint of a smile playing at her lips, in a gesture that could be interpreted any number of ways. He would engage in a whole host of things to know what Claudia was thinking at that moment. He knew what he wanted to be running through her mind and hoped with the fervent zeal of a true believer he was right.

"Wait, so you're all Sanos?"

The three women shared looks between them before Junior answered, "I'm Sano Rosales; she's Sano Pérez," she gestured to Claudia.

"And I'm Smith Sano." Alma finished.

"As in the Smith of Morenal Smith and Sano? You're double masthead?" Ian's shock made his voice rise at the end.

They laughed as Alma shook her head no. "That Smith is my uncle. He and her dad," she used her chin to point at Claudia, "are childhood besties. His older brother, my dad, married his baby brother's best friend's sister, my mom."

"But your office says Sano."

"Yes. Unlike her, I want everyone to know I'm management. With Smith, there's a small chance I could be unrelated. With Sano, I make it clear. I like them watching themselves around me. Sometimes gossip requires action, and I'd rather not know."

"I like to know." Junior gave him a speaking glance, "Especially if some gossip's action needs to be handled in an unofficial capacity? I like to know."

Claudia rolled her eyes, ignoring her cousin's very pointed threat. "Information is power. You're missing out, Alma."

"Says you. I have enough to deal with." Alma scoffed.

"But," Ian wasn't sure if this was appropriate to say, but he was missing something. "How don't they know?"

"*You* didn't." Claudia pointed out.

"Okay, fine. But once I did..." Ian widened his eyes, the 'obviously' hanging heavy in the air.

Junior's chuckle was a delicate, tinkling sound as she nudged Claudia's ribcage. "I really do like him, prima."

"How lucky for us all," Claudia said, her delivery dry and sarcastic.

Alma's phone buzzed in her hand and she made an exasperated face. "I don't even have to look. I'd better get back."

"I also have to go. Let me know if you want to carpool to my parents." Junior said, bending to kiss both women's faces. Back at her full height, she gave Ian a cheeky wink and made her way out the door while Alma hurried to the staircase behind the bank of elevators.

"I didn't mean to intrude," Ian said in the resulting silence. "Kinda feels like I busted up the party."

"You didn't. Sometimes working with your family means secret factions form to get things done."

He nodded, understanding the concept of it, if not the practice. Working with his family in no way shifted the seat of power from his mother's control. She was head of the household, head of the company, and head of her extended family. That Ian had been running it in her stead these few months was seen by all involved as an extension of her will.

"Is it hard having to work for your dad?"

"No." She laughed a little around the word, moving toward the elevators. He fell in step with her, and she continued, "I'm not his direct report and anyway, we both work for my uncle. Though, technically, my uncle works for his daughter. Her grandfather left her 27% of his company, making her the single largest shareholder, even above her mother."

Ian's eyes bugged out. Even without knowing how much money Claudia was talking about, he understood that to have it managed by this firm meant it was more than your run-of-the-mill Tax-Free Savings Account. It wasn't the kind of money his family would ever have.

"I knew you were fancy, Gossipika. I didn't realize you were *fancy*."

Claudia snorted, whether to both hide her flush of pleasure or to disavow him of the notion, he wasn't sure, but the idea pleased him greatly. "I'm not. Junior's maternal grandmother was a beauty queen turned actress and married a shipping magnate." When his jaw dropped, she added quickly, "I know. It's not really a *secret* but she doesn't like to bring it up so, you know, keep it to yourself."

"Because she's ransomable?"

"I..." She paused, her lips pushed out in an adorable frown of concentration. The furrow was a shallow indent between her brows, as though she rarely made the expression. He wondered how many times Claudia didn't have the answer at the tip of her tongue. If he ran his thumb along the gentle grooves, would he be able to tell how often information eluded her? "I've never really reckoned with that before. Maybe? It's more because it's her own business. She always says people get weird about money. I haven't heard anything about kidnapping protocols, though."

He gestured for her to go ahead of him into the empty elevator car. She swiped her pass and pressed the button. He settled in beside her, happy to have this moment of relative privacy to themselves. It wasn't as though he planned to stuff his tongue down her throat while rubbing her off, though he'd be lying if he said he was above such behavior. He just liked being able to keep their newly established intimacy without having to default to polite aloofness in front of other people.

"Anyway. My maternal grandmother was a functionally illiterate seamstress who married a hard-working construction worker. Believe me when I tell you, I am not fancy."

He understood the point Claudia was making and he knew there was an obvious difference in the women's backgrounds. But only a fool would ignore the proverbial elephant in her lineage. "And your dads? Your Sano family."

The left side of her face twitched in such a way that told him she was annoyed and impressed in equal measure. Taking a deep, dramatic breath, she said, "The Sanos have always been solidly middle class. The kind of middle class that meant good schools, new shoes whenever necessary, bikes for each kid, and a little extra something set aside to help struggling relations if needed."

Ian nodded his understanding. In Guyana, there was a different scale for wealth. Yes, there were the obviously rich, but the tiers between destitute, poor, working poor, lower class, and middle class looked different than they did in Canada.

The elevator dinged on the 11th floor, and he gestured for Claudia to proceed. They continued chatting as they made their way down the hall.

"My abuela raised her five children to operate like a...a..." She scowled as she searched for the word she wanted. "What do you call those robots that need a bunch of individual robots to make one big machine?"

"You mean like the Power Rangers?"

She snapped her finger in triumph. "Yes! The Sanos are like Power Rangers. Each one is successful in a particular skill or talent that complements the others so that they can chase success individually and collectively. When they reach for something, they do it like a single unit."

"Like this enterprise."

"Like this enterprise." She agreed. She swiped her key card to get in her section, then swiped it again to unlock her office. Setting her coat on the hook and her phone on her desk, she looked up at him leaning in the doorway with a shy, tentative smile on her face. "You're talking to me at work again."

He'd managed to swing by each shift for the past couple weeks to check in.

The key to his success had been not crossing the threshold, to not fully enter the office. By staying in the hall, he could keep it light and breezy. By staying in the hall, he could avoid the temptation of her lush mouth and curvy body.

He hung his head as his own shy smile spread across his face. He looked up at her through his lashes and said in a low voice, "It upsets you when I don't."

They stared at each other, neither knowing what to say next but unwilling to part. Finally, Ian cleared his throat, gathering himself. He had work to do. He didn't need more reason to be distracted by this woman. "Okay, well—"

"Would you—"

They both laughed at themselves. Ian gestured for Claudia to speak.

"Would you," she looked down at her desk for a moment before meeting his eyes, "do you want to grab dinner? There's a Vietnamese place in Leslieville that's really good."

"I would like that." He'd spent time with Claudia doing all manner of activities but none of them had been a date. And maybe this one wasn't either, but it was the closest they'd come, which meant everything.

"Thursday?"

He could hold out for two days. He nodded, "You've got yourself a date."

"Good."

Her reserved smile went straight through him. He knocked on the doorframe for something to do with his hands, a way to expel his nervous energy, more than any desire to make noise. His own smile bloomed on his face. "Great."

Then there was nothing left to do but leave. He pushed off the doorframe with a small salute before he made a fool of himself and Claudia reconsidered the invitation.

Chapter Eighteen

It was date night and Claudia was giddy with anticipation. Not even the cold bite of November air could dim her excitement. She thanked her driver as she grabbed her purse and exited the car. She made her way to the entrance and saw where Ian stood in the doorway waiting for her.

"Hi." She braced herself for his kiss, for the warm press of his lips against hers.

"There's no wait; I checked." He said in lieu of greeting.

It wasn't disappointment that flared in her belly. It was closer to embarrassment. The low-level shame of being caught out for reading the situation incorrectly. She rallied with a bright, "Good to know. You ready?"

His smile was a little tight as he held the door open for her to enter ahead of him.

Que Ling was a small house that had been converted into a Vietnamese restaurant with some of the best phở in the city. She hoped Ian enjoyed it as much as she did.

"Were you waiting long?" She asked, settling her purse on the back of her chair. It was a small, local spot with limited seating and a fairly bare-bones decor.

"Nah, I was just walking up when I saw you get out of the car."

They fell into an awkward silence. Why was this so weird? She knew why— she'd bawled in his lap like a baby, then rubbed herself all over like a horny teenager, before guilting him into hanging out with her during the day at work.

She'd officially made it weird.

She should have been mortified to admit such a vulnerability, to even acknowledge his effect on her, but her hurt feelings at Ian's indifference were bigger than her pride. Besides, at that point she hadn't had much else to lose.

"I'm sorry. I didn't even ask. Do you like Vietnamese food?"

"Yeah, who doesn't?"

Maybe the awkwardness wasn't entirely her fault. Ian had reverted to his taciturn one-grunt answers. She'd spent the last forty-eight hours restless with anticipation. Was he not as excited to be here?

Oh, God, had she guilted him into this date?

No. She hadn't forced or guilted him. To prove it, the Minister of Horniness elbowed Anxiety out of the way and replayed the moment she'd asked him out. The way his eyes smoldered and his lip caught between his teeth was genuine. He wanted to be here as much as she wanted him here. So this... reticence was something else.

She leaned forward on the table and gave him a pointed once-over. "Do you feel pressured into being here tonight?" Then, remembering how he toyed with her when she was initially looking for intel on Quincy, she added, "Do you feel like your job was in jeopardy if you declined?"

The way his eyes widened in shock before he caught on to her teasing shouldn't have pleased her as much as it did.

He rubbed his hands on his face and groaned a laugh. At himself? The situation? She wasn't sure.

"I'm sorry. I know I'm trippin' but I can't shake it."

Did it make her a bad person to feel relief at his discomfort?

She was about to ask what he meant when their server came to ask if they were ready to order. Both of them quickly scanned their options., They chose the house special phở each and an order of shrimp on sugarcane with vermicelli noodles to share.

"Oh! And can I please have two orders of spring rolls?" Ian added as an afterthought.

"That's a lot of food." Where did he put it all?

"I'm hoping something to nibble on, something to do with my hands, will help settle my nerves."

The Minister of Horniness, still standing at the ready, passed her a list of things he could do with his hands printed on thick, creamy cardstock.

With a prim shake of her head and a soft clearing of her throat, she asked, "We're a bit beyond nerves, aren't we?"

"I don't know. Are we? This is technically our first date. I want to make a good impression."

At that, Claudia tossed her head back and laughed. Her impression of Ian Yang had already been cemented. Her good favor was his to lose. In fact, at this point Claudia worried that even at his most atrocious, she might make space for him in her life. It was a worrying concept to grapple with. Luckily she didn't really believe he would behave anything but admirably and therefore didn't have to put her morals to the test.

"It's not funny, Gossipika. I've been twisted up all day."

"Ian," She stretched the word out to show him just how ridiculous she found it all. "You have a nickname for me. You know where I live. I've had my tongue in your mouth. I think it's safe to say you can skip past first date jitters."

"Yeah, but what do we even talk about now? I know too much."

She smiled at that. She completely understood what he meant. It was weird to be treating this as a first date when they'd already had so many other 'dates' over the weeks and months. And, sure, it was under extremely different circumstances. But the reality was, this wasn't a first date, per se. It was, to her mind, an evolution of their existing arrangement. One without a ticking clock attached to their outings.

"Okay, tell me about your parents. How are they doing? Is your mother still worried about the company being left in your questionable care?"

"They're good. My dad has another round of tests coming up, but everyone is pretty positive about the results. And no, I haven't run Sun Star Cleaning into the ground as yet, not that you could tell based on my mother's constant fretting."

This made Claudia laugh. Ian had changed his whole personality to keep from damaging the enterprise his parents had built, but still his mother behaved as though he was one lit match away from burning it all to the ground.

"Their company is called Sun Star?"

"Yes?"

"Don't say it like that," she balked. "Why would I know the name of the cleaning company?"

"Why wouldn't you? You seem to make it your business to know everything."

She gave a small nod, conceding his point. "Fair enough. But I don't have anything to do with HR or personnel and, if memory serves, their contract is with the building not specifically with MS&S."

Ian arched a judgmental brow at the amount of information she'd just disclosed.

"Okay, okay, but Miss Val told me that. I can't remember what we were talking about, though." Claudia's face scrunched up as she tried to recall.

"Well, to answer your questions, yes. Yang is Mandarin for sun, so most people in my family with any type of business or side hustle have Sun in the name."

"Do you speak Mandarin?"

"Nope! My dad's family has been in Guyana for four generations. None of them speak it. My auntie Eileen—my dad's brother's wife—is from China. She tried to teach me, but I just don't have the gift for language."

"William's mom, right?"

"You are truly dangerous, you know that?"

Claudia mimed tossing her hair over her shoulder. If Ian thought she'd forgotten the details he'd shared with her, she'd now cleared him of that notion. It pleased her to be thought of as dangerous in this way. It pleased her even more that Ian seemed to admire her more shrewd qualities.

"It's cool, but it's also a mess because, like, sun is super common in business names. So, when I finally go to register my business, it'll be a whole lot of cross-referencing against all the other existing companies. Luckily I have a top 5 list in case my first choice isn't available."

"Well? Don't keep me in suspense. What is it?"

"Sun Escapes Design."

"Sunny Scapes?" Claudia asked, her face telegraphing her confusion.

He shook his head and enunciated. "Sun. Escapes."

"Like Design is holding Sun hostage, and it's finally Escaped?"

"No, wise guy. Like you're escaping indoors to the beautifully designed outdoors. Where the sun is."

"Did you ask any ESL people to say it, because I think it'll come out as Sunny Scapes six times out of ten."

Ian laughed, shrugging helplessly. "I could call it 'Ian Yang Landscape Architect', and it will still be misnamed. I did think about it, though. I even toyed with being another Sun Star as a kind of callback to my folks, but it's their schmoopy backstory. I don't know if I could handle it day in and day out."

Claudia pressed her hands to her cheeks, feeling the warmth of her blush spread beneath her skin. It didn't surprise her in the least to learn Howard and Valerie Yang had a schmoopy love story that they built their empire on. For all the hustle and bustle and hard work they did, it was no secret to anyone that those two people were the center of each other's universes.

"Please don't swoon. I really can't handle it." Ian gave a disgruntled huff.

His spring rolls arrived, and he went to pick one up at the exact same time Claudia cautioned, "They're probably very hot."

"Ouch!" His brows met in the middle, a display of betrayal that his spring rolls would cause him pain. The way his face went from forbidding to expressive at the drop of a hat tickled her.

Ian stuck the pad of his finger in his mouth to soothe the burn and Claudia, in an act of supreme maturity and refinement, slid her ice water close to him without offering her mouth as a balm.

It was one thing when she'd been imagining what it'd be like to kiss him, to have his hands on her body, but now she knew. The feel of his hands gripping possessive, greedy handfuls of her flesh was like a brand on her memory, and to have not so much as kissed him since? It was a miracle she hadn't offered more than her mouth to soothe his burnt finger. Like her hot, wet—

Claudia wrangled the controls away from the Minister of Horniness and steered her brain to more appropriate ground. "Tell me about your siblings. Are any of them in line to take over Sun Star?"

Ian wiped the condensation off her ice water on his napkin and tilted his head to one side, seeming to consider the question. "My parents didn't really plan for that, I don't think. I mean, it was never a topic of conversation where they would bring up the future when one of us would carry on the family business." He gave the last a grave, somber intonation. "I think they were happy to provide us with a good life and, had any of us wanted it, they'd happily pass the torch."

"But none of you do?"

Ian looked down and to the side before answering. "Will it sound terrible if I say I don't think it occurred to any of us? We've all kind of taken it for granted that Sun Star exists. Filling in for them now has really opened my eyes to a lot." At Claudia's understanding nod, he continued, "I don't think any of us considered it as more than a guaranteed place of employment whenever we needed a job."

"Huh." Claudia hadn't meant to make the sound. But now that she had, Ian's full attention was all hers. "Sorry, I'm just... I'm amazed you were able to keep it separate. That is not at all my experience."

Ian's scoff was playful, "Then I've clearly misrepresented myself. There was no separation. All four of us have done our share of unpaid labor and have sat through countless 'business meetings' between my parents at the dinner table: so-and-so gave their notice, should we switch suppliers, those towels leave too much lint behind. What I was trying to say is we treated Sun Star the way any other kids treated their parents' job, y'know?"

It was weird to think about. They both worked for their family business, yet their circumstances couldn't be more different. Claudia often wondered what people thought when they heard the words 'family business'. As far as she was concerned, it could be anything from a local mom-and-pop business—dry cleaners, corner store, or takeout restaurant—to a corporate monopoly like the Canadian telecom family.

She didn't think Morenal, Smith & Sano qualified as either. Though the company employed multiple generations of family, it had only been operational for twenty-five years with the original leadership still in place. They hadn't been around long enough for the passing of the torch to raise eyebrows one way or the other. The 'shirtsleeves to shirtsleeves in three generations' critique that people lobbed at family businesses hadn't happened yet.

What they did have in common was the way home and business merged and overlapped until the boardroom was completely interchangeable with the dining room as far as locales for litigating decisions big and small. Sure, her cousin Alma's second pregnancy was announced at a family dinner, but it immediately turned into an update on 4th quarter projection targets. Yes, there was a monthly staff meeting, but as the rest of the staff trickled out, her Uncle was just as likely to hold her back to ask if she had spoken to her grandmother about holiday plans. There was no separation between the proverbial church and state, no escape from either source of conflict.

"I guess that makes sense." She allowed, as their plates arrived.

The steaming broth was fragrant, and Claudia inhaled greedily, wrapping her hands around the bowl and letting it chase away the last of the chill.

"Did you always know you'd work for your family? You're the only one who does, right?"

"Yeah, my sister Fernanda lives in Costa Rica with her tree-hugger husband and four practically feral boys, and Diego is, well, you know." Ian's laugh was bright and knowing. Diego was always Diego. "I didn't know I was going to get into this field. I'm cursed with a degree in history. I was halfway through my program when I realized that my historical knowledge could be useful in a peripheral way. So, I went and double-majored in economics. Lots of classes and tests and training and shadowing later, and here I am."

"But you could have done it somewhere else, no?"

"I could, and I couldn't." Claudia took a minute to think about her answer, to really give him the consideration he'd shown her. "Working at MS&S meant I was able to start my career a little closer to my destination instead of at rock bottom. I wouldn't have been afforded that luxury anywhere else. The downside, of course, is being surrounded by family at all times. There's no calling in with a dead relative for me. No," she made frail coughing noises, "'sick days'. And, sure, I'd get the time off if I asked for it, but then the family would know I asked. Like, I can't invoke the words 'mental health day' without calling down the full scope of my mother's fretting on my head."

"Because everyone knows you're related."

"Hence me using Pérez. It's not that my colleagues don't know or that using Pérez magically pulls the detail out of their memory once they learn the truth. It's more about being able to create a tiny bit of distance for myself with the clients so that my work is only judged and undermined because I'm a Black woman and not because I'm a useless, unqualified nepo-baby. It helps."

Claudia closed her eyes as she savored her first mouthful of pho.

"Makes sense. All those stories about men signing off as one of their female counterparts and realizing just how vastly different their working experiences are? It's wild."

"I mostly work with women and queer people, so I'm not as subject to it as other members of my department, but that struggle is very real."

"I worry about my sister pursuing her dream of becoming a physicist. Luckily she grew up with three older brothers, so she won't be run roughshod over."

"Aren't your youngest siblings twins?"

"Yeah, but," Ian slurped noodles into his mouth, "she's still technically the youngest of us."

Claudia rolled her eyes, and they continued eating, enjoying both their food and each other.

"Um," she started, knowing it was none of her business but unable to stop herself from asking, "How come you're the one supporting your family through this? Isn't that usually the role of the firstborn?"

Ian pushed his empty bowl aside. How was he finished? They'd started their food at the same time, hadn't they?

"My brother is painfully analytical. It's not a skill set that lends itself to caregiving, so he was released from duty almost immediately. The twins are still so young. They shouldn't have to give up on their goals and dreams to shoulder this. I'm willing and able, so… it's on me. Besides, they all contribute in their own ways. Desmond sends money and his opinions, Gavin researches additional services and programs we might qualify for and gives his opinions, and Renée calls every day to check in and run some interference so my mom's attention is split. And offers her opinions." He shrugged a careless 'it is what it is'. "We're making it work."

They continued to eat and chat and generally enjoy each other's presence. Every so often, Claudia thought she'd caught Ian giving her a heated look, but before she could capture it, truly seize it, he'd schooled his features, making her wonder if she'd imagined the whole thing.

Still, by the time they finished their meal, she wasn't ready for the night to end.

"Wanna grab some dessert? There's a French bistro close to here. We can split something."

"French after Vietnamese? How very colonizer of you."

Ian laughed at her teasing and took her hand in his. "Is that a no?"

"No," She smiled up at him, truly delighted by his company and the fun she was having on their first not-first date. "It's not a no."

"Alright then, Gossipika. Let's go."

"After you, Sunny."

"Sunny? Really?"

Her warm smile twisted into a challenging smirk as she dared him without words to push back on the new appellation. It was such low hanging fruit, there was no way she could pass it up!

He wisely said nothing more about 'Sun Escapes', and led her up Boulton Avenue.

He wasn't joking when he said it was close. They'd crossed Gerrard at De Grassi, and before she knew it, they'd made it to the next intersection and were at the door asking if they could be seated. She almost didn't feel the cold.

Almost.

No, that wasn't true. She was very aware of the frigid November air. She was simply more aware of Ian, of his hands wrapped around hers, of his warmth as he kept her tucked close to his side.

The ambiance here was entirely different than the casual eatery they'd just left. This place was also laid back but definitely had an air of classiness. They were seated along the wall, which still managed to feel intimate despite the tables that were no more than an arm's length from where they sat.

Ian immediately ordered the chef's special dessert and two glasses of a paired wine as they settled themselves.

They didn't speak, didn't make polite chit-chat about the decor or how Ian knew about the restaurant. They only held hands across the table, mooning at each other like goofballs. Claudia had never felt as content as she did in that moment.

When their dessert arrived, Claudia gasped. It was a tart topped with the most beautiful concentric circles of fresh cherries; she picked up her spoon but didn't want to slice into it. Ian, unbothered by such sentiment, sliced his fork into the pastry and held it out to her. She closed her mouth around the fork and moaned as the tangy lemon cream landed on her tongue.

"Oh, that's good." She made a slice of her own now that Ian had made the first move.

"Can I tell you something?"

She paused with the spoon halfway to her mouth and waited.

"I can't stop thinking about our kiss."

Everything inside Claudia clenched tight. "Which one?"

Was that her voice? When did it drop an octave? How did it get so husky?

"The first one."

Claudia put her spoon down and tried to compose herself under the weight of Ian's heated glaze. She wasn't sure if she was imagining the want she saw there or if she was projecting it, but her own hunger sparked hot and bright.

"Why the first one?" Apparently clearing one's throat doesn't rid it of horny hoarseness in any way. She'd make a mental note to remind herself about it later.

He gave a careless lift of his left shoulder. "Without that one, there wouldn't have been the other ones. Wouldn't have led to...

well." He paused as though suddenly aware of his surroundings. "The first one is the one I think about."

She couldn't help the blush that rose over her skin; all she could do was lower her gaze to stave off the sudden bashfulness that accompanied it. She caught her bottom lip in her teeth, a habit from childhood, as she tried in vain to compose herself. Every cell and molecule in her body remembered how it felt to be kissed by Ian.

"Can I tell you something else?" Ian's voice was sin and want and desire. He didn't wait for her answer. Not that she could do more than nod mutely when his raspy, fuck-me voice was lulling her into a trance. "When you do that, when you gnaw on your lip like that, it makes me feel like you're daring me to put your mouth to better use. Like you're waving a flag at a bull."

Claudia Sano was at a loss for words. Sure, people claimed they didn't know what to say, but she rarely suffered that affliction. Her problem was generally about what she wanted to say not lining up with what people expected her to say. But now, with Ian's heated gaze warming her from head to toe, she was so overwhelmed with the many thoughts clamoring for the spotlight, they seemed to cancel each other out, leaving her speechless, not knowing which to express first.

She wanted to enumerate the many things she was willing to do to him—with him, for him—with her mouth. But she also wanted to admit this was the best date she'd ever been on and tell him he was entirely the reason. She wanted to try to make him understand how much it meant to her that he knew even a fraction of the twisted path her mind took her on, seemed to accept it at face value with no tips or tricks offered, and wanted her regardless.

Instead, she continued blushing, tongue-tied like a skittish debutante, and brought the spoon to her mouth, desperate for the reprieve chewing her food might provide. Ian—keen, attentive

Ian—clasped her hand across the table and allowed the moment to pass. When their dessert and wine were finished, their lingering at the table arrived at its natural end.

Ian asked, "Do you want a ride home? Or I can wait until your rideshare shows up if you prefer?"

"I'd love a ride. Thanks."

Bundled up and back in the cold night air, Ian tucked her to his side, and she leaned into his embrace. The entire drive was spent talking about everything and nothing, her hand still in his. Before she realized, Ian had pulled into her complex's visitor parking.

"Let me walk you to your door," was all he said before he hustled around to the passenger side and helped her to her feet.

God, she wanted this man. And after this perfect night they'd shared, she'd take him however she could have him—a cup of tea while they chatted in the kitchen, some kisses by the doorway, maybe even another swing around second base. She just didn't want the night to be over.

"Do you want to come in?"

"I don't know if that's a good idea." His shuffling feet occupied his attention. He looked up and Claudia saw the truth before he spoke the words, "My thoughts are... not entirely chaste."

She could write a doctorate on the subject of not entirely chaste thoughts. Instead, she popped up on her toes to press her mouth to his.

She kissed him, a slow, languid tangle of lips and tongues. She broke the kiss with an indulgent mmm of enjoyment and stepped through the doorway. She turned to him, facing off over her threshold, and dropped her coat where she stood. With an arched brow, she said, "Good to know because mine are thoroughly carnal." She started to unzip her dress while she waited for him to make his choice. He laughed to himself because they both knew it wasn't a choice at all.

Ian stepped into her apartment and kicked the door closed behind him.

Chapter Nineteen

The door was still vibrating in its frame when Ian wrapped his arms around Claudia and pulled her in for a searing kiss. She tasted like lemon curd and sin.

"Claudia, please." His words were a gasping plea, "If we do this, she can't be here, okay?"

Before she could answer, he was at her mouth again, taking the breath directly from her lungs.

"I only want you, Claudia. I want you so much, I—" He was frantic, his mouth never far from hers, his lips sipping and caressing. "She can't be here. Please, okay? Put her away, Claudia."

He didn't want bubbly work Claudia. He wanted the snarling, angry woman, and he was desperate for her to put the other one away. Claudia's eyes darted between his as understanding dawned. He was surprised she could clear her thoughts enough to process his meaning since he was reduced to little more than grunts and half-formed words.

"That's what you want?" She asked him even though she knew the answer.

"Yes."

"What if I—?"

He cut her off, impatient for another taste of her. Her pouty mouth was swollen from his kisses. He needed to get back to them. "I don't care, Claudia. Whatever it is, I don't care."

"Don't say that." She pulled away from him.

"What should I say?" He brought her back to his body, unwilling to relinquish the feel of her pressed against him, even for a moment. "That I'm so crazy about you, I can't think straight? That the sound you make when you come has haunted me, and I'm willing to do anything—*anything*—to hear it again? Do you want to know about the new levels of depravity I've unearthed, depths I didn't even know existed, centered on the logistics of bending you over assorted pieces of furniture?" Her breath caught, and he felt like a titan. He leaned over, tugging at the lobe of her left ear with his teeth and whispered slowly, "I want whatever you want."

"What if I want to toy with you?"

God, yes! "Then toy with me."

"What if I hurt you?"

He tilted his head, studying her. "Do you want to hurt me?"

"No." The word came out rushed and vehement.

He nodded, removing it as a concern. "What else?"

"What if..." She gulped, unsure and possibly unwilling to continue her sentence, "What if you don't like it?"

He held her neck gently in his hands, tilting her face up so their eyes met. "I don't know what to tell you, Claudia. I can't imagine not liking any scenario that ends with you coming." Pulling her up to meet his kiss, Ian was driven by a hunger he couldn't fight. "Do your worst, Gossipika. I'm all in."

It seemed to be what she needed to hear because Claudia surged up, claiming him the way he'd wanted from the very beginning. She kissed him as if she was trying to make him understand that there was more to his request than a plea for her authentic self, but he didn't need her reassurances—he was looking for this exact type of abandon and wanted it from her. With her.

She wrapped her arms around his neck, holding him close as she plundered and took and pillaged, a frenzy to which he willingly surrendered. When they broke apart, gasping for breath, their gazes caught, and hot need reflected back on itself like an infinite loop of desire.

"Sit over there."

Ian held her gaze as he dutifully lowered himself onto the armless, open-backed chair at her dining room table, fully committed to whatever came next.

What came next was a tortuous striptease where Claudia finished unzipping her dress. She let the fabric pool at her feet, leaving her clad in a maroon silk slip and hose.

Claudia stood beside him and wrapped her hand around his throat, collaring him. He held her gaze as he swallowed, his Adam's apple moving against her palm. The rush of desire blew out her pupils as a small, needy sound escaped her parted lips. Ian had never been so turned on, so willing to be led to ruin; he was surprised to find he hadn't come right then.

He leaned further into her grip and watched her eyes widen.

"Put your hands behind you. Grab the chair legs, don't let go." Her voice was hoarse, and Ian felt the same mania flowing through his own veins.

He rolled his shoulders a couple of times, loosening up to make himself as comfortable as possible. He planned to enjoy every minute he could withstand.

She tipped his head up and licked into his mouth. It was a filthy, lewd kiss that went straight to his dick.

"I'm going to use your body to get myself off. Your job is to sit there and let me."

"And if I don't?"

"Then I'll know you didn't mean anything you said to me."

"Is this a test?" Didn't she understand? He was all in. Before she stripped down to a slip and garter belt, before she faced off against him on the other side of her door—even before she asked him out tonight—Ian Yang was all aboard the Claudia Sano Express, nonstop to the end of the line.

"Not a test. An attempt."

"I'm so hard, Claudia, I don't see me lasting longer than it takes to get my pants off."

Another sloppy kiss.

"It's a good thing I have no intention of taking your pants off." With that, she reached down, undid his zipper, tugged on his pants just enough to give herself room to reach in and pull his erection out from his boxers. It stood at attention, eager and willing to do her bidding. She swiped her finger over the wet, swollen tip, spreading the moisture around. His stomach clenched with the effort it took not to move, to not pump himself into her hand, to stay still while she explored.

"Would you look at that?" She said to herself as she ran the tip of her finger along the length of his dick. "I thought I made it up."

Ian could only manage a grunt in reply. His focus was required elsewhere.

With one hand still collaring him, she fisted him in lazy strokes that were too firm to be ignored but not hard enough to satisfy. "I thought some of it was the fabric or maybe even my imagination."

Finally letting go of his throat, Claudia reached under her slip to shimmy herself out of her underwear, gingerly plucking them from around her heel before standing over him and straddling his lap. He wanted to sink his teeth into the small expanse of skin framed by the top of her stocking and the ties of her garter belt.

She was preparing to lower herself by balancing her hands on his shoulders, and he couldn't help but taunt her, "Would your feet even be able to touch the ground without your heels?"

Straightening, she scoffed at him. "You're not that tall."

"I'm not," he agreed easily, happy to have a moment of distraction. A small window to shore up his defenses.

"And I'm not that short!" She sank onto his lap and he groaned from the feel of it. His arms twitched and flexed, desperate to hold her yet determined to obey. Did she notice? Could she tell he was fighting a battle that would end in his ruin no matter which side won?

Claudia leaned forward; her entire torso was plastered to his. Her tongue met his lips in little licks and swipes as she spoke against his mouth, "When I was grinding on you the other night, I thought, 'It couldn't be all him, could it?'"

"Claudia!" He pleaded, unsure whether it was for more, for her to stop, to have mercy.

"You felt so good last time. I wonder if it will be the same without the barrier of our clothes?"

Then she proceeded to do exactly that. She rubbed her hot, wet slit along the hard length of him, tormenting him with the promise of what she clearly planned to withhold. It was delicious torture and he fought against the pleasure. The heat and slick and friction all overwhelmed him, daring him to lose control.

Ian bared his teeth, breathing through it His wide nostrils flared, his chest heaving, as he did whatever it took to give this to her. When she came, the little spasm in her leg giving it away, she made the same pleased sigh, and Ian had to close his eyes to stop himself from spilling on his stomach. Again.

"You can let go of the chair leg now, but you still can't touch me." Her directive, issued in choppy, panting breaths, was meant to be a kindness and a cruelty. He'd squeezed the wooden bars so hard he was sure he'd feel the strain in his muscles for days. But if he couldn't touch her, then it was no kind of relief. His hands hanging at his sides, he let his mouth land on her face and neck, wherever he could reach.

She graced him with a long, languid kiss, humming her satisfaction into his mouth, into his marrow. "What do you think, Sunny? Was this about the same or better?"

"I think you should do it again, like a double blind."

"That's not what that means," she gave an indulgent nibble of his neck, "but you bring up a good point. We might be at a crossroads."

He raised a brow in response. Yes, his breathing was slowly regulating itself but he still didn't have full cognitive function.

"Generally speaking, I am not one of those women who have multiple orgasms. Not big ones, anyway." To demonstrate, she made explosion gestures with her hands and adorable 'bksshk' noises out the side of her mouth. Each explosion came with a tiny hip thrust that, in turn, pulled a grunt from him. Her demeanor was silly and comical, but he saw the fire in her eyes, his pufferfish staring back at him.

"Maybe you haven't tried hard enough."

"Exactly what I was thinking. But here's where it gets tricky: I have no idea how long it could take. And you've done so well," she gave his dick a gentle, reverent caress, "I'd hate for you to get benched while there's still so much game left on the clock."

"Why don't you let me worry about that?"

She answered him with a careless lift of her shoulder, as if to say, *Very well, then*. She moved off his lap, and he took a perverse pleasure in noticing the unsteadiness of her first steps as she ambled toward her coffee table.

Ian shifted in his seat. She hadn't said he could get up but she didn't say he couldn't move, either, so he took the opportunity to stretch and loosen his muscles. With some of the pressure easing from his erection, he found a bit of clarity. He was just starting to function without the haze of lust clouding his thoughts when he heard the familiar clinking sound of ceramics.

Claudia had opened the lid of a dish on her coffee table and pulled out a condom. She gave him a considering look, then chose a different kind before replacing the lid and walking back to him.

Just like that, his erection went from mostly hard to hard enough to crush rocks.

When she got within arm's reach, she pointed at him with her chin, "Arms behind your back. No touching."

Again, Ian settled into his body, getting as comfortable as possible. The back of the chair wasn't high enough for him to rest his head but it was wide and sturdy enough that he didn't worry about settling his entire weight into it.

She threw her leg over his lap, her silk-clad breast rubbing his cheek, and he tried to follow her, tried to get his mouth on her, but she leaned away with an admonishing tsk.

"You have a beautiful body, Ian. Have I told you?" She spoke to the head of his dick, "I don't spend a lot of time thinking about men's penises, but yours is truly a marvel."

He couldn't help but smile.

"Anyway, as I was saying," she gave her head a small shake as if to clear her thoughts as she looked at him, "we're going to attempt this multiple orgasm thing. Now, I acknowledge that there may have been too much time between them to truly count as multiple, so I'm willing to put an asterisk beside these findings. Either way, I'm going to use your body as I see fit, and you are going to keep your hands to yourself."

"Why not let my hands get in on the action? I'm certain they would be helpful."

She completely ignored him and went about rolling the condom on. She used a solid, efficient grip, covering him in no time. Then she leaned forward and proceeded to rub herself on his shaft again. Leaning close to his ear, she whispered, "Can you still feel that? I'm so wet, it's *indecent*."

"Claudia!"

"Do you think it'll help or hurt my efforts?" She sucked on the skin behind his ear. His hips kicked up in reflex.

"Pobrecito." She tutted with a sympathetic pout. "Are you losing control?"

"No," he rasped. His control was lost days ago, when he pulled her into his arms and felt the plush softness of her body pressed against him. There was no more control left. He had been distilled down to a simple objective—Claudia's pleasure—and he was devoting his entire being to the task.

"Good. Now let's begin."

Begin? Hadn't they already begun? She'd been rubbing herself on him lo these many minutes. How did that not count as beginning?

Claudia grabbed the base of his shaft and shifted her hips so she could spank her clit in a firm, continuous rhythm. By the fourth one, she started to moan and writhe in his lap. By the tenth, her eyes were closed, and she was playing with her nipple over the silk slip she still wore. It was hard and inviting, and Ian's mouth watered to feel it against the flat of his tongue.

"Let me touch you, Claudia."

"Shh." She admonished as she continued to play with herself.

"We can find out together if my hands add any appreciable value."

She continued to tap her clit with his dick, continued to fray the edges of his composure.

"Kiss me."

"Why?"

He was cross-eyed with lust. He needed some release, some valve to take the pressure off—a mouthful of her tits, a meaty thigh in his palm—something. Anything.

"Please, Claudia."

She leaned close, swiping his bottom lip with her hot, wet tongue. "No."

"Claudia…" Had he ever whined in his adult life? He had no idea, but he was reduced to it now.

She lifted herself up and sank slowly, tortuously, down on his sheathed erection.

Foreheads touching, they groaned and panted at the feel of their connection. She was so sweet, so perfect, he wanted to stay exactly where he was for the foreseeable future, food and water be damned.

"Ian." Her hushed voice was filled with wonder, as though she hadn't expected it to feel this way. And perhaps she hadn't if the way she twitched and clenched on his shaft was any indication. He closed his eyes, savoring the perfect hot grasp of her body on his, the perfect weight of her in his lap, her mewling little sobs as her body adjusted to the intrusion. "That feels so good."

She was talking to herself again, but Ian couldn't help but answer, "You're perfect, Claudia. Perfect."

If he thought he was in heaven before, he was unprepared for the feeling of Claudia starting to move. Her gorgeous body twisting and circling on him, her hips setting the rhythm she'd picked specifically to drive him mad. Every slide, every stroke, every drag of flesh set him aflame.

Ian kept heaving large, noisy breaths through his nose, trying to maintain his focus. Trying to clear the spots that were clouding the corners of his vision.

"Is that your big plan? Do you think ignoring me will help you last longer?" She ran her hands under his shirt, his skin bunching at her touch, and flicked his nipples with her thumbs.

She thought he was trying to ignore the pleasure but she was wrong. He was wallowing in it, sinking himself in its depths as he learned its dimensions. He was devoting himself to the study of the bliss Claudia wielded so he would always remember what it was to soar.

"This is what you wanted, to use me?"

"Shh." She let her head fall back. "No more talking."

"Then give my mouth something to do. Kiss me."

Instead of putting him out of his misery, she gave his nipple a scolding pinch, tutting, "Maybe I should trade you for one of those sex torsos. They don't talk back."

"But I'm way more versatile."

"Yet here you are, under me."

Yes, he thought, *I could spend the rest of my life with you above me this way.* He was sure he'd let Claudia do anything she wanted if it meant he got to stay this close to her fire.

"A whole new avenue of impure thoughts for me to explore."

"Ay, por dios!" She hooked her feet around the chair's back legs to anchor herself, then leaned back in his lap so her body stretched out before him like a buffet. All he'd have to do is bend at the waist to be face-first in her cleavage. But to reach her, he'd have to let go of the chair legs. Which she knew, the witch.

She pulled herself back up to sit on his lap. The shift and drag of her changed positions pulled a rumbling groan from his chest. Was that display of flexibility a taunt? Another way to drive him out of his mind? Before he could ask, she'd shoved something in his mouth.

"No. More. Talking."

They froze, eyes locked as she watched him, wide-eyed, both of them processing what she'd done. She'd used her panties to gag him and he struggled to breathe around the sudden intrusion. The hint of her arousal from the fabric was in his nose, on his tongue. The whole thing untethered something in his brain as a rush of pure, primitive need flooded him. He let go of the chair legs, his hand flexing as he reached for her.

Claudia was riveted. Her attention bouncing between his face and his now freed hands halted her movement.

The air around them seemed to vibrate with anticipation.

He wrestled himself back under control, fought his every instinct to reach for her, and settled back in the chair. His dick twitched in protest and she gasped at the feel of it.

"You like this."

Ian nodded.

"You like me." She breathed the words as though it only now occurred to her.

He spat the wadded fabric out, letting it tumble down his chest as he held her gaze. "So much."

"Fuck," she sighed, gnawing at her lip, "that was hot."

Ian's chest was still heaving with the effort to keep his hands to himself. Still, he managed to grunt out, "What did I tell you about that?"

Claudia leaned forward with her hands braced on his pecs and whispered with a devious smile teasing her pouty mouth, "Remind me."

Ian's breaths were labored, his body too overwhelmed by pleasure and frustration and restraint. His ability to carry a rational conversation was increasingly difficult when the pulse and grip of Claudia's body on his dick crossed his eyes with bliss. His heart was racing so fast, his muscles held taut, and this woman was rubbing herself against him, expecting answers to her questions? It was madness.

"You need something else to occupy that mouth."

"I do," she nodded, dove at his mouth, sucking on his tongue as she ground their pelvises together.

Ian was lost. There wasn't anything he could do about the desperate noises torn from his throat as he bucked up into her, hard and unrestrained.

She wrapped herself around him and moaned her frantic pleas directly into his skin. *Please. Harder. Yes. There.* He moved like a man possessed, as the feel of her hot, wet breath on his neck drove him heedlessly into ruin. Into salvation.

"Ian, please," She cried, blindly grabbing at his arms. "More."

It was all the permission he'd needed.

He wrapped her tightly in his arms and proceeded to move her body against his in brutal, teeth-clattering thrusts. It didn't take long until they were both caught in the tempest of their feverish coupling.

His climax raced at him like a storm on the plains. It rushed and it roared and it took and he let it because he didn't think he had anything left to give that wasn't hers by right. That she hadn't taken, demanded, by the sheer force of her will.

He didn't recognize the low guttural sound he made as he continued to pound into Claudia's body. Her own gasps of pleasure ricocheted throughout the room as he clamped her shoulder in his teeth in a futile attempt to tether himself to her in this moment.

Her mouth opened on a silent scream, her limbs stiff and jerking as though she were being electrocuted. All he could do was hold her close while her orgasm ravaged her tiny frame. The chain reaction was almost too much to take. Her spasms called an answering throb from his dick, which sent a shivering aftershock through her, which triggered his hips to thrust, and then the sequence would start all over again. They stayed that way, in a jittery, twitching loop, for what felt like an eternity.

When he could finally see past the blinding pleasure, he felt wrung out by the experience. The only thing centering him was the need to keep hold of Claudia, who'd fallen limp in his arms. Her eyes fluttered open, her voice sounding like it was coming from miles away, "We did it, Sunny."

"We sure did, Gossipika," he said, his voice tender and full of emotion while he brushed her hair back from her face to press gentle kisses along her damp hairline.

Her eyes rolled closed, her head lolled back and snuggled against him. She whispered, "Good job".

Ian held her tighter as he breathed her in. After everything they'd done tonight—the filthy talk, the wild, uninhibited sex, the chemistry-altering climaxes—this moment, Claudia sheltered and sated in his arms, was the most earth-shattering.

It was the moment he'd return to for as long as he lived.

Chapter Twenty

"Claudia," she heard the quiet rasp of Ian's whisper moments before she felt his soft kisses move down her forehead to the tip of her nose. "I have to go."

Claudia rarely woke up groggy or confused. Her mind was always racing, always engaged, so she woke up fully alert more often than not.

Which is why this, right now, waking on her couch, covered in the throw, and still wearing her slip, was so jarring.

Every single element of her present reality was a problem. First, she didn't sleep on her couch. Ever. Her sleep hygiene was such that her bedroom was set up exclusively for the practice of slumber.

Which also spoke to items two and three on the weird list: she had a specially calibrated weighted blanket and five pairs of identical pajamas for sleep clothes. She'd never use the throw or her lingerie for sleeping.

"Hi," Ian ran a gentle finger along her jawline. "How are you feeling?"

He was kneeling in front of her couch, his other hand wandered gently down her back as he kissed her awake. Instead of answering, because she didn't actually understand what was happening, she blinked mutely and nodded. Ian's smile and chuckle were soft, indulgent.

He pressed another quick kiss to her lips, stood, and said, "Take your time getting up."

Claudia lay still, working on getting her bearings. Her usually overactive mind was sluggish and uncooperative, which was a new, annoying development in their established Claudia's Brain Works Against Her routine.

"Honey or sugar?" Ian called out.

She shifted to see him puttering in her kitchen.

"What?" What on Earth was happening? Clearing her throat, she tried again, "Sorry, pardon?"

"I made you some tea. Do you take honey or sugar?" He was behaving as though this whole interaction was entirely normal while she was scrambling to put the pieces together.

It was too late for her to be drinking anything at all, but she didn't want to say that, so she answered, "Neither. I take it black."

He made a 'huh' motion with his head and set the tea on the breakfast bar for her.

Why couldn't she get her shit together? She went to stand, to go to him, and her entire core protested.

That familiar, delicious ache brought everything back. She and Ian had had sex. And not just any kind of sex. No, for their first time together, Claudia decided it was appropriate to fuck him in the kitchen like a bawdy house madam. She'd basically tied the man to a chair, edged him for a half hour, and then came so hard she passed out. He must have put her to rest on the couch.

Who does that? Who skips over the pleasantries to dive right into light bondage and orgasm denial? She'd stuffed her underwear in his mouth, for chrissakes! She didn't even let him *take off his pants*! The small scrapes on her nalgas from his zipper were confirmation enough of that fact.

As if she'd needed any more proof that there was something profoundly wrong with her. How was she supposed to face him now? 'Oh, hey, Ian. Thanks for sticking around and making me a cuppa. Really appreciate you indulging my pathological need for control. Hope your shoulders don't seize on ya overnight!' All that was missing were some finger guns. Fuck!

She dropped her face in her hands and groaned.

Fuck, fuck, fuck.

Claudia took a deep breath and tried to calm her racing thoughts. All she had to do was get through this awkward bit—the gods knew she'd been here before, though usually it was either her reassuring them she did have a good time despite her lack of orgasm or thanking them heartily for the orgasm she had managed while maneuvering herself out the door—and then try to put this all behind her. Except, of course, for the one, teensy detail of them working in the same building where they saw each other almost every day.

She could kick herself for telling him she wished they'd talked at work. Maybe, hopefully, he'd get the hint and go back to the way things were? It'd only been two weeks since they'd started socializing at the office. Twelve days since they'd started to orgasm together. Surely that wasn't enough time to irrevocably change things between them, right?

"Are you okay? Do you need anything else before I go?"

Go? Oh, yes! Ian can't stay. She'd tried to tell him he couldn't stay over, that she wasn't equipped for sleepovers, but he'd taken it as her acceptance of his limitations. She hadn't bothered to correct him with everything else that had happened during their movie date.

Okay.

She could do this.

Standing, she took care not to wince too much as her tender flesh protested.

"Oh, um, no. Thank you. The tea is perfect. You didn't have to do that."

She made her way to the foyer, where he gathered his things.

Where should she look? His ear was too obvious but she couldn't look at his mouth either. His eyebrow? Yes, that seemed to work.

"Claudia... is everything okay?"

"Oh, totally. Yes!" Ugh, her voice sounded weird even to her own ears.

He made a displeased growl and was looming over her in two long strides. He cupped the back of her neck, shaking her gently. "I thought I told you I didn't want her here."

"She's not!" This fucking guy. She couldn't even rely on her mask to get her through this? "She's not. I'm tired and a bit disoriented, and you have to go. I'm fine."

She felt him staring at her, assessing her, searching and sifting and parsing her words for truth. "Look at me."

That was the last thing she wanted to do, but if he got him out the door... She took a deep breath and looked him in the eye. She had no idea what he saw, but he let go of her nape and kissed her temple. "Good night, Claudia."

"You too. Drive safe." She was looking at his eyebrow again, so she heard more than saw his disappointed sigh.

Still, he let himself out, started his car, and pulled out of the visitors' parking space.

Leaning on the door, Claudia thudded her head repeatedly on the heavy oak. It wasn't going to change anything that happened in the last twelve hours, but maybe it would knock some sense into her for the future.

Looking around, she noticed her kitchen was clean. Ian had tidied their snacks and washed the few dishes while he was waiting for her to come to. A wave of emotion flooded her. He was such a good person and she'd behaved abominably. He deserved better.

Since there was no chance her mind would let her drift merrily off to sleep with this embarrassment heating her skin like a fever, she picked up the mug and took a sip of tea. Golden Yunan. Her favorite, brewed exactly how she liked it. She didn't have to wonder how he knew.

It was Ian. Of course he knew.

God, she'd royally fucked up this time.

***

Claudia was avoiding him.

He'd known she was tweaking when she woke up, but he'd already stayed later than he'd planned and needed to get home to make sure his parents were okay. He wished he'd stayed with her. He should have stayed to talk her through it because there was absolutely nothing about their time together he regretted.

Regret was so foreign a concept in this scenario. If scientists developed the technology to put the very concept of regret on the moon, it still wouldn't be far enough away from how he felt about sex with Claudia. She always held herself wrapped so tightly, kept every part of her tamped down, safe from judgment and recrimination. Seeing her let go? She was glorious. Hell, just thinking about her, wild and unleashed atop him, so very alive, made his dick jump and his stomach clench.

But now it was the middle of the second week and he hadn't spoken to her or spent any time with her. She'd been conveniently absent any time he checked for her, getting airy, bullshit replies like, 'Working from home! Happy hump day!' or 'TGIF! Have a great weekend!' whenever he texted. Sure, sometimes he'd seen her in passing, but she was always surrounded in a way he was unable to breach. He'd tried everything he could think of. He'd even tried a sneak attack by switching his schedule around, but she'd somehow known and also switched her hours to avoid having to share the same space.

Why was he surprised that she'd sussed it out? The woman traded in information. She knew more secrets than a CSIS agent.

The only thing that had stopped him from driving to her place and banging on the door was the fact he knew he'd see her at the holiday gala this weekend.

All the staff had been invited. He'd initially thought to decline, but Past Ian obviously knew something was coming and RSVP'd in time so Present Ian could have this standoff.

He sent a quick message to see if Domenic could get him a suite since the event was at his hotel. The way Ian saw it, he'd either be celebrating or wallowing, and both activities were enhanced by a luxury suite at a five-star hotel.

He had no idea what Claudia was thinking, but one way or the other, they'd sort this out.

Chapter Twenty-One

Claudia walked into the ballroom, taking in the dramatic lighting. The large chandelier glowed a soft, golden light, and everywhere she looked there were little tea candles and vases filled with floating votives. It was bright enough to see everyone while still maintaining a romantic atmosphere. Claudia supposed that for what they were paying, it made sense the ambiance was pitch-perfect.

What impressed her the most was how lively the party seemed. She'd purposely skipped dinner, knowing it was too much for her to manage. Since she couldn't beg off entirely, the compromise was a strong showing for the party. The arrangement worked well for her since she could flitter in and out of small groups, delivering empty platitudes with a wide smile, while never having to actually engage with anyone.

The annual holiday gala was a major event, and Morenal, Smith & Sano went all out. Part mixer, part staff party, part client appreciation event, every employee—whether on contract or a member of staff—was invited, as well as their entire client list. Over the years, the declines dwindled almost entirely as people made a point of fitting the party into their schedules. This year was no different. As she stood there in a gold, square sequin wrap dress with a plunging neckline, she let herself admit she'd put in the extra effort because she wanted to impress Ian even though she planned on limiting her direct exposure to him.

The thought had barely formed when a small commotion from the bar caught her attention. She turned in time to see the man in question, surrounded by a small cadre of the younger staff members, cheers-ing each other. Before he'd even swallowed the mouthful of beverage, Ian's hands were in the air, whooping at the song the DJ was mixing in. Apparently that was the signal for the entire group to start their own woo-ing and hollering, racing to the dance floor to let the entire party know, as was foretold long ago if the song's lyrics were to be believed, they had what was being waited for.

The frenetic joy displayed reminded Claudia of nothing so much as the late stages of a wedding reception when shoes were kicked off, ties were worn as bandanas, and everyone was deep into their drinks doing the Wobble. She was mesmerized. The only thing more surprising was the delighted smile that stole across her face.

"He's always been first on any dance floor that would have him."

Claudia turned to find Ian's mom, Valerie, smiling fondly at her son in the middle of the action.

"Miss Val. How are you? We miss you around the office." Claudia was genuinely happy to see her and allowed the woman to hug her.

"You cut your hair," she lamented, taking in the tousled bob Claudia sported.

She ran her hands through the shorn ends. It had been so long since she cut it, she almost forgot what her longer hair felt like.

Claudia tipped her head and shrugged a small 'what are you gonna do' smiling a casual, "I needed a change."

"Well, you look lovely. You always do."

"All smoke and mirrors, really, but I still like to hear it."

Her husband joined them then, bringing Valerie a drink. Claudia focused her attention on Ian's dad. He moved slower, yes, but he seemed exactly as she remembered: quiet, jovial, and completely besotted by his wife.

"Howard! We're so happy you were able to make it tonight. I was just telling Miss Val how much we miss seeing you around. It's not the same without your jaunty whistling."

He took her hands in his and gave them a gentle squeeze. "You're going to make an old man blush."

"Psh. You're not fooling me. I saw the woman in the green dress make eyes at you."

"You hear that?" He winked at his wife, "I still got it."

She teased him with a long-suffering sigh and sipped her drink, not acknowledging his words. His responding smile—pleased, smug, and a teensy bit mischievous—hit Claudia in her proverbial breadbasket. She'd seen Ian make that same face dozens of times. She looked at Howard anew, seeing what she hadn't before. This was Ian, thirty years in the future, from his high forehead and mono-lidded eyes right down to his slightly pigeon-toed stance.

Claudia couldn't help but wonder what his siblings looked like. Did they all share such a striking resemblance to their father? Maybe their mother? As someone who didn't look genetically related to anyone in her family, she was always fascinated by people who shared obvious and undeniable physical characteristics with their parents.

She turned her brightest smile on Ian's dad, "How lucky for you all your *it* still interests your wife!"

They all shared a laugh as Valerie raised her glass to Claudia. Their laughter was still ringing out when a keen awareness stole over her. She felt him and knew without looking that Ian was watching her. She needed to make her escape.

"If you'll excuse me for a moment." She smiled brightly as his parents waved her off.

She spent the next hour laughing and flirting and weighing in on rumored happenings, all while dodging Ian's attempts to get her alone. She'd left the group of interns she'd been encouraging with a quick "Oh! I'm being summoned", when she caught sight of Ian moving through the crowd. She'd disappeared to 'get another round' for her already tipsy team moments before Ian joined them. She'd even ducked into the washroom at the last moment when she heard his voice in the hallway.

Embarrassment had formed an alliance with Anxiety to overthrow the Minister of Horniness, making her already complicated feelings for Ian Yang downright chaotic. She wanted him. She couldn't have him. She'd ruined it. She was too much. She'd made a fool of herself. She couldn't face him. She wouldn't have to *face him* if his face was tucked helpfully between her thighs. On and on it went, and in the days that passed, the voices hadn't settled in the least. She was desperate for a reprieve.

Seeing Junior and Alma together without their spouses, she made a beeline for them to sneak in a quick bit of face time. It wasn't that Claudia didn't like Davis and Eddie; she really did. They were good guys who worshiped her cousins; what wasn't to like? It was more that she felt compelled to keep a version of the mask on for them in a way she didn't have to with her cousins. Though she made a point of not slipping in and out of her persona in public, sometimes it helped to take a breather and be herself.

"You took my advice and let your tetas out, I see." Junior complimented her very on-display cleavage. "Are you using the tape I got you?"

It would be generous to suggest her cousin was a full B-cup. Any tips and tricks that worked for Junior were ill-equipped for Claudia's bountiful bosom. Which she explained. Again.

"Then what sorcery is this?" Alma ran her finger down Claudia's sternum, indicating the open space between her breasts.

Her answer was a dry, sardonic, "The Russian woman on the Danforth and three hundred bucks."

"Holy shit, she's still there? I went to that boutique, I don't know, ages ago and got the best bra ever." Alma said, still marveling at Claudia's breastbone. "I should go back once this is resolved." She thrust her belly out for emphasis.

Junior nodded in agreement. "I've literally never been so thoroughly felt up without the promise of orgasm in my life. But you can't argue with the results."

Claudia stiffened when she felt Ian's eyes on her. She'd started to relax, let her guard down a bit, but she should have known he wouldn't give up. Her back was to the rest of the room and she didn't dare turn to look.

"What?" Junior's demeanor changed from teasing to high alert in an instant. "Dime qué pasó."

"Nothing happened, Hammer."

"Mira. Ahí." Alma elbowed Junior and pointed with her chin. Both women sucked air dramatically through their teeth. "That doesn't look like nothing to me, prima."

"Maybe not nothing, *Alma*," Claudia snapped, "but it's nothing you need to worry about." She immediately regretted it. "I'm sorry. I just... I need a minute to think."

Junior looked over her head and raised her brow, then quirked her head to the right with a small shake. She returned her attention to Claudia and soothed, "Okay. Fletcher is on a course to intercept. What else do you need?"

Her shoulders slumped in resigned defeat. "Do you have a time machine?"

"Long story short, go." Alma prompted.

Claudia took a deep breath and let all the words tumble out of her in a long, rambling stream of consciousness. "The first and only time we had sex, I basically tied him to a chair, stuffed my panties in his mouth, rode him like a bucking bronco, came so hard I passed out, but now I can't look him in the eye, and have been avoiding him ever since."

Both women stared at her, blinking slowly as they processed her words. She didn't blame them. The whole thing sounded outlandish, and she'd been there!

"At some point, in the very near future, I'm going to need every detail of the long story."

"Focus, Junior!" Alma scolded. "That man was looking at Claudia like she was due for a reckoning."

"I'm inclined to let him give it to her! Did you hear what she said, Alma? She came so hard she passed out!"

"Is Davis talking to him yet? I don't want to look."

Alma, who was most organically facing that way, moved her eyes and nodded her confirmation.

Claudia's relieved sigh was loud and full-bodied. "Okay, good. I know you said Davis is a Chatty Cathy, but he may have met his match in Ian."

"Verdad?" Junior shook her head in disbelief. "It's always the sociable ones, eh? Yapping their days away until they get you alone. Then they're railing you over the kitchen sink with a custom replica of their dick while eating your ass." At Alma's scandalized gasp, Junior gave a noncommittal lift of her shoulder, "Just as a for instance."

Alma pressed the heels of her hands into her eye sockets and groaned.

Junior's already legendary eye roll was spectacular. "Oh, and I suppose you got pregnant lying on your back in the dark thinking about how the Canal was built?"

"The fact you don't know is the point!" Alma countered. Junior made a dismissive noise, waving Alma's words away.

Ordinarily, Claudia would have enjoyed watching her cousins devolve into a petty bout of bickering, but she was on borrowed time. Davis was friendly and personable, but he couldn't stop Ian from disengaging, not without making it obvious he was running interference. She had to make her getaway and she had to do it now.

With air kisses and promises to call in the morning, Claudia made her way to the other side of the ballroom. She managed to participate in several conversations, always careful to keep herself hidden behind the larger bodies in the group. Even getting cornered by her parents, aunts, and uncle wasn't the excruciating exercise it normally was because Junior's mom was tall and Alma's mom was chubby, so they provided excellent cover.

When the coast finally seemed clear, Claudia made her way to the bar for some ice water.

"You've been avoiding me."

The sound of his voice, low and close, made her jump, causing a small amount of her drink splashed on her hand. She turned to see Ian grinning down at her. Trying to calm her racing heart, she tilted her face up to his and said with a bravado she didn't fully feel, "Why would I be avoiding you?"

He leaned in and spoke directly in her ear, the puffs of his breath tickling her skin, "Because I know bossing me around got you off so hard, you almost blacked out."

Yes, you do. She thought. *Would you perhaps care to try it again?*

Claudia closed her eyes against the provocative words, trying desperately to shake off the flutter in her belly caused by his nearness. It had been almost two weeks since she rode herself to orgasm on his lap. The memory of it, of the abandon of it, made her face flush.

Before she could come up with a snappy retort, something cool and aloof like 'you're not the only one' or 'join the club', he took her drink and set it on the bar behind her.

"Dance with me."

"What?"

"It's a party, Claudia. Dance with me."

Claudia didn't dance. It wasn't that she couldn't; she knew how. She simply lacked the capacity for letting go required to really dance. Sure, she could fake it for a song or two, throw her hands up, and swivel her hips to the beat. But she didn't think she could manage it with Ian so close, his warm skin and spicy aftershave clouding her senses.

"I should..." She tried to beg off, but he stepped even closer and ran his nose along the skin behind her ear. A searing arousal slithered along her nerve endings.

"Are you willing to make a scene, Gossipika? Because I will happily tell anyone who'll listen about how you fucked me almost unconscious but have been too much of a coward to tell me to my face you don't want it to happen again."

The challenge in his voice, the nearness of him, and his filthy promise gave the Horniness Minister the votes needed to topple Anxiety and Embarrassment and retake control of the House.

Nodding, because that's all she could do when her entire system had been overloaded with lust, Ian took her hand and led her to the dance floor just as the tempo was changing.

It wasn't an all-the-way slow song—the kind of fraught, clothes-rending ballads that obliged you to cling to each other for the duration—but it wasn't something fast enough to shake and shimmy to, either. She had no idea how to dance to something like this, and when Ian pulled her close, wrapping one hand around her waist and the other holding her hand in his, she was a bit overwhelmed.

In her experience, dancing in another's hold was either for slow dancing or Latin dancing. The mid-tempo R&B ballad wasn't familiar to her, but it was smooth and seductive.

Ian started to move—actually move—and she followed along, hoping to figure out the steps as she went. It was a curious mix of waltz and two-step, where they glided around the room while still pressed together. She'd never danced like this before, never been guided so effortlessly to graceful rhythm. It was almost as if a Spanish speaker described the bachata to a non-Spanish speaker. The spirit of it remained even if little bits got lost in translation.

She looked around to see other people dancing. Some in a similar style to her and Ian, others making their own way to the song. She marveled at how much it reminded her of a ballroom of yore.

"Your parents are giving a master class." Claudia said, a hint of wonder in her voice.

Ian hummed his acknowledgment. "It's their wedding song. They always dance to it."

"Really?"

He nodded. "I've been listening to this song since I was in the womb."

And, to prove his point, he started singing along under his breath so only she could hear. He sang about having waited for this moment, the dream come alive, and thanking heaven for sending him an angel of the night. He called her his lady soul, and even though she knew it was a song some forty years old, a small, traitorous part of her wanted to believe the words were for her.

She shouldn't want him because she couldn't have him. The truth of the thought made her stiffen, halting their movement.

When she started to pull away, Ian held her tighter. "Don't."

"Ian, I—" It was too much; she didn't know how to protect herself. She didn't know how to stop wanting what she couldn't have, how to save herself from getting in too deep. Before she could come up with a plausible excuse to flee, he went and said the most devastating thing.

"Stay with me, Claudia. Please. I miss holding you."

If she had any defenses, if she were capable of pulling the ripcord and saving herself, the window had closed and she'd lost the opportunity. All that was left to her was surrender.

Nodding, Claudia fell back into his arms and let him lead her around the dancefloor.

Chapter Twenty-Two

Ian loved to dance. His family teased him about it all the time. He took the taunting merrily because there wasn't anything to dispute.

Claudia in his arms, her body pressed against his as they moved to the music, was settling the part of him that had shaken loose since he'd left her condo all those days ago. He knew what it felt like to have her in his arms, soft and lush, and it had seemed wrong to not be able to relive the perfection of it.

She'd done her best; he'd give her that. She'd ducked and dodged, flitting about the room in constant motion. He thought he had her when she was smiling and laughing with his parents, but when he turned around, she'd disappeared. She'd been in the corner with her cousins, the three of them with their heads together, likely scheming ways to keep her out of his reach.

He'd been headed straight for her until a dark-haired man with an impressive bone structure and a piercing stare stopped to ask him about his grandfather's money clip. Ian wore it on his breast pocket, hanging like a military badge, in lieu of a pocket square. It was an ornate sun in Guyana's orangey yellow gold and one of his most prized possessions. Since he'd worn it specifically for the occasion, it didn't strike Ian as odd for it to be noticed. The man was friendly and asked insightful questions. Ian had genuinely enjoyed talking to him.

He should have known better. Not ten minutes after they'd parted ways did Ian see the man lay a proprietary hand on the small of Junior's back.

But none of it mattered now. He'd found her, caught her, and wasn't going to let her out of his sight until they worked this out. If that was to be their only time together, and he prayed it wasn't, he needed to make it abundantly clear he was a willing participant with nothing but eager anticipation for an opportunity to try it again. The last thing he wanted was for Claudia to keep walking around thinking she'd done something wrong.

She *had* done something wrong, he supposed. Icing him out the way she did was very wrong. But everything that passed between them until he laid her on her couch to rest was so very perfectly right.

Ian pulled a small plate from a passing server, handing it to Claudia.

At her blank look, he explained, "You haven't eaten anything since you got here."

She mulishly raised a challenging eyebrow. She had obviously confused escaping his presence with escaping his notice. Another thing he'd have to school his belligerent pufferfish about.

"You had both the sesame noodles and the tempura shrimp, but you didn't put either in your mouth. Eat, Claudia. Please."

He watched as she took a delicate bite of the brie and fig crostini. Satisfied she was finishing it, he waved over the spring rolls, chicken skewers, and ceviche, setting them on the high-top table in front of her. Slowly, wordlessly, she ate each small serving while he made congenial chit-chat with passersby.

"Thank you," she said primly when they were alone again. "I didn't realize how hungry I was."

A gruff noise in the back of his throat was his only reply.

There was so much he wanted to say to her; the words clogged his throat. He wanted to scold her for not taking better care of herself. He wanted to chide her for running away, for giving up. He wanted to ask her if she still felt him, like a phantom sensation, deep in her core. He wondered if she'd touched herself, hoping to recreate even a fraction of the pleasure they'd found together. But it was neither the time nor the place.

Not yet.

"I'll be right back."

Not this again. Ian looked to the ceiling for patience.

The higher-function part of his brain understood she was free to come and go as she pleased. Despite all of his behavior to the contrary, he wasn't her jailer. But the base, lizard part of his brain sounded the alarm, riding him to keep her from escaping.

Searching for calm, or if not that, then reason, he said, "You don't need my permission. You aren't prey. I'm not going to run you to ground." He gave a small, self-deprecating smile. "Again."

"You wouldn't have had to if I wasn't too embarrassed to face you. I shouldn't have done that. I'm sorry. Truly."

"If you want to go, you can just say that. I won't Hulk out."

She smiled, a real, genuine smile that sent sparks through his bloodstream. "I'll be right back. Promise."

Looking in her eyes felt like falling in your dream, your mind and body out of sync with what was real and what wasn't. There was an Ian who was standing in a ballroom, dressed in his finery, leaning on a table while people danced and milled around. There was also an Ian who was reaching for her, slipping down, down, down, into the freshly turned earth of her dark gaze.

Both of them were real. Neither of them existed.

She placed a light touch on his stomach, slamming the two versions into each other, causing his brain to short out for a moment. "Okay?"

"Okay." He was breathless from the mental collision. "I'll be here when you get back."

He watched her—gold and glittering and gorgeous—walk out of the ballroom. Watched as her cousins diligently followed her, Junior tossing him her now-familiar cheeky wink over her shoulder. Taking a large gulp of his drink, Ian tried to settle his nervous system. He was feeling a bit untethered and hoped his now watery Manhattan would help recenter him a bit.

"She's not who I would have chosen for you, but I can see why you like her."

"Dad!" Ian sputtered into a napkin. "What are you talking about?"

"You really think people are born big, eh?" His father's unmistakable Guyanese accent was the last thing he was ready for.

Howard smiled fondly at his son while he cleaned himself up. Of his four children, Ian was the son most like him in looks and temperament. It was often mistaken for quiet reserve. Howard didn't often socialize without Valerie, so people could be forgiven for not realizing, but Mr. Howard Yang was as social as his wife. The difference was he didn't require the spotlight and happily ceded it to Valerie, who thrived in it. Which he explained to his son.

"You're lucky your mom is too busy being in her element, or this would be a different conversation."

"I'd rather it wasn't a conversation at all." Ian grumbled.

His father laughed, lifting his own drink to his lips. "If that were true, you wouldn't have stalked the girl all night."

"I didn't—" His father's arch look cut him off and he started again. "It's not like that. I had to tell her something." All the things he planned to say to her were not for parental catch-ups, which Howard seemed to intuit by the gleam in his eyes.

"Was that 'talking' you were doing on the dancefloor, mashup so?"

Ian could only groan. There wasn't much he wasn't willing to do to have her lush curves pressed against him in every situationally appropriate manner available to him. A farewell hug after hanging out; her tucked against him on the sidewalk; curled in his lap on the couch while watching TV; an arm around her torso during sleep; her writhing, sweaty flesh beneath him, above him--he was open to it all. Putting up with his father's teasing was a small price to pay to have shared those dances with Claudia.

Didn't mean he had to like it.

"You're smart, always have been, so I'm not going to tell you to be careful."

"Thanks." He let out a relieved breath.

"What I am telling you is to be *careful*. Claudia is different. Special. She is not like those fast girls you're used to. She needs soft hands."

"Dad." Ian dragged the word out, his face hidden behind his hands. Was this really happening to him? Was his dad giving him dating advice in the middle of a work party?

It wasn't necessary. He could explain to his father all the ways in which he understood how much babying Claudia required. That he understood it more clearly than probably even she did. He could try to tell his dad that he'd already devoted himself to the task and all he was waiting for was that stubborn, impossible, glorious flight risk of a woman to get on board. He wanted to make himself understood but couldn't put it all into words, so instead he wrapped his arm around his father's shoulder and vowed, "I know, Dad. I swear."

They shared a moment, father and son, in the midst of the sounds of revelry.

"I can't promise your mother hasn't noticed," Howard drained his glass, "but I'll do my best to keep her distracted."

"Thanks, Dad."

"Thanks, Dad, for what?" Claudia asked, returning to his side like she'd promised.

Howard leaned in and whispered loud enough for Ian to hear, "I'm gonna see if it's not too late to make Ian another sibling."

"Oh my god!" Ian cried, squeezing his eyes shut, immediately clamping his hands on his ears in a futile attempt to block his father's words.

Claudia's playfully scandalized gasp and delighted laugh made it through the barrier. When he opened his eyes, it was just in time to hear her offer, "Are we about to witness a Christmas miracle?"

"It's a miracle I don't require more therapy." Ian grumped at his dad's jovial 'who knows' posture.

"What's so funny over here?" Valerie joined their little group, and Ian hung his head in defeat.

"Nothing's funny, woman. Come dance with me." Howard took his wife's hand and led her to the dance floor, where Ian heard him say, "Our son wants another sibling. I say we should give it our best shot."

"No, I don't!" He hollered after them.

His mother's voice floated back to him, "Through Jesus Christ all things are possible." Then his parents' uproarious laughter faded as they twirled into the party.

Ian pinched the bridge of his nose, waiting for the flush of humiliation to leave his skin.

"They're adorable." Claudia offered, smiling as she followed them with her eyes. She turned back to him. "He looks good, y'know? Clear-eyed and healthy."

Ian softened. Being annoyed by his parents was a blessing and a privilege. One he'd almost lost. "Yeah, he does."

"Wanna hear some gossip?"

"You want to tell me?" He wasn't sure if she was trying to save him from slipping into melancholy or if she truly couldn't wait to share the dirt she'd gathered tonight. Either way, he was ready for the change of topic.

What he didn't expect was a full breakdown of two marriages in trouble, an impending shake-up at one of their client's firms, a long-lost son given up for adoption and thought to have died in his youth showing up via a random social media exchange, and, hilariously, MS&S's championing of a healthy work-life balance inspiring one of their interns to leave finance altogether to become a dog groomer.

"Oh, and I gave my client's husband's ex-wife my card to see if her portfolio is something we can work with." Claudia added, brushing imaginary lint off her shoulder.

Ian's face was scrunched in concentration as he tried to work out the relationship. "Your client's…"

"They're co-parents. It's all very civilized, apparently."

"All that juicy intel and a potential new client? Your weekend's gonna be a non-stop celebration, huh?"

"Maybe." She graced him with a coy smile. "What about yours?"

"I have a suite for the night. Might treat myself to some room service or a spa treatment, who knows?"

"Really? Why bother when the subway is right there?" While she hadn't left his side and didn't seem to be under any explicit duress, she was definitely distracted by the remaining partiers, no doubt taking in any details she deemed relevant, filing them away for future use.

"My cousin hooked me up." A fleeting thought bubbled to the surface as he spoke the words. The MS&S Holiday Gala moved to this hotel shortly after his cousin Domenic's much-lauded promotion to management. Was this more of the Sano 'hand and fist' maneuvering? Had his mother's bragging about her nephew put him on the Sanos' radar? He made a note to ask about it later. "I might need a little pampering if things don't go well."

Right now, he was trying to regain Claudia's distracted attention.

"We have important things to discuss, Gossipika."

"Discuss?" She turned to face him.

"Yeah. But honestly, it's more of a monologue than a dialogue."

"What if I have something to say?"

"You'll have your turn. But if you find yourself unable to hold your tongue, we can stuff your panties in your mouth."

He had her full attention now. Her eyes went molten, and he knew she was remembering their night together as vividly as he was. Though, to be fair, he wasn't really 'remembering'. In fact, he wasn't certain he'd ever stopped thinking about that night. It has simply played on a loop in the background every moment of every day since, a constant source of relief and torment.

"You left me. After everything, you just... cut me loose."

Her face twisted into something between a grimace and an eye roll. "You walked to your car and drove away."

"Don't." His nostrils flared as he tried to keep his cool. He poked her forehead with a little more force than necessary. "In here. You left me."

Boney M's White Christmas probably wasn't the best soundtrack to this conversation, but he didn't suppose the DJ was aware of his emotional upheaval. He watched as a series of emotions played on Claudia's face. She pulled her bottom lip into her teeth, absently gnawing away on the plump flesh. He wanted to rescue it and kiss it better.

"I didn't think we were going to merge our calendars or anything, but I thought I was more than a dirty fuck you could ignore for ten days. Did I read this wrong?"

Her eyes filled with tears. He watched, mesmerized, as she willed them away. God, she was amazing. Stronger and braver than probably even she realized. With her composure intact, she took a deep breath and admitted, "You didn't read it wrong. I freaked out. I'm still freaking out. But I shouldn't have ghosted you. It was shitty, and I'm sorry."

"What happened? Why did you freak out?"

Her eyes went wide with shocked disbelief, as though he'd asked why you shouldn't cuddle a koala. "Ian... the things we did, the things *I* did were—"

"Consensual?" He interrupted. "Mind-blowing? Staggering? So much fucking fun?"

Her mouth hung open slightly, the gloss on her lips reflecting the twinkling fairy lights on the table beside them, as she struggled to come up with an appropriate response.

"Did I somehow give you the impression I wasn't right there with you, every step of the way?"

She shook her head slowly, something lightening in her posture. Her eyes seemed less haunted, less wary, and her shoulders less tense.

"Do you believe for one second I wouldn't do it all again if given half the chance?"

She looked down for a moment. If it was to hide her blush, she'd wasted the effort. She shook her head while still looking at their feet.

"Would you?"

He heard the quick intake of breath right before she met his eyes fully and gave, a slow, single lowering of her head.

"Claudia." He followed the motion of her gently heaving breasts. "Will you come up to my room with me so we can sort this out?"

This was the moment that would decide their future. While she looked off to the side performing whatever calculus she needed, his heart slipped into arrhythmia. She was the bouncer at the velvet rope while he stood in the cold waiting to be let in.

When she returned her attention to him and nodded, he almost fell over from the relief.

"We can leave now. Unless you need to say goodbye to anyone?"

She shook her head.

"Then let's go."

He led her out of the ballroom, grabbing her coat on the way to the bank of elevators, trying to maintain an outward appearance of cool. Inside he was a riot of emotions, and he wasn't entirely sure his brain hadn't conjured this whole thing to protect him.

"My room is on the ninth floor, third door on the left. You have until we get there to decide what happens once I unlock the door." Claudia followed Ian into the elevator. Swiping his card for his floor, they stood facing each other as it climbed higher and higher. When the doors opened at his floor, he gestured for her to go first, and she walked dutifully to his suite.

Ian held the key card out in front of the security pad. "Have you decided?"

She nodded eagerly.

"Why aren't you speaking, Claudia?"

"You said you'd stuff my mouth shut with my panties if I talked out of turn during your monologue, but I'm not wearing any panties, so…" She gave him an impish grin, pulling her bottom lip in between her teeth in that adorable, aggravating way she had.

Ian used his thumb to pull her bottom lip free. It was plump and moist and wicked. "What did I tell you about that?"

"If I didn't stop, you'd give my mouth something to do." Her voice was thick with lust. The sound of her want sent a shiver through him. His own desire dotted his skin like a sheen of mist.

"But since you're not wearing any underwear," he took a sinful inhale of the skin behind her ear and whispered, "we'll have to find something else to use."

"God, I hope so." She breathed, leaning in to him.

Any thoughts of discussion vanished like smoke in the breeze. Ian clasped her wrist, swiped his keycard at the door, and dragged her into his room.

Chapter Twenty-Three

They came together in a fevered rush, pulling and tugging at clothes and kicking off shoes. They were a messy clash of teeth and tongues, and Claudia felt like she was chasing Ian's desire to the finish line. They tumbled to the bed, she in only her slip, he in his underpants, hands roaming wild and unencumbered as they gave in to the need to touch and explore.

Ian kissed her, his whole body invested in the process. His arms caged her head, his hand holding her face, running gentle fingers along the column of her neck. His body pressed against hers, the delicious weight of him, hard and lean, meeting her where she was soft and smooth.

How many times had she lain there, the mask on, while a man stumbled into pleasuring her, accidentally tripping into the act of administering an orgasm? Too many. It wasn't that Claudia was unwilling to tell them what she needed—she was happy to give them step-by-step instructions. And, sure, some men found being told what to do hot; too many others took exception to her guidance, too overconfident in their stroke game to fear failure.

Yet here was Ian, who saw too much to be fooled, who was willing to cede every moment of this encounter to the altar of her control.

"Don't hold back. I want everything we did that night and more."

How could she deal with such a request when her entire body ached for more of his touch, when she thrummed with need? How was she supposed to order herself enough to reconcile such a request?

She couldn't.

She brought him to her mouth, captured his bottom lip between her teeth and tugged. With his lip still caught, Ian licked at her mouth.

"Okay, Sunny." She kissed him, a lewd swipe of her tongue against his. "You wanted me; you got me."

His groan, a deep rumble that sounded like it was mined from his very soul, sent a flutter of anticipation down her spine. She placed her free hand on his shoulder and pushed him down the length of her body until his face was nestled in the cradle of her thighs.

"No hands."

He gave her a look so hot, so filthy, that she moaned in response. As if to assure her of his ability to meet the task, he rolled his tongue into three separate shapes in quick succession, rasping, "bet!" before setting himself to the task.

The first pass of his tongue had her hips lifting off the mattress. Then, when she thought she was fully prepared for what was in store, Ian lunged forward, placing his face firmly at her core, making obscene, greedy noises as he proceeded to eat her out with his hands clasped behind his back.

Claudia was so overwhelmed with feeling, the sharp sizzle of her release barreled down on her, and she couldn't do anything to stop it. Her whole body seized, voice caught in her throat, as she tried to process the rush of sensation. Ian didn't stop, didn't slow down, seemed to be completely unaware of the crisis he'd caused her, licking and sucking away at her as though he was content to remain face first in her crotch for the rest of the night.

When she was able to think clearly, the room was completely dark, except for a sliver of moonlight slicing through the curtain and the small amount of ambient light spilling in from the other room. Ian's pleased noises as he hummed his enjoyment and her heaving breaths were the only points she could focus on in her dazed state.

"Ian... I..." She tried to push herself up on her elbow to see him, but, in an impressive display of core strength, he lifted himself enough to use his head to push her stomach, sending her sprawling, and returned to his private conversation with her clit.

She couldn't concentrate with his mouth on her. Ian was robbing her of her control while doing exactly as she'd asked. Could she let him take it? Should she? He claimed to know her, to fully see her, and she believed him. With her orgasm still fizzing in her veins, she wondered what it would be like to pass the baton of control between them.

"Enough." The word was barely sound, caught on the way out of her mouth on a sob of pleasure, but he heard her. He ran his mouth along her inner thigh, placing wet, open-mouthed kisses on her skin as he rose. The hungry way he looked at her felt like a brand, claiming her and her pleasure for his very own. God, she wanted that. She wanted him to have it and nurture it and tend to it.

"Now only your hands."

He didn't ask any questions, only grabbed her left ankle and raised her heel to his mouth to place a small kiss right on the sole of her foot. He then ran his hand over her calf, down her thigh, his hands warm and questing as he took groping handfuls of her flesh until he was right back at the puddle of desire he'd created. Without taking his eyes off her, his curious fingers trailed all over her skin, tapping on her clit in the exact same rhythm and pressure she'd used with his dick, mapping out the terrain of her sex. Claudia's hips moved, prompting him to go where she most wanted him, but he refused to be hurried. Refused to be led away from his purpose.

Claudia's skin was so sensitive, his touches setting her nerve endings aflame, she couldn't help the desperate sounds he was pulling from her like some type of carnal symphony conductor.

Ian dropped forward, her left knee hooked on his elbow now brought to her shoulder on the mattress while the other hand continued to tease and explore. His low, gravelly voice landed hot against her neck. "Is this another test?"

She shook her head, too lost to speak.

"You think I don't know what you want? What you need?" He didn't give her a chance to respond before spearing her with three of his fingers.

The pleasure of it crossed her eyes. She cried out, "Ian!"

"Because I do. I know exactly what you need."

And, God help her, he did. His fingers were in a constant state of motion while his thumb stroked and toyed with her clit. She couldn't think, couldn't worry, couldn't spiral. Ian made sure all she was able to do was feel the pleasure he delivered with his eager hands and mouth.

She was ready for it to be his eager dick.

"Tell me, Claudia." It was a plea and a demand. "Tell me what happens next."

She collared his throat with her hand, putting enough pressure behind her grip for him to feel her intention. The feel of his Adam's apple bobbing under her palm filled her with such primal satisfaction, she worried she'd combust on the spot. She brought them nose to nose, eye to eye. "You're gonna wrap that monster up and make me come. Right now."

"Say less." Ian caught her chin in his teeth for a playful tug.

She was so blissed out with wanting, she had no idea where the condom came from, only that she heard the crinkle of the package and watched him roll it on. Without preamble, he braced one knee on the mattress for leverage, folded her in half by bringing both of her knees to her ears, and rode her hard and fast. One hand played with her nipple through her slip while he sucked on her pulse; the other hand held her still under the onslaught of his thrusts.

"Ah, Ian, yes!" Claudia babbled, too overwhelmed to do more than grunt her pleasure.

And then he started to talk, punctuating his words with each thrust of his hips.

"Is this what you wanted? I can do it. Trust me." Thrust, thrust, thrust.

She was lost. Lost to the sensation, lost to the words. Ian leaned over and kissed her, stealing her breath with his consuming kiss. When the dam broke, she was flooded with a toe-curling climax that rolled her eyes into the back of her head and left her gasping. It was like deliverance and freedom and she wanted to cry, it felt so good.

"That's it. Let it all go." Ian soothed while riding her through it.

She was barely through the surge of pleasure when he buried himself deep in her body and groaned his own release. "God, fuck!"

The feel of him throbbing hard and thick inside her tripped her into another shallow orgasm, leaving a trail of shivers all over her skin. He peppered her face with kisses, then collapsed on her, their ragged breathing coming in noisy, gulping lungfuls.

Claudia wrapped her legs around him to hold him in place when he made to shift his weight off her and whispered, "Stay."

He held her face, looking at her with such tender affection, Claudia closed her eyes against the crush of emotions tumbling through her. He placed a sweet kiss on her lips and said, "For a little while. Then I have to deal with this." Ian flexed his hips so she could feel his now softening length.

She breathed him in as they lay there, her hands roaming freely. Eventually, he raised himself off her and, with a quick kiss, left for the washroom. He returned and settled himself beside her, his arm across her torso and curled under her shoulder, his leg tossed proprietarily over hers. Claudia allowed herself to enjoy the moment, the simplicity of it. Her default instinct was to figure out how to remove herself from any post-coital episodes. But for the first time in a long time, she didn't want to leave.

She let herself marvel at the quiet of her mind. It wasn't silent—she didn't think it ever could be—but it was a perfectly ignorable bit of white noise that allowed her a moment of calm. Lying in Ian's arms, she contemplated the cause. It wasn't a result of the orgasm. Or not solely. She'd had orgasms before. Lots of them. Good, memorable ones and utterly forgettable ones administered by interesting and unremarkable men alike, and her mind never calmed. She didn't want to consider the possibility this had something to do with Ian specifically. It was too surreal to contemplate. But here she was, languishing in a relative bit of mental silence, and he was the only uncommon denominator.

What was the expression? If you hear hoofbeats, think horses, not zebras. Well, in this case it was: if your normally overactive mind calms after a mind-blowing orgasm, think specific partner, not the general act of sex. She told herself she had five minutes to wonder what it might mean for Ian to have such an effect on her before putting the thought in the impossible bin where it belonged.

She must have fallen asleep at some point because she woke up blinking into the dark room.

She had no idea how much time had passed. Her phone was somewhere by the door and she couldn't move to see if any amount of light was coming from the sliver of space in the curtains since Ian was still curled around her.

Her sleep getting disrupted was a frequent enough occurrence; Claudia usually used the time to practice a bit of mindful meditation. She knew better than most a body was capable of finding a measure of rest even without sleep.

She lay flat on her back, with her arms at her side, her palms facing up—or, as up as the one trapped between Ian's stomach and her hip could be—and started her routine. She was just starting to move her Intention from her abdomen to her back when Ian's large hands twitched, taking a greedy handful of her hip in his sleep.

Even though her rational mind knew it was only a reflex, the Minister of Horniness, House ever in session, imagined he was claiming her even in his dreams. She managed to successfully swallow her moan, but the restless fidget caused by the squeeze of her thighs couldn't be helped.

"Why are you awake, Gossipika?" Ian's sleep roughened voice did nothing to quell her burgeoning arousal.

"I don't sleep well," she whispered into the darkness.

He pulled her closer, his strong body on its side bracketing hers, and she fought herself to keep from curling into the warmth of his embrace. "What's wrong?"

What was wrong? What wasn't wrong? "Everything. Nothing. My anxiety gets the best of me sometimes."

Any other time, with any other man, she would have demurred, citing an unfamiliar bed or being unused to someone sleeping beside her, but Ian already knew about her brain. He'd already seen through her carefully constructed coping mechanism to tell she'd be crying. He knew she wanted to introduce a generation of adolescent girls to the power of their rage. There was simply no point in putting any lipstick on this proverbial pig.

Her curiosity whispered into the darkness, "Do you have any experience with it?"

"Who doesn't fall victim to their intrusive thoughts from time to time." He pressed a kiss to her forehead. "But, no. I don't suffer from anxiety."

"When it's really bad, it feels like I'm stuck in a crowded room where no one can hear me call for help. They can't hear me or see me, and I get carried away with the crowd against my will. I'm paralyzed by the stress of it."

"Fuck. That sounds like a nightmare."

"Ian," she breathed through the hot throb of her clit when his hand roamed up her body to rest on her neck. Her words were thin and breathy. "This can't be what you want to talk about."

"I already told you; I'm willing to talk about literally anything with anybody for any length of time." His thumb drew aimless circles on her jaw. "Since it's you, I'm devoting my considerable attention to the matter."

"Your considerable attention should have a worthier focus."

"You don't have to talk about it if you don't want, Claudia. But I want you to know you can. It's not going to change how I feel about you."

Claudia's gossiping had started as a way to fit in, to deflect attention away from herself and onto anyone else. Then it was her best chance of knowing if people were talking about her, if her attempts at hiding were working. As she got older, it became clear to her that there was power in knowing, a currency to barter with. And in all that time, she'd never met anyone who'd prised her truths open as effortlessly as Ian Yang had.

"How do you feel about me?"

Ian put his arm between her thighs, grabbed her by the hip, and hoisted her body atop his now supine position. She had no idea she'd be so into being manhandled but, she guessed, it was never too late to learn new things about oneself.

"Don't pretend like you don't know."

Don't know? Don't know what? Claudia had lost the conversational thread, so swift and consuming was the desire that swept through her body.

"I'm crazy about you and have been from the very first moment I saw you. You're smart and gorgeous and endlessly fascinating. I knew it was over for me when I watched you manage a room full of people, telling the one blowhard to get fucked, without ever once dropping your smile even though your eyes were *vexed*."

He didn't need to elaborate. She remembered that day perfectly. It stood out as one of the few times she'd almost gone mask off at work. It was her third meeting with a potential client. The first two meetings had gone well, and she'd sent the woman, an author of a mystery series that had been adapted into a popular television show, home with materials to review. At their third meeting her husband showed up to piss all over the boardroom in a show of dominance so transparent, so pathetic, he might as well have had a banner made reading 'I live off of my wife's success and contribute absolutely nothing to our bottom line no matter how many times I claim to be a photographer.'

He was exactly the type of man who waxed poetic about the good old days when only straight, white, cisgendered, Christian men reigned supreme. She had wanted to launch herself over the boardroom table and slam the door on his head. Repeatedly. She'd had no other choice but to shut him down and politely suggest MS&S wasn't the right fit for them.

"Yeah?"

"Yeah."

He pressed his palm in the middle of her shoulder blades to bring her down to his mouth for a kiss and Claudia let herself get lost in the feel of his lips on hers.

"For example," Ian continued, but she interrupted him.

"Example of what?"

He nipped her bottom lip in a playful scold. "An example of how you fascinate me." He ran his hand down her spine, dragging the silk of her slip on her sensitized skin. "How many of these do you own? And why don't you ever take them off? Do you suffer from gymnophobia?"

"Do I... what?" Claudia shook her head, laughing.

"Is one nipple bigger than the other? A different color?"

Her laughter shook her shoulders as she sat up on his lap. "You're being ridiculous."

"I have to admit, I kind of hope it's both." Ian ran his hand up and down her sides. "You don't have to show me if you're not ready. You can just blink once for yes or twice for no."

She didn't have to wonder if he was serious. His growing erection said more than his words ever could. She slid off his lap to return to her spot beside him on the bed. It was easier to think without his hard-on rubbing against her core. It also allowed her a moment to panic. Claudia let herself have the small internal freakout. It was better than trying to stifle them, which only worsened them.

The truth of the matter was inhibitions and reservations had gone out the window four spine-contorting orgasms ago. Whatever happened next was going to be what it was.

"I have a lot of them, actually." She inched the fabric up her thigh until she could gather the hem. Taking a deep breath, she added, "They make sure my clothes hang properly," and pulled her teddy over her head. "And they help keep my under fashions from showing through my clothes. As well as other things."

Chapter Twenty-Four

"Holy shit." He breathed, his eyes roving all over her body, not knowing where to focus first. "Look at you."

In the time since Ian took his leave of absence, he'd often had the itch to pick up his pencil to sketch something. He'd always had his notebook with him, where he'd scribble ideas, shapes, concepts. His general exuberance for life meant he found inspiration in all sorts of places and liked to be able to doodle his notes.

He'd never before been so desperate for a pen and paper as he was in that moment. Claudia was stretched out before him, fully nude, revealing an elaborate sternum tattoo. Finely done, intricate patterns in a red, henna-like color cradled the underside of her breasts and flowed down to her side.

"I get the distinct impression that it isn't my naked breasts that have your attention. Are you disappointed that my nipples are fairly symmetrical and appropriately brown?"

He looked up at her teasing tone but couldn't hold her gaze for very long before her tattoos commandeered his attention once more. "These are magnificent. I want to get a sheet of graph paper and a ruler. I need to make notes."

Claudia's laughter filled the room. "Seriously, Sunny?" She gave her chest a wiggle so her breasts bounced invitingly, "Tetas!"

He lunged up, catching her mouth in a searing kiss. This was what he'd hoped they'd share last time. Her playful, put-upon pout as they laughed and enjoyed each other. He'd take it now, no questions asked, knowing how awful the alternative felt.

"Tits with an intricate design. Christmas came early!"

"It might be the only thing that comes at this rate. This is not the reaction I was expecting." She grumbled. "I feel like I'm being pressed between glass slides to be put under the microscope."

"There is no way you thought I wouldn't be obsessed with this. Look at this line work, the craftsmanship. Was this done freehand? Does this pattern have a deeper meaning?"

Ian placed his hand under the curve of her breast so his thumb was in the middle of her chest and his index finger stretched toward her side. He continued perusing this way, this rudimentary examination, while delighted sounds rumbled in his throat.

At first glance it seemed like lace, but the more he studied it, it became clear it was a complicated series of symbols in a repeating pattern formatted to look like lace. If he didn't know better, he'd have guessed it was some type of stimming-type doodle, but something about the repetitive nature of it snagged in his mind. Could it... Would she...

"What does it say?" He asked, watching her face for her response.

"Say? It's a design, Ian."

Oh, but she was good. It was indeed a design, a design that was very clearly in code. "Fine. Don't tell me." Ian hauled his naked behind out of bed, went to the window, and pulled the curtains wide open to let in the pale light of the early winter morning, ignoring her laughing entreaties to come back. Then he went to the desk where he'd dropped his satchel and pulled out his notebook and pencil. Thinking twice about it, he brought the entire satchel into the bedroom with him, dropped it on the floor by the nightstand, and got back in the bed.

He opened his notebook to a blank page and set it, with the pen in its gutter, beside her naked body on the bed. Every single thing about this tattoo dinged the pleasure center of his brain. The intersection of design and function and hidden meaning was pure dopamine to him.

Ian ran his hands along the edges of the design, then moved back to where he started with just the tip of his finger. The climate control kicked in caused her nipples to harden slightly.

"I know it's cold," he gave one a gentle kiss. He kissed the other. "Be good and I'll give you a surprise when I'm done here."

"What kind of surprise?"

Ian pressed another soft kiss between her breasts and chided, "I wasn't talking to you."

Her outraged gasp devolved into a throaty moan as he sucked the skin of her ribcage into his mouth, worrying it with his tongue in a love bite. When he was done, he freed it with a pop and placed a quick, soothing kiss there.

"Talk to me about this beauty." Ian's hands were back to her tattoo.

"I can't think!" She cried. Her restless fidgeting shook him and the bed as he tried to recreate the pattern in his notebook.

He gave the side of her breast a bite, scolding, "Try again. All you do is think."

"Not when your hands are," she broke off in a tortured moan as Ian ran his hand down her belly, letting his finger play in the curls above her sex. "Not when your hands are toying with me!"

Ian positioned his arm around one of her thighs. He grazed his teeth along her hip and let his finger roam further. "How old were you when you got the first one?"

Claudia panted as she tried to direct his finger where she want-ed it. Realizing he had no intention of offering her the relief she was chasing, she slumped back onto the pillows and huffed, "Uh, um, it was after university. Twenty-two? Twenty-three?"

He rewarded her by slipping a single finger into her soft warmth. It wasn't enough to satisfy her; he knew that much. But it would help keep her ever-whirring mind with him in the moment. He twirled his finger lazily around, enjoying the access and the exploration. When she settled into the sensation, he picked up his pencil with the other hand and started to sketch.

"Do you remember which one was first?"

"No," she shook her head, trying to keep the thread of the conversation with his finger moving aimlessly, inexorably, inside the heat of her body. "Not anymore."

Her reward for that was a swipe of his thumb against her clit.

"Did you already have the design in mind that first time?"

Claudia ran her hands lightly over the top of her breasts while she tried to work herself on his finger. He stilled all movement and let out a disapproving tsk. "So impatient. What do you normally do when this masterful artist works?"

Claudia's palms covered her nipples while holding her breasts high on her chest, out of the way.

"Good. Keep them there until I'm finished." He said sternly, poking her gently with the end of his pencil while trying desper-ately to mask his enjoyment of the entire ordeal. "Now, go on. Did you already have the design?"

He listened as she explained that she had an idea of a concept of a design, but wasn't entirely sure how to bring it to life. When she went in for the consultation, she and the artist collaborated.

"I knew right then it was going to be okay," Claudia said, sighing as Ian slipped two fingers in. "From the very beginning, Missy understood what I needed and was open about how to make it happen. She's done every single line, dot, and squiggle. I don't know what I'll do when she retires."

Still copying the pattern of her tattoo, Ian started to move his fingers almost imperceptibly. She was warm and pliant around his fingers. He was giddy with the freedom to touch and lick and explore she'd allowed him. The feel of her arousal was intoxicating, and he enjoyed merging the two activities this way. Mapping her pleasure, her body, and her tattoo all tweaked the same thing in him. Ian wondered if the wires were now indelibly crossed. The steel rod that was his dick certainly seemed to agree.

"Tell me about Missy," Ian said, dragging his lips along her stomach. The flex of her abs and the tightening around his fingers brought him an unspeakable amount of pleasure.

"Her name," Claudia moaned in response to his fingers finally starting to really move within her, "is Melissa. She's Italian."

It took some time, Claudia's hitched and gasping breaths stalling her train of thought as Ian wound her up, but she finally got the story out. Missy G, originally from Niagara-on-the-Lake, had rosy, freckled cheeks, big, sable curls, whisky-colored eyes, an undercut, and a museum's worth of art inked on her skin. She was quick to laugh and compassionate in a way that made Claudia feel safe.

The woman had a house in Puglia where she and her long-haul trucker girlfriend lived half the year, and Claudia was afraid of the day the move to Italy became permanent.

"Right now, she's gone sporadically—a month here, ten weeks there—but since I don't need her on any kind of foreseeable sched-ule, it works. But if she moves to a straight fifty-fifty split, or leaves altogether," Ian gave a brutal press on her clit and bit into her meaty thigh to bring her back. She'd veered too close to the edge of her worry. Her bucking hips and thrashing head told him it was working, so he stayed on her, continued stimulating her.

"Shh," he soothed. He licked the underside of her breast, catching the knuckle of the bottom finger covering her nipple. "I'm almost done, Gossipika. Hang on, okay?"

Claudia breathed in through her nose and out through her mouth a couple of times before nodding. Her eyes were glassy, and a delicious flush crawled up her chest. It made the rich, warm brown of her skin glow. Ian couldn't help but lean over to taste her there.

"I would wake up like this every morning if I could," he murmured against her throat.

"I could do with," she gasped as he flicked his thumb across her clit, "a little less," he did it again, *flick, flick,* "lingering."

Ian pumped into her, hard and deep. The sound she made in her throat rumbled through him, and he had to concentrate to keep himself from rutting her through the mattress.

"Ian!"

"You're right, you're right," he captured her mouth in a sloppy kiss. "Back to work."

He settled back beside her and retrieved his pencil from where it rolled off his notebook and into the mess of their rumpled sheets, to finish the last row of the lace pattern.

At any other point in his life, if you'd asked him, he would have told you this type of zeal was only triggered by art. By the beauty of creation. He'd always placed the joy and satisfaction of sex in an entirely different category. One of passion and pleasure, yes, but different from the way design consumed him. Little did he know all it would take was to add an intricate pattern in fine-lined artistry to the skin of a woman he was head over heels for to merge those two states of being together.

"Did it hurt?" His left hand had slowed to a gentle exploration, and he nibbled gently on the skin at her flank while he worked.

"Yes? Not really?" He looked up at the reedy sound of her voice to catch her stroking both nipples.

Ian pulled his fingers out of her body to swipe feather-light caresses on her clit until she was writhing under his touch. "Stop cheating and answer the question."

"The pain," she said on a choppy exhale, "is kind of the point. I get the tattoos when I need to be anchored to my body."

He gave her tattoos another once-over, double-checking that the patterns were identical on both sides and that he'd made a faithful, accurate recreation of her right breast and ink; he pushed the notebook away, focusing fully on Claudia's answer. "Pain anchors you to your body?"

"Not the pain specifically. But the buzzing and the itching and the care of the tattoo force me to notice my body when my mind would leave me otherwise untethered."

When her mind would leave her otherwise untethered.

If he hadn't already committed himself to her, if he hadn't already known, deep in his marrow, that she was someone who needed gentle tending, learning she had a secret tattoo that existed solely as a measure of her determination to regulate her anxiety would have tipped him over.

"Do you need to notice your body now?"

Instead of answering, she released her breasts and wrapped her arms around his neck, bringing him to her mouth for a scorching kiss. The feel of their bodies, skin to skin, top to bottom, was heavenly. She was warm and soft and lush and her curves welcomed him eagerly.

"I believe you made promises to my tits." She said between kisses.

"I did."

"They were very, very good."

"They were." He agreed, groaning into the skin of her throat.

"Then I think it's time you kept your word."

So, he did.

He gave her everything her body demanded and a little more besides until they were both limp and breathless. Ian gathered Claudia in his arms, fitting her into the curve of his body, pressing chaste kisses along her hairline, vowing that he'd only rest for a moment before getting up to prepare for check-out. Which is probably why the polite but insistent knocking on the door was so jarring.

But not more upsetting than the knowledge Claudia was gone.

He hadn't fully opened his eyes, but he knew. More than the missing warmth of her tiny, curvy body, more than the barest hint of lavender fading from the pillow, more than the shadows growing on the wall as the sun made its way higher in the sky, he knew.

Opting for the immediate problem, he dragged himself out of bed and pulled the robe on as he made his way to the hotel room door. He had no idea what time it was, but it was probably bad if the hotel sent someone to his door.

"Oh, uh… Mr. Yang?" There was a very flustered, very skittish member of hospitality at his door with a room service trolley. It could be because Ian's naturally forbidding face now telegraphed confused inconvenience. It could also be because, on the surface, Ian wasn't what people expected a Mr. Yang to look like. Either way, the young man regained control of himself. Straightening, he said, "Your order, sir."

Ian was tired and cloudy-headed from being unceremoniously roused from sleep. He was frustrated and disappointed that Claudia had snuck out without so much as a word. He was also a little antsy because he was worried about causing problems for Domenic by missing check-out. With all that swirling in his head, he hoped he would be forgiven for snapping a terse, "I didn't order room service."

The young man looked at the door number, then confirmed it against his notes. Nodding to himself, he pulled the envelope nestled between the two cloches, handing it to Ian. "This is for you."

He felt ridiculous having this conversation, this misunderstanding, in nothing more than a hotel robe, so he opened the note without comment, reading the bold-yet-feminine penmanship:

Sunny,

Thank you for the lecture. It was very informative and highly enjoyable. I will be thinking about it for a long time as I very much look forward to continuing with this subject. Unfortunately, my schedule required me elsewhere, and I couldn't stay. To show my gratitude for your rigorous labors, I have taken the liberty of ordering some light refreshment.

Yours, G

PS: Take your time; the room is paid for until tomorrow.

The smile that bloomed was an expansive, reckless thing that took over the entirety of his face, practically closing his eyes. All the groggy irritation he'd felt moments ago vanished, replaced by a giddiness he hadn't felt in a long time. Yes, she'd had to go, but she didn't *leave*. There was an again; there was more.

A delicate throat clearing brought him back to the moment. "Your order?"

Ian stepped aside to allow the trolley to be wheeled in. Still a couple steps behind, Ian scrambled to find his wallet. What were the odds he had cash? Good apparently, as he pulled a bill out to tip the man for his trouble. "Thank you."

With a slight bow and a bemused grin, he left Ian standing in front of his impromptu breakfast of assorted pastries, finger sandwiches, a fruit plate, and a side of bacon. The carafe of ice water was sweating beside the thermos of boiled water for tea. He popped a grape in his mouth and went to find his phone. He had a call to make.

Just as he'd unlocked his screen, a text came in from Domenic. **'If you needed a later checkout, all you had to do was ask, you name dropping bitch.'**

Ian doubled over laughing.

Looked like he had two calls to make.

***

Claudia stepped out of her shower, secured her linen towel under her armpits, and started applying the many serums and tinctures she believed helped keep her face looking supple and healthy. She'd had a surprisingly good sleep the night before. The orgasms and the vigorous way in which they were achieved were definitely a factor.

She was the first to admit she didn't have a lot of experience sleeping with men. Yes, she'd had her fair share of sex, but she generally got up and left when it was over. It was always understood that Claudia was for the proverbial streets, not their sheets. Yet she'd slept with Ian, actually slept, his body in constant contact with hers, and it wasn't awful.

Her aunt's words came back to her.

'*Men* want *to have sex with you. They will say anything to make it happen*', her tía Yesenia repeated numerous times until she was sure the message stuck. *'It doesn't mean you're special; it means you're available. Make sure you're prepared for the consequences of that availability'.*

She remembered all the times her aunt cautioned them, her daughter and her niece, two girls on the brink of puberty, about the changes their bodies were going through. It was a frank, stark conversation she'd never had anywhere else. Her beautiful, accomplished, Toronto-born aunt—also a surgeon, an heiress, and daughter to a beauty queen-turned-actress who knew every way a woman's body could be commodified—gave them this knowledge openly, without hesitation.

Now, all these years later, Claudia had made the choice to make herself available to Ian, little by little. And at every turn he'd rolled with her punches, moved within her limitations.

Her face moisturized, she opened the jar of her favorite body butter from Cocoa Butter Kisses, a local husband-and-wife small-batch creator from Ajax she'd stumbled upon at a craft fair. Claudia inhaled the cloud of shea and lavender, scents she wasn't sure would work together before, permeating the still warm bathroom.

Looking at her body in the full-length mirror, taking in all of her dips and curves and contours, remembering how it felt to have Ian trace every line of her with reverence and awe, Claudia smoothed the butter into her skin. The single-mindedness with which he examined her tattoos, making notes and sketching recreations in his notebook while idly nipping and kissing and suckling at her wherever his mouth happened to land, whenever the mood had taken him, humbled her. His absentminded compulsion to have her skin in his teeth while he worked brought a shiver to her spine all these hours later.

Ian Yang had proven himself to be the exception to every rule. He was devilishly handsome and very aware of it, but didn't think it was a carte blanche invitation to selfishness in any aspect. He was accomplished and successful, yet moved through the world with humility. He was a silly chatterbox with a keen sense of empathy but didn't hesitate to stare down an adversary with his forbidding Doberman glare.

He was going to upend her world into chaos and disorder, and she wasn't sure she would do anything to stop it.

It made her feel reckless. It made her feel uninhibited.

It made her feel free.

At this point of her routine, Claudia would be beginning the process of getting 'camera ready'. It was an expression she'd learned from Junior, who worked in film and television production in the city, filling her lexicon with such industry terms.

As with most things she did, Claudia got dressed with intention. Every piece, every step of the ritual, prepared her mentally to face the outside. The many layers felt like armor protecting her, holding her together, while she battled both her demons and society's. Claudia would be the first to admit modern-day garters and corsets had basically become fetish wear, but thighs like hers needed more than a bit of elastic to keep her stockings up. Her outside clothes—soft and feminine in the finest materials, delicate cuts, and colors—were a crucial part of the facade.

Her sleeping clothes were entirely different. There was no slimming, shaping, or smoothing required. Her nightshirts were chosen for comfort and durability. She needed the fabric to be soft, yes, but she also needed to stay cool and dry during the few hours of sleep she managed each night.

Pulling the slip-like garment over her head, Claudia relished the feel of the thick, smooth fabric draping her body as it covered her various marks from view. She was usually hiding them from the world, but today she felt like she was saving them, keeping them as souvenirs of this milestone. The thought made her flush with emotion.

Looking at herself in the mirror, clean and moisturized and ready for a little downtime before attempting sleep, Claudia repeated the words that helped her out the door, "Every breath is worth it. Every step is a victory. Every day is a celebration."

Satisfied with her efforts, she grabbed her phone off the charger to deal with the flashing notifications. It was probably missed calls or texts from Junior and Alma being nosy, or Fernanda complaining about... knowing Nanda, it could be any host of things. Picking it up, she scrolled through to see she'd missed a call from Ian, but there was also a text from him waiting.

'Sorry I missed you. The refreshments were greatly appreciated. Though had I known vacating the premises was optional, I would have much preferred continuing our discussion. We can add it to the docket for our next meeting. Give me a call at your convenience to discuss scheduling.'

Checking the time, she wondered if he was still in the room. Had he opted for a spa treatment in the end? Tapping the phone icon, she sat on the edge of her bed and held her breath while it rang.

"Gossipika." Ian's raspy voice was low and sinful in her ear.

Claudia let the sound settle over her like a blanket, smiling to herself in the fading evening light. She tucked herself into bed, making herself comfortable while answering, "Hey, Sunny."

As they filled each other in on their happenings since they'd parted three hours ago, Claudia caught herself thinking, *Christmas was still two weeks away, but this is the best present of all.*

Chapter Twenty-Five

Ian loved when his family gathered.

Being half Black and half Chinese of Guyanese descent meant his family ran the gamut of human phenotypes. People liked to call Toronto a melting pot, and it was. But it had nothing on the composition of Guyana. A British colony until the late sixties, the country's population was a reflection of the empire's reach. It showed in the food, the language, and the people.

Especially the people.

The third largest ethnic group was "mixed", after East Indian and Black. If that wasn't a mosaic, he didn't know what was.

The simple act of hanging around with his family, his actual genetic one and not the found family of most Caribbean households, was a trippy experience. His cousins, William and Domenic, fifteen and twenty months older than him respectively, were like a Rorschach test. When he stood with William, who had a Chinese Guyanese dad and a Chinese Chinese mom, most people recognized Ian's own Chinese heritage. When he stood with Domenic, who had two Black Guyanese parents, his Chinese heritage vanished without a trace. Which was weird since he had his father's monolid eyes and could sink into the Asian squat unprompted.

"What up, player? Uncle Howard's looking good!" Domenic raised his fist for Ian to bump.

"The doctors gave him a clean bill of health. It'll be a bit more physical therapy, but the worst is over."

"My mom's been leaving offerings at the temple since it happened." William clinked his beer bottle against Ian's.

"All prayers are welcome, man."

They were leaning on the banister overlooking the living room of his parents' Scarborough backsplit. The house was full of people celebrating both Christmas and the good news about his father's health. The music was blaring, the people were mingling, the dominoes were out, and the food and drink were in almost endless supply.

"How was your trip?"

William was a commercial pilot for the country's national airline. Though the company itself had a bad reputation, William was thriving.

"Good. I got Q and Dom to roll with me for a long layover."

Domenic chuckled. "I love seeing how they change their tune once Big Willy over here hits them with the flawless Mandarin. I can't get enough of it."

William groaned his frustration. His mother, Ian's Auntie Eileen, raised her two sons with the food, language, and customs of her small village in China, yet he always got written off as a lao wai when he visited the country. To this day William couldn't figure out what it was about him that signaled *foreigner*.

"It's not enough that I spent literally every summer of my youth in China and can close down a mahjong den? It's wild, man."

"Tell me you didn't fly fourteen hours just to play mahjong."

"He might as well have; he's been banned from most tables from here to Mississauga." Domenic laughed.

"Haters." William grumbled. "And it's closer to sixteen flight hours, thank you."

Ian kissed his teeth at the needless correction. "No, but for real, what did you guys get up to on a weekend in Hong Kong?"

He listened as his cousins regaled him with the details of their whirlwind trip. He could picture it now: William flew them there, Domenic got them a luxury suite from one of his hotel's branches, and Quincy made a call to comp them some sort of exclusive experience from one of his many contacts in premium sales. The three men—each conspicuous in their attractiveness—would have been a sight. William, tall and lean, carried himself with the cool arrogance befitting a pilot. Quincy, plus-sized, impeccably dressed, and adorned in expensive watches and assorted jewelry, was never more than a smile away from garnering a woman's attention. And Domenic, who was built like a wide receiver, always turned heads in his custom flashy suits.

"Here. We got you this." Domenic pressed a small tissue wrapped package in his hand

Ian loved getting presents and souvenirs. He especially loved getting postcards. He'd demanded they be mailed from their point of origin until his friends staged an intervention. They claimed finding post offices wasn't on their list of things to do when traveling, so he would have to be satisfied with getting them handed to him when they returned from their trips. It wasn't the same as having the postmark on them, but he accepted the demotion.

Tearing into the wrapping, Ian let the small stone block fall into his palm. He looked, recognizing the character for yang on the rubber stamp, and smiled. "Dope! Thanks."

His Auntie Eileen had tried, and failed, to get his brain to absorb Mandarin but she did teach him to write his surname. But while he was willing to use a sun in his company name and logo, he was hesitant to make any moves with the written character lest he come across like all the hapless tourists before him insisting their tattoo meant courage or strength when it really read as barbecue or sofa.

"This is great."

"Yeah, we thought you could use it as your, like, signature on your designs and whatnot. Like in the corner of the blueprints." William explained.

It was such a thoughtful gift; he didn't have the heart to tell William that he hadn't used paper in his work since university.

"Fool. They do all that shit on computers now. The fuck are you talking about?" Domenic, it seemed, had no problem disavowing William of his romantic notions.

"I definitely plan to incorporate it as a calling card of sorts somehow." Ian quickly added, hoping to soothe any wounded pride.

"We were at the chop stall for so long; it was the least we could do to buy something else from that poor man." Domenic explained, looking over Ian's shoulder at the small hand-carved stamp.

"What do you mean?"

"What I mean," Domenic sighed heavily, "is Q was obsessed with getting the perfect souvenir for the woman who'd curved him."

"Like, spectacularly curved him," William added for emphasis.

"It took forever."

"Yeah, those stalls are already crammed full, so the lengthy process took even longer while he debated between the material and whatnot. He was torn between getting táo for peach or something that translated well for li. Do you know how many words use the sound li? He was finally happy when I found the character for pear, which was somehow a substitute for peaches, but I have no idea how. That man has got it *bad*."

Ian laughed, trying to picture handsome, immaculately groomed Quincy poring over hundreds of samples until he found exactly what he was looking for, while two of his best friends suffered in unlikely silence at his side.

He and Claudia had never talked about the dirt she'd gathered on Quincy, but it was clear it was for someone she and Junior knew. Did that mean Claudia had given her seal of approval? His phone buzzed in his hands.

Speak of the devil.

Merry Christmas, Sunny

You too, Gossipika

Ian smiled to himself. He wasn't entirely sure if they were dating or not, but he'd spent the last few weeks wrapped in her arms, feeling the way she came apart again and again as he learned all the variables of her pleasure. Yes, he wanted more, but if that's all she'd ever give him, he knew he'd remember the feeling of her soft curves filling his hands for the rest of his life.

Was Santa good to you?

He refrained from answering anything too lewd in case she was, like him, surrounded by family. **Yeah. I was a very good boy this year. Santa had no choice but to show out**

She sent an eye roll and a crying laugh emoji in response. He could picture her making those faces so clearly, his own smile bloomed unbidden.

I know I don't have to ask about you. He sent it with a wink emoji.

It's better you don't ask. But maybe if you're really good, I'll show you instead.

God, he couldn't wait. **You're a menace**

Yes, I am. Feliz Navidad, Ian

Merry Christmas, Claudia

He put his phone in his pocket and tried to relish the warm feeling that was settling on him. His cousins, however, were in no mood for his fuzzy feelings.

"You dirty little bitch." William accused him with a playful shove.

"What?" Ian pushed him back while also dodging a punch from Domenic.

"It be ya own people." Domenic lamented, shaking his head in what Ian supposed was penitent sadness.

"What are you assholes talking about?"

"You, Gabby O'Talksalot! We're talking about you!" William emptied his beer in a noisy swallow, putting the bottle down on the table beside him. He pulled up his Day Ones group chat and scrolled until he found what he was looking for. He turned it to Ian, who read aloud, "Anyone know a 'Claudia from work'? She seems to have a lot of information about me and the mandem."

Ian grimaced. His chickens, it seemed, had come home to roost.

"That was almost a month ago."

"He also brought it up when we were away." Domenic added.

"There I was, swearing up and down that I had no idea who would give up all those details." William made a big show of his disappointment. "Meanwhile, my cousin—my father's brother's son—sold us out!"

"Easy there, Mona Lisa Vito."

"Doesn't family mean anything to you? Is nothing sacred?" Domenic was being equally dramatic, which was saying something because William was unquestioningly channeling Marisa Tomei. It would surprise most people to know that the man who looked like a high-ranking member of the Triad claimed *My Cousin Vinny* as his favorite movie.

Ian's sigh was deep and weary, knowing he both had no interest in their scolding and had every minute of it coming to him. How could he explain to them that he had been so desperate for Claudia's attention, for any excuse to get close to her, spilling whatever he knew about Quincy Temple seemed a small price to pay? Would they understand the compulsion he had to make that woman happy, to be the cause of her smile? They couldn't possibly understand how easy it was to just spill his guts to her, her keen gaze sharp and eager to be the repository of any and all details.

Could he tell them that for this woman he'd do it again with no hesitation?

"You're being ridiculous. How do you even know that I'm the one who knows the person you're talking about? Claudia isn't an uncommon name."

"Don't make your eyes pass me," Domenic said in a perfect Guyanese accent. Ian had always found the expression equal parts nonsensical and amusing.

"I'm not! I'm simply wondering how you can be so sure it's me." He really had no idea why he was pressing the matter. It wasn't like he was innocent of the charges and, in fact, had given up their details for a song. Still... "What about innocent until proven guilty?"

William leveled him with a look that dried all subsequent protests in his throat.

"Okay, okay but you don't understand—"

"Oh, I understand alright." Domenic's grin was smug and knowing. "You thought you could impress a woman by airing all of Quincy's business."

"First of all, they aren't secrets if you dummies keep putting every single thing on social media. Second, I wasn't spilling his secrets necessarily. I was letting Claudia know he was a good guy.

So, in a way, you should be thanking me for his current happiness." Ian gave them a winning smile to drive his point home.

His cousins stared at him, stone-faced and disbelieving, until William broke the standoff. "I'm telling your mom."

Ian looked at him as though he'd announced he planned to carve a pentagram on his forehead before dinner. William raised his chin in defiant challenge, knowing Valerie Yang would lecture him about putting people's business in the streets.

Ian decided to meet him on the battlefield. "I'll tell your mom you wore a green hat at your week-late thirty-first birthday party."

His aunt was supremely superstitious and believed in the absolute power of feng shui, a practice that went far beyond where your furniture was placed. She took the practice so seriously, she checked birth charts, applied color theory, and even christened each of her husband's sibling's kids with auspicious names in Mandarin. His name, Yang Guang, meant sunshine.

Hearing her son had taunted Luck would be cause for a full week at temple to cleanse his qi.

William reared back as though he'd been slapped. "You wouldn't dare."

"I have date-stamped pictures. You were blowing out candles." Ian threatened his cousin with his locked phone.

"Alright, alright. Everyone calm down." Domenic got in between them with his own phone held aloft. "No one is going to tell anyone's mom anything. Snitching is what got you into this mess."

"I'm not in a mess," Ian sniffed.

"Fine," Domenic allowed with an impressive eye roll. "But you did snitch. We're just asking why."

"What are we, twelve? It's not snitching to answer the question, 'Tell me about Quincy'."

"Yo, are you dumb?" William asked, then repeated it in Mandarin for good measure. "That's the literal definition of snitching."

"And all for a woman Q said was," Domenic looked at his phone and read, "a 'beautiful misanthrope'?"

Ian couldn't help but smile, a broad, goofy thing that took over his entire face. "That she is."

"Oh, for fuck," William shook his head in dismay. "It's too late. He's already cooked."

"It's something in the water. Has to be." Domenic took a large step back from Ian as though Ian's state of infatuation was contagious.

"I keep forgetting you're a softboi." William accused. "You look like a stone-faced assassin and sound like you gargle with shards of glass, but in reality you're just," he moved his hands in a talking motion in Ian's face, "yap, yap, yap. Nonstop."

"Let's see a pic."

"What? No!" Why Domenic thought he'd entertain the request was beyond him.

"Don't we at least get to see the woman who's got you so down bad?" William argued.

"I'm not down bad." Was he? Didn't being down bad imply one-sidedness? Or was it about the all-encompassing way in which he wanted her?

Both cousins leveled him with scathing gazes.

"I'm not!"

"Pics or I tell Quincy I found the narc."

"You're gonna tell him anyway!" Ian huffed, unmoved.

William's entire posture confirmed Ian's assertion. It was a small miracle he wasn't texting Quincy right then.

Domenic chose to come at him from the other side of Persuasion Street. "Throw up her IG or something. What's the big secret? What are you worried about?

Ian considered it. What was he worried about? Nothing that these two chuckleheads had to say, certainly. He shook his head. "No. You'll see her once I'm ready and all this is settled."

"All what?" Domenic demanded.

"All this," Ian gestured to the chaos of his family gathering for Christmas. "Who wants to take all this on?"

"Are you on crack? She'd be lucky to have you, to even have a taste of this."

"Word." William eagerly agreed with Domenic. "This entire clan is made up of top-tier specimens. You're already a catch, but then she'd get access to all this? Ole girl is sitting on a winning lottery ticket and has no idea."

The speed with which his cousins pivoted gave him whiplash. They were clowning him for being a chatty softboi, but now he was suggesting a woman wouldn't want to take on the responsibility he shouldered—that he didn't want to ask her to—he was a fool for not seeing himself as a catch? They were impossible.

Ian straightened his clothes from their roughhousing and said, "I am a catch. Or I could be. What I want with her, the vibe I'm tryin' to be on? That requires more than I have to give right now." He looked between his cousins to see if they were following. Domenic nodded along while William's face was twisted with skepticism. "But if she gives me the slightest hint she wants it too? I need to have everything locked down and in place. I need to make sure she has nothing to second guess when it comes to me."

William's pessimism seeped out in a noisy exhale. But Domenic squeezed his shoulder. "I hear what you're saying, I do. Just... sometimes life doesn't work out that way, you feel me? You can plan and strategize but you can't control when shit happens."

Ian took in Domenic's words. He was all too aware of life not working the way you planned. His whole axis had been tipped off orbit by happenstance. He knew things 'just happened' all the time. Hell, Claudia was a force that had slammed into him when he wasn't expecting it. He was still reeling from the collision.

His cousins didn't understand all the weight Ian carried. Not fully. Supporting his family and having Claudia existed on two separate sides of this new temporary reality. His former life was still waving at him in the wings, and he wasn't entirely sure it was compatible anymore. Further to that, he wasn't sure he would go back to that life—his life the way it had been—if it meant he couldn't keep her. And wasn't that a huge, inconvenient, throat-clogging something to chew on?

For all Claudia's discomfort with new people, he knew the right combination of factors existed to make it manageable for her to show up and charm her way into their hearts. No, his large, chaotic family wasn't the problem. He was. Until things with his family were settled, he couldn't make any tangible plans.

He wanted to create a life with her, to give her everything he had. But how could he when his life wasn't his own? How could he start something with her by asking her to both accept this responsibility while also having only parts of him?

He clasped Domenic's forearm and put his other hand on William's shoulder. "That's why I'm taking each day as it comes. I just need a bit more time."

As soon as he figured out what his future would look like without the looming threat of weighing her down with his familial obligations, he'd be able to make a move.

Chapter Twenty-Six

"Are you ready for your day of personal inventory?" Claudia asked Ian as he settled himself on the floor between her legs.

It was Claudia's monthly self-care day. She'd been noticing the term 'Everything Shower' bandied about lately and rejected it wholeheartedly. Her ritual didn't begin and end with the shower. It was a full day of routine maintenance and a full accounting of her internal baseline systems. If something was off with her—changes in her sleep or digestion, for example— it could require an alteration to meds or worse. She'd worked too hard finding the balance; she *had* to pay attention to her care for her own good.

A thing she'd ranted about to Ian, which is how he ended up participating in the ritual now.

"I am. Still surprised you subscribe to such individualism, though." Ian teased.

She laughed as she settled the towel over her lap and his shoulders and started to unbraid his hair. Her rant about "self-care" and "everything showers" may have veered slightly into white women's habitual co-opting of the language of resistance, the way they congratulated themselves for taking time to recover from the work they'd yet to do. Or maybe it was something else he was teasing her about. The possibilities were truly endless.

"Admit it, you missed me."

"You know I did. Why else would I subject myself to this painstaking process?" He said, critiquing her speed in unbraiding his hair.

Claudia rapped his scalp with the comb, threatening, "It's not too late for you to go to your spot."

"It is, actually. Besides, I can't do this at the salon." He turned his head and placed an open-mouthed kiss on her inner thigh.

She gave the braid she was working on a playful tug. "Stay still or we'll be here all night."

His only response was to recline more fully in her lap, forcing her to spread her legs wider as he used her knees as armrests. This position was arguably worse for trying to detangle his hair, but she loved the feel of him leaning against her, the full weight and heat of him, the softness of his curls between her fingers as she freed each lock one by one, the way he idly ran his fingertips on her calves. She happily sacrificed speed for the pleasure.

When she finished, she gave him a gentle shove. "Up."

He leaned forward, sending his curls forward like a curtain hiding his face. Claudia freed the scrunchie from her wrist and gathered Ian's hair in a loose knot atop his head. To the uninitiated, it looked like their hair was the same length, but because his curls were tighter, more defined, his hair was actually much longer than hers.

Claudia wrapped the comb in the towel and headed to the kitchen with the bundle tucked under her arm. Standing at the sink to wash her hands, she called out, "We need music. Care to do the honors?"

"You're trusting me with such power?" His voice was comically breathy, like an old-timey Southern Belle.

"Great power, great responsibility, and all that."

Over the running water, she heard the groan he made as he stood from his cross-legged position on the floor. Moments later, the familiar strings of the Ninth Symphony filled her home, and she gasped when she turned to find Ian right behind her.

"Beethoven," she said on a surprised exhale as warm affection flooded her.

"I've had a bit of an education on classical music recently." Ian leaned forward to place a soft kiss on her lips. Without fully retreating, he said, "Turns out, he's the coolest."

She nodded, her movements big and uncoordinated like a Dollar Store bobblehead figurine. He added, as though just one performance of her favorite composer wasn't enough, "It's a couple hours of your boy, Joseph Bologne, Florence Price, and George Walker. Is that long enough?"

Her two favorite composers, Beethoven and Chevalier, and two iconic Black composers of the 20th century that she'd mentioned in passing. Too overwhelmed by the implication of his playlist, her eyes searched his for any explanation other than the obvious. Realizing she hadn't answered, she gave a small, breathless, "It's perfect" hoping it conveyed everything her overloaded mind could not.

Ian placed a chaste kiss on her forehead. She closed her eyes and leaned into his touch in an attempt at gathering her slowly fracturing wits. Taking a deep breath, she straightened.

"Okay," her voice was shockingly steady, "now that we have the playlist sorted, let's get to it."

She led him the short distance to the downstairs bathroom, where she'd laid out all their supplies. On balance, this bathroom was slightly smaller than her upstairs ensuite, but it had more counter space and a walk-in shower, which worked better for their current needs.

Starting from the bottom, she pointed to each piece in the folded stack of fabric she passed him. "Bathrobe, bath towel, hand towel, hair wrap, face cloth."

Ian inspected the items, feeling their texture by rubbing them randomly on his cheek, ooh-ing and ahh-ing about their softness. "What next?"

"Next is hair treatment."

Following her lead, Ian removed his scrunchie and held out his palm so Claudia could add a vitamin treatment to his palm. When they both finished massaging the oil into their scalps and running whatever remained through to their ends, Claudia secured her twisted hair with a clip. "You, too." She said, handing him a tortoiseshell clip.

It was only because she knew better, had seen the truth of his personality over these many months, that his reflection—stern-faced and severe with his hair twisted in such a haphazard way—made her laugh.

"What?" Ian's affront screwed up his face.

"For someone with as much hair as you have, you're not very good at putting it up." She gestured to the lopsided clip barely hanging on to its quarry.

He huffed his indignance. "It's either loose, braided, or tied in an elastic. What else do I need to do with it?"

"Come here," she gestured, not even bothering to disguise her laughter. Twisting and clipping his hair, she nodded. "While the hair mask is working, we use the dry brush."

She pointed to the two brushes on the counter. "This one," she gestured to the one with the long-handled brush, "is boar's bristle. And this one," she showed him the one with a strap to secure it to your hand, "is sisal. I like them both, but the boar's bristle takes a bit more getting used to."

Ian took them both, again the texture of the brushes dominating most of his attention. He rubbed each of them on the back of his hand, then on the tender skin of his inner bicep. She was fascinated by how seriously he was taking this. Instead of just grabbing a brush and going to town, he was actually intending to make an informed decision.

"It's to exfoliate?" He was running the sisal brush on his collar.

"Yeah," she answered, transfixed by the path of the brush on his skin, "it's also a mini massage that's supposed to help stimulate circulation and help reduce cellulite, but," she gestured to her thigh and shrugged a nonplussed 'results may vary'. "You start at your feet and work your way up in a wide, clockwise motion. Some people like to incorporate positive affirmations, but I prefer to do those later."

Nodding his understanding, he gave her the sisal brush and began undressing.

Claudia had seen Ian naked many times in many situations. She'd been over him, under him, and tangled between his limbs. They'd been naked vertically, horizontally, seated, kneeling, in a squat, and one time, by accident, diagonally. She'd had the pleasure of seeing his body in the moonlight, daylight, candlelight, and in the soft glow of her bedside lamp.

What she hadn't experienced was Ian removing his clothing in a clinically efficient manner, pulling his sleeveless t-shirt over his head with one hand before stripping out of his shorts. Ian folded his clothes in a tidy pile as though he were at a doctor's appointment.

Picking up the brush from the counter, he hiked the legs of his boxer briefs up, winked at her reflection, and got to work.

He was so good-looking, it always derailed her concentration. He was all smooth, brown skin over taut muscle, with no real discernable marks or scars on his body. Before she could get too distracted, she got busy with her own body brushing.

"Time for the shower," she said when she was done. The Minister of Horniness hovered at the sidelines, conferring with Embarrassment, as neither seemed sure who should have the reins with Ian standing stark naked, completely unaffected in the bright lighting of her downstairs bathroom, with the thick length of him hanging unbothered between his legs. It was her anxiety propelling her forward for once.

Her need for routine and familiarity overrode all else. Anxiety seemed to say, 'Today is self-care day, so that's what was going to happen whether this penis haver is here or not'. "We're going to wash and condition our hair, then shower, then apply a leave-in."

Ian pulled his hair free of the clip. The oil treatment gave it a sheen that reminded Claudia of the way it looked when he was sweaty on the cricket pitch.

Swallowing the surge of lust that threatened, Claudia gave him a fair warning. "Just an FYI, the water temperature will start at lukewarm and work its way to cool."

"Like at those Nordic spas? I went to the Scandinave in Tremblant a couple years ago. Have you been? I highly recommend it."

Claudia tried to stifle her laughter. Ian just loved things. His joie de vivre was staggering. "No, Sunny. Not hot, then cold. Tepid, then cold."

"It's the beginning of January!" His eyebrows rose with the register of his voice. "We're not having a steam first? Just straight into cold showers?"

"Lukewarm," Claudia corrected. The thread of sympathy in her tone changed nothing.

"Okay." Ian nodded. He rolled his neck on his shoulders, then bounced on his toes, shaking his arms loose at his sides. "Okay, let's do it."

All through the process, Ian gamely followed along. At no point did he make a face or mock or scoff at any of the steps. He didn't provide any suggestions, much to her Horniness Minister's disappointment. He didn't rush through the process. What he did do, to Claudia's endless delight, was sniff and touch and ask the most random questions about matters big and small. When was water-based better than silicone-based? Was all-natural to be taken literally? Was there a fundamental difference between cocoa and shea? Would a curl cream that worked for him be too heavy for looser curls like hers? Did the conflicting smells of the assorted products help or hurt?

Claudia wasn't sure what she thought sharing this experience with Ian would be like. When she'd invited him over, it was more abstract in her mind. But once he started stripping, once the practicalities were in her face literally and figuratively, she'd had a brief moment of doubt. What if this was awkward or too personal? How many people were involved in the minutiae of their intimate partner's grooming? Would this look behind the curtain ruin the magic?

It hadn't. Instead, as she led him through her routine, they'd simply taken care of each other. She listened to his stories about being stuck in the tub with his brother because it made sense for them age-wise, despite what their physical bodies had to say on the matter. She laughed until her stomach hurt when he tried to wrap his hair in the towel unaided. They painted face masks on each other and made silly faces in the mirror to see how much they could move their features while the masks dried.

Claudia wasn't sure if she'd ever shared such non-sexual intimacies with a sexual partner before, and she didn't know what to make of it. Didn't know if it was a commonplace occurrence or if it was something unique.

Sitting on her couch, cleaned and moisturized in their robes in front of the fire, Ian pulled Claudia's foot into his lap and started to massage her instep. His firm kneading felt so good, she couldn't help the groan that rumbled through her.

Ian chuckled and brought her foot to his mouth for a quick kiss.

Claudia wriggled her toes in his grasp. "Less kissing, more massaging."

"You have a ten-step process to bathe and wash your hair, but you don't have foot massages built in when you stomp around in those ridiculous shoes all day?"

"Shh," Claudia closed her eyes, sinking deeper into the couch. "Don't bring your logic over here. It doesn't fit the vibe."

"Apologies," he intoned gravely, pulling on her pinky toe as he teased her. "If I weren't here, illogically massaging your feet, what would you be doing?"

Claudia wiggled her toes again, urging him to continue his ministrations. Ian's hands on her body was always a cause for celebration. But this easy intimacy wasn't something she was used to. She'd never shared this with anyone before, and she was finding the companionship pleasant. Soothing.

"Honestly, you're the biggest difference." She poked his side with her other foot. "You and the music."

"Really?"

Ian resumed the massage, and Claudia sank further into the couch on a pleased sigh. "Yeah. Sometimes I listen to my abuela's folk music or salsa, but mostly it's a white noise playlist like in a yoga class or at an actual spa."

"Makes sense," he agreed, then added with a wry note to his voice, "I noticed your boy likes to go hard every now and again. Might not be great for relaxation".

Beethoven's excess was legendary but she was still too moved by the gesture, too overwhelmed by the implication, to discuss it. All she could manage was a small, "This is nice," as she tilted her head to indicate the classic music playing in the background.

She thought about all the things she'd shared with him up to this point, all the little things she'd allowed him to access. Despite Anxiety's tutted disapproval, she decided to grant him this one additional tidbit.

"At this point, I usually do a detailed review of the month. My sleeping patterns, how many days I exercised and for how long, my hydration goals. Things like that."

"Do you have a habit tracker?" Ian sat up, his grip on her foot tightening with his excitement. "Better yet, a bullet journal? I've successfully trained my algorithm. I can show you some if you want."

Claudia laughed at his exuberance. Of course his social media feed was filled with journals and stationery and fancy writing implements. "Thanks, Sunny, but I have an app on my phone."

The way he deflated almost made her regret not having a bullet journal.

"And?" He continued, "How are your numbers?"

She hadn't really looked yet, but there wasn't much change. If there was a positive to the way Anxiety plagued her, it was that she lived a fairly routine life that didn't fluctuate much in either direction unless something drastic happened.

"Not wildly different from last month. Which is good."

They slipped back into an easy silence, and Claudia let her eyes close as she enjoyed his attention. The only sounds were her sighs of pleasure and Ian's huffs of laughter at her vocal appreciation.

He finished one foot and started on the other. With his head on the back of the couch, he asked, "You said something about affirmations?"

If Claudia had to choose only one thing about Ian that impressed her, it would be how he managed to pay attention—to retain details—while bouncing energetically from thought to thought and topic to topic. He was always noticing, always observing.

"Yeah," she smiled, "but it's probably not in the way you're thinking about it. It's more like... gratitude."

He made a sound in his throat that she interpreted as a cross between curiosity and acceptance.

It wasn't that Claudia had an opinion one way or the other on traditional affirmations. It was more that she found the act of acknowledging her wins—being thankful for them—helped her counter Anxiety's droning negativity.

"What are you grateful for this month?" Though his demeanor remained languid, she felt consumed by the intensity of his gaze. There would be no hiding from him, even if she wanted to. She had his full attention; he would miss nothing. Claudia didn't doubt that for a second. Taking a moment to gather her thoughts, she looked into the silent flames flickering around the logs. Misreading her silence, Ian rushed to add, "You don't have to share if you don't want to."

She smiled her appreciation. "I don't mind. I'm just not used to saying it out loud in any sort of cohesive manner."

He gave her foot an encouraging squeeze.

Claudia started with the bigger things and worked her way inward. She was grateful for the two referrals she signed. Existing clients bringing her new business was always a point of pride. She was also proud of herself for getting in on the ground floor on some Nigerian investments. Over fifty percent of their population were under eighteen. Once that demographic came into its buying power, the demand for goods and services promised to be record-breaking. Instead of playing nice, swallowing the bile of her disappointment, she'd told five different people to fuck off for one well-deserved reason or another. A win in her books. She found a brand of trousers that fit her waist, hips, and thighs, with a shorter inseam. "Pants that I don't have to take to the tailor? I bought three pairs!"

When Ian laughed at that, she continued, "I'm also grateful for the health and well-being of my family. All of them. No matter how annoying some of them may be."

"Yeah, I feel that."

Of course he did. His family was still working through a very serious health scare; she should have been more sensitive. Embarrassment sent her a reproachful glance, and Anxiety seemed poised to join in on the scolding.

"Hey," he tugged on her foot. His eyes were clear as he admonished, "None of that."

He really was more than she deserved.

When she nodded, he continued, "Besides, I'm grateful for lots of other things."

"Yeah?"

"Uh-huh. Like, I started seeing someone. She's pretty amazing." Claudia squirmed a little as a furious blush raced up her neck and face. "My cousins heard that she's a 'beautiful misanthrope', gave me shit about spilling all their business to her."

"Your cousins heard that I'm beautiful?" She cooed.

Ian arched his brow. "Seriously, Gossipika?"

Well? Who didn't like compliments? Being a misanthrope wasn't any worse than anything else in the balance. It wasn't like she had any control over either thing. Her genetics were luck, and her aversion to mankind was common sense. Especially when humanity had done everything in its power to earn her ire by being on the wrong side of history, refusing to learn from its mistakes, time and time again.

Claudia channeled all that into a cute, flirty head-tilt-shrug combo, which earned her a bite on the heel Ian had been massaging.

She pulled her foot from his lap, making note to avail herself of his skill in the future, and shifted herself to his side. His arm automatically pulled her closer, his hand settling with a comfortable familiarity on her hip.

Her eyes fluttered closed when he pressed a gentle kiss on her forehead, warming her more completely than her fireplace ever had. It spread from her belly outward and she couldn't imagine being anywhere else but right here with him. Claudia didn't put herself out there often, didn't press herself to broaden any type of horizon. She stayed in her lane where it was safe and predictable. But this? This gamble had paid off. Sharing this day of quiet retrospection with Ian was so much better than she'd imagined.

"Hey, Sunny?" She felt his answering 'hmm?' vibrate through his chest. "Where's your phone?"

"Right here." His face buried against her head muffled his voice, but she felt him shift to reach for his phone on the end table. "Why?"

She smiled up at him, her heart full. Feigning a careless nonchalance, she shrugged, "I was wondering about the difference between a bullet journal and a habit tracker."

"Oh, my god!" His eyes widened with glee as a wide, dopey smile spread across his face. He sat up, pulling her with him, as he scrolled excitedly through his phone. "Okay! First, we'll start with this year's winner of Japan's Stationery Award!"

Claudia allowed herself to be swept away by the force of his enthusiasm, weighing in on everything from binding style to deckled edges.

Safe and cared for in Ian's arms, she quietly added another thing to her gratitude list.

Chapter Twenty-Seven

It was Home Food Friday, the monthly potluck where the staff were welcome to bring in a homemade dish to share. Bonus points if it was something culturally familiar or a childhood favorite. Over the years, there had been as many as twenty-six dishes and as few as five, but it was always a celebration that included everyone that worked within the halls of Morenal, Smith & Sano.

January was usually subdued; everyone was still food-and-drinked out from their holidays. But today, the first Friday of the new year, was still appropriately festive.

Claudia watched as Jorge, her father's assistant's assistant, made his way around the offerings. The layout for these feasts was so involved, custom signage had been designed so participants could easily indicate the dietary information with a simple circling of the icons with a dry erase marker. It was Jorge's delicate palate that necessitated the inclusion of a spice meter.

"Jorgito," Claudia called out to the younger man, "try the ropa vieja. I promise it's not too spicy."

"This one is good." He gestured to the bistec he had on his plate. "It has the right amount of spice."

Kyle whispered under his breath, "Isn't it just a grilled and sliced flank steak seasoned with salt and pepper? He's killing me!"

"Shh!" She jammed her elbow into her departmental admin assistant's ribs as they both tried to hide their snickers.

Claudia didn't make it a habit of othering people for their limitations. She had just never met a Latino with zero capacity for spicy food before. Young Jorge was an anomaly that prompted her to find the boundaries of his tolerance.

Moving closer to the spread, Kyle rubbed his hands together in anticipation. "Looks like there's mie goreng and chow mein." As he piled his plate high with the noodle dishes, he warned everyone within earshot, "If you're looking for me later, I'll be under my desk in carb overload."

The room erupted into playful taunts and chuckles.

"Did you eat?"

Claudia turned, smiling up at Ian. He hadn't been in the room when they started, so she wasn't sure she should expect him to join. If her memory served, and it often did, this was the first time he'd partaken in the months since he'd stepped in for his parents. A small part of her preened at the thought he'd broken his 'do not engage' rule for her.

It was a shallow, primitive, pheromone-driven part that she wasn't proud of but had decided to embrace anyway.

"I already stuffed three empanadas down my throat. I'm attempting decorum by not following it up with a plate of pierogi. Why, you want me to fix you a plate?"

"You want to?"

She considered it.

They hadn't done anything overt or conspicuous at the office—no giggling together in corners or 'meetings' behind closed doors—but after the way Ian stalked and captured her before leading her out of the ballroom and to the bank of elevators at the holiday gala, anyone who was paying even the slightest bit of attention recognized they were more than polite acquaintances. But Claudia had cultivated her reputation as a friendly, bubbly sort. Why wouldn't she help Ian choose his lunch at this, his inaugural Home Food Friday?

"Yeah, I want to."

He smiled, wide and winning. "Okay, Gossipika. Do it up."

"Any food allergies or preferences?"

"None. I eat everything."

She knew he was only answering her question, saw it in the guileless smile on his face, but her Horniness Minister was always hard at work where this man was concerned. Tamping down her baser instincts, Claudia made her way to the table and filled two plates—one for Ian and one with the pierogi she hadn't really intended on skipping.

Ian took one look at the plate she'd made for him. "Damn, Claudia."

"I'm Latina." Was her only explanation for the mountain of food she'd chosen. "We like to feed people."

He shook his head disbelievingly but took the plate and wrapped cutlery from her. She settled into the seat beside him and started in on her own plate.

"You notice how every culture has a food stuffed in dough?" She asked the room at large, "Empanadas, dumplings, pierogi, patties. What is that if not proof of the Almighty?"

There were a couple of playful 'Hallelujahs' and some tittering laughter, but otherwise, everyone was happy to enjoy their meal in the company of their colleagues. Claudia continued to tease and joke with the people closest to her until her plate was empty. She turned to let Ian know she was going to get an empanada for dessert and watched wide-eyed as he put the last forkful in his mouth, chewing methodically around the mass.

Ian swallowed the last of his food. The aggressive bobbing of his Adam's apple called forth a phantom sensation in her palm. He took a long drink from his water can then wiped his mouth with the napkin.

"Jesus," she breathed.

"I'm Caribbean," he said in answer. "We like to eat."

"But... I..." She snapped her mouth shut against the stammering and started again. "I brought you a little of everything so you could pick what you liked. I wasn't throwing down a gauntlet, Ian!"

"I'm a growing boy, what can I say?"

"How is your stomach not distended right now?"

"There'll definitely have to be some extra reps at the gym tonight. You wanna join me? There's a location by you." She didn't answer right away, so he added a little guilt to the mix. "It's the least you can do since you tried to stuff me full like some storybook witch."

Claudia's laughter honked out of her, and she slapped a shocked hand over her mouth. She looked around frantically to see if anyone noticed. To her horror, some had and were laughing at her reaction.

"I'm willing to bet good money you have a gym bag packed at the ready. Why not join me for a quick circuit?"

She was annoyed that he knew her so well but pleased at not having to hide the strange, quirky bits of herself. Yes, she had a bag packed. It made the times she needed the outlet of an extra, more demanding workout easier to maneuver.

"How close to my place is it?"

"Walking distance in good weather." He assured her.

"Okay. Let's do it."

His pleased grin had her leaning close. Thankfully she caught herself before she pressed herself against him and started making out in the middle of the boardroom. He must have noticed because his grin tipped over to a devious smirk as he said low and sinful, for her ears only, "Later."

Claudia's head moved in a jerky sort of nod, her entire body flushed with arousal. "Later."

With that settled, Ian excused himself from the table with their plates, loaded them in the dishwasher before sauntering back to his duties, leaving Claudia to wrestle with her libido. She heaved on the reins of her self-control. She still had the entire afternoon to get through. There would be plenty of time for Ian's promises later.

HE'D SET THEM UP IN a corner of the main weight room. Using the step platforms and risers, he'd created an all-purpose station that could function as their bench, their seat, or their box jumps. He'd just finished wiping them down when she made her way to him. His double take was both adorable and flattering.

She was wearing what she normally wore for exercising: an industrial-strength sports bra underneath a knee-length, tank-sleeve bodysuit. She completed the look with a high ponytail, a sweatband on her edges, and a cropped top. It amused her to know, even after exploring every inch of her naked body, this look was enough to have Ian swallowing his tongue. Which is exactly what she told him.

"I can't talk right now, woman. I'm battling seasickness."

She swatted him, rolling her eyes while secretly preening at the compliment to her curves. It wasn't that Claudia didn't know she was attractive. She wasn't being conceited in acknowledging she knew what she looked like. It was more the reality that, despite how deep she tried to bury herself behind her bubbly persona, she still managed to call attention to war crimes, social injustices, and the rise of the Christo-fascist right when people were expecting polite chit-chat about whether popcorn was better sweet or savory. Even the biggest tetas in the world couldn't disguise that for long.

It was supremely satisfying to have her physical appearance appreciated by someone who was fully aware of her inclination toward nihilism.

"So, what am I in for?" She asked, pulling her right elbow across her chest in a stretch.

"How do you feel about a mixed circuit of free weights and body weight?"

Claudia usually practiced a strengthening stretch program that was challenging in its simplicity. She didn't use weights often but felt fairly confident she wouldn't overextend herself if she kept them light.

"Sounds good to me."

"Great. Let's grab some dumbbells, a bar, and some plates before we warm up."

Ian's gym was an old-school, bare-bones type of establishment. The people here kept their eyes on their own proverbial paper and didn't seem concerned with trends or clout. On the way to the free weights, Claudia noticed a woman filming herself on the squat rack but it only took a moment for Claudia to realize the woman wasn't looking at the camera or talking about what she was doing and surmised she was recording herself to track her own form and progress.

They settled their assorted weights at their station and began warming up. Ian seemed to have a routine he preferred that consisted of lots of big motions and jumping. She decided to do the warm-up from her own hybrid routine and got to it. Almost instantly, Claudia was lost in the familiar flow of the movements, her body limbering with ease. When she stood upright again, she was startled to see she'd garnered Ian's full attention.

"What?"

"I think I didn't fully appreciate how bendy you are because you're so small. I mean, don't get me wrong, I think about how I've folded you in half all the time but my focus is always on how your hot, tight—"

"Ian!" Claudia hissed, looking around frantically.

"I'm sorry. I can't help it! You have no idea how good it feels to be gripped by—"

She poked him in the rib. Hard. "Cállate, Sunny. No jodas!"

"I'm not fucking with you, Gossipika, I swear! If I were you, I'd walk around introducing myself like that all the time. 'I'm Claudia. If I decide to grace you with the opportunity, don't miss the chance to experience bliss. Be prepared to kiss your pull-out game good-bye, for real'."

She couldn't help but laugh at that. Affecting a haughty tone and posture, she said, "I'm probably gonna keep that information to myself. It's a supply and demand thing, you understand."

"More than you know."

They began their circuit, Ian telling her the reps and sets so she could choose her weight accordingly. It didn't take long for Claudia to lapse into the high of exercise. She was so focused, so locked in to what she was doing, she was surprised when Ian said they would finish with a set of burpees. She looked at the large clock on the wall in the cardio room and, sure enough, forty-five minutes had gone by since they'd warmed up.

Maybe she should look into adding more of these circuit-type programs to her rotation. She felt challenged but energized, her whole body thrumming with a pleasant level of exertion, despite the burpees.

The cool firmness of the mat was like a 5-star mattress as she sprawled out, taking a moment to catch her breath. Rolling into a seated position to start her cool down, Claudia startled at the sound of Ian's voice.

"I'm struggling with some logistics." Ian said, while Claudia held the soles of her feet to stretch her hamstrings. He continued once she'd turned to give him her attention. "I think it would be a superlative experience to fuck you while you're in the splits."

It was probably the very last thing she expected him to say—the shock of it sent spittle down the wrong pipe, making her cough uncontrollably.

"What?" She wheezed.

"Nothing so basic as you doing the splits on my lap, of course. I'm thinking of spreading you out and taking you from behind."

Everything in her body went molten. "Go on."

"Here's where the logistics come in. I need to find a surface at the right height that is both sturdy and hypoallergenic. We don't want exposure to any... contaminants while your swollen, needy clit rubs all over it."

"Obviously." Sure, her voice was still scratchy from her coughing fit, but the added hoarseness was due to the Minister of Horniness being too busy compiling options to allow her words any additional oxygen.

"I suppose a solution to that would be to keep your panties on. I could pull 'em to the side, use the fabric like a harness or a handle. Plus, it would add to the friction."

Claudia looked around. No one was close enough to hear them, and nothing about Ian's posture suggested he was spilling this filth in the middle of the training mat. She was aware there were security cameras, but unless they had a professional lip reader zoom in on his mouth, she was the only victim of his depravity.

He continued casually, heedless to the need he was stoking in her, "That might even be better, actually. You do tend to squirm and wriggle as your orgasm approaches—you're so impatient when you're on the brink of coming—and I'd want you as stationary as possible while I worked you over as your orgasm barreled towards you."

A small whimper escaped.

Ian pulled his arm across his chest and twisted at the waist. "Anyway, as I was saying. A countertop might be too high, and a kitchen table isn't sturdy enough. A dresser might work for both height and sturdiness, but it lacks the depth needed for me to press you face down on its surface."

Claudia could feel all of it. Her heated skin on the cool wood, her face sticking to the lacquered finish, while Ian stuffed her full. His hands would be on her back. No, on her thighs, running outward as far as he could reach before coming back to palm her ass. He'd spread her cheeks to—

"Claudia?"

"Wha... yes?" She blinked to clear the vision, but the slick desperation flooding her bodysuit was unfixable. It was only the engineering of her high-impact sports bra that kept her nipples from making a vulgar show of themselves. As it was, she felt them harden to an almost painful degree. "Sorry. I didn't hear you."

"Were you imagining it?" The self-satisfied grin told her everything she needed to know. He clasped his hands behind his back, puling them slowly upward to stretch his chest and shoulders. "Were you able to come up with any solutions for how I could achieve my goal?"

During their workout, she'd figured their thoughts had been running along a similar appreciation for the feats of physical fitness their bodies performed. A general call to horniness, as it were. He was strong and focused, and the way his muscles glistened and rippled was a delightful reward for the grueling circuit they'd completed. She would have never guessed this type of detailed, lewd filth had been running through his mind while maintaining perfect form during twelve reps of upright rows. Claudia was seriously considering filing a motion of contempt against her brain's Horniness Ministry for failing so utterly at rising to this level of debauchery.

Ian twisted at the waist a couple of times, windmilled his arms, then rolled his shoulders. He did the now familiar bounce on his toes while shaking out his arms before settling.

"I didn't mean to interrupt your cooldown. I apologize." Claudia didn't buy it for a moment. Nothing in his tone, his posture, or the wicked curve of his full lips said contrition. "Why don't you finish up while I put all this away?"

Trying to come up with the appropriate, most effective piece of furniture, and the resultant desire of Ian's proposal had tripped the Minister of Horniness into a frenzied 'all hands on deck' type of hysteria. Claudia couldn't see straight for all the chaos happening in her mind. She hadn't moved, hadn't continued her stretches, just sat there reeling.

"Ready?" Ian held his hand out to her. Shaking some of the confusion loose, she let him pull her up.

Big mistake. Now she was pressed against his chest, crumbling her fragile focus.

"I'm gonna get changed." He spoke low, against the side of her face. "My suggestion? Don't put too much effort into cleaning up. You're only going to get dirty again when we get back to your place." He nipped at her earlobe and added in a sinful register, "Besides, it's not like you could wash it away even if you tried, could you?"

Then he walked to the changerooms, leaving Claudia coiled tighter than a spring trap, liable to go off at the slightest amount of pressure.

The monster.

Chapter Twenty-Eight

They'd barely made it in the door before they'd dropped their things, mauling each other.

"Now, Ian. Please. Now."

What was he supposed to do when she begged so prettily? She was practically crawling out of her own skin with want, making him drunk off her desire.

He'd barely blinked, and she'd already managed to step out of her panties and unbutton his pants. Needing no further prompting, Ian pushed his pants and boxer briefs down his hips, freeing his erection from the confines of his clothing. Before he knew what was happening, Caudia had the condom unwrapped and rolled down the hard length of him.

"You really mean business, don't you?" He rasped.

"This is all your fault," her words came out in a breathy whine. "You started it; now you're going to finish it."

There was no arguing there. He most certainly did start it, he most definitely would finish it. Ian lifted her up against the wall and slid himself fully into her warm readiness.

The way she sobbed her pleasure while her body contracted against his erection made him dizzy. "Fuck."

She sighed and closed her eyes while she tipped her head back, letting her limbs fall lax at her sides. He realized Claudia's shoulder blades were against the wall, but her feet weren't on the floor. She was essentially dangling off his dick.

For a moment, she seemed content just to be filled by him, to have the ache he'd created temporarily soothed. Then she said, "Don't move. I'm going to play with my clit until I come."

Her pupils were blown out in the way he'd come to recognize meant she was out of her mind with arousal. The hornier she got, the more outlandish her demands: *I'm going to try to pour this rum down my body and into your mouth without spilling any while sitting on your face!* With pleasure! *If you figure out what word I'm tapping out on my clit in Morse code with your dick, you can choose where you come.* Yes, please! *Let's see if I can get you off using only the muscles in my throat. Stay still!* Anytime!

And now this.

The sight made him quiver. He gripped her thighs, determined to both have his hands as full of her as possible and to help keep her upright and spread open while her busy hands went to work.

She worked herself over at a furious pace, squirming and writhing as she chased the pleasure that seemed just out of her reach.

He looked down, the place where he disappeared into her body capturing the totality of his attention. Nothing had ever been more noteworthy, more riveting, than the sight of Claudia Regina Sano Pérez pinned to the wall by his dick.

Which he told her, not that she could hear him. She was too far gone.

"You fill me so good. I want you to feel how good when I come." Her words were choppy and breathless, but he hummed his agreement all the same.

She tossed and thrashed while she breathed noisily through her nose. The guttural sound of her pleasure rioted through her small foyer as she gritted her teeth through her climax. Ian was transfixed by the sight. Claudia's left hand roamed her body, squeezing her breast in a punishing grip, while her right one still played fast and loose with her clit.

She'd told him not to move, and he prided himself on following her rules when they played these games. But she was so out of her mind, blissed so completely out, she might have very well forgotten he was there.

He'd never seen anything so erotic in all his life.

Her eyes snapped open, laser-focused on his. It was as if the relief of her climax acted like an asthma inhaler, clearing her head so she could take a full, clear breath. The curve of her smile signaled a depravity he'd come to expect, and he knew without a doubt he was going to do whatever she said. The charged moment between her opening her mouth to speak and the words landing in his brain fizzed through him.

"My name is Claudia. I've decided to grace you with the opportunity to experience bliss." Ian's grip on her thighs tightened reflexively. "Are you ready to kiss your pull-out game goodbye?"

For one searing moment everything slowed down. Ian's senses were hyper-focused. He heard the wubb wubb of his blood rushing in his veins harmonizing with the throb of Claudia's pulse. He was certain he could see the overhead lights reflected in each individual bead of sweat dotting her hairline. Then, just as quickly, the room returned to regular focus, and all he could feel was the sweet grip of her dying climax.

"Pull-out game? I never met 'em."

She managed to shift herself in his hold, grab him by the collar, and pull his mouth to hers. Ian responded to it like a starter pistol. It only took twelve brutal strokes, which was honestly eleven more than he thought he had in him, before he'd pressed them both into the drywall while he emptied himself into the condom with a shuddering groan.

The kiss was less feverish now that the storm of lust washed over them. It was the slow, languid kisses of a summer afternoon swinging in a hammock.

"Come on, Gossipika. Let's get you cleaned up."

She nodded peacefully and wrapped herself more firmly around his torso. He loved how agreeable she was after an orgasm. The high of it leaving her blissed out and pliable. Knowing he contributed to her mindless state was a high all its own.

With his pants still unzipped and barely balancing on his ass, he carried them to the bathroom and set her on the counter.

He rolled her stockings off with practiced ease before searching her dress for the zipper.

"It's on this side." Claudia leaned over to show him the placket.

With that sorted, he lifted it off her head and placed it neatly on the toilet seat. She was still wearing her sports bra, apparently in too much of a hurry to fully change back into her outside clothes.

He ran his hands over the fabric covering her flesh, marveling at the construction. He couldn't feel anything of her body underneath it. Sure, he'd appreciated how little bounce there'd been while they jumped and stretched and lifted, but seeing it, feeling it, brought the efficacy of the garment's construction into clear focus.

Reaching behind her, he undid the four clasps and groaned at the relieved sigh Claudia let out. It wasn't exactly like the one she made when she came, but it was close enough that his dick poked its head out to see if its assistance was required.

Freeing her of the underwire, he looked down at the reddened lines left on her breasts and tsked a scolding, "Look what you've done to my girls."

Ian's touch was soft and reverent as it traced the indented markings on her skin.

"*Your* girls?" Claudia asked, her head leaned back on the mirror and her eyes closed as she enjoyed his ministrations.

"Well, you obviously can't be trusted to care for them. Look at this!" He cried, only partly joking. He bent down to place gentle kisses all over her abused flesh. Even her tattoo was disfigured by the angry red lines running through it.

"I promise you, I'm quite capable of managing the care and maintenance of your girls." She said the last mockingly, but Ian didn't care. They were his. All of her could be his if only she'd accept it.

"I'd like to apply for the position if it's all the same to you. I'm eminently qualified." He cupped a breast in each hand, nuzzling them.

"You're so silly." She mushed his face and tried to slide off the counter but he was too fast. He put his large hand on her stomach to keep her still. "Fine. You win. I'm too worn out to fight you."

Ian proceeded to show Claudia exactly why he was the right one for the job of Chief Claudia Operations Officer. He started by collecting the few locks of hair that had come loose from her ponytail and securing them with a clip. Then he pulled a microfiber towel from one of the drawers and expertly tied it around her head, covering her hairline while leaving the majority of her face uncovered. Then he took out the cleansing mask she opted against on their self-care day and applied it with a small disc of plastic that looked like a putty knife to her face and neck.

"Mmm... that feels good." She hummed, eyes still closed.

"Eucalyptus."

Claudia looked so peaceful on her bathroom counter, fully naked with a thick layer of green clay on her face, he almost didn't want to move her.

He grabbed two towels from the cubby shelves behind the door, kicked off his pants, and fiddled with the controls on the shower console to make sure only the removable shower head turned on, setting the temperature to a lukewarm 37 degrees.

He relished the feel of her naked body against his as he brought her into the shower and held the spray to her neck to prevent her hair from getting wet while the water fell all over her body. The washcloth maintained enough lather for the entirety of her lush curves, between her toes, and weirdly shaped belly button, despite her squirming giggles.

"Tip your head back; I'm going to rinse your face."

She did as instructed, and he proceeded to sluice the water over her, moving and arranging her limbs as needed.

He raced through his own shower, sparing none of the gentleness he'd had for Claudia for himself. He wrapped them both in her fancy Turkish linen towels before running a whipped body butter over her damp skin, massaging her overworked muscles as he went.

Her pleased and satisfied hums caused a bubble of pride to swell in his chest. He would happily spend the rest of his life taking care of this woman, easing her aches and pains so she had the strength she needed to slay more villains, to face down more threats. He knew it the first night she came apart in his arms, just like he knew it now. Claudia was all the woman he needed, and he hoped one day he could tell her that without her pulling the ripcord and hightailing off to perceived safety.

He was safety. He wanted to be her soft place to land. He wanted-ed to love her and have fun with her and encourage and support her. He wanted it all.

But he didn't know how to say it. Not in a way she'd receive it, anyway.

So instead, he led her upstairs to her bed and let his body do the talking.

Slow kisses, gentle touches, lingering caresses, soft swipes of his tongue had both of their bodies straining for completion. But he didn't want fast and fevered. So he continued to take his time, savoring the murmured sighs and breathy moans. It didn't take long once he'd rolled the condom on. And when they both tipped over the edge, their lips grazing as they panted their pleasure, all he could feel was the truth pulsing through his body.

I love you.

I love you.

I love you.

Chapter Twenty-Nine

It had been over ten years since Ian roamed these halls as a student. It felt eerily familiar, yet completely foreign. Muscle memory told him to watch for the edge of the vending machine at the corner, but the label on said machine was all wrong.

Being in the architecture building, seeing students running to and fro, warmed him with nostalgia. They all looked so young, so fragile—so *new*. He couldn't even remember what was going through his mind at the time, but his life at thirty-one, as it stood, was beyond his wildest dreams. Contemplating the steps necessary to hang his own shingle? Preposterous.

He didn't often give in to such navel-gazing. Even at eighteen, he knew his scholarship deal wasn't his endgame. Pursuing an actual education instead of being treated like a commodity before he'd ever had a chance to fully develop was the right decision. He didn't have any regrets about the path his life took. Following his dream to become an architect, a dream he hadn't fully tested the scope of in high school, was worth more than the murky promise of going pro in a sport that wasn't wildly lucrative in the first place.

He found himself in front of Jonathan's office. It was Thursday, his one lecture hall that he extended to include in-person office hours. Since Ian was in the neighborhood, he thought he'd take a chance to see if Jonathan was available for a quick visit.

Sure, he could have called or texted, but Ian didn't want to make a big deal out of it if Jonathan was busy. This way, his brain could accept the missed opportunity as chance instead of dwelling on the way they weren't in each other's daily lives anymore.

Jonathan's door was ajar, so Ian knocked on the frame. "S'up?" He said, gently nudging the door open.

Ian noticed the back of someone's head in the chair facing his friend and former mentor and instantly started to apologize.

"Yang! How perfect. Come in!" Jonathan waved him forward.

"Are you sure?" Ian glanced nervously at the student trying to speak one-on-one with their professor.

"Da da da." Jonathan's exuberant Romanian affirmative welcomed Ian, easing the tension from his shoulders. "Your timing couldn't be better!"

Making his way further into the admittedly small, cluttered space, Jonathan came from around his desk to wrap Ian in a bear hug. "It's good to see you, frate. I've been terrible about keeping in touch. How are you? Estás bien?"

Jonathan's familiar indiscriminate blending of English, Spanish, and Romanian made Ian's heart hurt. He missed his friend. Missed his life, if he were being honest, and wished he'd had a way to make more time for catching up. Instead of wallowing, he smiled. "Yeah, my dad is up and around, and all the doctors have been positive about what his future looks like. It seems the worst is over."

"Gracias a dios. I want to hear more, but for now I'd like to introduce you to one of our recent graduates, Zavier Henshaw.

This is Ian Yang, one of my former students, now a valued team member and friend."

Ian turned to greet the young Black man. "Zavier, I believe we have plans to meet later today."

He stood up and gave Ian a solid handshake. "You're Ian Yang? I'm sorry, I didn't—"

He cut himself off, probably realizing how inappropriate it would have sounded. Ian knew what he thought and couldn't begrudge him the confusion. His grade nine science teacher was a petite white woman named Pauline Kishimoto. Sometimes surnames didn't tell the whole story.

"Yeah," he smiled good-naturedly, "Chinese Dad, Black Mom, both from Guyana. I never had a bad meal growing up."

They all laughed and settled themselves in their seats.

"What brings you by?" Jonathan asked, sitting on the edge of his desk in front of them.

"As I mentioned, I was meeting Zavier here at the Maddy and thought I'd take a chance at catching you in office."

The Madison Pub was an institution for University of Toronto students, and Ian thought it would both make Zavier feel comfortable in familiar surroundings while also being a small 'full circle moment' for him, who'd spent enough of his own misbegotten youth in those four floors.

"The alumni association put us in touch, and we'd been emailing back and forth," Zavier added. "I have an interview coming up, and I'm feeling a bit nervous, so Ian said he'd help me prepare."

"Is it a paid internship?"

He nodded.

"Do you mind telling us the company?" He did, and Jonathan whistled. "Impressive."

"If you can, get a tour of the studio. Look for evidence of team-building events or other signs of personality in the space.

The last thing you want is to end up in a company where people are uninterested in each other, or the culture feels toxic or devoid of life. Your CV, your skill, got you in the door, right? This is your chance to figure out if they're the right people to hone and cultivate it." Ian added. It was a subject he was very passionate about, which is why he tried to always be available to his fellow alums.

"See why we snatched him up right off the stage?" Jonathan beamed with pride.

Ian made a 'this guy' face but soaked up the praise all the same.

An electronic chirping started and everyone looked to Zavier who stammered out a nervous, "I, uh, I was hoping to get some stuff done before we met but, um, I—"

"I'm still happy to meet later if you want."

The young man's relief was visible. "Yes. Thank you. I'd like that."

"Good luck, Mr. Henshaw. Don't forget you're interviewing them as much as they're interviewing you. Make sure they're worthy."

"Thank you, Professor Bendea."

Zavier quickly gathered his things, gave them both another wave on his way out, and then they were alone.

Ian settled more comfortably in the chair, his coat unzipped and scarf hanging loose around his neck. "He seems like a good kid."

"He is. He'll do well in the right place. I have high hopes for him."

They got caught up as Ian gave him the update on what was happening with his dad and his tentative prediction for when he'd return to work. He wasn't willing to commit to returning full-time until they were able to see what his father could manage—if there were any lapses in his recovery from overdoing it.

Knowing Howard Yang the way he did, Ian didn't trust his father to stick to modified duties.

Jonathan let him in on the faculty dramas that never seemed to improve despite everyone involved being fully grown adults, which naturally transitioned to some industry gossip. As he listened, he thought of Claudia. Of her insistence that gossip was vital and, in some cases, lifesaving. He wondered how many people engaged in this very type of 'behind closed doors' info dumping would consider themselves gossips. Most would likely turn their noses up, believing themselves above it.

He laughed to himself and made a note to tell Claudia about it when he spoke to her later.

"What's that?"

"What?" Ian's brows furrowed.

"That look on your face, chacho."

Ian let a shy smile escape. Domenic had taken to calling it the Claudia face, so he didn't bother wondering how Jonathan noticed it. "I'm seeing someone."

"Pe bune? You're not playing with me right now, are you?"

Ian laughed at Jonathan's melodrama. He'd often chided Ian about his single status, insisting he was too young to already be so jaded, that there was more to life than casual hookups. It didn't matter how many times Ian explained that he wasn't jaded or cynical or anti-relationship; it'd simply been years since he'd found someone he wanted to spend more time with after a handful of dates. The reaction was the same. 'Put yourself out there. The right person will come along.'

And now she had. Maybe.

He hoped.

"She's actually one of yours." Ian teased.

"Eastern European?"

He shook his head. "Latina. From Panamá."

"Oh, mi prima! Did you know Panama was part of Gran Colombia until they declared their independence in 1903?"

Ian gave a dry, "I didn't. I'm sure she does."

"Okay, okay. Tell me everything. How long have you been dating? What's her name? Where did you meet?"

"Easy! Slow down!"

"Por favor! I've been waiting years for this moment. I want every detail. Ahora! Dale!"

And since Ian was desperate to talk about it, he gave Jonathan exactly what he asked for. He told him about seeing her around the office, about the way she hides her keen, cutthroat nature behind a bubbly, gossipy facade. When he got to the part about her walking in on him post shower and discovering she was Diego's sister and their father was one of the named partners; Jonathan's hand shot to his throat as he gasped.

"It's like a telenovela."

"You're telling me. Her family even calls her Gossipika because of how much she loves the drama."

"They call her... what?" Jonathan's usually smooth brow was lined with his confusion.

"She said it means gossipy woman. I know." Ian shrugged a helpless 'what are you going to do?' at Jonathan's disbelieving face. "She said unflattering nicknames are common in Latine families."

"They are..." Jonathan said slowly, as though he was trying to solve a difficult math equation. "But a gossipy woman is a chismosa."

Ian's eyes bugged out. *Chismosa*. Diego had called her Chismosa, not Gossipika. All this time, she smiled a private smile, he thought it was because he was using her family nickname when in reality it was because he'd butchered it so profoundly.

The truth was written all over his face because Jonathan brought his fist to his mouth in a futile attempt to muffle the sound of his uproarious laughter. "Please tell me," he said in choking gasps, "tell me you've called her Gossipika. Por favor!"

"All the time!" Ian confessed from behind his hands as they dragged down his face.

Jonathan wiped tears from his eyes as he begged, "Stai, stai—it's too much! I can't!"

Ian shook his head in stunned disbelief. What was he supposed to do now? Confront her with his newfound knowledge? Apologize? Ask her why she let him run around calling her a made-up word like a fool? Why hadn't she corrected him?

"I think it's sweet."

Ian was still too mortified to deal with Jonathan's swooning. Of course he thought it was sweet; he wasn't the one being laughed at! "Ugh, how do I even bring it up?"

"You don't." Jonathan disregarded Ian's scowl, insisting, "I'm serious. She obviously doesn't mind, or she would have said something. One day, when she's not expecting it, you can hit her with the correct word like you've been in on it this whole time. But for now, I say, leave it."

Ian considered it. He supposed it made a certain amount of sense. He couldn't think of a scenario where Claudia would let something go unchallenged. So if she didn't want her family nickname to be used, to be butchered, he would've known about it. God, it was so mortifying; it didn't matter how much she did or didn't mind.

Jonathan cut his floundering short. "Okay, okay. Finish what you were saying. She sounds amazing."

"She is." Ian sighed and proceeded to confess everything.

He told Jonathan how she's a ferocious little thing that stomped through the world in four-inch heels and wanted to raise an army of equally ferocious girls so they can accurately harness their rage as women. How she didn't think he liked her because he'd been trying to keep a professional distance. When Jonathan stopped chuckling at that, he went to explain about the deal to get information on Quincy and how it led to them hanging around. How they kept hanging out together until one time they were kissing, and now he couldn't imagine a life where he didn't get to kiss her. He admitted to all the little pieces of her that he'd gathered, afraid to hold them close and break them but unwilling to relinquish them for fear of losing them forever.

And because he trusted Jonathan, because he was his teacher, then his mentor, then his employer, but most importantly, he was his friend, he leaned forward—his head in his hands, his elbows on his knees—and told the truth he'd been hiding from for weeks. "What if this thing between us doesn't work when I'm no longer in crisis mode and I go back to my regular life? What then?"

"What? Why would that matter?"

"No, listen. It works right now because I can't ask for more. The light at the end of my tunnel is a pin prick—it's so small it might as well not be there. I literally do not have the bandwidth for more. We don't spend nights together, we don't do group hangs or double dates, we don't spend weekends at apple orchards or wineries. We don't get tickets to games or shows. I see her at work where we touch base about our day, we text back and forth, and maybe one or two nights a week we have a meal together, top it off with a little action, then go our separate ways."

"Ian..." Jonathan's sympathy was not what he needed right then.

"Think about it. What happens when even one thing is off my plate? My availability, my lack of it, is not a problem for her." He hung his head and spoke around the lump in his throat, "I'm crazy about her. What happens if I'm capable of wanting more but she's not interested?"

He felt Jonathan's arm around his shoulder moments before he was caught in a crushing embrace.

"If she doesn't, then you bring her to me for a regaño."

Ian couldn't help the bark of laughter that erupted when he thought about Jonathan trying to give Claudia a talking-to. The small amount of levity was exactly what he needed to break him out of the spiral. Yes, he was worried about it, but it—the looming, nefarious it—was still a ways off. Things had changed so much from when he'd told his cousins his vision for the future. He wanted what they had right now, and bringing his fears about the future into their current happiness was a recipe for disaster.

He extracted himself from Jonathan's hug and tried to let go of his agitation.

"I won't pretend it won't hurt," his friend said with his hand still gripping his shoulder. "I won't even lie and say it's the kind of hurt that you'll get over in time. That's not for me to know."

Ian nodded. He appreciated this pragmatism when romantic sentiment might have prevailed.

"What I do know is you're smart and hard-working. You have a big heart, an easy laugh, and an unassailable moral compass. Your temper has a long fuse, and you have a face that could launch a thousand ships. If your Claudia is all that you say she is, she's aware of these truths. If, knowing all that, she doesn't want more, then there isn't anything you can do or change or adjust to make her want it. It just isn't meant to be."

"Fuck, Jonno, how's this helping?"

"I'm supposed to be helping?" He teased. At Ian's petulant look, he raised his hands in surrender. "Alright, alright. What I'm trying to tell you is to trust her. Trust that she can make the right decision for herself. If you care about her, then you need to trust that she's making the right choice. Even if it isn't you."

Ian sat there, a little stunned and a lot overwhelmed, as he absorbed Jonathan's words. As much as he hated it, he knew Claudia was allowed to not want more than this. She was allowed to not want it at all. He understood that she was well within her right to pull up stakes at any point and wasn't obligated to do more than tell him she was done.

Knowing it, accepting the truth of it, didn't make the possibility of it hurt less.

"You're right. I know you're right." He said on a weary exhale.

"Doesn't make it any easier to hear, does it?"

Ian gave a rueful laugh. "No, it doesn't."

"Well, luckily for you, I'm not right that often. Just ask my sister, Amelia."

They sat together in companionable silence as the last of their laughter died. Ian wasn't sure when he'd get another chance to visit with Jonathan this way. This moment felt stolen—Jonathan was at work, Ian was on his way to meet with young Zavier—which made it all the more precious.

"Professor Bendea?" A young woman's voice came tentatively from the door.

Both men turned to look at her. She seemed tiny and skittish, and Ian couldn't believe he'd ever been that young, that green, even though every moment of his undergrad felt like yesterday. "Is this a bad time?"

"That's my cue. Thanks, man." Both men stood, and Ian clasped Jonathan's hand. "I'll let you know how it works out."

"Please do." He gave Ian's hand a meaningful squeeze before turning to usher the student in, with a warm, "Not at all, Ms. Huyck-Morgan. Come in. Mr. Yang was just leaving."

And with that, Ian headed to the Maddy. It didn't escape him that he was about to offer life advice when his own world was mired in chaos. Luckily, Ian had always been clear-headed when it came to his career.

If only his personal life were as easy to manage.

Chapter Thirty

"The rules are fairly simple." Claudia had brought her laptop into her bedroom and was connecting it to her phone while Ian lay sprawled on her bed, waiting gamely for whatever was to come next. "Red light means stop, green light means move. The first one to come loses and has to wear whatever the winner decides for one two-hour outing."

Ian opened his mouth, but Claudia put her finger up to stop him. "The choice cannot cause illness, injury, or incarceration."

They'd been discussing the absurdity of Western media's interpretation of the Korean series—how could mowing down a room full of civilians in a hail of bullets be anything other than an indictment of late stage capitalism—when Ian mused he'd at least make it through the red light/green light round. Claudia was so taken with the idea of making it sexy, she'd found an app that changed the screen from red to green in random intervals.

"You are going to look so cute in a Cheer Bear t-shirt and a pair of matching pink velour track pants. We'll be twinsies."

Claudia shuddered, knowing he was dead serious. "You're willing to spend money to buy these clothes? Because there's no way you think I own anything remotely similar."

"I'm willing to do a lot of things to see you in a t-shirt and messy bun out in the streets, Gossipika. You've taunted the wrong man."

"To get that, you'll have to outlast me. I'm not too worried."

"Please. One swipe on your needy clit, and you'll be shooting off like a Roman candle." Ian picked up his phone from the nightstand and started scrolling, presumably shopping for these mythical items. "Will medium fit, or is that too big? I want a nice, snug fit on your curves."

"I said move, not touch. We both have to keep our hands to ourselves. I don't touch you, and you don't touch me, either."

Ian scoffed, his tossed phone clattering on the wood surface of her night table. "Any other secret rules I should know about?"

Claudia enjoyed their playtime. It wasn't that they didn't have sex without some type of rule or scorekeeping; they did. Often. It was more that she liked how Ian gave her the freedom and comfort to suggest these outlandish things. She didn't need them, she wanted them. She enjoyed them, and being with Ian allowed her this outlet of expression she never thought she'd have the chance to explore.

"Nothing unless you have any addendums."

"Red Light, Green Light, and we keep our hands to ourselves. Do we change positions between Green Lights?"

She tilted her head, tapping her index finger on her lips. She hadn't considered it, hadn't factored in all the ways sex could be performed.

"What do you think?"

"I think if you don't want to wear a Cheer Bear t-shirt, missionary is out of the question."

They both laughed at the truth of his claim. It was remarkable how easily Claudia was brought to climax when Ian was on top. She was convinced his hip was somehow double-jointed. She couldn't explain the way he moved within her otherwise.

"That's magnanimous of you."

"I don't want to hear your excuses when you lose. Get up here." He ran his hands over his thighs in invitation. "This is the best way to abide by the rules."

She climbed onto his lap, and he pulled her close. "What else? Can we talk?"

She nodded, sinking into the comfort of his hold.

"Can we kiss?"

She nodded again, raising herself up to press her mouth to his, her tongue immediately finding and caressing his. "Yes."

"Okay. Are you ready, or do you need to warm up?" His hands made their way up and down her spine in a soothing motion.

This was the other thing about playing with Ian that was so amazing. While they were in the midst of whatever wild and depraved things she'd suggested, he matched her step for step and stroke for stroke. But before, while he was gathering details and establishing her boundaries, and after, when she was limp and sated and near out of her mind on dopamine, he was full of tender care and gentle affection. His hands running softly all over her body while he cuddled her and pressed sweet, chaste kisses on the side of her face and on the tip of her nose was always the perfect balm as she floated back down from her high.

No matter what they did together, she never felt judged or objectified, only cherished and adored.

Simply thinking about how he cared for her, how good it was between them, was enough to get her engine running. Her kiss was a sloppy, filthy thing that tipped her arousal over the edge from a banked fire to a full-blown inferno.

"No," she sighed, "You?"

He shook his head, though she didn't need his answer. She felt the hard ridge of him underneath her.

Claudia shifted off Ian's lap and closed the curtains to block the noon sky's brightness. As typical of Toronto winters, the late January sun was for light, not heat. She pulled her teddy off while Ian shuffled out of his briefs and got back into her bed. Grabbing a condom from the dresser, Claudia climbed onto her mattress and crawled to where Ian waited at the head of the bed.

"How do you want to do this?"

"I think I should," he said, taking the foil packet and sheathing himself.

With one knee on either side of his hips, Claudia lowered herself until she felt the tip of his erection at her entrance. She put her hands on the wall on either side of his head and awkwardly, slowly, tried to sink onto him.

"Maybe we need to touch, just this once," Ian suggested through gritted teeth.

"Yeah, okay," she breathed, reaching for the base of his erection. Holding him steady was still an effort, but Claudia managed it with far less fumbling. She leaned over to tapped the screen on her phone, and the monitor lit up with a countdown circle, beeping its way down from five.

When it got to zero, the entire room was cast in a green light from the monitor, just as she'd hoped.

Claudia leaned forward and kissed Ian. The feel of his lips against hers as they licked and sucked and tasted was probably a mistake on her part if the goal was to last the longest, but she couldn't resist.

The room was suddenly glowing red, and she stopped, their chests heaving, breaths ragged.

Now that they'd started and the full scope of the game's rules were upon them, Ian smirked, "This is going to be a problem."

The room went green again, and this time she worked her hips in a slow, winding rhythm. The feel of him, hard inside her, solid beneath her, stole her breath.

Red light. Green light. Ian took some control and moved, driving his hips upward. The mattress didn't allow him much range of motion, but it was enough to make her breasts jiggle as she bounced on his lap.

Red light. Claudia leaned forward, resting her forehead against his. The feeling of his exhale, the spicy scent of the cinnamon gum he preferred on his breath, made her want to snuggle into his chest.

Green light. They were both moving now. Ian drove upward while Claudia rode the motion. The drag of him as he ramped up her pleasure was too much. She needed a distraction. She needed to think of anything besides the feel of him, perfectly filling her, stroke after stroke.

"I still haven't decided what I'll get you to wear," she panted.

Red light. Green light. Red light. Claudia was barely hanging on, and Ian seemed perfectly unaffected. She didn't want to lose, of course. But more importantly, she didn't want it to be over yet. She should have known, though, how good it would feel to have Ian this way, how her body would be rearing to race to the edge. Could she... could she create a little distance there? Fighting against the rise of her climax, Claudia decided on a calculated risk and slowly, just a teensy bit, started to remove herself from her body.

Green light. Ian looked up at her through hooded eyes. She had no idea what he saw, but he must have sensed her plan because his gaze went from half-lidded lust to a flinty-eyed assessment.

"Look at your poor nipples, peaked and aching." Dear God, the man was a menace. "They're waiting for me, aren't they? Waiting for my touch, for my mouth." Claudia let out a desperate whimper. The more he talked about them, the more aware of them she became. The more aware of them she became, the more they ached. "You don't even have to touch them. Just lean forward and put one right here on my tongue so I can make it better." Now even her clit was throbbing at the promise of his mouth on her tits. The bouncing of her breasts as he drove up into her only added to the urgency of her need.

Red light. She slumped forward, and the feel of his chest hair on her now oversensitized nipples was almost painful.

"You think rubbing them on my chest will help," Ian continued his assault on her composure, "but it's not the same, is it?"

She shoved her tongue in his mouth just to shut him up, but he nipped it, sending her yelping back off his chest. "It's a red light, cheater."

A frustrated sound clawed its way out of Claudia's throat. She hadn't thought this through. Obviously. The no-touching element made sense when she'd said it, but now, with the need to hold him, the desire to feel his hands on her, anchoring her, it could not be more clear what a miscalculation she'd made. "Fine!"

Green light. Kicking it into high gear, Claudia pressed against the wall as leverage and rode him like a vaquera. Finally, there was a crack in Ian's placid demeanor. His breathing was labored, and he was gritting his teeth against the pleasure. She took advantage of his momentary lapse and ground herself against him, squeezing her inner muscles.

"Fuck!"

Ah, there it was. She was too close to the edge herself, but it was entirely worth it.

Red light. Green light.

Now that she felt she'd leveled the playing field, Claudia slowed down. Even with Ian moving beneath her, the pace was unhurried and leisurely. The sensation of his long, slow slide was pure bliss. Ian reached up and sucked her bottom lip into his mouth. Her contented hum was almost a purr.

"I think instead of Cheer Bear, I'm going to get you a tight t-shirt that says Lollipop Guild. It'll look deliciously perverse with the two Os framing your hard, needy nipples. What do you think?"

Claudia's gasp of outrage had her sitting bolt upright in his lap. Red light.

"Admit it," Claudia demanded. "You're thinking about, like, baseball stats or whatever."

"I don't know any baseball stats and you made it so I can't think about cricket without getting hard."

She let out a lusty sigh at the memory. "I never knew shin pads could be so arousing."

"Your beautiful, depraved mind." Ian's praise was equal parts admonishment and adoration. The way he looked up at her, right at her, made everything inside clench tight. "Stop that."

"I can't help it." She was powerless against her body's reaction to him. "Thinking about you looking through your mask at me kneeling on your shin pads as you spilled down my throat." A shudder ran through her. "I...oh God, Ian!"

"Shh," he soothed. "Not yet, Gossipika. Think of something else."

"Like what? My brain has locked in." She was close, too close; her words came in on a choked sob.

"Anything. I'm putting the alphabet in alphabetical order."

"You..." Claudia had never heard anything so perfectly illogical in her whole life. The mere concept of it was enough to pull her from the edge as she tried to grasp the meaning of his words. "What?"

"The alphabet in alphabetical order would be: A H R B D W E F L M N S X I J G K Q O P C T V Y U Z."

He wasn't joking. He was literally alphabetizing the alphabet.

"Tell me again." When he repeated it, Claudia paid close attention, visualizing each letter and its phonetic spelling. "Wouldn't X come before E and Q after C?"

Ian leaned up and kissed her in the green glow of her room. He let out a little laugh against her lips. "I cannot believe you are litigating this."

"Well, believe it!"

Claudia never really knew whether her first language was English or Spanish. Spanglish was the *lingua franca* in her home and she'd spent a lot of time trying to make sense of a language that didn't play by its own rules. Thinking about how to spell a letter? It was the exact type of thing English's nonsense would complicate.

"Okay, I'll give you *cue* instead of *kew*, but there's no other way to spell X."

Pfft. That's where he was wrong, and she was going to prove it. Reaching for her phone to gather her proof, she remembered her sister's long-ago complaint about their cousin's accidental video call. *Why she was reaching for her phone while* that *was happening, I have no idea.* At the time, Claudia hadn't given it any thought. Being exposed to Junior's sex life was simply a given, the way taxes were the price you paid for participating in civilization.

But now that Ian had brought her to this crossroad where intercourse could be playful and erotic, she was considering it. She wondered what it meant that she now had her own valid reason for reaching for her phone while she was crammed full of Ian's hard dick, her nipples aching and clit throbbing, as she fought off her impending climax.

It was more than wanting to win this battle when she knew she was about to lose the war.

She enjoyed this man. Everything about him was a delight—from his passion for his work to his inexorable joie-de-vivre—Ian made her feel like she could be more than the sum of her parts. Being stark naked as they fucked each other to the finish line didn't mean they couldn't tease each other, couldn't challenge each other's trains of thought. That wasn't the way Ian operated. He lived boisterously, embracing life's complexities at face value, and invited Claudia to do the same.

Offered her the freedom to try.

Her adult life to that point had been about damage control, about mitigating problems. She'd never lived without limitations. She'd never had another way made available to her until now.

Until Ian.

His grumbling about getting in shit for trying to help her step back from the ledge recentered her focus.

She dropped her phone on the bed, no longer concerned with how to spell the letter X. "That's on you for letting up when you had me against the ropes. You, Sunny, lack a killer instinct."

"Maybe I have one but don't apply it to you."

He couldn't keep saying things like that and expect her to let it slide. Her feelings for this man were unwieldy and without structure. She worked so hard at processing all these big emotional swings, his casual declarations overloaded her already taxed system.

"Then prepare to lose!" She gloated, attempting to steer them to safer waters.

Ian was impervious to her efforts. He kissed her, slow and sensual. "I already have."

The solemn certainty in his voice, the laser focus in his eyes when he said those words, toppled Claudia's crumbling defenses. She had to admit to herself, if no one else: she'd fallen in love with Ian Yang.

It was too late for her to leave this thing unscathed.

Chapter Thirty-One

Claudia had waited days—months, if she was being honest—for the article to go live. She'd happened to find herself at the same table as a celebrated investigative journalist at one of the many functions she forced herself to attend. And, though she kept the details to herself and her integrity completely intact, something told Claudia to pay attention to the woman's work. With a bit of instinct and a whole lot of luck, Claudia stumbled upon it: an exposé of the tech giant who'd engaged in a laundry list of ethics violations. From child labor to exploitation to environmental travesties, they were about to be exposed as the very worst kind of predator.

It took a couple of months and lots of careful movements, but Claudia had moved all of her clients' money out of anything that even so much as brushed against them to protect their investments from the inevitable fallout. The reverberations would be felt for years to come, and Claudia intended on shielding her clients from the worst of it.

Now, at the beginning of February, as she refreshed the news wires, she once again took comfort in the knowledge—the incontrovertible truth—that gossip saved lives.

"Finally!" Claudia clicked the link and began reading. As she suspected, it was a damning account of unfettered greed and corporate negligence. The journalist wrote in a way that was clear and informative with lots of cited sources that proved unequivocally that the mining disaster that had held the world hostage was not an unforeseeable accident but a malevolent pattern of disregard. "Fucking leeches."

She finished reading the article and immediately started it again, this time making notes of the different governing bodies who'd either looked the other way or were flat-out party to the corruption. She'd followed up to see if there was any overlap with her clients' money and immediately set about rectifying the problem.

That was the thing about Claudia's success. It was more than knowing the historical ebbs and flows and market triggers. It was about applying said knowledge to the best conceivable outcome. It was acknowledging climate change was a devastating problem for humanity, *but also* some winters weren't cold enough to produce large enough quantities of maple syrup, thereby skewing the supply and demand. It was looking around at governments who'd slashed social programming budgets to pad already bloated police budgets and accurately predicting where such shortfalls would have the greatest impact on social safety nets and infrastructure and pivoting her clients' money accordingly.

It was expecting the worst at all times while being prepared to react even when your heart was sick at the blithe indifference to suffering all around you.

Satisfied she'd done all she could, Claudia closed the article and tried to get some work done. It was hard; she was practically vibrating with the knowledge that consequences would be meted out. When she went to bed that night, it was with the brittle comfort that some small measure of justice would prevail.

She checked the markets when she woke, but there wasn't any change. She told herself it was still early; the article hadn't been up for a full twenty-four hours yet. There was still time. She'd reasoned giving it two full business days to really make waves would be enough. Claudia had thrown herself into her work and availed herself of the delicious distraction of Ian's body in the meantime. He seemed to sense something was wrong but also that she didn't want to talk about it, which she appreciated.

His ability to read her, understand her, should have been cause for alarm. Months ago it had been. But now, she accepted it as the magic of Ian. So even as she spent her adult life railing against the destruction greed wrought, she was swept away by her greed for this man, willing to lay ruin to all her barriers to have more of him.

"Morning!" Kyle, her department's administrative assistant, called out. "Anything new and exciting?"

"Not yet!" She answered while she watched him hang his coat and settle himself. "How was hydrotherapy?"

"So good! I feel completely reset!"

She chuckled to herself. Claudia really liked Kyle. He was smart and capable and handled the demands of the job with ease. Why he felt the need to float in scented water bi-monthly to refresh himself was none of her business.

"I have back-to-back meetings today, but after I'm going do-not-disturb."

"Got it!"

She often stacked her mornings thusly. It kept her busy and engaged while leaving her plenty of time to unwind after. There were times when an evening appointment couldn't be avoided, and she did her best to balance her schedule in those instances, her sleep hygiene chief among them, but at this stage in her career, it was fairly easy to make it work. Besides, Claudia had always preferred to wake up early and get the day over with than to have an obligation hanging over her head well into the evening.

By the time she'd returned to her office, she was happy to lock herself in and turn the harsh overhead fluorescent lighting off in favor of the gentle light of her two standing lamps. The rest of her department teasingly referred to it as Claudia's Zen Den, promising to get her a small gong, but otherwise left her be.

She settled in, scrolling through social media. People were definitely talking about it. Good. Mainstream media had lost almost all its credibility. Message boards and chat rooms were a more reliable barometer of public opinion. Regardless of the rage-baiting echo chamber of it all, it still was more current and more accurate than any of the traditional methods.

She checked the markets again. Still nothing.

Taking a deep breath, she went to the country's national broadcaster. There it was on the main page. Lots of think pieces and talking heads weighing in, as well as the CEO's statement refuting the allegations. *Allegations.* Claudia rolled her eyes at their temerity.

Still, the markets showed no change. No notable fluctuation from Tuesday to now. Four days! The world had been hearing about this for almost a week, and nothing?

Could it be that people didn't understand the implications? No, she'd spent hours on social media reading takes that ranged from nuanced to full-on red pill.

She knew there was a large population who relied on the mainstream media for their news, that there was a huge divide between the chronically online and the so-called blue-collar working class. Still. The truth she didn't want to face was becoming undeniable.

Nothing was going to happen.

They'd been outed as the very worst type of predator, and the world was going to keep turning.

Something deep inside Claudia fractured. She didn't have much faith in humanity—people were a constant source of disappointment. But she'd thought, believed, society had collectively drawn the line at the maiming and murder of children. She held it as a red line against even the bottomless pit of corporate greed: children had to be exempt.

Society had failed to keep the planet safe for them, had failed to keep their drinking water clean, had failed to ensure them equal opportunity for education and a future free of crushing debt in the pursuit of said education, and now it was failing to keep their tiny bodies from being thrown into the gristmill.

The horror of it stared Claudia in the face.

All that evidence, all that work, was basically for nothing. They would face no consequences and, worse, would be emboldened to double down knowing there would be no fallout. Knowing no one would stop them.

Claudia couldn't hold a thought in her head. Her mind ran an endless loop of facts and figures, of historical atrocities, of hypocritical immorality reframed as progress and freedom and self-defense. All of it mocking her for daring to think change was possible.

Her rage was like incense. Even unlit, you were aware of its presence. Now ignited, its smoke was everywhere, agitating Embarrassment and Anxiety. The three made a dangerous alliance, enabling every destructive thought and impulse she had.

An angry, riotous mob of voices swept through her mind armed with a sickeningly long list of evil prospering. It got louder and louder until she couldn't hear, couldn't see, couldn't escape. She fought to find a plausible explanation for this apathy, but the more she struggled, the further she sank. It was too big, too insurmountable. The death tolls kept climbing and climbing, sweeping Claudia away in the tide of humanity's failures.

Chapter Thirty-Two

"Another night in the zen den?" Ian teased from outside Claudia's office. He wasn't sure if she could hear him through her closed door.

This was the fourth night he'd come by to find her overhead lights off and only the two floor lamps on. On Tuesday, she said she'd gotten a headache while waiting for Tokyo. Last night, she'd seemed impatient and distracted as she muttered to herself that she must be missing something.

Tonight, when he opened her door to say goodbye, he immediately knew something had gone very terribly wrong.

In the last month, he'd thought he'd seen all the versions of her. The one he held while she roamed the dark corridors of her mind, the one whose sex drive came with a deliciously depraved edge, the one whose keen mind found patterns and connections in unconventional places to best serve her clients. Ian even loved when she was raging against the injustice surrounding her. He just wanted to see her, unfettered, without the mask she wore. He preferred her fiery and alive, her cynical gaze missing nothing.

Sometimes she snarled at him, sometimes she cooed and purred. Sometimes she teased and giggled. But always—*always*—her eyes burned with her banked fire. No matter what, he could look into her eyes and see his pufferfish, cute but deadly, staring right back at him. But now she was gone. There wasn't the blank slate; there wasn't the empty vessel. There was nothing at all, and he felt sick.

"Claudia," Ian tried to keep his voice modulated, but his panic was choking him. "Claudia, please."

She didn't respond or react to his presence in her office in any way. He looked around frantically but couldn't find the source of her trouble. Her two monitors were off, as was the TV mounted in the corner. She just sat there, staring into the middle distance, with her phone clutched in a death grip in her hand.

He approached her slowly, unsure what would happen if he touched her. "Claudia? Claudia, can you hear me?"

Still nothing. God, how long had she been sitting like this in the dark? Tentatively, he put his hand on her forehead. It was cool to the touch. He used both hands to feel the side of her neck. That was where your thyroids were, weren't they? He wasn't entirely sure what he was looking for, but there had to be something he could point to, something he could work on making right.

Something to bring her back.

"Claudia, can you stand up? Please?" Nothing.

Ian swallowed thickly, fighting the tears that were burning in his sinuses. She'd told him sometimes she felt like she was being carried away, swept up in the crowd where no one could hear her call for help. Is this what that looked like? Had the crowd in her mind taken her away? Fighting for calm, Ian tried again. "Claudia?"

She blinked, a slow, disengaged motion that didn't provide him any type of comfort. He wrestled with whether to call someone, but... as much as he was very clearly out of his depth, something told him she wouldn't want that. He was sure if he allowed the voice to keep talking, it would say she wouldn't want *him* there either, but that was a problem for another day.

With all the gentleness his spiraling mind could muster, he helped Claudia to stand. He got her coat and scarf off the rack, draping both over his arm. He found her purse in the bottom drawer of her desk. He gave it a quick shake, searching for the telltale rattle of her keys. Satisfied he had the essentials, he tucked Claudia against his side and walked her down the hall. It was a listless set of stumbling steps, stopping when he stopped, moving when he moved.

Fuck. How was he supposed to get her to her car without being suspected of some kind of foul play? All the common areas were monitored. Anyone could plainly see the woman was barely moving under her own steam while he had all of her belongings in his possession. There was no way this looked reasonable. There was nothing for it; he'd do his best to explain if it came to it, but he needed to get her home.

No sooner had he gotten her in the elevator than the intercom crackled to life. "Mr. Yang? It's Ruben, head of security. Is everything alright?"

"No, actually. Ms. Pérez isn't feeling well and I'm trying to get her home."

The resulting silence didn't bode well, but the elevator didn't stop, and he didn't hear any emergency sirens. That was good, wasn't it? Logic and rational thought had taken a backseat to worry, now riding shotgun with panic.

The doors opened to two waiting security guards.

Ian held Claudia tighter, tucking her head into his chest, and faced them down. He would put himself between anyone who thought to separate them. He'd risk everything to protect her during this vulnerable time.

"Ruben sent us. He said we're to make ourselves useful to you in getting Ms. Pérez home safely and to ask if you want Ms. Sano to turn the lights on?" The young man's voice kicked up at the end as though he didn't quite understand the last part of the directive.

Understanding flooded Ian's system. If he wasn't so consumed with keeping Claudia upright, he might have collapsed from the relief of it. Ruben must have experienced this in the past and had called Junior to help. It didn't make him feel better to know this was a recurring episode, but knowing Claudia had people watching out for her, that they'd created their own support system to protect her, gave him a small amount of peace.

"Yes, thank you." He unloaded the bundle of her coat and scarf into the one man's arms and wriggled her purse off his wrist and piled it on top. With his arms free and the support of the other two men, Ian lifted Claudia in his arms, bride style, and started for her car. Luckily, the car unlocked when it sensed the fob nearby, so no one had to rifle through her purse. Ian strapped her into the passenger seat, closing the door as quietly as he could manage while her belongings were placed in the back seat. Ian took a couple of deep breaths and made his way around to the driver's side, having come to a decision. He could do this.

He had to do this.

"Please let Ruben know that I'll turn the lights on. Ms. Sano can confirm in the morning."

He watched as the older of the two men relayed his message via walkie and heard Ruben's chirped "Copy that" reply.

That settled, he got in her car, adjusted the seat and the mirrors, and started for her place. By the time they arrived, between his nerves and the snowy, icy streets, he was so tense and unsettled, the muscles in his hands were cramped from squeezing the steering wheel. Claudia sat there, the same vacant look staring back at him. If it weren't for the motion of the car jostling her body, she'd have remained exactly as he'd placed her.

Once they were inside, things were slightly less urgent but he was still strung tight with worry; it almost paralyzed him. Should he set her on the couch or straight to bed? She was a nighttime bather but was obviously in no condition to be left alone in the shower. Tea! He could make her a big mug of tea, but what if she wasn't... aware enough to go to the bathroom and she soiled herself? She'd be horrified.

He stood with her in his arms in the foyer with his thoughts piling on top of each other, creating a logjam of indecision.

"Snap out of it, Yang." He muttered to himself.

Putting one foot in front of the other, he laid Claudia on the couch. He watched, rapt, as she curled in on herself. It was more movement than he'd seen since he found her in her office. "Claudia?" Nothing. He lowered himself to the couch and ran his hand gently along her face. "Claudia?" He spoke so softly so as not to startle her. "I'm going to lock things up, okay? I'll be right back."

She didn't respond, didn't indicate that she'd heard him, so he pressed a kiss to her temple and hurried back out to her car.

Not concerning himself with more than retrieving her belongings and making sure everything was locked as it should be, Ian hurried back into her condo and kicked off his own coat and shoes and set the entire handful of her coat, scarf, and purse in a pile on top.

"Okay, Gossipika," he said as he lifted her off the couch. "Let's get ready for bed."

Ian proceeded to narrate every action he took, explaining everything from why they had to have a shower but couldn't brush their teeth to how convenient it was to have his soft pants left behind from their spa day. He was quick and efficient and took pains to care for her body as best he could without her participation or input.

He kept talking as he carried her to bed and tucked her in, pulling her flush to his side. He ran his hands in a continuous, soothing motion along her body, up and down, while he let his lips linger on her forehead as he tried to gather the fracturing pieces of his sanity.

"Have you read much James Baldwin? We've never talked about it." Ian asked conversationally, in this troublingly one-sided exchange. "I've always been fascinated by him. By everything he was, the legacy he left. I devoured anything I could about him. Interviews, biographies, his fiction, and his non-fiction. He was a complicated contradiction."

He held her closer, shifting her so that she wasn't resting the entirety of her weight on her one arm.

"His quote about being a conscious Negro reminds me of you. Do you know it?" He didn't expect an answer, but he still waited on the off chance one would come. "It goes, *'To be a Negro in this country and to be relatively conscious is to be in a state of rage almost, almost all of the time.'* Sound familiar? He goes on to say, *'And part of the rage is this: It isn't only what is happening to you. But it's what's happening all around you and all of the time in the face of the most extraordinary and criminal indifference'.*"

He tucked a stray curl behind her ear, watching for any kind of reaction.

"It's the indifference that hurts you the most, isn't it? I try my best to fight against it, to focus myself on one thing I can do consistently and well so I don't burn myself out. But that doesn't work for you, does it, my ferocious little warrior?" Ian started to gently rock her as he spoke into the quiet of her room, clinging to the hope he was speaking into the tumult of her mind, "You throw your whole self into the fight day after day. But it's okay to rest now and then. It's okay to breathe."

Ian took his own advice and focused on his breathing. His bloodstream was still spiked with adrenaline, his heart was beating erratically in his chest. Pressing a kiss on the top of her head, he continued, "But you know that, don't you? It's why you have those reminders inked into your skin."

Still nothing.

"I don't know which battle you were fighting, but you aren't defeated, okay? You can retreat and regroup, but you're still in this fight—they haven't won, they haven't beaten you." Ian swallowed thickly, his throat tight. "I'm going to wait right here for you to come back, Claudia," he vowed, his voice cracking as the tears he'd been fighting finally spilled down his face. "I love you. I love you, and I'm not going anywhere, okay? So take as long as you need because I'll be here waiting for you to come back. Please," he sobbed, holding her limp body to his chest. "You have to come back to me."

Ian continued to talk to her, bargaining and cajoling, in hopes his voice would act like a beacon she could follow out of the emptiness and into animated consciousness. He made offers and bets and promises and repeatedly told her how much he loved her. He talked and talked, and when his voice went dry, he whispered his words to her between kisses and caresses. Even as he fought against sleep, the exhaustion of the day catching up to him, he persisted until he drifted off mid-sentence with his mouth on her temple.

Chapter Thirty-Three

Claudia's body shifting beside him roused him from his sleep. She might as well have blared an air horn for the way Ian's body reacted to the small movement. He had no idea how much time had passed, but the pins and needles tingling in his arm, and the crick in his neck, said it had to be at least a couple of hours.

Moving as gently as possible so as not to rouse her further, he slid down on the pillow so they were face-to-face in the darkness of her bedroom. He inhaled the crisp night air coming through the bit of window Claudia maniacally insisted on keeping open. Snow didn't have a smell the way rain did, but it had a sound, and Ian let the familiar scrape-and-crunch of a sidewalk being shoveled lull his racing heart.

He scanned her face, wondering what was happening in her chaotic mind. Would she remember what happened? Was she aware that she'd disassociated? She'd told him bits, here and there, about her mental health journey. He'd understood it was something she'd been dealing with since childhood, something that affected her relationship with her mother and family members. Was this what they worried about? Claudia, somewhere, vulnerable and unable to help herself?

If that was the case, Ian couldn't say he blamed them.

His breath caught in his throat as Claudia's eyes started to move rapidly behind her lids. Slowly, as if to torture him, her eyes fluttered open.

"Hey," he whispered as she groggily took in her surroundings. "Welcome back."

She shifted warily, her eyes taking in everything from his presence in her bed to the length of the shadows on the wall cast from the streetlight below. His pufferfish was back, and he'd never known such bittersweet relief.

"How do you feel?" Ian let her settle herself on the other pillow. Her autonomous movement mattered more than her proximity to him.

Claudia's words were low and cautious. "You brought me home?"

Ian nodded. She obviously understood her last known location was her office. That was a good sign, right?

Whatever calculus she was doing had produced an answer because she slumped back on her pillow and exhaled a frustrated "Fuck!" to the ceiling.

Slowly, gently, Ian reached across the quilted patches of her weighted blanket and rested his hand next to hers. When she held it, tangling her small hand with his, he gave it a squeeze and let his jaw unclench. The message that the immediate threat had passed hadn't made it to the tension in his muscles, but at least he could take a full breath again, knowing she was safe.

"Do you want to tell me what happened?" His thumb made circles on her hand, though he couldn't say who the gesture was supposed to be soothing.

"I failed."

"What are you talking about?"

"I... I thought I had it."

Ian listened as she recounted the last six months of work, and it was worse than he thought. This wasn't her failure. This wasn't something she'd attempted and gotten wrong. This was society's failure. Society had collectively turned a blind eye to craven greed, and it had broken her heart. His poor, fearsome pufferfish wasn't a victim of her own high standards. This episode hadn't been caused by her biting off more than she could chew. Ian was faced with the brutal reality: her stability wasn't based solely on any action of Claudia's; it could also be affected by the world's inability to do better.

He held her close as she cried for the lost lives, for the destroyed communities, and for the soulless greed that would continue to reign terror and destruction on the world unabated because their money shielded them from consequences.

He held her as his own heart broke. Ian didn't believe in a specific afterlife, didn't think it mattered which gods held your allegiance, so long as your intentions were good. When things like this happened, when they kept happening, he felt the initial shock. He looked to community leaders for best practices, for ways his compassion and empathy should adjust his behaviors for the better, and tried his best to put more into the world than he took out.

Claudia's moral compass demanded justice and consequences. For all her nihilistic grumbling, Ian knew she raged the way she did *because* she felt so much. It was a miracle she made it through each day, that she managed to eat and think and function, with her tender heart so close to the surface.

"Shhh..." he soothed. "I know it sucks, and I know you're disappointed. I am, too. But you didn't fail."

He wondered if her clients knew how much of herself she gave to the fight of securing them some type of financial freedom. He doubted it.

"Your clients are safe, Claudia," he pressed a kiss to the side of her head. "You've made it so they can lay their heads down at night with clearer consciences. None of their money is tied to these atrocities. You did that."

She clung to him, her face buried in his chest, as her sobs died down.

When he was sure she was able to hear him, he continued, "Those monsters didn't get what they deserved, but you won. You saw what was happening and you did something about it. You took that money out of their hands and put it somewhere worthy."

Her nodded acceptance didn't take the sting out of her mumbled, "It still hurts."

"I know. But it won't last forever. Nothing lasts forever, not even the bad things."

She gasped and raised herself up on his chest so she could see his face in the scant light. "You figured it out!"

"I did." His smile, the first one since he stepped into her office, hurt his face. "It took me a minute, but then I figured it out. Braille. In Spanish." He kissed her smirking mouth. "So sneaky."

She kissed him. Her lips were salty as they explored his. They lost themselves to the pleasure, letting the moment stretch and swell.

"Thank you, Sunny."

He furrowed his brow, still breathless and dizzy from the kiss. "For what?"

"For being there. For helping me." Her breath caught as though she wasn't sure how to get the next words out. "For staying."

He cupped her face, bringing his mouth to hers. With their noses touching and eyes locked on each other, he said, "You don't ever have to thank me for that, Claudia. Not ever."

Her shallow nod and visible swallow were all the acceptance he needed. He settled them into the bed and held her until she fell asleep, no more words needing to be said.

When Ian was jolted awake for the second time, Claudia's gasp as she sat bolt upright was the cause. The sound of keys in her door sounded like cannon fire in the silence of her home.

"Shh," Ian soothed, "It's Junior. Ruben asked if he should call her to come help, but I said she should wait until the morning." He checked his watch. "7am. Seems she took it literally."

Claudia pressed her face into the pillow and groaned. She didn't seem upset so much as annoyed, the kind of irritation only loved ones could inspire.

"She's worried." Ian whispered, pressing kisses to the side of her face.

"I know." She peeked out from her cocoon and rolled her eyes. Then, with a devilish smile added, "I suppose we should be grateful she didn't show up at 5. I'll have to send Davis something to thank him for the assist."

Chuckling, Ian pulled her to him for a kiss. "Go get cleaned up. I'll buy you some time. Take as long as you need."

Ian got out of bed and pulled a shirt on as he made his way downstairs. He was going to hold Junior off until Claudia was ready, then he was going to do everything he could to support her. He'd read any article, speak to any professional, study any text—whatever it took, so he'd be prepared.

The bitter taste of bile from his earlier helplessness still coated the back of his tongue. He had committed himself to taking care of her, to having her back, and when she needed him the most, he choked. He'd been slow. His panic and worry had made him sloppy. Inefficient.

Because he hadn't understood. But he did now.

Ian vowed to redouble his efforts. Claudia needed soft hands, but she also needed strong shoulders to lean on when her own burdens were too much. He would be better about reading the signs. He would plan for any eventuality.

He would be ready the next time.

Chapter Thirty-Four

I t had been...tense waking up from an episode to find Ian there.
It wasn't the first time she'd woken up with someone watching her, but it was the first time she'd felt protected. It wasn't her mother's fretting or her sister's worry that felt oppressive and exhausting, nor was it her abuela's pleased certainty that prayers had done the trick. She preferred the disorienting fogginess of emerging alone to either of those.

Ian's simple care for her, for how she felt as she came back to the reality she'd run from, was so foreign, so different from everything she'd experienced up to that point, she didn't know what else to do except pour her broken-hearted guts out in the darkness of her bedroom.

Even Junior's compassionate indifference didn't garner such a reaction.

She'd been nervous, hesitant, about what it would mean for their relationship, but he had been so accepting, so *Ian*, she could almost believe she'd imagined the entire thing.

Claudia was generally distrustful by nature. Her anxiety thrived on pointing out patterns and likely outcomes. Even a week later, Ian's regular behavior hadn't convinced Anxiety the other shoe wasn't waiting to drop.

She pushed the thought out of her head as best she could and made her way to the kitchen.

"What's wrong?"

Ian was at the sink cleaning up from breakfast. Brunch, maybe? It was later than Claudia usually broke her fast, but it was the first time Ian had stayed the night—she wasn't counting that night. She was doing everything she could to pretend that night had never happened—and she wanted to commemorate it. Except, of course, waking up with Ian in her bed was a recipe for distraction. So, now here she was with the beginnings of a headache.

"Nothing," she said as she grabbed some ibuprofen from the cupboard and a glass. Passing him on her way to the fridge, she placed a quick kiss on his shoulder blade on her way to the fridge for some juice. "Just a headache I'm hoping to stave off before it gets worse."

"Should you be taking those? With grapefruit juice?"

"I like grapefruit juice." She wasn't sure if he knew that, if they'd had occasion to discuss it. They must have at this point, right? But here he was, questioning her juice choices, so maybe not.

"Neither mix well with antidepressants. Together they could be problematic." He was watching her as though she were about to do a shot of ammonia with a bleach chaser, as though she couldn't manage the simple task of swallowing pain relievers without supervision.

"I beg your pardon?"

Ian obviously missed the warning in her voice because he continued, "I've been doing some reading. There are lots of everyday things that counteract their effectiveness, people don't even realize."

And there it was. The thing she'd been dreading. The kind of *concern* she'd been trying to avoid.

"Thank goodness you were here to protect me from myself. Who knows what kind of damage I might have caused left on my own for *eleven years*?"

This was the part she hated more than all the rest. Yes, she struggled; yes, her mental health was a factor; yes, it could be debilitating at times; but for the fucking love of common sense, did people think she woke up every morning with all prior knowledge and coping mechanisms erased from her memory? Why was it the default to treat her like she had no idea how to take care of herself, like she hadn't been managing her life with her specific strengths and weaknesses for literal decades?

This, from Ian, hurt the most.

Ian, who she'd confided in about these things, who hadn't treated her any differently, only like the complex woman she was as a result. Now he'd turned into one of them who reduced her to her anxiety and wanted to sit her in a corner covered in bubble wrap. It was all so tedious.

Tedious and disappointing.

Of all the things EvilCorp had done, the fallout of their avarice now included stealing this from her, too.

"Claudia..." He trailed off, still leaning on the counter, arms crossed, as he tried to parse the shift in her tone.

"For your information, Ian, I'm well aware of the drugs that don't mix well with my meds. I also know that grapefruit isn't great for any medication. It's not great for most things, if you're keeping score. Luckily for me, it's not a factor."

"You stopped taking your meds?"

His horrified gasp snapped the last of her tether. She let out a string of Spanglish curses that would have impressed her father and scandalized her mother. "No, I didn't stop taking them. Not that it's any of your business!"

"But—"

"But nothing!" She shouted over him. "But nothing! I don't need a keeper. I don't need you tiptoeing about like I'm a landmine you need to navigate around. If you've suddenly forgotten, I've been here, surviving, on my own, long before you showed up, and I'll continue even after you leave!"

She was overreacting, she knew, but she was so tired of this. So tired of being made to feel like a burden. She couldn't deal with it from Ian. It was too upsetting.

"Why are you being like this? I'm trying to help. I want to be able to support you during your next episode."

"My next *episode*?" She hissed.

"I didn't mean it like that," he sighed, shoulders slumping.

"Then how did you mean it?"

It seemed Ian had lost control of his tether, too, because now he was yelling, arms flying out from his side. "I walked into your office, and you were gone, Claudia! Gone!" His voice cracked, but he kept going. "I didn't know what was happening or how to help you. It was fucking terrifying. I never want to feel like that again!"

Anxiety lifted a smug brow at the sound of the other shoe finally dropping.

Everything in her went still as she absorbed the blow. Claudia couldn't hear anything over the sound of her heart breaking.

"Then don't." Her voice came out flat. A huge contrast to the rioting emotions she was feeling.

"Don't what?"

"No one is forcing you to be here. You're free to go at any time."

His manic laughter and incredulous words barely registered over the rising sound of static in her ears. "Are you seriously suggesting we break up? Is that what you're saying?"

"You don't want to feel like that again? Then go. Now. While you're free of my 'fits'."

"Goddammit, Claudia, that's not what I meant and you fucking know that!"

"Do I?"

"Yes, you fucking do!" He snarled. "I have checked in on how you sleep, how much you've eaten, whether one of the many vessels on your desk each night was for water. I have been 'your keeper' for months. Why is it suddenly a problem now?"

She huffed an impatient, scornful noise.

"Because you're deciding how I feel. Again."

"No!"

"Yes! Yes, you are and I want you to fucking quit it!"

"Well, I want you to leave!"

Ian hung his head and pinched the bridge of his nose. "Don't do this, Claudia. Please." He pressed his palms together, his eyes flooded with emotion. "I love you!"

She flinched, as though the words had physical weight. "Don't!"

Claudia couldn't deal with his declaration, couldn't process the implications of it. Not with Anxiety goading her with all the reasons such a thing was impossible and Embarrassment, who had been waiting impatiently in the wings for its cue, finally letting the words she'd been dreading fly. Even Rage added a little something to the racket, condemning Ian for bringing it up now, like this.

She was starting to feel sweaty and short of breath. Her riotous thoughts made it hard to focus. The constant barrage of every awful thing she'd ever thought, every failure, every disappointment made her feel loose at the seams. After everything, there was no way she'd allow Ian to see her unravel. Not when Embarrassment was still stomping around reminding her of what he'd already witnessed and Anxiety promising he'd never look at her the same way ever again as a result.

"What do you mean, 'don't'?"

"It's not what I want." She said, cruelly lying right to his face.

"It's not?" Ian was equally caustic. "Do you even know what you want?"

Now she was truly done with this conversation. She was done feeling like she was a problem to be solved. Tired of attempting palatable. She didn't want to be tolerated; she didn't want to be suffered. What Claudia wanted was to stick in the throats of every single person who crossed her.

"I do, actually!" She started pacing as she spoke. "I want a single member of government, at any level, to prioritize the people instead of corporations. I want bigots to get punched in the teeth, early and often. I want the bloated police budgets reallocated to community programming. I want churches to pay taxes." She'd crossed the short distance from her kitchen to her front door and opened it, the cold bolstering her actions. "And I want you, Ian Yang—with your sunshine and rainbow bears—to *leave*."

"You're making a mistake," he warned, his voice tight with emotions she didn't want to examine.

"Add it to the list!" She shot back, full of belligerent bravado.

She stood there defiantly while he stared at her. He could search her face all he wanted; it changed nothing.

Sighing his resignation, Ian stuffed his feet in his boots, snatched his coat off the rack, and stormed out.

The door hadn't fully closed before all the fight left her, and she crumpled to the ground, heartsick. She'd lost him. She'd lost the funny, caring, interested man who saw the reality of her life.

She was back to being alone. And for the first time in as long as she could remember, Claudia was not looking forward to the solitude.

CLAUDIA FINISHED PUTTING THE LAST of the groceries away and realized she'd been zoned out the entire time.

She tried to remember the last couple of hours, but it was spotty. She remembered parking her car but not driving to the grocery store. She remembered being in the aisles but not paying. She remembered walking in with bags but not unlocking the door to let herself in. It was disconcerting but not entirely unexpected.

Claudia was numb.

This wasn't the usual void she sometimes fell in, the kind Ian had nursed her through, where she couldn't break through the proverbial surface of her thoughts. Those episodes were akin to being trapped in a crowded room, unable to be heard when she called for help. It was like being paralyzed. This was different. She felt... haunted.

When Claudia was ten, she and her siblings, along with some of the neighbor kids, snuck into a construction site on their bikes. They ducked under the chain meant to prevent their entry, granting them unfettered access to the lot where they created a fanciful world vanquishing evil with their weapons atop their mighty steeds. Claudia had found herself at the top of a gravel hill and somehow got it in her head to race her bike down its slope. The exhilaration she felt, the g-forces in her belly, the wind in her face, was unparalleled. She was laughing and shouting her joy until the moment her tire hit a rock and sent her flying over the handlebars. By the time she rolled to a stop at the bottom of the hill, she was scraped and bloodied and had swallowed her loose tooth.

Her relationship with Ian was like that day at the construction site. A wild, intoxicating thrill that ended in a sharp, unforgettable pain.

The realization changed the abject nothing to a stinging burn, like the road rash from wiping out on her bike. Ian, open and curious and genuinely delighted by the world around him, wasn't cut from her same cynical cloth. She would keep pressing on the pain of that bruise as many times as necessary to get the message through her thick skull.

Ian was gone. She'd sent him away, and while she knew it was for the best, she hated knowing he'd seen her at her worst. That he'd live the rest of his life with the memory of her sitting listlessly at her desk. That he'd had to carry her home and tuck her in like a child.

It didn't matter. What was done was done. She'd simply find a way to move on. To face him during the day without the flames of her embarrassment crumbling her to ash.

A furious pounding on her door stopped her from getting too far into her spiral.

Heart racing, she took a cursory look around. A reflexive action from her youth borne from her mother's constant fretting about having 'her depression' strewn about. She gave her head a shake to clear her thoughts. She wasn't a child. She was a grown woman in her own home.

Another round of what could only peripherally be considered knocking echoed through her quiet space. The security screen mounted on the wall in her foyer showed an irate Ian staring right at her.

Taking a minute to compose herself, Claudia tried to regulate her heart's frantic rhythm.

"It's okay," she promised herself, anxiously rubbing her palms on her thighs, "you've got this."

She opened the door and was forced back a step by the intensity of his stare. It had been a long time since Ian looked at her from behind his mask of reserved indifference. She hated it. She missed his goofy grin and the way his eyes danced with amusement for every little thing she did. Even still, in his indigo shearling-lined parka and baggy jeans stuffed haphazardly into his boots, he was the most handsome man she'd ever seen.

"You owe me 90 minutes, Claudia." He said in lieu of a greeting. "Let's go."

"Ian..." She thought she'd said everything she had to say to him. She wasn't ready to face him, had no idea what was left to discuss. "Ian, please."

He tilted at the waist so he was nose-to-nose with her. Despite the cold air whipping around them, she still felt the heat radiating off him.

Everything in her body reached for him. The memory of his spicy aftershave, his always too hot skin, and his fierce gaze were all working together to dare her body to ignore him. Too bad it wasn't her body that needed convincing. Her broken heart and battered pride were the ones holding the line.

"You think you're the only one who's angry? You think I don't feel rage?" His scratchy voice was low and tight. "I waited. I gave you your space. It didn't work. So go put on one of your fancy outside outfits. Or don't. I don't give a fuck. You owe me 90 minutes." His hard stare froze her in place. "Get in the goddamned car, Claudia."

Sure enough, his car was idling at the curb in front of her door directly underneath the 'no stopping' sign.

He stood to his full height, and Claudia was mesmerized by the way the muscles in his jaw worked, flexing and bunching. He'd never spoken to her that way before, and she didn't know how to take it. Any other man at any other time would have been told to fuck his dickhole with his demands before the door slammed on him.

But this man at this time…his devastation, like hers, was etched in the planes of his face.

"Right now." Ian's eyes were lit with his fury, and, after everything, she felt like she owed him this much. Especially since she knew it wasn't his rage calling to hers that she needed to fear.

Looking down, she was in a pair of warm leggings and an oversized cashmere cowl neck sweater. She was dressed appropriately for almost any scenario. Seeing as it was just after noon, she couldn't imagine where he'd be taking her, but before her brain did its usual song and dance about leaving the house, she was pushing her feet into her heeled boots, grabbing her coat, scarf, keys, and phone, and following him out the door. Apparently her body had wrested control and was willing to follow wherever Ian led.

Even rigid with temper, Ian held the car door for her. He made his way to the driver's side and, after buckling his seatbelt, set the heat controls and cracked the window the way she liked without saying a word. His care, his steady concern for her comfort, had always been a tacit responsibility he committed to with eager resolve. The misery of missing something she'd never known she'd gone without, something she would never have again, caused a sharp stabbing sensation in her sides.

They made their way slowly east along Dundas. Every time she thought to ask where they were going, his forbidding profile dried the words on her tongue. Being this close to him while the gulf of their separation yawned endlessly between them was a wretched punishment. It made her think of all those retro shows where the parents caught their kid with a cigarette and made them chain-smoke an entire pack to discipline them out of the act.

She could be forced to smoke entire cartons, and it wouldn't be enough to make her not want this man.

Eventually, he pulled into a parking lot at the top of Alma's street that looked abandoned, for all that it was a block east of Carlaw in the heart of the trendy and desirable Leslieville neighborhood. Leigh's bakery was only a couple of blocks west on Gerrard. Between her cousin and her friend, she felt her odds were good of finding a soft place to land should she need it. It gave her a small amount of comfort to have an exit strategy. She wasn't afraid of Ian, but old habits died hard. Her anxiety demanded she always be able to make a quick getaway, should it become necessary. Especially since she still had no idea where they were going.

Silently, he gestured for her to follow, staying close in case she slipped on the icy concrete but not touching her either. When they got to the corner, Claudia figured out their destination.

"Ian, please..." Of all the things Claudia didn't want to do, seeing any sort of performance at the Crow's theater was high on the list.

When the light turned green, he grunted, "Let's go," and crossed the street.

They made their way to a different entrance where Ian had a brief exchange with one of the staff, who moved aside to let them in. Knowing Ian, it was just as likely he'd befriended a stranger over some Tiny Tom's donuts at the CNE once upon a time and was now calling in a favor as any other explanation for why they were using this entrance.

They walked the couple steps down a wide, well-lit hallway to another set of doors that opened onto the stage. She startled a little when she realized the actors were essentially in place waiting for the curtain to open. They didn't seem nearly as disturbed by her as she was by them. There was no time to dwell on it—she was led through the backstage area down the aisle in a matter of moments.

Claudia, usually sharp and keenly aware of her surroundings, stumbled to her seat beside Ian just as the house lights lowered. Even with all the confusion and secret passages, once the play got going, it didn't take long for her to figure out Ian had brought her to see Medea.

As uncomfortable as she was in the situation, she appreciated the way the playwright stayed true to the original Greek tragedy while deftly modernizing its themes of betrayal, revenge, and ambition. The original play had a minimal cast and was largely centered around the main Medea character, which this production upheld.

Medea was played by a pretty white woman with dark, curly hair and blue eyes that were so pale they seemed silver. She wore a shimmering champagne-colored slip dress of gauzy, layered silk. The exaggeratedly feminine look—her big, bouncy curls falling around her shoulders and delicate costume swishing invitingly over her form—was a stark contrast to the hardened savagery of her character. She was captivating as she snarled and stalked and raged from one end of the stage to the other.

She poured her fury out, making the audience complicit in the crimes against her—convincing everyone in attendance that they, too, would receive her vengeance just as soon as she was done with her faithless husband.

Claudia not only understood Medea's judgment of them, she welcomed it.

She was so taken with the performances that the sound of a lone oboe surprised her. Judging by the reactions of her fellow patrons, they also weren't expecting Medea to be moved to song. It was a haunting, bile-spilling number of lament and regret and the inevitability of consequence. Even as she cried for the loss of her two sons, whose lives were cut short by her own hand, she remained steadfast and unapologetic about the punishment she intended to mete out. The repercussions she'd been *forced* to mete out.

The justice she would not be denied.

It was all too close; she started to feel singled out, like the patrons sitting around her could sense her failures. Why hadn't she fought harder, they demanded. Why hadn't she delivered justice?

There was too much emotion, too much unresolved in her own life; she simply couldn't stand it anymore.

Looking around, Claudia found the door closest to her. She had no idea where it led, no idea if she was entering prohibited space. All she knew was it wasn't marked as an emergency exit and therefore was her path to freedom. Without thinking twice, she was out of her seat and through the door. Before she could make it through the next set of doors, Ian grabbed her shoulders and hauled her into the light lock.

Wrapped in the familiar warmth of his embrace, all the confusion, frustration, and longing came pouring out, breaking the floodgates in the small transition space between the lobby and the auditorium.

"You think you're special because you're angry, but being angry doesn't make you special at all." Ian's voice was low despite the criticism in his words. "Lots of people are angry, Claudia. Lots of people struggle. You don't have some rare affliction. You aren't an oddity."

She clung to him as her tears soaked his clothes. She didn't have the breath to beg him to stop, to let her go. She missed him too much to spare herself this torture.

"There are people all over who see the world the way you do, doing what they can to make a difference. Some people make art to comfort or inspire. Some people are on the ground organizing in their communities. Others are waging small acts of rebellion where they can. People are fighting every day in all sorts of ways, Claudia." He pressed a kiss on the top of her head, and she was grateful she couldn't feel it. "It's your compassion and your fearlessness and your willingness to keep fighting that make you special! This isn't something you have to tackle on your own. You don't have to be alone."

God, she loved him. And because she loved him, she couldn't think of a worse, more selfish thing than to sentence him to a life with her instability. No, Ian deserved joy and laughter. He deserved someone who could stop and smell the flowers and appreciate them for the beautiful bits of nature they were instead of someone like her who couldn't see past the ecological damage the potential extinction of bees would bring.

And what did she deserve?

Up until that moment, Claudia hadn't given it any real consideration. She'd lived her adult life convinced she'd found the best version of fulfillment available to her. She had a single handful of friends she trusted implicitly—two of whom she could probably harvest organs from in a pinch—satisfying, if insubstantial, hookups when the mood struck, and a career she was proud of and challenged by.

A man like Ian was beyond her wildest imaginings. She needed to make him understand the truth. She would suffer this heartache a hundred times before seeing the light in his eyes fade to regret. Or worse, resentment.

"It doesn't work for me, okay? I've tried it. I've *tried*!" The words felt like they were mined from her very marrow, leaving a burning trail from her esophagus to the pit of her stomach. "I have nothing new to say, nothing different about my progress. I breathe, and I visualize, and I write in the fucking journals, and it doesn't matter! Nothing changes. I still wake up every day and force myself through the front door."

She hoped their heated whispers didn't carry. She didn't want to disturb the theatergoers more than she already had, but her hold on her composure was fraying.

"But that's just it, Claudia. You keep walking through the door!" He ran his hands up and down her back, trying to calm her. "Just because your joy doesn't look like giddy acceptance doesn't mean you're wrong or broken. Doesn't mean you don't have it. Joy is not about ease; it is the refusal to break. If you can still have hope for more, for better, then you're still in the fight. You're still a threat."

He cradled her head in his hands and stared intently down at her. His every emotion was there for her to see.

"It hurts because you give a shit what happens. You care enough to keep fighting. And I'm telling you I will be there, right beside you, to clean your wounds and hold you close and give you whatever you need so you *can*!"

How dare he? How dare he dangle such an impossible offer, knowing what it would do to her when it came crashing down around them?

It was so typically Ian. Looking at the bright side, thinking of the best without concern or consideration for the very real downsides. His sunshiny optimism had no place here.

"No." It was resolute and final. The last thing she wanted was to be another obligation weighing him down.

The man lacked all sense of self-preservation. If he wasn't willing to avoid this head-on collision, she'd have to do it for him. She'd have to love him enough to protect him from himself.

"Claudia, I–"

"Don't!" She hissed, stepping away from him. "It's over."

The door to the lobby opened behind them, flooding the small alcove with light. Taking the opportunity, she ducked around the startled staffer and headed out the front door, away from the promises Ian made.

Chapter Thirty-Five

Ian chased her out of the theater. Unwilling to barrel over a small group of elderly ladies, Ian let them pass, convinced she could only go so far in those shoes in this weather. Too bad for him, she was already across the street, and the lights had changed by the time he'd made it to the corner.

He considered going after her, but all their things were still in the seats from when she'd run off. Reluctantly, Ian returned to the playhouse, the lobby now crowded with people exiting the auditorium. After a brief bit of explaining to one of the ushers, he was allowed back in to get their few abandoned belongings, and, not knowing what else to do, Ian slumped in the chair and hung his head in his hands.

He'd done everything he could think of to convince her that he loved her, that her episode hadn't changed anything, yet still she'd run from him.

His heart had already broken. It had shattered eight days ago. All that was left was for the last few pieces to fall now that they were no longer being suspended by hope.

He must have made a miserable sight since the staff seemed to be giving him a wide berth. He had no idea how long this grace would last, but he was grateful for the reprieve all the same.

Where was Claudia going? Was she safe? Did she have cards or ID to get home? Should he have chased her down the street like a madman? He thought perhaps he should have. He could have bought another coat. He would buy twelve more if it meant he could get Claudia to stay and listen to him.

He felt someone standing over him and figured his time must be up. With a weary sigh, he said, "I'm sorry. I'm leaving now."

"Don't rush out on my account."

Though it hadn't been so long since he'd last heard the deep, flirty voice, he would know her face anywhere.

"Junior? What are you doing here? Is Claudia with you?" He looked around frantically but they were the only ones in the auditorium.

"She's safe at Alma's."

"Alma's?"

"Yeah, she lives just over on Boston between a DJ and a publicist." She answered his unasked question with a simple, "I happened to be in the neighborhood at my favorite bookstore bakeshop. I've been tasked with collecting her things." Junior gave a meaningful glance at the piles of fabric Ian held in his death grip.

He was a little relieved to know that she was somewhere safe and warm even if his lungs still weren't working to their proper capacity.

"You mind?" She gestured at the seat beside him and he shook his head mutely. "Do you know how your parents ended up working with mine?"

Ian was both stunned by the direction of the conversation and amused at her use of the word 'with' as though their parents were collaborators.

Obviously not requiring his input, Junior continued, "One of your siblings broke their arm in five places. My mom was their surgeon. Your mom, relieved and reassured by my mom, got to talking. She told her about how she met her husband working at the Mariposa hotel in Georgetown. How, when they came to Canada, they thought to make a go of all the experience they'd gained in service."

Ian knew this story. All of his siblings did. Their mother, a young, hardworking chambermaid—prettier than all the others—caught the eye of the handsome, reserved maintenance worker. They dated, got pregnant, then got married. His dad's brother sent for them, and they uprooted themselves and their young son for a new life in Canada.

Junior was telling the story the way he would, with a familiarity born from repetition. "Apparently, they'd hit it off over the many appointments, and my mom took it upon herself to champion your mom, suggesting her services to people and so on."

He didn't want to be rude, but he had no idea what was happening. Why was she telling him all this? "Junior, I–"

"The thing is, we never had cleaners when I was a kid. Like, ever. So imagine my surprise when my mom was promoting your mom's business amongst her peers and I still had to wake up to mop the floors every Saturday." She gave a rueful shake of her head that he figured must be at least 43% genuine. "Anyway, I bring it up to tell you that our moms might not be friends, per se, but they have a deep respect and affinity for each other. It's impressive because my mother, like her mother before her, doesn't trust easily—she doesn't let people in. In that way, she's always had more in common with her niece than her daughter."

She spoke with her hands the way Claudia did. It was probably a family trait. Junior and Claudia, so similar and yet so different. The large green gemstone glinting in the auditorium's light, made

Ian briefly wonder about the hurdles Davis might've had to jump to win her.

"You seem like you're pretty discerning."

Her laugh was a husky, throaty thing that coaxed the first semblance of merriment from him in eight days. "It's a skill I had to hone and cultivate. Claudia has always had a finely tuned bullshit detector."

"She said you had similar issues growing up."

Junior's expression was pensive. "They only looked similar from the outside. I was a desperately lonely kid that had to learn who and how to trust. Claudia spent a lot of time alone, but she's never been lonely a day in her life."

Ian made a face. He didn't want to argue with her, but surely everyone has experienced a bit of loneliness at some point in their lives. She must have seen his disagreement on his face because she raised an expectant brow that was so like Claudia, he had to blink to clear the image from his mind.

"Alone is neutral. You are not with others; therefore, you are alone." Ian nodded his understanding. "Loneliness is about connection, about feeling disconnected. But imagine being four years old with a sneering distrust you can't vocalize, incapable of 'going along to get along'. Imagine trying to explain not wanting what everyone seems to take for granted. Disconnected was a reprieve. Being alone was always easier for her."

He nodded.

Empirically, he understood what Junior was saying, he even believed a lot of it was true. He knew firsthand Claudia spent a lot of time by herself and didn't seem to struggle with it and, in fact, needed the alone time to recharge and regroup. That didn't mean he believed she didn't want connection. Not when he'd witnessed her with her cousins. Not when he knew what it was like to sit in the quiet with her and feel at peace. Not after he'd been held rapt by her fiery gaze as they came apart, again and again, in each other's arms.

But he didn't want to think about all he was losing, and he certainly didn't want to argue with Junior, so instead Ian pictured a tiny Claudia, fists clenched in outrage, and let the flood of emotion warm him. "I bet she was adorable."

Junior gave him a long, assessing glance as though she were reading something written on his forehead. She declared her verdict with a simple, "I knew I liked you." She stood, putting her hand out for Claudia's things. "She'll come around. She just needs a minute."

Ian nodded dumbly. What else could he do? There was nothing he could say to change the fact that he was there with her cousin instead of her.

"Are you going to be okay to get home? Can I call you a car service or something?"

It was such an incredibly kind thing to say to him in this moment when he was positive nothing would be okay again.

"Thanks, I'm good."

She searched his eyes a bit before nodding her acceptance. She shifted the load in her arms and exited, leaving him to his misery.

And it was misery. He'd stewed in the fury of Claudia's rejection; he gnashed his teeth trying to make sense of how she could walk away from what was so obviously the best thing that had ever happened to him. Then he'd made his big play. He'd brought her here to show her that beauty could be found in the midst of anger, that rage wasn't an isolating state she needed to suffer alone.

He'd swung for the fences, but it wasn't enough.

Jonathan's words came back to him. *Trust her to know what she wants, even if it isn't you.* Why had he ever agreed with that lunatic? This pain, the loss of her, wasn't something he'd simply accept. How could he? His heart was squirreled away somewhere on Boston Avenue in Leslieville, surrounded by her fiercest and staunchest allies, where he couldn't access her.

Still.... Junior had said, 'wait', not 'leave'. Ian had no doubt in his mind that woman would have had him trussed and gagged in the back of a windowless panel van if she thought he posed the mildest of threats to Claudia. And though he hadn't had a lot of exposure to Alma, it wouldn't surprise him to learn his entire digital footprint could be wiped clean off the World Wide Web at her whim.

Ian took another moment to center himself. He gathered his shattered pieces as he resigned himself to the truth: He loved Claudia Regina Sano Pérez. He would wait as long as it took. He had absolutely nothing else to lose. There would be no one else, so either he was alone while he waited or he was alone with his memories. The end result was the same.

It was time to go.

This part, at least, was familiar. He would go home—alone and exhausted—and count the moments until it was time to see Claudia again.

Chapter Thirty-Six

Claudia banged on Alma's door, shivering and numb, willing her cousin to be home. She knew the code; everyone did—it was the last four digits of her childhood landline number. If anyone knew her then, or knew her mother now, as it was in tía Lovie's Instagram handle, they had full access to Alma's house. But as much as she had been desperate to get away from Ian, she didn't want to be alone.

"Claudia! Qué pasó?" Alma looked up and down the street trying to figure out what was wrong. "What are you doing here? Where's your coat?"

Claudia stumbled across the threshold and into her cousin's arms, sobbing.

"Shhh… dime, prima." Alma rubbed soothing circles on Claudia's back even though she was on high alert for whatever brought Claudia to her door in this state.

She couldn't pull a clear breath into her lungs. "He knows, Alma. He saw everything."

"Ian?"

Claudia could only hang on to Alma as though her life depended on it. And, she supposed, it did. She felt like she was adrift in the endless black of the Atlantic, the familiar yet mercurial ocean that battered its moodiness on the beautiful coastline of her mother's home in Bocas del Toro.

Her breaths were no less frantic but somehow she was able to access enough higher function for Alma to lead her into the house and set her on the couch without once letting go. Claudia burrowed into the familiar stability of Alma's soap-clean scent, her ginormous belly no obstacle to the safety she sought.

"He told me he loved me." She gasped in noisy hiccupping sobs, still too raw to process the implications of it all.

"That's good, no?" Alma's tone was gentle and cautious. Some small part in the back of Claudia's mind accepted that she was little more than a wild, feral thing. Alma was right to not make any sudden moves.

"No!"

Alma pulled the throw off the back of her couch, wrapping Claudia in the soft, thick fabric without saying another word.

What was there to say? This was a disaster. The worst part was knowing she had no one to blame but herself. She'd known from the very start Ian Yang wasn't for her. She'd known it was no use, and she'd let it happen anyway. She could lie to herself in a million different ways, tell herself it was because she had wanted to get the information for Junior to help Leigh, tell herself that she'd made a deal and had to honor it... tell herself anything other than the truth. She'd wanted Ian Yang from the moment she'd laid eyes on him and had been willing to do whatever it took to get close to him, no matter the cost.

Even when the cost was her broken heart.

Claudia's sobs had petered out to choked sniffles. Her tears had dried, but the pain in the very marrow of her was still raw.

Alma kept her wrapped in her soothing embrace as they sat in silence.

Eventually she was calm enough to speak. Her voice had lost all its strength. Claudia's throat was tight, but she was able to get the words out to explain to Alma what had happened. The lack of fallout from EvilCorp, her episode, Ian finding her in the dark of her office; how he cared for her until she came to the next morning.

"Él es una joya."

The scared, savage part of Claudia's heart curled protectively around the small, battered part that agreed with Alma. He was a gem.

"He was normal, you know? I woke up, and he asked me what happened. He joked about being on a watch list because Ruben was probably after him. Then when Junior burst in, he handled her like a pro. Seriously, Alma—I've never seen anyone stand up to her like that. No one."

"I'm sorry I missed it."

It wasn't really a laugh that sputtered out of Claudia; she was still in too much pain for humor. "Yeah, too bad it won't happen again. Junior was too stunned to react, or else I'm sure she'd have put a machete to his throat."

"Prima, none of this sounds like a bad thing. What happened?"

Claudia closed her eyes against the memory of their fallout. It was worse for the fact she'd known. She'd known things couldn't go on as they had, but she let herself believe otherwise. She allowed him to cloud her better judgment. Which was the biggest insult of them all.

Ian Yang made Claudia believe things could be different for her when she knew good and damn well they never would.

"I believed him, Alma. I believed I could have what everyone has." The hot sting of her shame brought fresh tears to her eyes.

She buried her face in the blanket and sobbed, "For the first time in my life, I let myself believe, and I was wrong."

Alma listened calmly while Claudia explained and railed and cried. When she'd run out of words and tears, Alma held her close, letting her wallow.

Claudia had no idea how much time had passed when the voices of Alma's menfolk broke the silence of the house.

"Mami!" Lalo came running to the couch, his toque still on. "Tia Chichi!"

Alma deftly gathered her son into her arms, peppering his face with kisses without dislodging Claudia. She really was the best of them, Claudia thought. The new baby was lucky to be getting Alma as a mom.

"Ay, Lalo, what's on your face?"

Before Alma got an answer, young Eduardo lunged forward and held Claudia's face in his cold little hands and gave her a sticky, toddler kiss.

"Gracias, Lalito." Claudia mustered a smile for the child's benefit. "I feel better now."

He babbled something at her from around his pacifier with a serious expression.

"Sí, mi amor," Alma answered, apparently fluent in this foreign dialect. "Her heart hurts."

Lalo smushed his little fist into her boob, in an approximation of where he thought her heart was. "Aquí?"

"Sí." She nodded. Since the child was taking it seriously, she decided to answer honestly. "Me duele tanto."

His face fell, eyes wide, pacifier tumbling as he let out a horrified little gasp. He wriggled out of Alma's arms and took off down the hall.

"What just happened?" Claudia's mouth was agape as she looked to Alma for answers.

"Give it a minute." Alma rubbed her belly, obviously very used to this reaction.

No sooner had she said it, Claudia heard Lalo's little feet thundering back toward them. He slammed into Claudia's legs, holding up a bandage with a little Black girl in pigtails and a white lab coat. She made a big show of accepting his offering and wrapped him in a hug while raising a questioning brow to Alma over the child's head.

"Doc McStuffins," she mouthed.

Nodding, Claudia helped Lalo put the bandage on her heart that hurt so much. He rubbed the spot consolingly, babbling babbled more serious words at her. Alma opened her mouth to translate, but Claudia stopped her. "I understood that time." She turned to Alma's sweet-faced son and nodded, "Mucho mejor, gracias."

It wasn't at all better now. It probably never would be again. But this exchange reminded her of the truth she'd had inked into her skin.

"Nada dura para siempre, incluso las cosas malas." She said it to herself as much as to Lalo.

It sucked, and it hurt, and she might never get over it, but *nothing lasts forever, even the bad things.*

Chapter Thirty-Seven

Claudia lay in bed, staring at the ceiling, letting her mind drift aimlessly from thought to thought. She didn't interfere, didn't try to restrict its path. She simply let the thoughts flitter in and out of focus while she lay there, unmoved and unmoving. None of them mattered, anyway. Not really.

Not anymore.

Was the world on an extinction-level event trajectory due to climate change? Probably. Should she try to fit a workout in? Yeah. Did the growth of BRICS signify the potential for a foundational shift of the global market away from the US dollar? It sure seemed like it. How many meals could she get out of an extra-large pizza? Three. No, four if she was strategic. How long would Panamá be excluded from the conversations around the creation of Reggaetón? Indefinitely, apparently. Were there really no cats that could both roar and purr? Nope!

The revolving door of disparate concerns held equal weight in her mind.

She thought she heard a key in her door but dismissed it as a figment of her unregulated imagination.

"Claudia, I'm serious, okay? Turn on your fucking phone!" Diego hollered from her foyer as he, presumably, removed his coat and boots at the door.

After Silvana had moved out, the only members of her family that had keys to her place were Junior and her brother because they, she'd believed, could be trusted not to show up unannounced, disturbing her peace.

Obviously she'd been wrong.

She dragged herself out of bed to look down at him from the banister of her loft bedroom. "Diego, please. What are you doing here?"

"You look like shit."

Since it didn't seem like Diego was looking for a response to his proclamation as she made her way down the stairs, she didn't bother providing one. It was only luck that he found her within forty-eight hours of her last shower, a feat she could barely accomplish most days.

He sprawled on her couch, stuffing his face with something from a paper bag. "I just left Mami's. She has Nanda whipped into a frenzy because you won't leave the house. I legit think she was moments away from swiping my key to make a copy out of dough like some deranged bakery spy."

Claudia was surprised that she'd gotten away from their scrutiny for this long. She was sure the National Guard would have been called in at the end of the first week. But now, at the end of the third, she was still working, exercising, shopping—everything—from home. It made the spontaneous fits of tears easier to deal with when she didn't have to explain their existence to witnesses.

"And your presence on my couch, Rico Suave?"

"Are you listening?" Diego pushed his mouth in the bag and took another mammoth bite. Around the mouthful of whatever he was chewing, he continued, "The only reason Mami's not at your door right now with a priest and a shrink is because I said we had plans to go look at new patio furniture." He swallowed thickly and crumpled the bag. Lifting its mangled remains for her to see, Diego added, "She sent hojaldres, by the way."

Diego interpreted the noise Claudia made as a scoff. He likely thought she was berating him for eating their mother's offering because he shrugged a simple "protection fee", rose to his feet, and ambled over to her kitchen, where he threw out his trash before rooting around in her fridge.

The truth was her body had experienced a visceral reaction she wasn't fast enough to curtail. The last day they'd spent there, the day she'd chased him from her home and her life, she'd made the fried bread for Ian for breakfast. He'd told her it was similar to what he called bakes, a misnomer he was well aware of based on the many other, more logical names used throughout the Caribbean.

They'd laughed and talked and teased each other. She was so happy, it was probably why she landed so hard when she finally fell back to reality.

"Do you want to talk about whatever it is that has you holed up in here?"

"Not particularly."

"Do you actually want to come with me to check out patio furniture?"

Claudia's laugh was a wheezing chortle as she sat at her breakfast bar. "Not even a little."

Diego sighed a multi-leveled show of his thwarted efforts. "Well, then you're gonna have to get dressed enough to stand on the street so I can FaceTime your sister who can call off your mother."

"Mine, are they?"

"When they're being like this, they certainly aren't mine!"

Diego used the back of his phone case to open the beer Claudia was sure he'd left the last time he'd been over. No other enjoyers of stout had ever crossed the threshold of her home.

Claudia watched as Diego drank his beer while scrolling on his phone. Her baby brother, handsome and ridiculous and cosseted by their parents, was a man. A fuckboy to his core, to be sure, but also the owner of a successful business. At some point when no one was looking, she and her siblings had become bona fide adults. Yet he was here, in the midst of all that he had going on, to stand as her shield against the invasion known as their mother.

The genuine gratitude and affection she felt for him threatened to spill over. Not needing to contend with any more maudlin thoughts, Claudia cleared her throat and asked, "How's work? Anything new and exciting?"

She listened attentively as Diego gave her the updates on his life, grateful to have something else to focus on even for a little while. It allowed her mind to wander in a productive way, thinking about different investment avenues to pursue for her clients and burgeoning industries that might make bigger waves down the line.

It was only because she'd let her guard down like a fool, allowed herself to be lulled by the familiar rhythm of her brother's self-assuredness, that his words sent her reeling.

"Remember my buddy Ian Yang?"

"Ian." His name left her lips on an exhale. She hadn't said it out loud in twenty-three days. She'd missed the taste of it, the way it moved along her lips. On her tongue.

"Yeah, Ian. You got his number off me so you could apologize for being such a bitch that time?" If only Diego knew how many more times she'd been a bitch to him— even the times that were for his own good—her brother might never let her live it down. "Anyway, I heard he's slowly stepping his toe back in the waters, so I think I want to ask him for a competitive bid on The Place. That's Marta's department, right?"

Peristeria Place was the apartment complex in the Beaches she owned with her girl cousins. Since Regina's fourteen grandchildren were split fifty-fifty down gender lines, Junior had, in her typical over-the-top way, gathered them together to propose the venture in response to an opportunity she was locked out of by their older boy cousins. Each of them was responsible for a specific aspect of management based on their profession or expertise.

She couldn't concentrate on that, however, with news about Ian thrashing about in her skull. What did it mean? Was Howard out of the woods and Ms. Val retaking control of the day-to-day again? Was Ian going back to the design firm? This was good news, wasn't it? What did 'dip his toe' mean, exactly? Her brain raced to put the pieces together, to formulate answers.

"Have you talked to him directly? Is he okay?" Claudia's hands braced on the countertop as she lifted off her seat.

"Is he..." his voice trailed off in confusion until understanding dawned and he let out a violent "puta madre!"

His outburst startled her, and her tiny yelp of surprise only served to irritate him further.

"Really, Claudia? Of all the guys, you had to pick one of the few architects I actually like and respect?" Diego spat, dragging his hands down his face. "Now instead of a nice bit of catching up, I gotta wonder if he's gonna have an attitude because of whatever fuckery went down between you two? I don't want to have to beat his ass, Claudia, but I will if that's what's up."

"What are you talking about?" She asked, brazening it through. Diego had obviously put the pieces together based on her one simple question, though she had no idea how.

Instead of answering, her brother continued to mutter to himself, "Here I was, worried that you're in the middle of some kind of crisis when this whole ashy, shut-in, llorona thing is over a guy?!" He threw his hand up in frustration and paced her small kitchen. "Fernanda called me *four times.* Four! You know I talked her down from getting on a plane?"

While Claudia was sure Fernanda had been ready to book a flight, Diego's word alone wouldn't have stopped her. She must have also heard from Junior and Alma.

Diego was still ranting to himself, "Mami was going on and on about how to make you show up at the office. I had to listen to her every crackpot theory just to keep her from storming the gates. And for what?" He raised an accusatory brow at her. "I could have avoided a lot of the drama from our annoying sister and frantic mother if you'd just said it was garden-variety relationship bullshit and not your freakazoid brain."

"But it is my freakazoid brain!" Claudia exploded, tired of her brother centering himself in her heartbreak. "This," she waved her hand over herself in a wild pattern, "is entirely because of my brain."

"What happened?" Diego sighed. He still wasn't exhibiting the amount of Claudia-centric concern she wanted but at least he'd stopped lamenting his woes.

"I—" Fuck. She'd gone over this a dozen times. A hundred. A million! She still couldn't accurately articulate what happened.

She'd been a hysterical, sobbing mess when she told Alma. She knew that it had come out a disjointed, barely comprehensible jumble of words. Alma had summarized for Junior when she'd shown up with Claudia's coat, but while it was technically accurate, it still lacked nuance and context. Claudia was just too heartsick at the time to correct her.

In the days and weeks since, she'd combed over every moment, every single interaction, looking for... something. She wanted to know if this outcome was as inevitable as Anxiety kept insisting. Could this misery have been avoided?

She decided to give Diego the summary Alma gave Junior. It wasn't as though her brother had any use for nuance or context. Diego was about as subtle as a freight train.

"Okay, so? What are you making shit weird for? He knows you're a basket case and wants to put all his eggs in there anyway. Let him." Diego shrugged as if it really was that simple. Which is exactly what she told him.

Diego was unmoved. "If he knows about all your bullshit and still wants you, that's his problem."

"And if one day he decides he doesn't want to deal with my bullshit anymore?"

"What, you're worried you'll forget how to be alone? I'm sure Mami will be happy to cure you of that." His shoulders shook as he laughed at his own joke.

"Your swing from compassionate understanding to wildly inappropriate is astounding." Claudia rolled her eyes. "I'll be fine on my own, thanks."

"Mentirosa."

"I'm not a liar!" She objected

"You are because you're skipping all kinds of steps and pretending you're safe at the finish line." Diego gave an unimpressed shake of his head. "That's not how shit works. Besides, you keep complaining you wish you were like everyone else. Take a chance and get your heart broken. What's more basic and 'everyone else' than that?"

"Oye, bobito—I don't want a broken heart." She couldn't believe she had to explain something so obvious.

"A chance, Chismosa. There's a *chance* you might. Besides, you told him that you struggle with anxiety, and he was willing to rock with it. Then he saw the extreme version of your disability and held you down, ready to ride. Right? Entonces explícame cuál es el problema?"

"The problem, *Diego*, is I don't want to feel like a burden."

"Claudia," Diego huffed through an eye roll of his own, "You and Nanda let Mami make your anxiety a bigger deal than it is."

She absorbed his proclamation with a small amount of skepticism. It was true that Diego was the least concerned by her limitations, but she'd always assumed it was because her limitations weren't about him.

"What do you mean?"

"Look around, Chismosa. You live in this bomb-ass condo and have your fancy-pants job where you help people secure their futures. You're not living on a sheet of cardboard and eating your hair."

"Diego!" Chastising her brother's language was easier than reckoning with his words. He could be so inconsiderate at times.

"That's not me! That's how Mami behaves—like you're an unstable risk to yourself and society. But you're fine. Mostly." He shrugged. "You've lived alone, you've lived with roommates, and nothing catastrophic has ever happened. So you like to check out from time to time. Who the the fuck doesn't?" Diego rinsed his beer bottle and placed it in the recycling. "At least you know. At least you're doing something about it. How many ahuevados are walking around, undiagnosed, just inflicting their crazy on unsuspecting bystanders?"

"Seriously, man, you can't talk like that."

"Okay, okay. But you know what I mean."

She rubbed her temples. God, she hated when Diego was the reasonable one in the room. It was the surest sign of how low she'd sunk in this mess. "Yes, Diego, I know what you mean."

Claudia watched as he made himself comfortable on her couch. His legs were stretched out as he arranged the pillows to his liking. "Now what are you doing?"

His face twisted in a derisive 'isn't it obvious?' scowl. He pulled the throw over his feet and said, "I'm gonna wait here 'till you finish your overthinking spiral and go running to him. When you do, I'll be there, ready to take proof of life footage to send to Nanda."

Chapter Thirty-Eight

Diego insisted on driving. He started a video chat with Fernanda as soon as they crossed out of the recognizable landmarks of her neighborhood, claiming more distance was better for convincing their watchers this outing was legit.

He wasn't wrong.

Nanda worked herself into a full-throated lecture almost immediately. Neither Diego nor Claudia was in the mood for her high-handedness even though they both knew it was unavoidable. Claudia was busy thinking of ways to excuse them from the conversation when Diego whistled the familiar melody of their youth. It was loud enough to make Claudia's ears ring in the cab of his truck, but she couldn't complain. As it had when they were kids, it was like a siren for Nanda's four sons who came crashing into the room. Their excitement at having both aunt and uncle on an unscheduled call pushed Fernanda and her lecture to the background.

She was grateful for her nephews' gleeful chatter. It provided a reprieve from her sister's interrogation and also helped keep her mind off the impending confrontation. She was winging this whole 'spill your guts' situation, and Anxiety was having a field day criticizing every aspect of her grand gesture.

She'd never had a picture in her head of what love meant, what it would look like. There were no boxes to tick because she couldn't imagine the combination of traits a man would need to override all of her... *Claudia*. But this thing with Ian had her reconsidering everything she thought she knew. Maybe it wasn't about a set of preconceived traits measured against society's arbitrary standards and more about the person noticing all the things the world said had to stay hidden—all the anxious, messy, volatile parts she hadn't been allowed to show before—and accepting them as part of the greater whole.

Maybe it meant something as simple as believing you could be loved, exactly as you were, and then giving someone the chance to try.

Ian had pleaded with her to let him try, and she'd refused him. She hadn't been able to see a way where this condition of hers didn't bury them both. But Diego was right—as galling as it was to admit—hiding from the worst without allowing even the possibility of something good was disingenuous.

So now here she was, on the porch of Ian's semi-detached house in the trendy Beaches neighborhood, trying.

She'd teased him about calling it the Beaches when he was so close to the area's northern Kingston Road border but he'd simply scoffed and told her to ask his property taxes if he lived there or not. The sidewalk teemed with strollers, dog walkers, small children on bikes and scooters, and joggers in stylish athletic wear. As she double-checked the address—Ian said his Auntie Eileen approved of the three 3s because it was a lucky number—Claudia admitted she owed him an apology.

She'd have to add it to the ever-increasing list of things she needed to apologize to him for.

The door flew open, and his cousin William stood at the threshold, both of them startled by each other's presence. Claudia clutched her racing heart through her heavy coat. "Um... I'm looking for Ian?"

William looked down at her without speaking and Claudia straightened her spine as she stared right back at him. His hair was shorter than in the pictures she'd seen, but he still carried himself with the same cool, aloof bearing she remembered.

"Yo! Get over here. It's her."

Before she could say anything, the door opened wider so Domenic could squeeze into the doorway. He looked the same as his pictures—well-muscled and well-dressed. His gaze glittered with interest as he tracked her from head to toe. "He didn't say she was short."

Ah. This was the gauntlet she'd have to run if she wanted access to Ian. Fine. She could put up with their hazing if that's what it took.

Claudia's chin lifted as she arched an expectant brow at them. "William. Domenic."

William's own brows raised slightly. "Impressive memory, Gossip Girl."

"Is he here?" She wasn't terribly concerned with impressing his cousins at the moment. Claudia could lead a long and healthy life without ever once trying to please someone determined to not like her. This little power trip burned through her anxiety, clearing the way for her rage. If they wanted it, she had thirty-odd years of ire to spill.

"He's—"

"What's it to you?" William spoke over Domenic. "Haven't you done enough?"

Claudia opened her mouth to let him know exactly what she was capable of doing, but Domenic's hushed "Shit, he's back" stopped her.

"If you'll excuse us for a moment," Domenic said solicitously as he stepped back into the house. William continued to look down his nose at her, so she curled her lip at him and sneered. Illogically, William smiled and offered a quick, "Just a sec", before closing the door gently in her face.

Claudia paced on his doorstep, as close to her bare-bones self as she'd ever managed. Standing on her flat, sneakered feet was disorienting. Outside of the gym, she didn't spend a lot of time negotiating the world at her natural height, and it was humbling to accept just how short she truly was. The extra three to four inches she added every day had become her normal and having even that stripped away was sobering.

She was completely unadorned. No tailored clothes or towering heels. Nothing to protect herself from the very reasons she'd needed the armor in the first place. Knowing she managed the little standoff with William was oddly invigorating, all things considered.

When he opened the door, her breath caught in her throat. Ian—beautiful, athletic, rangy, Doberman-faced Ian—looked like hell.

"Claudia," he was clearly surprised to see her there, but she hoped he wasn't angry.

Not waiting to find out if she was welcome, she started without preamble. "I'm not great with new people. New experiences are difficult for me. I don't generally like extending myself outside of work, and even then, it's on a very specific, structured path." She took a deep breath and looked him in the eye. "You were many firsts I wasn't prepared for."

"Claudia," this time when he said her name, it was a plea.

"I obviously know how to function in the world. I'm not a recluse." She rolled her eyes at her nervous babbling. "I just usually need a lot of lead time. I like to know exactly what I'm walking into and what my escape options are. It's hard for me to open up to new people, so I like to limit the number of times I have to do it."

"Come inside, Claudia. It's freezing."

She shook her head. Adamant that she would get these words out. "Thank you, but no. I... I'm not ready."

"Ready?"

"I have things to say and I'm not ready to step inside." She didn't want to know what the inside of his home looked like, didn't want to see what kind of art hung on the walls or how many throw pillows he did or didn't have. She didn't want to see the pictures showcasing his loved ones, the awards chronicling his every achievement. She didn't want to know what she was going to lose out on if he didn't want her to stay.

He nodded but said nothing, simply reached behind the door, and pulled out a parka. It looked worn and stained. It was probably what he wore to shovel the walk and other winter chores.

Another deep breath, and Claudia continued, "For as long as I can remember, I've gathered information and applied the knowledge. I'm good at my job because I have a wealth of history to draw from. The cyclical nature of market losses and gains, its response to global stimuli and political maneuverings, are fairly reliable. But you..." Claudia's mouth opened and closed again. She didn't know how to get around the lump in her throat, so she didn't bother. "I had no history on you. No history for this." She looked away. The breadth and scope of the man was too much for her to process in her fragile state. "You're terrifying." The words came out quiet and unbidden. She hadn't meant to say them out loud.

Ian exhaled noisily through his nose but maintained his silence.

She didn't know what else to say except the truth. "I was scared. I'm sorry."

"That's it, you were scared and you're sorry? You think that makes it better? It's been three weeks!"

Oh, Christ, he wasn't interested in her words. It was too late. Her mind raced for something to say but all she did was stammer, "I...."

"I told you I loved you, and you said, 'Don't.' I said I wanted to be there for you when things got hard, you said, 'No'."

His detached delivery made the words land that much harder. Claudia's eyes filled with tears, and she fought to keep them from falling.

"I can't keep putting myself out there only to be discarded when you don't feel like dealing with me."

"No, Ian, it's not–"

"It's not what, Claudia?" He demanded, cutting her off. "The ball has been in your court the entire time. I was happily going at your pace, but you still found a way to leave me behind!"

She wouldn't cry. No matter how much she wanted to curl herself into a ball on the cold concrete and sob, she wouldn't put that on him. She'd earned every bit of his scorn, and she would take it all because she owed him that much. But, God, did it hurt.

"I'm sorry, Ian. I am so sorry! I thought I was doing the right thing. I thought I was protecting you from a life of having to deal with this." She waved her hand in front of her body. "I was wrong, and I hate that I hurt you."

"I didn't want to be protected from you, Claudia." The scold, like everything else he'd said, was dispassionate. A simple recitation of facts she couldn't dispute.

"I know!" Her hands balled into fists in frustration. "That's what I came here to say! I fucked up!"

Ian dropped his head, and the finality of his posture almost choked her. This couldn't be it. Yes, she'd made a mess of everything, but wasn't love supposed to be bigger and stronger than that?

She didn't know, but she had to try.

Because that was the thing about trying. You had to keep trying until you got it right. Then, when you got it right, you tried until you got good. You tried until you were so used to trying it didn't feel like effort at all, but you never stopped trying.

Love worked the same way. She understood that now.

She rushed forward, ducking under his lowered head, resting her hands on his chest so she could look him in the face.

"Listen. Please." Her eyes darted frantically between his. She wasn't sure what to make of his blank expression, but since he hadn't slammed the door in her face, she kept going. "I was thinking about what you might lose committing to a life with me. I thought the worst thing that could happen was saddling you with more burdens and obligations. But deciding for you wasn't my place." She swallowed thickly, losing her fight against her falling tears. "That was my mistake."

He leaned his forehead on hers, and she could smell the cinnamon gum on his breath. Was this goodbye? Would this be the last time she felt his body against hers? She inhaled deeply, trying to absorb as much of him as she could in 'case she never got another chance. His lips were so close, her body twitched involuntarily to feel them against hers again.

"I love you. I did it the wrong way because I didn't know how before. I won't make that mistake again. I can love you better, Ian. If you let me, I will love you properly."

"Claudia," he said gently, slowly, as though he'd been repeating himself all afternoon. He held her face in his hands; his touch was remarkably warm against her cold skin. "None of that matters if you won't let me love you."

"I..." God, what she wouldn't give to have her Ian back. This stern, detached man made her feel edgy and unsettled. She had no idea what he was thinking, no way of knowing where she stood. But she had no pride when it came to him, had nothing to lose, so she closed her eyes, clutched her fists in his shirt, and begged him to hear her. "Ian, that's what I'm trying to tell you. I want you to love me."

She felt him moving his head back and forth. Was he saying no? Her stomach dropped as she choked back a sob. She couldn't fall apart. Not now.

"Prove it."

Wait, what?

Her eyes snapped open and he was there—silly and smiling and hers. She was so lightheaded with happiness, her words sputtered out in a mix of sobbing laughter. Claudia followed his lead, repeating her words from their long ago exchange. "How can I prove something like that?"

He moved his head again. With her eyes open, she could see he wasn't shaking his head but nuzzling her. This time he let his lips brush her skin and she sighed at the sensation.

"Easy. If you want me, you can meet me somewhere and sit down to a civilized conversation." He brushed his thumbs on her cheekbone in a futile effort to stop her tears.

Claudia didn't care that she was hiccupping and sniffling. She launched herself at him for the kiss she'd been desperately missing for weeks now. All that mattered was Ian wrapped his arms around her, hauled her higher on his chest, and kissed her back. The Minister of Horniness linked arms with both Embarrassment and Anxiety. When Embarrassment started to fuss about her runny nose and questionable attire and Anxiety tried to point out all that could yet go wrong, Horniness clamped a hand over their mouths, shushed them, and returned to the joy of Ian's kiss.

They broke for breath, puffing little clouds in the scant space between their mouths. "Are you ready to come in yet? I'm freezing my nuts off!"

Claudia nodded quickly and returned to his lips. She had a lot of lost time to make up for. She wasn't going to squander it with rhetorical questions.

They stumbled into the house, Ian kicking the door closed behind them, as they clung to each other while clumsily removing their shoes and coats. Claudia had no words for the rightness that settled over her. All she knew was she was going to dedicate herself to making sure Ian never had a single moment's regret about taking her back.

"I love you," she said against his lips. Ian stiffened and didn't respond.

Lord, she couldn't possibly have screwed up already, could she?

"What are you still doing here?" Ian demanded.

Claudia finally took in her surroundings. William was lazing in an armchair, and Domenic was helping himself to something out of a canister in Ian's kitchen. His reaction wasn't about her. Phew!

William made a pointed look to the front door they'd just been blocking. Ian responded with an equally pointed look at the back door in the kitchen. Domenic, who clearly spoke this eyebrow-centric language, said, "Wasn't sure how it was going to play out. We thought you might need us."

Ian snorted an incredulous, "And now?"

Domenic made a careless 'what are you gonna do?' gesture and tossed more of the snack in his mouth before putting the canister away. Claudia hid her face in his chest to hide her reaction. It amused her to see that Ian had the same dynamic she did with her cousins. Amused her to know he might very well be the Alma of their trio.

"We realize you two have some... catching up to do, so we're going to let ourselves out." William announced as he gathered his belongings. Then he added, as though it was completely reasonable, "At your earliest convenience, my mother is going to need the date, time, and location of your birth so she can check your chart and get you the proper Buddha."

Domenic, not to be outdone, added, "And my mom is going to want a list of any food restrictions. I know spice tolerance isn't universal among Latin Americans, so if you could include that, too, it would be appreciated."

"We can make adjustments, if necessary." William's voice was heavy with reluctance as he waited for Domenic at the door. "But we'd rather not have to bland up the food, y'know?"

Claudia's laughter sputtered out like a car struggling to turn over. The two men who'd tried to intimidate her earlier were replaced with Orientation Volunteers welcoming her to Camp Yang. She supposed it was only fair. She was the source of pain for their kin before. Now she was his. Fully.

"Later, Gossip Girl." Domenic saluted as he shrugged on his coat and pulled the door closed.

Before the latch caught, Ian called out, "It's Chismosa, not Gossip Girl!"

Claudia spun on her heel and gasped an affronted sound. "Not to you, it's not!"

"What?" Ian frowned his confusion.

"I realize we've just overcome a hurdle, and it was basically all my fault, but that's no reason to abandon our proper relationship names!" Claudia didn't care how irrational it sounded; she was unwilling to compromise here. Fighting for him included his perfect butchering of chismosa.

Ian reached for her, tugging her giant scarf loose. "Is that right?"

"Claro que sí." She insisted with an obstinate tilt of her chin.

Chuckling, he tossed her scarf onto the armchair, pulled her close, buried his face in her neck, and inhaled deeply. "I love you, Gossipika."

Claudia pressed herself closer to him, her elation bubbling over. "I love you, Sunny."

He trailed a line of kisses up the column of her neck. When he got to her ear, he whispered, "Ready for the tour? There are a couple of pieces of furniture I'd like to introduce you to."

Claudia's Minister of Horniness's hands rubbed together in anticipation. "It would be my pleasure."

Epilogue

"Turn right at those lights," Claudia instructed. It was the end of May and, in typical Toronto fashion, after a week of beautiful sunny spring days, it was cool and overcast as their progress along Kingston Road was being hindered by a streetcar, a cyclist, and delivery truck.

Without the city's ever worsening traffic, it should've been a quick jaunt to their destination. As it was, following her directions through the back-streets took almost fifteen minutes, and her silent disapproval at how close they were cutting it did not go unnoticed.

"We'll get in and out so fast, your being a teensy bit late won't even register."

Claudia snorted her disbelief. "I want you to remember this later when I have to literally drag you from the premises."

God, he loved her.

"Of an 82 year-olds birthday party in Scarborough?" He gave a considering tilt of his head. "I can't deny it's a possibility."

Her pleased laughter rang out in the small space. She knew he was teasing. They'd been out socializing a handful of times in the past three months and each time Claudia's tank hit empty, they'd left immediately, no questions asked. No party on Earth was more important to him than her. Ian would rather not go at all than put her at risk

"There's a spot there." She pointed to the short row of spaces at the curb and he easily backed his car into the available spot.

Ian rolled his shoulders as he made his way to the passenger side. The accidental nap they'd taken had put a crick in his neck. It was a small price to pay for the eye-crossing pleasure they'd found edging each other with remote controlled insertables, but he'd barely felt the hot water of his shower when Claudia started rushing him to hurry up and get ready.

Now standing in front of Peristeria Place, the apartment complex she owned with her cousins, Ian was already looking forward to resuming his truncated shower.

It didn't look like much from the street, but Ian knew the bland exterior was by design.

Behind the concrete wall was a veritable oasis. The four-story building was set in a u-shape around an open courtyard area that included an in-ground pool and six circular tables with umbrellas. There were lots of trees and tall grasses around the perimeter that provided both shade and privacy. Ian had been vibrating with the effort it took to keep his cool in front of Diego during the site tour he got in advance of putting in a bid to design the proposed rooftop terrace. Well, as cool as possible when they weren't busy cracking jokes and goofing off.

It hadn't occurred to him to be concerned about Diego's reaction to his relationship with Claudia until his name lit up Ian's phone a couple days after they and Claudia emerged from their... marathon reuniting. Somehow, even knowing they were siblings, Ian still considered Diego part of the "work life" he'd walked away from, and therefore had no connection to his life with Claudia.

The offer to throw his hat in the ring for this project was as unexpected as it was thrilling.

"I love finding places like this, just tucked away," Ian mused, taking in the quiet residential street in the Birch Cliff neighborhood.

"Yeah, Junior used to live over by Victoria Park across from the cemetery." Claudia crossed herself, and continued, "And she generally fraternizes with both boat people and member club people, like the Toronto Hunt over there," she gestured vaguely to their right, "so this neighborhood was definitely on her radar."

"I, for one, am glad we're still gatekeeping Scarborough. Let the haters stew in their ignorance."

Rolling her eyes, she swatted his side, chuckling. She was beautiful in a dress that flared out at her hips and fell in a row of small, neat pleats at her knee with a car coat, and leather booties all in monochromatic blush. Ian pulled her close and pressed a quick kiss to the top of her head as they made their way along the path.

Immediately, the sounds of merriment floated to them.

"Ugh, I told you!" Claudia muttered.

Ian was desperate to meet the birthday girl. Claudia, as a rule, didn't get places on time and the people in her life had come to accept it. Why she worried about being late to this party was an intriguing mystery.

"You still have six minutes, Gossipika."

"I'm sorry." She exhaled slowly after confirming the time on her fancy watch. "I guess I'm nervous about introducing you to Mavis."

"Is this the level of freak-out I should expect when it's time to meet your folks?"

She stopped in her tracks, stricken, as though she hadn't considered the reality of him meeting her family.

Laughing, he nudged her back into motion with a teasing, "I'll take that as a yes."

Ian was glad they'd decided to leave the parents out of things for now. It was enough that their cousins and siblings were involved. William and Junior were already acquainted, apparently having met at both of Quincy's birthday parties in February. They didn't need any more melding of worlds for the time being. Besides, it's not like this reprieve would last much longer. His Auntie Eileen had already sent a Sunday Buddha for Claudia's mantle with strict instructions to have the statue face east.

An unfamiliar accent called out, "Darling, I'm so glad you came!"

Ian turned to see a striking woman in a fabulous pantsuit striding over. Her medium brown complexion was made up flawlessly and her skin still held a firmness many women her age lacked. When she extended her hands for Claudia to take, Ian was torn between focusing on her jewelry and her manicure. Both were conspicuously dazzling.

"As if I'd be anywhere else!" Claudia pressed kisses to each cheek.

This could only be Mavis.

"And who is this?" She gave him an appraising once-over, making him stand taller under the scrutiny. "He's quite handsome."

"Mavis, allow me to introduce my boyfriend, Ian." Claudia beamed at him, his chest puffing slightly. He'd never get tired of being claimed by her. "Ian, this is Mavis. She's both the oldest and eldest tenant here."

"The stories I could tell."

Ian smiled at her false modesty. There was no doubt in his mind she told all sorts of tales. "Happy birthday, Mavis. Thanks for having me."

"Oh, and such manners." She hooked her arm in his and started walking toward her party. He looked over his shoulder to find Claudia grinning with her lip caught in her teeth as she gave him a conspiratorial wink.

In the short time it took Mavis to lead Ian to the rest of the revelers, she managed to inform him that she and her husband moved from Nova Scotia for his job some fifty-odd years ago and had lived in the same apartment ever since. He was "called home to glory" three years ago, leaving behind their daughter, two grandchildren, and two great-grandchildren—the joys of her life. Ian had a whole host of follow-up questions on the tip of his tongue but had to keep them to himself as Mavis sing-songed "Look who I found!" and swept her arm out to reveal Claudia, standing just behind them.

It was a group of about thirty-ish people of all different ages, races, and gender expression. Not unlike a high school cafeteria, there seemed to be obvious factions based on the assorted groupings around the tables.

"Buenas tardes," Claudia said, dipping into a small but exaggerated curtsy. "You can start the party now."

This bit of bravado didn't seem to faze anyone here and, in fact, set one table into hysterical applause. Two people from said table rushed over, enveloping Claudia in a gushing, fawning, tangle of limbs.

Ian looked over when he heard a particularly scandalized, "Is that who I think it is?"

Claudia chided a young Black man with bleach blond micro braids and matching bleached eyebrows in a playful scold. "I don't know, Luc. Who do you think it is?"

"Yeah, Luc. Who do you think it is?"

Ian stifled a grin at the inquisitive way the young woman's gaze darted between Luc and Claudia.

"Hi." Ian extended his hand which she shook confidently. "Ian."

Claudia wrapped herself around his arm again, and gave the two a dazzling smile. "This is Luc and his sibling Lola. They've been here almost a year."

"We live with our cousin who is not our dad."

Ian noticed the very specific way Lola answered the question he didn't ask. Not that Ian had a chance to ask questions. Luc had immediately swept Claudia and Lola up in an animated retelling of an incident at his job.

He felt Mavis tug on his elbow and Ian stuffed down the little spike of disappointment. He'd ask Claudia how the story ended later. Her grip was firm as she shifted them slightly away from the group.

Once she was assured of their temporary privacy, Mavis let her bright, cheery smile drop. Her words were pitched low, for his ears only. "She's a good girl, that Claudia. Comes to check on me, sits and has tea, listens to my stories. First started coming around when her brother was doing some work around here. Ever since I met her, she's been an absolute doll."

Ah, so that's how Claudia fulfilled her ownership role. He'd wondered about the feasibility of an owner gauging "tenant satisfaction". His clever pufferfish did what she did best: gossiped. He didn't doubt for a moment that her affinity for Mavis was genuine, that her visits with the woman were sincere as they bonded over their shared commitment to chisme. But he did wonder if Mavis knew Claudia was her landlord.

Mavis continued, pointing a bedazzled nail at him, "I'll have no truck with any leaving ghosts read nonsense. You hear me, young man?"

The only Earthly reason Ian could conceive for why he didn't so much as crack a smile at the octogenarian's mangling of 'leave on read' and 'ghosting', was because he understood he was being put on trial. Understood the devotion his tiny dynamo engendered. Respected it, even. Ian spoke his truth openly and without reservation. "There'll be no ghosts, ma'am. She's the best thing that's ever happened to me."

Her shrewd gaze was replaced by a wry, pleased smile. "That she is."

Just then, a hushed ripple of anticipation ran through the crowd. Luc and Lola were practically buzzing with it.

A large man walked through the courtyard. He was impeccably dressed in a charcoal gray three-piece suit. His dress shoes were shiny enough to see your face in, and his thick beard was trimmed to neatly frame his mouth.

He strode out to a waiting town car idling on the street without giving his gathered neighbors more than a cursory nod.

When the car pulled off, the party erupted into excited chatter.

"What just happened?" Ian was asking Claudia, but would take an explanation from anyone who offered it.

"I know, right?" Lola said, though it wasn't any kind of answer.

Luc picked up the conversational thread, "Every other day of the month, he looks like he smells of Funyuns."

"Seriously. He usually looks like he forages for his necessities in a burnt out dumpster." Lola interjected, in case Ian didn't understand Luc's reference. "The textbook definition of unkempt."

"That's if you see him at all." Mavis leaned in to add her two cents to their little circle. "That boy barely leaves his unit to throw out his trash!"

Luc and Lola were nodding enthusiastically.

"Then, once a month, out of nowhere, he started going out looking like that!" Lola pointed to the curb where the car had idled.

Ian nodded along, waiting for the punchline.

Luc tossed his braids over his shoulder. "We're all desperate to know the story. We've made it a bit of a sport. So far, it's been the same outfit down to the pocket square and tie clip."

"Any guesses?" Ian could speculate about something like this for hours.

"Lots. We're about to make it interesting!" Mavis said, a mischievous twinkle in her eye. She clapped her hands, calling her guests to attention, and instructed, "Alright, everyone! Write your best guess down and put it in the bag!"

Ian took in the flurry of activity as people scribbled their words on strips of yellow note paper. He couldn't be sure, but it seemed like many of those participating were doing so specifically to appease Mavis, and not for any real investment in the comings and goings of their neighbor. Still, those who were into it, were really into it!

A middle aged South Asian woman in a pretty, sage green salwar kameez signaled to Mavis from the archway.

"Oh. Looks like lunch is ready. Susanna, darling, be a dear and collect the votes. We'll tally them after we eat!"

The child picked up the iconic purple velvet bag and skipped from table to table, accepting the folded bits of paper.

Claudia took his hand as they followed the crowd inside. A quick double take had her veering away from the party room and toward the lobby.

"Just a sec," she assured him quietly as they hung back from the crowd. "Silvana said she had the desks moved around. Something about it being better for deliveries. I just wanna see."

She poked her head around the corner, making a curious 'huh' sound when she saw the long table in the alcove. Then she crossed the hall to a closed door, looked around to be sure the coast was clear, and let herself inside.

"Oh. Okay, that makes more sense." She said, once they were both in what appeared to be the leasing office. Claudia smiled up at him. "That's it. I'm good. We can head to the party room, now."

Ian wasn't. Ian's entire focus was on the large, sturdy wood desk that came up to his hips in height.

The solution to his logistical prayers.

He was mesmerized. Of all the pieces of furniture he'd had the pleasure and privilege of bending Claudia over, this was his white whale. His holy grail.

"Sunny, did you hear me?"

"I... can you... it's..." Ian stammered, excitement clogging the words in his throat. He put a gentle hand on the back of her neck and bent her forward. Fuck. Just as he suspected, it was the perfect depth for her torso. He quickly pulled her back up and answered her sputtered confusion with a kiss. Desperation made his already raspy voice even raspier. "Claudia. This is the one. I found it!"

She looked between his wide, nearly manic eyes and the desk as understanding dawned. Claudia, his perfect, depraved pufferfish simply said, "I think this was already here when we took over, but I can ask Silvana to be sure."

Ian was taking pictures and typing away on his phone. "No need."

Claudia ran her fingers along the desk's surface thoughtfully. "It might be too big for your place, Sunny." She checked it with her hip. When it didn't budge, she added, "The delivery alone will be exorbitant for a piece this big and heavy. This is quite a purchase to make on the fly."

"It's an *investment*, Claudia. You of all people should understand about the benefits of long term rewards. If it's even half as good as I think it will be, it will pay for itself in one afternoon. I'm willing to empty my entire house of all existing furniture to make space for this beauty."

"You know," Her bottom lip was caught in her teeth in that adorable, aggravating way she had. "We could probably arrange a test drive of sorts." He was too intent on his image search, he didn't catch her meaning. She gave a pointed look behind him and said, "The door locks."

Ian stopped what he was doing. All focus on sourcing the desk was replaced by a hot, primal hunger. He didn't need to be told twice. "Then lock the fucking door, Gossipika. What are you waiting for?"

***

Author's Note

Anxiety disorder is a very real and very personal condition. While I do not share this diagnosis, I am keenly aware of the barriers imposed, and the way society both stigmatizes and downplays the effects of mental illnesses. Claudia's attempt at self-regulation is a work of fiction. It is in no way an endorsement, nor is it an indictment of coping mechanisms. If you live with any type of mental illness, please continue to work with your doctors to find the best solution for your needs. I hope you received my fictional tale about thriving on your own terms with the grace and respect intended.

Acknowledgements

Thank you, gorgeous reader, for making it to the end of my *third* novel and the end of the Queens City Queens series. When I started this journey, I had one story in mind and didn't think it would ever leave my immediate circle. Three years, three novels, a short story, and a novella later and I still have more to say! Who knew?

Again, I would be nowhere early readers and champions. Thank you to AC, D, Hockey-Name, Catherine, and Jenni—your notes and enthusiasm for this story made all the difference.

Ian Yang's job as a landscape architect is a direct result of having the privilege of knowing my sister-in-law, Chrissy. She is kind and generous (also a hugely talented landscape architect), and I am grateful for both her friendship and invaluable input to the process of making Ian and his passion for his job believable.

My ball of sunshine character needed a name that reflected his personality and I'd like to thank Rong for helping me come up with his Chinese names. Thanks also goes to Alexandra who made sure six Romanian words I know were used correctly, and to Monica for making sure my Spanish landed the way I intended.

Thank you to Josefina, Ofelia, and Jorge for sharing your family idiosyncrasies with me. Josefina has multiple drinking vessels on her desk, Ofelia's IG handle contains the last 4 digits of her old landline, and Jorge thinks salt and pepper is the right amount of spice in his food. I hope your enthusiasm for being immortalised in my naked kissing book was rewarded!

Claudia and the way she experiences mental health struggles are entirely made up. I don't know if anxiety attacks feel like being swept away by a stampeding crowd or if disassociating to a field of wild flowers helps manage big emotions. What I do know is Claudia's refusal to 'stay down' when shit gets hard and her brain works against her is inspired in part by my friend Sara. She is stronger and braver than even she probably knows, and I am so lucky to know her.

While I didn't have to resort to the same level of thievery I did on Dickface and Peaches when crafting these characters, I remain an unreformed bandit of identities. Big love to Amy, Candice, Catherine, Francine, Gabriella, Jennifer, Jeremy, Jill, Karla, Kyle, Laura, Leah, Lin, Loffieann, Marr and Martha, Nicole, Paula, and Tina for the inspiration.

As ever, I'd like to thank the collective known as Romance-landia. Whether its on social media, or in person meet-ups and retreats, I'm grateful for the support, comradery, and generously shared knowledge. I'd specifically like to thank Anuska Sikdar, Té Russ, Tif Marcelo, and Mia of Ardently Bookish for donating their time and expertise (of which I am a proud beneficiary) to raise funds for Lift 4 Autism. You make it easy to continuously celebrate Happily Ever After in all its forms.

I want to thank my big, loud, supportive, Latino-Caribbean family for filling my life with love, inspiration, and endless laughter.

And, finally, to my husband. He's listened to me rant and brainstorm and spiral without once doubting my ability to make it to the finish line. Thank you for taking all of this in stride!

Stick around to see what hijinks arise in the next series, Peristeria Place!

xx

About the Author

Lindo Forbes is a first gen Canadian who lives in Toronto where you can find her at her day job or procrastinating on social media – sometimes both, simultaneously. She speaks enough French to not disgrace herself when she visits Montreal but not enough Spanish to please her abuela. She's also been known to spend her free time working on her works-in-progress, battling with the Libby App, thinking of varied ways to corrupt her nieces and nephews, holding grudges against fictional characters and celebrities she's never met, and/or searching for the world's best street food with her husband.

Join her mailing list to get updates on these very noble endeavors.

www.ingramcontent.com/pod-product-compliance
Lightning Source LLC
Chambersburg PA
CBHW010423170726
48283CB00011B/3024